W9-BVY-210

CROWN OF
STARS

Also by James Tiptree, Jr.
published by Tor Books

Brightness Falls from the Air
The Starry Rift

JAMES TIPTREE, JR.

A TOM DOHERTY ASSOCIATES BOOK
NEW YORK

SBUIA
Collection
PZ
690
I68C7
cop. 2

This is a work of fiction. All the characters and events portrayed in this book are fictitious, and any resemblance to real people or events is purely coincidental.

CROWN OF STARS

Copyright © 1988 by the Estate of Alice B. Sheldon

All rights reserved, including the right to reproduce this book or portions thereof in any form.

A TOR BOOK
Published by Tom Doherty Associates, Inc.
49 West 24 Street
New York, NY 10010

Library of Congress Cataloging-in-Publication Data

Tiptree, James.
Crown of Stars/James Tiptree Jr.
p. cm.
"A TOR book."
ISBN 0-312-93105-0: $18.95 1. Science fiction, America. I. Title
PS 3570. I66C76 1988
813′ 54—dc 19 88-19234
CIP

First edition: September 1988

0 9 8 7 6 5 4 3 2 1

Acknowledgments

"Second Going" copyright © 1987 by the Estate of Alice B. Sheldon. Originally published in *Universe 17*, edited by Terry Carr (Nelson Doubleday & Co., 1987).

"Our Resident Djinn" copyright © 1986 by James Tiptree, Jr. Originally published in *The Magazine of Fantasy & Science Fiction*, October 1986.

"Morality Meat" copyright © 1985 by Alice B. Sheldon. Originally published as by Raccoona Sheldon in *Despatches from the Frontiers of the Female Mind*, edited by Jen Green & Sarah Lefanu (The Women's Press Ltd., 1985).

"All This and Heaven Too" copyright © 1985 by James Tiptree, Jr. Originally published in *Isaac Asimov's Science Fiction Magazine*, Mid December 1985.

"Yanqui Doodle" copyright © 1987 by the Estate of Alice B. Sheldon. Originally published in *Isaac Asimov's Science Fiction Magazine*, July 1987.

"Last Night and Every Night" copyright © 1970 by James Tiptree, Jr. Originally published in *Worlds of Fantasy* issue 2.

"Backward, Turn Backward" copyright © 1988 by the Estate of Alice B. Sheldon. Originally published in *Synergy* 2, edited by George Zebrowski (Harcourt Brace Jovanovich, Inc., 1988).

"The Earth Doth Like a Snake Renew" copyright © 1988 by the Estate of Alice B. Sheldon. Originally published in *Isaac Asimov's Science Fiction Magazine*, May 1988. (Written in 1973 as by Raccoona Sheldon.)

"In Midst of Life" copyright © 1987 by the Estate of Alice B. Sheldon. Originally published in *The Magazine of Fantasy & Science Fiction*, November 1987.

Contents

Second Going

I didn't mean to start like this. I wanted to make it a nice formal Appendix, or Addendum, to the official Archives. The account of man's first contact with aliens: what really happened.

But I can't find any bound copies of the White Book, not even in the President's office. Except one somebody got mustard all over and another piece the rats got at. What I suspect, what I think is, *they never finished it*. All I can find is some empty cover-boxes, so I'm going to put these discs in one of those so people will know it's important.

After all, I am the official Archivist—I typed the promotion myself when Hattie went. I'm Theodora Tanton, Chief NASA Archivist. And I'm seventy-six years old, as of this morning. So is everybody old —everybody who can remember, that is. So who's going to hear it, anyway? You with your six fingers or two heads or whatever?

You'll be around, though. They promised us that, that we wouldn't blow ourselves up. They said they fixed it. And I believe them. Not because I *believe* them exactly, but because I think they just might want to come back someday and find more than ashes.

They didn't command us not to fire atomic weapons, by the way. I guess they knew by that time that when a god commands Don't Eat Those Apples, or Don't Open This Box—it's the first thing men'll do. (And manage to blame it on a woman, too, if you'll notice. But I digress.)

No, they just said, "We fixed that." Maybe the Russians have found out what they did by this time. Or the Israelis. What's left of the Pentagon is too scared to try. So, Hello, Posterity.

This is about what really happened, to add to the White Book, if you ever find one—Oops, that was a rat. I have a Coleman lantern, and a hockey stick for the rats.

Start with First Contact.

First Contact took place on Mars, with the men of the First Mars Mission. The two who had landed, that is. The command module pilot, Reverend Perry Danforth, was just flying orbits, looking down and seeing peculiar things. Meeting them on Mars confused everybody for a while. They were not Martians.

The best account of the meeting is from Mission Control. I found a man who had been a boy there, sort of a gofer. In that big room with all the terminals, you've seen it a million times on TV if you watched space stuff. So this first bit is dictated live by Kevin ("Red") Blake, now aged 99.5 years.

But before him I want to say a word about how everything was. *So normal*. Nothing sinister or dramatic going on. Like in a ship that's slowly, very slowly listing to one side, only nobody's mentioning it. That's all underneath. But little things give it away, like this one Kevin told me before they landed:

It was a long trip, see, two years plus. They were all in the command module, called *Mars Eagle*. James Aruppa, commanding, and Todd Fiske, and the Reverend Perry, who wasn't going to get to land. (Personally I'd have broken Todd's arm or something, if I'd been Perry, so I could get to land. Imagine getting so close—and then flying circles for a week while the others are on *Mars!* But he acted perfectly happy about it. He even made a joke about being "the most expensive valet parking service ever." Very cooperative and one-for-all, the Reverend. I never did find out exactly what he was the Reverend of, maybe it was only a nickname.)

Anyway about five or six months out, at a time when they were supposed to be fast asleep, they called Mission Control. "Are you all right back there?" "Sure, everything's nominal here. What's with you?"

Well, it turned out that they'd seen this flash, some trick rock reflection or something that made a burst of light right where Earth was. And they thought it was missiles, see, World War III starting . . . anybody would've, in those days. That's what I mean by the feelings just underneath. But nobody ever said a gloomy word, on top.

There were other things underneath, of course, different for different people, all adding up to The End. But this is no place to talk about the old days, it's all changed now. So that's that, and now here comes Kevin:

"I can remember it like it was yesterday. All morning had been occupied with the Lander carrying Todd and Jim Aruppa, coming down and finding a flat place. I nearly got thrown out of the control room for sticking my head in people's way to catch a glimpse of a screen while I was bringing stuff. The amount of coffee those NASA boys put away! And some of them ate, one man ate seven egg sandwiches, they were all keyed up like crazy. All right, I'll stick to the point, I know what you want to hear.

"So by then it was coming pitch-dark on Mars, only the Lander's lights glaring on a pebbly plain with cracks in it. The computer colored it red, I guess it was. Mission Control wouldn't let them get out then. They were ordered to sleep until it got full light again. Ten hours . . . imagine, *sleeping* your first night on Mars!

"The last thing was, Perry up in the command module reported a glow of light on the eastern horizon. It wasn't a moon rising—we'd already seen one of those. A little greenish crescent, going like crazy.

"So during the night Perry was supposed to check on what might be glowing toward the east—a volcano, maybe? But by the time he came around to where he could see the place again, the glow had faded to nearly nothing, and next trip there was nothing at all to see.

"At this time a relief crew was on the CRTs in Mission Control, but every so often one of the men who were supposed to be sleeping in their quarters next door would come in and just stare at the screens for a few minutes. All you could see was a faint, jagged horizon-line, and then the stars began.

"First light was supposed to be at five-fifty A.M. our time—(see, I even remember numbers!)—and by that time the whole day crew was back in the room, everybody all mixed together, and all wanting coffee and danishes.

"On the screens the sky was getting just a little lighter, so the horizon looked sharper and darker until suddenly a faint lightness came on the ground plain in front of the mountains. And then came a minute I'll never forget. Like the whole room was holding its breath, only whispering or rustling a little around their dark screens. And then Eggy Stone yelled out loud and clear:

"*'There's something there! It's big! Oh, man!'*

"That made it official, what the sharp-eyed ones thought they'd been picking up but couldn't believe, and everybody was jabbering at once. And the voices of the astronauts cutting through everything, with that four-and-a-half-minute lag, about how this Thing was sitting in front of them unlit, unmoving, no indication of how it had come there, whether it crawled or flew in or bored up out of the ground. Of course, they thought it was Martians.

"What it was was a great big, say fifty-meter-long, dumbbell shape lying there about a hundred meters in front of their main window. It was two huge spheroids, or hexa-somethings, connected by one big fat center bar—really like a dumbbell. Only in the middle of the connection was a chamber, say three meters each way. We could see right in because its whole front side was folded back like a big gull-wing door. It appeared to be padded inside. The computer called it light blue, with two rust-colored lumps like cushion seats back on the floor inside.

"And both of the big dumbbell chambers at the ends had like windows spaced all around them.

"And filling the window of the end nearest us, the window we could see into, was something moving or flickering slightly, something shiny and lighter blue. It took a second or two to recognize it, because of its size—it was over a meter long, almost round.

"It was an eye. A great, humongous, living eye, blue with a white rim. And looking at us.

"Like the creature it belonged to was so big it was all curled up inside its compartment, with its eye pressed to the glass. For some reason, right from the start we knew that the creature, or being, or whatever, had only one central eye.

"In addition to looking at us—that is, at the camera, most of the time—the eye was also swiveling to examine the Lander and everything around.

"Now all through the excitement Todd and Jim in the Lander were trying to tell us something. I wasn't in on this, but whenever I could get near Voice Contact I heard things like, 'We are not crazy! I tell you we are not crazy, it's talking in our heads. *Yes*, in English. We get two words very distinctly: *Peace* and *Welcome*. Over and over. And we are not out of our minds, if I could figure a way to get this on the caller you'd hear—'

"They sounded madder and madder, I guess Mission Control was giving them a hard time, especially General Streiter who was sure it was a Soviet Commie trick of some kind. And of course there was no way for them to get a mental voice on the antennae. But then the aliens apparently solved that for themselves. Just as Jim was saying for the tenth time that he wasn't crazy or hadn't drunk too much coffee, all our communications went blooie for a minute and then this great big quiet voice drowned everything.

"'PEACE . . .' it said. And then, 'WELL-COME!'

"Something about the voice, its tone, made Mission

Control sound for a minute like a—well, like a cathedral. 'PEACE! . . . WELCOME! . . . PEACE . . . FRIENDS . . .' "

"And then it added, very gentle and majestic, 'COME . . . COME . . .'

"And Mission Control became aware that Todd and Jim were preparing to go out of the Lander.

"Pandemonium!

"Well, I'll skip all this bit where Mission Control was ordering them to stay inside, on no account to even put a hand out, to unsuit—Jim and Todd were calmly suiting up—and anything else they could think of and General Streiter ordering courtmartials for everybody in sight, on Mars or Earth—it even went so far as getting the President out of bed to come and countermand them in person. I found out afterwards that the poor man got so mixed up he thought they were *refusing* to go out onto Mars, and he was supposed to tell them to! And all with this four-and-a-half-minute lag, and this great hushy voice blanking everything out with 'PEACE . . . WELCOME . . .'

"Until finally it was obvious even to the general that nothing could be done, that forty-four million miles away two Earthmen were about to walk out onto Mars and confront The Alien."

(This is Theodora putting in a word here, see, everyone had been so convinced that there was no life on Mars above something like lichen that absolutely no instructions had been thought up for meeting large-scale sentient life, let alone with telepathic communications.)

"Well, they evacuated the air, and as they went to go down the ladder, Jim Aruppa grabbed Todd, and we could hear him saying in his helmet, 'Remember, you bastard! Count cadence, *now!*'

"And nobody knew what that was until we found out there'd been this private arrangement between the two men. After all those months together, see, Jim wasn't going to take all the glory for being the First Man on Mars. As he put it to Todd, 'Who was the *second* man to step onto the Moon?' And Todd had to guess twice, and nobody else knew either. And Jim wasn't going to let that happen again. So he ordered Todd to descend in synch with him and make an absolutely simultaneous first-foot-down. That was one of the little squabbles that kept Mission Control lively all those two years. Some kind of guy, Jim.

"So there they were counting cadence down the ladder to Mars—to *Mars*, man!—with this alien Thing a hundred yards away staring at them.

"And they walked over to it slowly and carefully, looking at everything, the eye following them. And there were no signs of how it had possibly moved there except by some kind of very gentle flight. But no machinery, nothing at all but these two big hexagonal spheroids with windows. And the compartment between. The first word Jim sent back was, 'It seems to be entirely non-metallic. Not plastic, either. More like a—like a smooth shiny dry pod, with windows set in. The frames are non-metallic too.'

"And then they got to where they could see the windows on the farther-off spheroid—and there was another eye looking out at them from it!

"It seemed exactly like the first eye, only slightly larger and paler. The flesh around the eyes registered blue too, by the way—and there was no sign of eyelashes.

"And then both Jim and Todd claimed that this eye *winked* at them and Mission Control went back to calling them crazy.

"When they got back in front, by the open compartment, they made signals as though they were hearing something. And then the voice we could hear via radio changed too. 'Come,' it said in sort of grand-friendly tones. 'Come . . . Please come in. Come with. Say hello friends.'

"Well, that sent Mission Control into a new spasm of countercommands, in the midst of which the two men set the camera on its tripod outside, and walked into the open alien compartment, bouncing a little on the padded floor. Then they turned around to face us, and sat down on the seat-cushion-looking things. And at that the big overhead door slid smoothly forward and down and closed them in. It had a window in it—in fact it was mostly window. But before anybody could think of any reaction to *that*, it opened up again halfway, and Todd and Jim stepped out. Four and a half minutes later we heard, 'They say to bring food for one day.'

"And the men went back up into the Lander to collect supplies.

"Somehow the ordinariness, or what you might call considerateness, of this just took the wind out of a lot of angry lungs.

" 'No water necessary, they say,' Jim Aruppa told us as they climbed back out of the Lander. 'But we brought some just in case. I never thought I'd be glad to see a can of Tab,' he grinned, holding up his little camp basin. 'But we can at least wash our hands in it.'

" 'Jeez, it's getting like a god-forsaken *picnic!*' Eggy Stone shouted over the general uproar.

"Well, the door snapped over and shut down again. We could see them through the window, waving. And then the thing simply lifted up quietly and flew like magic toward and over the camera, and over the Lander, and we couldn't pick it up again. And that was absolutely all for thirty-six long hours, until—

"—Say, Miz Tanton, haven't you got the tape of what they said when they came back? I just can't talk one word more."

So here's a break. All this next part I put together from Jim and Todd's report-tapes of their trip, plus the officially cleaned-up version of it that was in the *Times*. I found a stack of archive tape dupes in the janitor's cubby.

But before that, I should say that the Reverend Perry had been busy, up in the Martian sky. Mission Control at least had one astronaut who would take orders, and they'd told him to try to check out where the Thing had come from during the night. So he got busy with his 'scopes and sensors, and about the time Jim and Todd were going back for their chow, he had a report. A Martian building, or structure, "like a big mound of bubbles" was located in the foothills of Mount Eleuthera to the east. But as a city it was strange—it had no suburbs, no streets, not much internal differentiation, and no roads leading to or away. (Of course not, we know now it was a ship.)

So when the flying dumbbell bearing the two Humans went off NASA's cameras, Perry knew where to try to pick them up. And by the way, although Perry was obedient to orders, he too was acting strange. He didn't volunteer anything, but on direct questioning he admitted that he was hearing voices in his head—at first he said something about a "ringing in his ears"—and when the aliens' voices cut in on the radio wavelength, Perry pulled himself down to his knees and NASA could see enough to realize he was trying to both pray and weep. This didn't disturb them overmuch—considering what else was going on—because the Reverend was known to indulge in short prayers whenever some special marvel of space came up, and he was addicted to brief thanksgivings at any lucky break. He was quite unself-conscious about this, and it never interfered with his efficiency, so maybe NASA figured they were covering all bets by having him along. General Streiter asked him if he was all right.

"I shall say no more about this now, General," Perry replied. "I recognize it is inappropriate to this phase of our mission. But I sincerely believe we have contacted a . . . a Higher Power, and that some very great good may come of this if we prove worthy."

Streiter took this in silence; he knew Perry as a congenial fellow Commie-hater, and he had expected him to see Red skulduggery in the sudden materialization of the Thing. But Perry seemed to be taking another tack; the general respected him enough to let him be.

So back to Todd and Jim who were being flown silently, magically, over the Martian landscape. They were at the big door-window. The lift-off was so gentle that Jim said he wouldn't have known they were moving if he hadn't been looking out. This reassured them about the absence of any straps or body-holds in the padded compartment they had entered.

They were of course looking for a city or town, or at least the openings of tunnels, and the "mound of bubbles" Perry was reporting took them by surprise. Near the top of the mound was an opening where a sphere or two seemed to be missing; as they came over it, they saw that their craft exactly fitted in. Forward motion ceased quietly, and with a soft, non-metallic brushing sound the modules that carried them dropped into the empty slots. Todd was inspired. "Hey, that's all one huge ship—and this is a dinghy!" His mind had broadcast the right picture; "Yess!" the aliens chorused, "Our ship!"

Before they could see anything of the interior, a side window in their compartment opened, and a light-blue, leathery-looking trunk or tentacle about the size of a fire hose appeared. "Hello!" said the voice in their heads clearly.

"Hello," they said aloud.

The tentacle extended itself towards Jim's hand. Involuntarily he drew back. "Hello? Hello? Friends!" said the soundless voice. "Touch?"

Gingerly Jim extended his hand, and to his surprise, after a little confusion, the contact the alien wanted was achieved.

"It wants to shake hands!" Jim exclaimed to Todd.

"Yes! Friends! Shake!" And a similar window in the opposite wall opened, revealing the other alien. Its tentacle was larger, more wrinkled, and lighter blue. "Friends?"

A round of enthusiastic hand-shaking ensued. Then the second alien wanted something more. Its tentacle's tip pulled clumsily but gently at Todd's glove, and he got a confused message about taking it off and speaking.

When Todd got his glove off and took the alien's flesh bare-handed, he gasped and seemed to stagger.

"What's wrong? Todd?"

"Okay—it's okay, very—try it."

Jim ungloved and grasped the tip of the alien limb. Then he too gasped—as contact occurred, there came with it a rush of communication, both verbal and pictorial, in which he could pick out bits or sequences of past events, present communication, speculations, images—including a vision of himself—plans, questions—he was all but *inside* an alien mind!

They were both laughing, delighted at this immense novelty to explore—and from the other sides of their padded walls came echoing chuckles. A pleasant fragrance like cinnamon was coming through their air filters, too. They were the first Humans to smell the spicy odor emitted by these aliens when excited and interested.

"This is going to take practice," Jim gasped. He tried to convey the idea to the alien whose blue tentacle he was clasping, and received a strong feeling of assent. Delicately, it moved its tentacle within his grip, so that only certain surfaces were apposed, and the rush of mindflow quieted down.

Then it tapped his palm in a way that they soon came to recognize as meaning "I have something to tell/show you." And he found himself seeing a connected, coherent "movie" of the alien's bubble-craft approaching Earth sometime earlier, sampling the airborne communications—both radio and video—and selecting the large landmass of North America to linger near. "All same language," said the voice in his head. "Many pictures—teach much." And then a sample of what they had set themselves to learn—recognizable segments of *Dallas*, *All My Children*, *Sesame Street*, newscasts—and ads, ads, ads unceasing. "Much do not understand."

Whew! Jim tried to interrupt, but the flow went on. From it he gathered that the aliens had evoked a few hostile reactions from US Air Force installations. Also the aliens soon learned that great intergroup hostilities existed on Earth. They had actually been on the verge of leaving—"Go look better planet"—when they learned about the Mars mission. It seemed to them that this would be the ideal place and way to meet Humanity. So here they were, and here were our two astronauts—deep in converse, without having seen the forms or faces of their new friends. (For from the start, there had seemed to both men no question that a *friendly* meeting was in progress, and friendship was growing between them every moment.)

"Now you want say Hello others, so we talk more?"

"Yes indeed."

A picture-sequence in their minds prepared them and then the whole back wall of their compartment irised open, giving onto a great, softly glowing space. When they went to it they saw that the "mound of bubbles" was actually a shell around an open core; all the "bubbles" gave onto a common open space, in which were a few structures whose use or meaning they couldn't guess. All around the walls, ceiling, floor were the openings of compartments similar to their own, some brightly lighted, some dim, some dark, so that the whole formed a kind of grand auditorium or meeting hall. At the mouth of nearly every individual compartment was an alien, or two or more, all with their great single eyes turned eagerly in their direction.

And here I have to pause, or put in asterisks or somehow prepare you before I describe what you notice I've omitted so far—the aliens' shapes.

The color of course you know—sky-blue in the main, with here and there blues lighter or darker, from slate to peacock blue, from pale blue foam to deep marine. And the great eyes were quite Human-shaped, though the size of foot-lockers. And the tentacles you have met—each had groups of sucker-discs which were apparently quiescent unless the owner wished to cling.

It is their general shape you don't yet know.

There is one, and only one, earthly animal that they resembled, and they resembled it very closely. To put it bluntly, the aliens looked like gigantic cerulean octopuses.

Image-wise, of course, it was terrible.

In addition to being unspellable (octopuses, octopusses, octopoi, octopi, octopodes?), it conjured up every old horror cliché. And it was undeniable—they *were* in fact simply big air-breathing octopuses; we all learned later that they had evolved in their planet's oceans, and slowly adapted to land as their oceans dried. Their mantles had lost the propulsive function, and four of their back tentacles had evolved to limbs suitable for walking on land, leaving the other four to take on hand-and-arm and telepathic transmission abilities.

Their heads were large and bald and shiny above the single

eye, and their mantles began where a chin should be, concealing their noses and mouths, or beaks, or whatever. Also to be glimpsed beneath the mantle's rippling edges was a mass of darker blue fur-like organs, among which seemed to be some very small, delicate tentacles of unknown use.

In all, had it not been for their truly lovely coloring and odor and the expressive friendliness of their large eyes, the first impression of the aliens to a Human, would have to be revulsion bordering on terror.

The Earthly media of course went wild at first—GIANT BLUE OCTOPUSES ON MARS! shrilled even the staidest. Octopus!—the name alone makes for the world's worst PR. That's why I've given you all this preliminary stuff, instead of just dictating from the newsclips.

The photos, when they came, made things a little better, because their postures were so versatile and graceful. And their basically radial bodies were obviously in transition to a bilaterally symmetrical form—the four "back" leg-tentacles were much larger and longer, to free the front four. In fact if—as happened later—a small one wore a long robe with a hood to conceal the shiny bald dome above the eye, it could pass for a large, somewhat top-heavy human form. And they spent much of their time thus upright, looking rather like multiply-armed Indian deities, and smelling delightful. So that, as soon as Earth saw more of them, the original "Sci-Fi" horror images were seen to be ludicrously inappropriate, and forgotten.

While Todd and Jim were taking in the nature of their audience, and vice versa, their new friends were folding back the walls of their compartments and dragging the cushions to the edge of the front.

"We speak one-to-all like this. We show you." And they motioned Todd and Jim to take seats. "No fear fall off, everybody catch."

Then they stationed themselves on each side, laid their transmission-tentacles across Jim and Todd's shoulders, and seemed to listen.

"No—clothes too thick. Can take off, please? Air good here." So the men first gingerly lifted off their helmets—getting a real blast of carnation scent—and then started peeling down. They felt a bit odd about it in front of all those eager eyes, but what the hell, their bodies were no more to the aliens than a wombat's to them. So they sat back down again, nude, and the tentacles came back. "Ahhh! Good!"

And with that the two big aliens stretched their other transmitter arms out to the aliens in the compartments next door, and these did the same to those around them, so that in a minute the whole great amphitheatre was intricately laced together, with the men as foci.

While this was happening, Todd felt a plucking at his shins. He looked down, and there was this dark-blue tentacle coming up at him from the compartment below. He heard, or sensed, what could only be a giggle, and next instant three big round bright eyes were staring up at him over the edge of his floor. A spicy fume of interest wafted up.

The alien next to him emitted a reproving sound, and batted at the eyes with a spare limb. "Young ones!" Peering down, Todd and Jim saw a cluster of smaller aliens in the chamber below, evidently trying to get in on the network by short-circuit. "It's okay." He grinned. "No problem to us."

So their two big friends let the little fellows sneak tendrils in to touch the men's legs and feet.

"Okay . . . You go first?" said the one next to Jim. "Oh, wait—Us name Angli. An-gli," it repeated aloud. "You name?"

"Hello, Angli!" said Jim to them both. "Us name Hu-mans. But"—he pointed at the other—"You have special personal name, for you only?"

Well, that was their introduction to the one great difficulty of mind-speech—asking questions. It took minutes for them to get sorted out as individuals, and even so they weren't sure they had it right. Jim said, "The customary thing here seems to be to call up a quick flash-image of the person, or his eye, or something special about him or her. I don't think verbal names are used much. But our friends seem to be something like Urizel and Azazel, for what it's worth. We'll try calling them that and see if it works." Then he put his arm around Todd. "We together, Hu-mans," he said. "But *he* alone"—gesturing—"is *Todd.* I—me, here—am *Jim*. Todd . . . Jim. Jim . . . Todd. Get it?"

"Me Jane, you Tarzan," muttered Todd.

"Shut up, you idiot, this is no time to clown . . . We'll have to be sure somehow that they know what a joke is . . . All right. Urizel, Azazel, and all the rest of you Angli—what do you want to know about us Humans first?"

And so started the greatest show-and-tell anthropology class of their lives.

Surprisingly soon, it got itself organized with their two friends alternately passing questions to the men. Not surprisingly, in view of their TV fare, the first queries were mainly about economics. Todd had the pleasure of trying to answer, "What is 'money'?" He managed to form a picture of a medium of exchange passing from hand to hand in the Human world. And luckily the Angli seemed to have something to relate this to; Jim got a visual image of furry brown creatures carrying on their tails stacks of big square things with holes in them, that had to be clumsy coins.

"Gosh, what does a really rich one do?" Todd didn't expect an answer, but the Angli had picked up the drift of his query, and he got a clear mental picture of a pompous-looking brown alien followed by a formal train of specialized coin-bearers, their long tails erect and loaded to the tips with big discs.

Both Humans and Angli laughed.

"What do you do with 'money'?" Azazel asked. Jim gulped and tried to visualize a bank teller, vaults, checkbooks.

"I fear I'm not doing justice to the international banking system," he said to Todd. "But dammit, ours has to make more sense than carrying your money around on your tail!"

"I'm beginning to wonder," Todd muttered. "No, no," he said to Azazel. "Not important."

It was now very apparent that the Humans were by no means

the first new race the Angli had met. Fleeting images of many other aliens, worlds, cities, ships, crossed their perceptions from various Angli minds. These aliens seemed to have spent years jaunting about the Galaxy, meeting people and things.

As to the Angli's own home world—the notion that they were Martians was disposed of very early—they were shown an image of a planet not unlike Earth, but greener, near a GO-type sun. A view of the nearby constellations enabled the men to guess that it was near the nebula in Orion's sword. A close-up view showed a lush, attractive landscape with a bubble-dome town.

And the Angli were not alone! Another intelligent race lived there—no, wait, *had* lived there once—"many times ago." The blurred image of a porpoise-like creature with legs seemed to have passed through many minds. "They go"—but whether they had left or died off was never clear; these Angli perhaps didn't know. The Angli were alone there now.

One last fact that came out was sensational; the "bubbles" the men were in wasn't their only ship. They had maybe half a dozen ships and stuff parked on Luna, on the back side of our moon, where we couldn't see them. One or more contained a lot more Angli, who wanted simply to sleep until a really promising planet was found. ("Wake us when we get someplace!") Very young Angli were also asleep there. Another one—or more—contained members of another race, whose planet had been in trouble, so the Angli volunteered to find them a new one. (In their experience, the Galaxy seemed to be full of all kinds of planets just waiting to be found.) This particular race needed an aquatic environment, it seemed.

Another ship seemed to contain assorted seeds and supplies; despite their casual behavior, the Angli really had great practical sense about essentials. And at least two were empty—one had contained a race the Angli had successfully relocated. And a final one contained a spectacular cargo we on Earth were soon to get a view of.

(Of course, on learning that other ships existed, the general and others promptly began to suspect that the Angli also had battleships or other military capabilities parked up there, and many covert plans were laid to sneak around Luna and peek. But they all came to nothing, and nothing hostile ever showed up.)

Each query raised a dozen others; the hours passed like minutes. Finally a growing emptiness in their middles forced the men to call a halt.

"We eat now?"

The Angli too, it seemed, were tired and hungry, although so fascinated that they seemed ready to go on indefinitely. But at Jim's question a cheer broke out among the young ones below. In no time they had produced great baskets of what looked like hardtack, and were carrying them around the auditorium, passing a container out to each row. Each Angli in turn helped him—or her—self to a piece, and tucked it neatly under a mantle-fold in their central bodies, where the men had surmised their mouths, or beaks, might be.

"We've got to get this gender business straightened out," Todd said with his mouth full. "Oh, cripes. How do we do *that*, Tarzan?"

"Maybe we don't, until we can produce a real Jane." And so it turned out. He seemed to evoke a response to his first tries at describing Human sexes—"Humans like Jim and me here"—he indicated his genitalia —"we call 'men.' Other Humans have lumps *here* but not *here*—we call them 'women.' And it takes both the two kinds together to make young ones," Todd continued. "How do you make young?"

But here all impression of understanding faded, and an Angli question, "What you call Mathlon?" stumped everybody. Mind-visions of an Angli picking things out of a puddle didn't help.

. . . Theodora Tanton here again, I just excerpted all that above from Jim's long report, to give the atmosphere and show some of the problems; I guess that some parts belong in the after-lunch session. And don't shoot me, sisters, about the gender part and the "lumps," that's just what the man said. I put most dialogue as if it were ordinary speech instead of explaining whether it was telepathy or audible speech each time. Men and Angli were developing a sort of half-speech/half-thought lingo that worked well.

The afternoon, or what was left of it, went as fast as the morning, and soon the sunlight that filtered through into the great central dome was visibly reddening into a typical Martian sunset.

"We go back now, please," the men said. "Our people have much fear."

"Ohh-Kayee!" said Urizel, and they all laughed. One thing the men couldn't get over was how human their laughter was—and they thought ours was incredibly Anglian.

So they closed up the doors, the Humans suited up, the module lifted away silently from its slot, and the trip repeated itself in reverse. They tried again—it had come up all day—to understand the source of its power, but always the same answer baffled them. "We do with bodies. Like so"— and the speaker would loft himself a few meters, apparently effortlessly, and descend again. "You no do, eh? We find many races no do, only one we find can do." And a picture came in their minds of a large ray-like being, sailing and flapping above an alien landscape. The Angli tapped his head regretfully. "Fly pretty, but not have much brain. Come later, maybe."

Now on their return trip they could see their friends loading in, and it was obvious that they propelled their craft by simply *pushing* it up from inside, as a man under a table might lift it with his back—but with no need to press down on anything. Nor did it seem tiring.

"Antigravity is the best guess we can make," Jim told Earth later.

One more item they were shown—in both the end compartments was a window in the floor, beside which was a bank of what turned out to be outside lights—including infra-red. They were powered by small batteries.

"Use up fast," Azazel said, frowning. And they didn't turn the lights on again until they were over the Earth Lander. This contraption was the first construction of metal or wires the men had seen. It looked handmade. "We get from special people," Azazel said, and transmitted a brief shot of some sort of aliens in an apparent workshop. "Not on our home."

"We make light too," Urizel sent, and from under his (or her) mantle suddenly came a soft blue glow, which brightened to a point, then turned off. "Is work," the big Angli said expressively. Light was evidently strictly for emergency use. They seemed to have fantastically good night vision; the men suspected that their use of the floodlights as they neared the Lander was more for the Earthmen's sake than their own. "You no see so good in dark."

"Maybe they were surprised when we didn't seem to see their approach last night," Jim said.

And then it was time to say goodbye and get back in their own little craft. And report to Mission Control.

"I bet they don't let us off the hook for hours and hours and hours," Todd said. And he was proved right. Kevin remembers vividly the shout that rang through Mission Control when the camera picked up their approaching lights. And then it took half the night to relay and record what I've put down here, plus a lot of repeats and mix-ups I've cut out.

Oh—I've forgotten one big thing. Just as they were leaving the dome a senior-looking Angli sent them a message through Azazel.

"He say, why not we take you home to Earth? Go quick, like maybe thirty-forty your days. We get Human now up in sky, leave your ships here, you come back and get some other time. And you help us say Hello and make friendship with Earth?"

What an offer! "And with a soft landing at the end," crooned Todd ecstatically.

"Tell him yes, most happy," replied Jim. "Say—is he your leader?"

Now that brings up another subject I've been postponing—their government. As far as we ever found out, they virtually had none. The older Angli formed a loose sort of council that anybody who wanted to could be in. Any question, like where to go next, or what to do about a specific problem, was apparently solved by informal mind-melding. People would put up ideas, and they'd be mulled over until a consensus evolved. What happened in the event of a serious disagreement? But there doesn't seem to have been any. "Oh, we take turns," said Azazel negligently.

. . . Anyway, thus it was that the great homecoming of our successful Mars mission was in an alien ship in no way under the control of NASA, although they politely accepted all our communications. And they seemed surprised at the close supervision expected from and by Mission Control. On their home world, apparently, people just wandered hither and yon, off to a moon, or whatever.

One of the rites of growing up, it seemed, was making your own vehicle (they were indeed gigantic dried seed-pods) and fitting it out for long trips. With their long-range mind-speech capability there were no problems about getting lost, and their world seemed to have had few dangers. About the only mishap that seemed likely to occur to young ones jaunting about was when their presence or chatter annoyed some elder citizen who would complain to the council, and have them grounded for a week or two. Like youngsters everywhere, they prized mobility and were always putting in work improving their craft, which virtually served as alternate homes. The climate, one gathered, was very benign.

It sounded idyllic; I wasn't the only one to start to wonder why, really, they had left. . . .

The day of their arrival on Earth has been so amply covered in schoolbooks that I have only small pieces to add, like about the riot. What went on at first was all standard—this great beige bubble-nest wafting down toward a cleared-off area in a sea of people, escorted for the last miles by practically everything the Air Force could put in the air. It sat down resiliently and before it had finished heaving, Angli all over the top began opening doors and looking out. A group escorting the three astronauts got out together and flew them down to where a cordoned and carpeted way to the receiving stand was marked off.

There was Urizel and Azazel, and a pair of aged senior councilors the men had persuaded to come along. Their progress was highly informal; people could see that the men were trying to report back to their Commander-in-Chief in a stylish, military way, but the Angli were hard to keep in line. They began thought-broadcasting to the crowd in general, right over the heads of the officials. And then they hooked into the PA system with "Hello! Peace! Friends!" And the press corps broke the lines by the ship and began infiltrating everywhere. Kevin was with the NASA press contingent, he passed me a few tidbits. And the aged councilors, to whom one Earthman was much like another, began greeting the police and Secret Service men who were standing, arms linked, with their backs to the ship, trying to contain the swaying crowd. And during the official party's slow progress to the stand, Angli began coming out of the ship and making short flights over the heads of the crowd.

The stage was set for trouble, and it happened—five or six dark-blue young Angli came out together with their arms full of something and flew over the crowd to the right, looking for a place to land and calling out "Friends!" and laughing that Human laugh. What they had was blooms from the ship's hydroponics, big fragrant stalks that unfortunately looked a bit like hand grenades. The crowd was too thick below them, so they began dropping the flowers onto people's heads. At that, the Humans below started to mill, some people backing away in alarm while others pressed forward curiously. And the youngsters circled close overhead, laughing and pelting people with flowers.

Suddenly someone took real fright, and a small local stampede away from the Angli started. Others, seeing people running and feeling themselves pushed, began to run and push aimlessly too. Shouting broke out. The pushing intensified fast—and a woman screamed and went down.

All this showed only as a confused place on the edge of the TV screens, while the astronauts and the Angli were still straggling up the cordoned pathway to the stand where the presidential party was waiting. As the sound of shouting rose from off-screen, the United States Marine Band broke into a louder march-piece, which amplified the confusion over an outbreak of real screaming and yells.

Urizel, sensing what was happening, dropped Todd's arm and flew over the tangle with the idea of shooing the youngsters back to the ship. But the arrival of this monster of much greater size frightened more people. The fallen woman was trampled and began to shriek. Urizel, spotting her, dived to the spot and sent his long tentacles down to extricate her, really scaring the people nearby.

About then, police sirens started up, and an ambulance got its warbler going and began pressing into the scene. This excited more people outside the immediate nucleus. Some tried to gather their families and run, while others ran toward the uproar. The yelling developed a panicky, ominous beat. Meanwhile, those on the red carpet were still making their slow way to the President on the stand.

Now, every telepathic race is well aware of the terrible danger of contagious panic, the threat of a mind-storm. Both inside the ship and out, the Angli became aware of what was going on, and about to get much worse. Their response was automatic.

In perfect synchrony, they all stopped whatever they were doing, and sent out a united, top-power mental command: "*Quiet! Be calm! Sleep!* . . . QUIET! BE *CALM! SLEEP!!!*" It blasted the field.

So powerful was this thought-command that by the first repetition the yells and shouts died in people's throats. The uproar tapered down to a strange silence, in which the band raggedly played on for a few bars before they too were overwhelmed. Running people slowed to a walk, to a standstill; their heads drooped, and they saw the ground looking invitingly comfortable, attracting them to relax down. And suddenly, all in the moments that the great command silently went out, what had been a wildly agitated mob became a field of peaceful sleepers. Some slept sitting with their heads on their knees, others sprawled full-length, their heads on any neighboring body.

The police and Secret Service men were of course affected too, and after a moment's heroic resistance, they went down in waves atop their sleeping charges.

The band and the PA system were silent, and on the receiving stand the dignitaries retained presence of mind only to locate a convenient chair before collapsing into sleep. The President was already dozing; he opened his mouth and emitted a few snorts indicative of deeper slumbers, while his lady slept decorously beside him. A stray seagull alighted on the Secretary of State, and went to sleep on one leg.

Close overhead, at what had been the center of the disturbance, floated Urizel, the woman he had rescued sleeping in his grasp. He spotted the stalled ambulance, which emanated images of physical aid.

"Wake up," he said to the crew. "Here is Human hurt." They snapped back to consciousness rubbing their eyes, and jumped to man the stretcher.

"Put her here."

A press photographer beside them also woke, reaching by reflex for his camera, and got the banner headline shots of his life—Urizel stooping low with the unconscious girl draped photogenically across his tentacles, his great eye luminous with compassion and concern. "ALIEN RESCUES WOMAN FROM CROWD! ALIEN CARRYING GIRL HE SAVED TO AMBULANCE!"

(I found out from Kevin, who had been there too and waked first, that the photographer had luckily missed an even more sensational shot. Urizel, noting that this Human he carried seemed to differ from the astronauts, had seized the opportunity to check out the locations and nature of those "lumps" Todd had told him of—in the process rearranging quite a lot of her clothes.)

The woman turned out to be a Mrs. C. P. Boynton. She was only slightly bruised, and her statements to the press were ecstatic.

"I was so scared, I knew that hundreds of people would trample on me and I'd be killed. I just prayed to God, 'Help me!' And suddenly there was this great blue being flying over me like an angel, and he just reached down and pulled me out from under all those terrible feet! And oh, he smells so lovely!"

What I want to convey is that the Angli would be getting a very good press, right from Day One.

Back at the stand, the official greetings to and by the President finally came off. Perry tactfully roused the great man by murmuring, "Sir, I believe you were about to say a few words," and he automatically rose up into his speech—just in time to divert the aged councilors from returning to their ship. And the band began to play, rather disjointedly—but it isn't true that they then or ever played "Nearer My God to Thee." And the reception rolled off.

When it came time for Todd, Jim and Perry to part company from their alien friends, with whom they'd spent over a month of intimate travel, things got pretty emotional. During the voyage home, the Rev. Perry had been observed to attach himself to Azazel in particular. Now, up on the receiving stand, the great blue forms of the Angli were turning away, to go back to their ship and leave the Humans to their own. They were up on their back tentacles, their heads towering above everything as they bade polite farewells to the President, his lady, and the Secretary of State, now minus his seagull. Perry quietly moved closer. Suddenly he dropped to his knees and flung his long arms around the tentacles Azazel was standing on. (Perry was a huge man.) After a moment of confusion, it became clear that he was simply hugging the alien, his face laid against Azazel's side, and weeping. He was also mumbling something that sounded so private that no one listened, except Kevin. And no one knew what thought-speech he was sending to his big alien friend, or receiving back from him.

The strange tableau lasted only an instant. Then Perry got up with great dignity and stepped back into line with Todd and Jim. And the moment was swamped by the hand-tentacle shaking going on all round.

Kevin, who had been just outside the stand, told me afterward that at the end, Perry had said clearly, "*Non Angli sed angeli*"—and if you don't place the quotation at first, listen on.

Now to sum up the impression the aliens were making, I'll give you a letter I received in response to my first appeal for eyewitnesses. It was written by one Cora-Lee Boomer, aged eighty-nine, like this:

"Of course I only saw it on TV you know. Maybe I saw it better that way. The Army cleared off this big sandy place, Dry Lake Something. And they had guards all over. But the people just filled it up. And about eleven A.M., I remember because it was time to feed the baby, Donald, we saw it coming down in the sky. It was like a big bunch of grapes only no stems.

"And it kept coming down, real slow, I guess not to hurt anything, and pretty soon a helicopter was going around it, taking pictures. It was kind of tan colored, with antennae sticking out. All these round things pressed together like something I used to see—honey-combs. When they sent pictures from close up you could see all these blue eyes inside looking out. So beautiful. Excuse me, I can't say it right.

"Mostly I try not to think about it, even today I can just see it. But that man I had then, he thought he was so smart. And I was a young fool, I did whatever he wanted. He said that it was all no good. Stay away from Whitey shit, he said. Excuse me. I was so young.

"But when they landed and got out with the three men and I saw their eyes close up, I had a feeling he was wrong. They looked so beautiful. Like caring and understanding. And smiling too. I should have believed my own eyes.

"So I only saw things start. He came in and saw me looking

at it and turned the set off—it was on all the channels, see—and said, 'Get my lunch.' So I never saw much of them after that. And of course I never got to go.

"I think now he was wrong, he was crazy. They were good, good. But I was so young and the baby kept me pretty busy, and with my job. Now I'm old I know there's more to life. I wonder what it be like. George, he's long gone.

"I just remember that big loving eye. Sometimes I cry a lot.

"I hope this is what you said you wanted. Sincerely, Cora-Lee Boomer."

This is Theodora Tanton again, saying well, that was the way the Earth's first meeting with the Angli went. I know the White Book doesn't tell about the riot, and the little points Kevin saw. But they're important, to show how people were starting to *feel* a certain way about the aliens, to explain part of what happened later.

People could have been disappointed, see, or bored. The aliens brought no hardware. And all the films and fiction we used to see kind of assumed that our first contact with ALIENS was going to result in a lot of new fancy technology, or at least a cure for the common cold. Goodies. But as Urizel said, these people brought us only peace and friendship—at least on the surface people could see. Their own goodies, like antigravity and telepathy, were just in their bodies—they could no more explain them or transmit them than we could hand over our sense of smell.

And then more things happened to excite the press. To everyone's surprise, the big ship simply broke up next day, with Angli flying pieces of it all over. Soon there was nothing left in NASA's guard ring but some struts and potted plants.

"ALIENS WANT TO SEE WORLD! ALIENS TO VISIT CATHEDRALS! ALIENS STUDY WORLD RELIGIONS! CALL FOR LANGUAGE-SPEAKERS! ALIENS DO NOT READ OR WRITE! ALIENS WANT TO MEET EVERYBODY ON EARTH!" (That would be some of the youngsters chatting up the press. People had trouble sorting out the kids' stuff, at first.)

So Angli started turning up in little groups, or even alone, all over, at any time of day or night. Of course that gave the security forces of all the big nations total fits.

It turned out they needn't have worried too much about the Angli's safety. (Their own security was another matter.) But it's hard to assassinate a telepath—hostile thoughts blasted out signals to them long before the thinker could act. I don't know if this is in the White Book or not, but just to show you:

One afternoon some Angli were in Libya, chatting with people at a market by a highway where cars were whizzing by like mad amongst the livestock and all. Suddenly every Angli grabbed a nearby Human or two and shot straight up in the air, maybe twenty meters. At the same time, two more Angli grabbed a certain car, and flying with it, simply flipped it tail-over into the empty space they'd made. Next second there was an explosion as a bomb went off inside the car, and a few people got cuts. The would-be bombers were dead.

It all happened so fast people were totally bewildered, they had to piece together afterwards that some crazies had been going to blow the Angli up. And the Angli had taken defensive steps both for themselves and nearby people. That part of it was what stuck in people's minds when it was all over—that Angli automatically rescued you.

Then there was another big episode that may be in the White Book. It was when an Angli named Gavril was being taken on a scenic drive down the great road called the Corniche, in France. Gavril got tired of looking at the dirty Mediterranean—I guess he could hear the thoughts of dying fish and seabirds—and started casting about.

Next thing, he had flashed up onto the air from the open convertible, paced the car briefly, and then come to rest on a railway overpass. A rail line ran below the road. By the time his hosts got back to him, he was standing with closed eye, so evidently deep in concentration that they just waited.

Then train hootings began in the distance and Gavril opened his eye.

"Is O-kayee now," he said. "People see people." And he lofted back into the car, offering no explanation. Of course his hosts began questioning, especially as there seemed to be some excitement starting, down by the railroad.

What had happened, it transpired, is that Gavril had picked up the thoughts of two trainloads of people approaching each other at terrific speed in the tunnels below. Happening to notice that the line was single-track, he became concerned and hopped off to check.

Yes, he realized. They were heading for a frightful crash. Gavril shot strong mental blasts at the trains' engineers—it was hard work aiming simultaneously at targets speeding opposite ways—"*Danger!* STOP!" As I said, it was difficult. When he finally brought them to a stop, the headlight of each train was just visible to the other.

Well, when his hosts realized what he'd done, they called in the press, and hundreds of grateful passengers besieged the scene. A photo of Gavril hovering over a locomotive, captioned "ANGE DE MERCI," appeared in all the big French papers that night. Apparently about six hundred people would have died without his intervention; somebody, presumably terrorists, had buggered the automatic switch and alarm systems.

Well, of course there was no holding the media after that, and scads of episodes, true and concocted, were headlined. There grew up a feeling that Angli were symbols of benevolence or good fortune and that it was lucky to be in the presence of one. People actually began plucking at them, hoping to tear off a little scrap of "armor" to carry with them like rabbit's feet, I guess. But of course they weren't wearing armour, they were in their skins. The situation would have been dangerous and painful had it not been for their telepathic warnings. As it was, a couple of youngsters got scratched, and they all took to wearing flowing scarves they could cut up and pass out. "Is a little cra-zee, people your world," Todd said Urizel told him. Of course profuse apologies were extended by all authorities, but there is no controlling mobs. And the Angli began drawing *mobs*, crowds of very emotionally wrought-up people, quite different from merely the curious or sensation-seekers.

During this period, there were things going on that I should know and tell you, because for sure they're not in the White Book, but you know, I never completed my research—never began it really. To do so I'd have had to go to what's left of a dozen countries, and get into the USSR and even find certain hospitals. For the Angli were visiting places and talking to people they never saw fit to mention to NASA or anybody here, even to Todd, Jim and Perry who had become their more or less official escorts.

Well, you may ask, what kind of inside story do I have, if I never did the research? Oh, the research was just an ornament I envisioned, to the real tale that fell into my hands—wait!

And that aside about the hospitals is a guess, by the way. It could have been university labs, or even private industry facilities. The gist of it is that somehow some Angli found the means to do a spot of sophisticated scientific research into Human physiology. And they seemed to have an instinct for places where the press was strictly controlled, but that only came out later.

What came out then were two things of overpowering interest.

First was their plans to leave.

To leave? To *leave?* —To just go jaunting off somewhere out in the Galaxy—and maybe never come back?

This was a jolt. Maybe some higher-ups somewhere had done some serious thinking about how all this would end, but it hadn't reached the public. In fiction and films there was always some sort of permanence after the great Earth/Alien meeting; either the aliens were trying to take over, or Earthmen had beaten a path to their planetary doorstep, or *something* implied that there would be more contact, or at least some permanent effects. Not just this, "Hello, Nice-to-meet-you, Bye-bye" business the aliens seemed to have in mind. A *visit*. Was that all this was?

The answer seemed to be, Yes.

Why? Not that anyone had thought seriously of their staying around forever, but, well, why leave so *soon?*

Answer: They had things to attend to. There were all those beavers, or crocodiles, or whatever, sleeping up on the moon, waiting for the Angli to find them a water-world. And there were—God, there were all those *other* Angli up there, waiting to wake up when they found a real planet! And of course Earth wouldn't do. Here the Angli tried to be tactful, but it soon came out—Earth was to them a sort of planetary slum, too dirty and polluted and used up and overcrowded to live in. "An interesting place to *visit*, but—"

Not, of course, that any government had actually extended them an offer of real estate. (Some private citizens, especially those from Texas and Australia who seemed to own extraordinary amounts of the Earth's surface, did make some offers to "interested Angli families.")

What would be really nice, people thought, would be if the Angli were to settle on the Moon, or someplace relatively close. What about Venus or Mars? Couldn't they remake one, with some magical planet-shaping devices? And stay around?

Answer: Too bad, but we really haven't any magical planet-shaping tools, and everything else in your particular solar system is quite, quite uninhabitable. Sorry again.

As all this went on at an accelerating tempo, various people extended to the Angli some truly remarkable job offers, or suggested ways that they could make a living on Earth. Even the Mafia turned out to be very interested in their possibilities as security guards, with that telepathic alarm system. Strange Arabs called upon them at night. Several large churches even offered them substantial sums to stay and lead services. And a great many national intelligence or security agencies tendered proffers.

All of these the Angli listened to with good-humored mystification. One evening when Earthly economics were being discussed, an Angli pulled out a coconut-sized pod filled with what appeared to be five- to ten-carat diamonds of exquisite color. "Like these good?" he asked. "We pick up, over there"—waving a tentacle in the general direction of Alpha Centauri. "Go get quick." By the time the matter was explained the bottom had fallen out of the diamond market from Pretoria to Zurich. And it was intimated that they had resources of gold, or anything you cared to name, cached about.

What they really liked, personally, was flowers. Particularly dandelions of large size. Private applications to the Angli took on a distinctly different tone after this.

But it did not affect the public's emotional view of them as simply benevolent miracle-workers, angels of mercy—or, now that we are getting nearer the point, simply angels. Clearly a great outcry of mourning, a great weeping lay ahead. The day they would leave would be so black. People couldn't think about it.

And then came the second event, or shock.

The Angli seemed to be completing their study of our cultures and especially our religions—if "study" isn't too formal a term for what they did, which was simply to ask questions. They were very interested in anything we were doing, whether it was running a paint factory or conducting a service in Notre Dame. But they always asked people about their beliefs, or rather, about their god or gods. And one question which never failed to come up was, "Where is your god?"

After they had received an inventory or description of, say, the Hindu pantheon, they always wound things up by asking, "Where are they? Where are they *now?*"

They got strange answers, of course. People pointed to the sky, or Westminster Abbey, or the Golden Pavilion; one man took them to the Grand Canyon. But when it came to *seeing* a given god or gods—well, we had to struggle with terms like "immaterial" or "transcendent" or "immanent." And they seemed, not exactly disappointed, but very serious.

Finally one day Todd turned the tables on them. "Do you have a god?" he asked.

"Oh yes. Many."

"And where are your gods?"

They were talking on a balcony overlooking the moonlit Great Pagoda of Moulmein. Azazel waved a tentacle moonwards. "Up there."

"Your gods are up there with your ships? In spirit, you mean?"

"No. Gods—there! Many. Most medium, some very old, one new big one, the greatest now. In ship."

Well, everybody figured they were sculptures, or images, or sacred relics of some sort. But the Angli assured us they were alive, very much alive. Only sleeping, like the other Angli.

Well, uh, er . . . could they be seen? Could we go there and see some?

But they were asleep, Azazel repeated. Then he and Urizel conferred.

"Maybe is good they wake up one time," Urizel concluded. "Travel sleep long. You want we bring them here, show you?"

Did we!

Three reporters were present.

"ANGLI HAVE REAL GODS. ASLEEP ON MOON." "ANGLI GODS TO VISIT EARTH!"

And so an Angli delegation took off for Luna, to prepare their gods. And USA officialdom prepared to receive a supernatural visitation. Of course they didn't believe, then, that they'd be getting anything supernatural; their thinking ran to imagining Angli dressed up in costumes.

But the Angli seemed to be taking this very seriously. They returned from all over Earth, and their original ship reconstituted itself. Seeing this, the Reception Committee decided they had best take it more seriously too, and a committee of Earth's religious heads was convened to be in the reception stand. The Pope at that time was a great traveler, and very with-it; he insisted on being present. Of course, this threw official ecclesiastical circles into turmoil, as sanctioning a pagan religion. But he said, "Nonsense. All of us better come, to see what they've got." And the Patriarch of the Greek Orthodox faith for once agreed. The two British Archbishops were naturally eager. And the Protestant denominations joined in. So, seeing this unprecedentedly ecumenical gathering of Christians, the heads of other faiths were stimulated to attend, and what started as a simple showing of alien idols, or something of the sort, grew into the full-scale world-wide summit meeting of every religious affiliation that we all saw on TV. It all required a special super-committee, and the protocol was a nightmare.

What it was really like, by the end of a few days, was a sort of confrontation of all Earth's religions with their alien counterparts. But it was a confrontation we'd lost from the start: while we had Human officials in all kinds of fancy garb and ceremonial ways, they had—gods.

As we soon saw, when, that night a week or so later—another great bubble-ship came drifting, moth-quiet into the searchlights' glare, and settled into its cleared landing-spot. (The officials had learned from the first fiasco; there was a carpeted path to the Reception Committee but the whole area alongside the ship where informal Angli excursions might take place was cleared too. And the crowd was held well back, behind some temporary banks of seats to which admission was charged. Great video screens hung over the field, so all who came could see.)

And they came! The stands were soon overfull, with people crammed in everywhere.

As the ship settled, it could be seen that this was a larger craft, with bigger "bubbles," and a huge central bubble or dome. All the Angli were now present, lined up in a cordon around the perimeter in an unusually orderly fashion. And with them was a troop of Earth children, their arms full of flowers to present to the visiting divinities.

An outer door opened, and out shambled a huge, somewhat decrepit Angli figure, his great eye watering and blinking in the glare. He was festooned all over with what appeared to be animal remains, especially fish-heads and tails, and his head bore the gigantic mask of some unknown beast.

"An—er—animist totem of early days," said the announcer's

voice. "Surprisingly long-lived." Angli attendants handed the tribal godlet a dripping morsel to eat, and led it to a roped-off area of resting couches. It sprawled on tentacles rather than walking upright, being evidently from a time when the Angli were still semi-aquatic.

Next to emerge was a swathed barrel-shape, obese and possibly somewhat senile. Its eye rolled in what appeared to be malevolent confusion, as it was led away waddling, leaving a wet slimy trail.

"An early fertility-deity" the announcer—a hastily-summoned anthropologist—explained. "The next to appear will be avatars of this early form. You will note the increasing cultural complexity."

(The more alert members of the press, seeing the trend of events, were sending out emergency calls for anthropologists, ethnologists, and anyone who might interpret matters.)

"This," said one of these, as the file of ever-taller and more impressive Angli divinities made their various ways down the red carpet, "would represent about the Earthly level of Astarte or Ishtar."

The Angli goddess, a veiled form undulating past him, turned her huge eye and sent him a look that made him drop his note-pad.

By this time it was evident, from the height and demeanor of the newcomers, that they were not ordinary Angli dressed in costumes, let alone statuary or mobile idols. No; this was another order of beings, coming into view before them in the night, and the crowd grew strangely silent. Even today, we don't know what they were. We only know we saw gods.

The last in this first group struck even Earthly eyes as a radiant figure, and she alone appeared conscious of the dignitaries' stand. The dazzling lights, her sparkling, shimmering form and veils, made her—for it was to all earthly eyes a "she"—at one moment a bizarrely seductive alien, at the next a surpassing Earthly beauty. As she paced gracefully down the carpet, she flung up one cerulean limb, and out of the dark overhead a nighthawk dropped to it and perched there. From somewhere strange music played.

With a slight air of disdain she let her attendants turn her into the roped-off waiting area, and as she turned, her painted eye shot straight at the Papal Eminence an unmistakable wink. Then she stooped to accept an armful of flowers from a bedazzled child, proceeded into the reserved area, and stretched out upon an oversized, scroll-ended divan.

It needed no commentator to tell the viewers that great Aphrodite had passed by.

Behind her came a vast grizzled figure who limped, as had the Earthly Vulcan. And after a little space, a towering, commanding figure who glittered with menace, as he strode contemptuously down the way, alien weapons held high. Yet his eye seemed clear and boyish, though all else spoke of war and wrath; even so had Mars appeared to his mother.

Then came troops and bevies of bewilderingly decked and jewelled figures, some carrying emblematic instruments—minor deities, as they might be Muses, or Nereids, Oreads, Dryads of the Greek pantheon, or Peris and Algerits and Indus of others. These danced along under rainbows, piping or singing, to herald the advent of a grand, hoary elder figure, the inevitable old male of unlimited power and authority, whether Zeus, Jove, Wotan or Jehovah. Although the night was perfectly clear, the rumble of far-off thunder accompanied them.

Singing had broken out among the Angli as they all passed by; it was the first time Humans had heard the Angli sing, and they found the chants both strange and pleasing.

And on and on they came, deities resembling nothing familiar to Western eyes but more familiar to Persian, Indian or Chinese; some in weird built-out costumes and serpentine decorations, great curled and feathered headpieces representing frowning grins, or elongations of the eye to dreamlike proportions. In hieratic poses, they made their ways to the appointed spot, and attendant heraldic animals came with them. Also in the air were random sparks, or flames, that looked sometimes like flowers, sometimes like snowflakes, but seemed to have a life of their own as they danced and clustered here and there.

Finally, in the midst of what appeared to be a throng of patriarchal tribal or national divinities, there stood out one of seemingly great power, draped in long white robes. He was oddly attended by what looked at first like small mechanical toys in the shapes of alien children, with sweet luminous eyes. But they were alive.

"A culminant patristic deity," the announcer explained. "He repeatedly reincarnated himself in his own son. Evidently he still has a few believers left. And now—" He went into a huddle with his Angli consultants.

In the pause that followed, all could see that one of the small son-figures had slowed to a stop, and seemed disoriented or ill. But a nearby Angli stooped and patted it solicitously, and it soon revived and ran on.

The somewhat shaken commentator was asking the Angli, "Why do you carry with you these—uh—apparently living gods of old dead religions? I'd think that your one real god or gods would be enough?"

"Ah," said the Angli (some of whom could now speak several Earth languages quite well), "but you see, the minds and spirits of those who worshipped those gods are still in us, under the surface of civilization. And civilization can fail. When we notice that one of those old divinities is growing in vigor, in vitality, yes? it gives us warning. Too many among us are unknowingly worshipping those qualities again. So"—he made stamping motions—"like small fires, we put out quick. You see? But now—"

The singing had fallen silent, and for a few breaths no one moved; there was a feeling of Something impending.

Into the silence there stepped, or materialized, a tall, robed and veiled figure twice the height of any that had gone before. It was definably female. As she came down the way, her face turned toward the dignitaries' stand; she gave no sign, but there was a concerted indrawing of breaths, almost a gasp. Across her single eye was a domino mask; in the depths of its opening could be seen a deep spark of smoldering red-gold. But where the rest of her face and head should be was only black emptiness under the hood. Her garments moved as though covering a gaunt figure, but no feet or hands revealed themselves. Where she passed, children hid their faces in their flowers. And the line of Angli bowed like willows in a silent wind.

Beside her paced an alien animal that she seemed to be restraining on a choke-chain; one of her long sleeves descended to its head, but no hand could be seen. Below the creature's eye was a tangle of tusks and cruel fangs; its limbs were coarsely padded and savagely spurred, and its expression was a blend of coldness and hate. Once, as she moved, her beast lifted its head and gave out a long-drawn baying sound, and the distant thunder growled.

As this apparition neared the stand, it was seen that a great single regal seat was placed for her apart from the others. In this she seated herself impassively. The surrounding Angli had dropped to what would have been a kneeling position in Humans, and the nearby Humans involuntarily turned their eyes away, and dropped their heads low.

"This is she whom we now worship," the Angli by the announcer said. "She has many names but only one essence. Here you might call her The Law of Cause and Effect."

"What is the . . . the animal?"

"That is her instrument of vengeance of all who violate her commandments. Either knowing or unknowingly. Listen!"

From all around the horizon came the echo of a baying sound.

"Alas, my poor friends on your Earth—you do not worship her, but I fear your race has done violence to her Law. It may be that some terrible punishment is readying itself for you innocent ones."

Bravely, the Human commentator asked, "You mean, like meddling with the atom?"

"No. That is just what I do not mean. That might have fretted only one of our tribal gods. The Law of Cause and Effect has no objection to inquiry, and she will always answer. Her vengeance is reserved for those who activate a Cause without desiring its Effect. Like the failure to anticipate the result of accelerated multiplication upon a finite surface."

"But—"

"Hush." To the crowds, who had heard little of this complex interchange and were becoming restless, he spoke out: "Please do not rise now. There is one more to pass."

But nothing seemed to come from the great ship. Only those nearest to it suddenly shivered, as though a cold wind had passed, though nothing stirred. It reached the stairs to the reception stand, and apparently flowed upwards; several dignitaries were seen to hug their elbows to their sides and shudder.

Far away, lightning flashed, once. Then all was over.

"That was the shadow of the God to Come," the announcer said clearly. "Though what it will be we know no more than you . . ."

Did you see the Pope cross himself?

Well, the rest you all must have seen; they took the ropes down and invited everyone who wanted to to mingle with the gods. (Luckily the security forces had been prepared for some such Angli-type informality, and got things organized in time.)

"In their present incarnate form, our gods are quite harmless," the announcer said. "But they do have a habit, when bored or restless, of dematerializing into pure energy—if I grasp your language correctly—and in that form they can be very dangerous indeed."

Even as he spoke, there came a high tinkling crash like expensive crystal breaking, from the direction of Aphrodite's couch, and it was seen that the Goddess had vanished, leaving only a cloud of white particles like doves or long-finned white fishes, who danced in Brownian motion before dispersing.

A moment later the original old tribal animist deity also took himself out, with a minor boom, and the dancing of a few unidentifiable particles in the air where he had been.

But all this you have seen, and seen also the preparation of the Angli for immediate departure, after they took their refreshed gods back to Luna in the morning.

Their preparations also were highly informal, consisting merely of getting into their bubbles and reconstituting their ship with what souvenirs they had picked up. (They were partial to postcards of cathedrals and bathing-beaches, and dried flowers.)

Aghast at the suddenness of all this, the Earth prepared to mourn the departure of these wonderful visitors. And then the great announcement came. That you must remember. A senior Angli simply asked, "Anybody want come with us? We find good place."

Yes, they meant it. Would Humans care to come a-roving with them? Not to be parted, but instead to find, with their dear new friends, a pristine Earth of clear sky and blue waters? A whole fresh start, with guardian angels?

Would they? WOULD THEY?

They would!!!—In such numbers that the Angli had to announce a limit of a million, to be accommodated asleep in their empty bubble-ships. There would be, by the way, no aging or death while in cold-sleep.

Their selection process, like everything else, was simple and informal. In the US, Angli simply asked for room in parking lots (every shopping mall owner in the land offered one) and stationed themselves in any convenient place, holding a football-size pod that had an open end. Applicants were invited to hold one hand in the pod for a minute or two, while the Angli stared at it. The pod felt empty inside. Applicants could wiggle their fingers, hold still, or feel the sides; it seemed to make no difference, and the pod did not appear to change. After an instant or so the Angli simply said Yes or No, and that was that. Those accepted were told to go out to the ship with three kilos—6.6 pounds—of whatever they wanted. Suggested wear

—this got printed on a slip—was one comfortable exercise suit, work gloves, sun visor, and sneakers.

What basis were they chosen on, for this momentous voyage?

"They take the ones they like," Waefyel told me.

"But what does the pod do?"

"That way no arguments." I remembered these people were telepaths. An Angli could investigate a mind in depth while its owner was holding his hand in a pod.

But who is Waefyel?

Well, I forgot to tell you about meeting my own special Angli friend. Most of the rest of this comes from him. I met him, like so much else, through Kevin. Waefyel was acting as gofer for one of the aged councilors, who turned out to enjoy meeting Humans at those big receptions. The aged councilor would run out of water, or that hardtack stuff, which was all they ate, and Waefyel would get it for him. He met Kevin bringing coffee to a Human counterpart.

Technically, Waefyel was a young adult, male—question-mark—we NEVER got that straightened out—and as nice as an Angli could be, which was very sweet indeed. But nice as he was, he couldn't get me accepted to go after I flunked the pod test. I tried again—they had no objection—and again and again, but it was always No—and then they were over their million.

"What's the matter with me, Waefyel?"

He shrugged, an impressive gesture in an octopus.

"Maybe know too much."

"*Me?* But don't you people like one to be smart?"

"No, *we* like. Only some kinds smart get killed by other Humans."

"Oh." . . . But I knew what he meant.

However, the Anglis didn't take a million boneheads, or a million anything. The group, what I saw of it, when I went out to the ship, was as close to a random sample as you could come. (One selector *had* a weakness for redheads.) However, they did appear to eliminate obvious no-goods, junkies, the badly crippled—I tell you, *everybody* tried, before it was over!—and a lot of people I personally didn't like the looks of either.

The ones who got to go had a stamper pressed to their foreheads. It didn't leave any detectable mark, and they were told they could wash the place, or whatever. (That had to be printed too, the Angli got tired of answering.) At the ship, an Angli just glanced at the spot.

I asked Waefyel if it was a thought-imprint, and he laughed. "No need." I kicked myself mentally—of course, if a telepath looked there, the person's thoughts would automatically tell whether he'd been stamped or not.

Oh—one more thing about the selectees: at the ship, the men got misted with an aerosol and were given an injection.

"What's that for?"

Waefyel giggled.

"For fertility. You make too many young ones, no can educate."

"You mean they'll all be infertile? Won't they die out?"

"For twenty of your years only. Then another twenty. Then another." The concept in his mind was *cycle*. "Yes,—that way no spoil everything, until learn better."

"How do they do it?"

And here's where I learned about the sophisticated research. Apparently some Angli who like fussing with bio-science had found an opportunity to gene-splice a bacterium that would cause a Human male's immune system to destroy, or rather inactivate, his own sperm. The antibodies, or whatever, wore out after about twenty years, thus allowing the man a couple of fertile ejaculations; but the system was self-renewing, and it kicked back in and the infertility closed down for another two decades. And so on. It was also dominant-inheritable.

Neat, no?

It seems there was an argument about the twenty years. Some Angli opted for forty, but they were persuaded that they were overreacting from revulsion at the state of our affairs.

And of course you know all about the rest.

I remarked to Waefyel, a pity they couldn't do it to all Earth. But the men's objections would be violent. He giggled again.

"You no see sunsets? Pretty green lights, no?"

"Well, yes, but they've been explaining that—"

"We do it already," he said. "Coming down in air now. Trouble, whew! To make so much. Good your bacteria breed fast too."

"What???"

Well, as I say, you know all about that. I was just the first to happen to know. Lord, I remember all the to-do, the fertility clinics besieged—of course it was blamed on women first. But finally it became too clear to ignore, especially as it affected a few related primates in a partial way. And the men had symptoms, too—they got sore and puffy when a large number of active sperm were getting killed.

But you know all that; how we have an oldest generation of mixed ages, like me and older, and after that one generation all aged about forty, and then another about twenty. And then nobody, but some women are just getting pregnant now. ("MOTHERHOOD AGAIN!" "HUMAN BIRTHS RESUME!" "WILL IT LAST THIS TIME?" . . . It won't, I promise you.)

This was their going-away present to us, see.

"We do good thing you," as Waefyel put it. "Now maybe bad trouble coming not so bad."

And it hasn't, has it? We did just tiptoe by the worst of the war scares, but everyone worldwide was so preoccupied with trying to make babies that things quieted down fast. Of course it was hell on economies that were based on the asinine idea of endless growth, but that's a lot better than being exterminated. People who really go for the idea of a planet with fifty billion people standing on top of each other were disappointed. But all the ecological stuff, the poisoning and wastage and sewage and erosion, all became soluble, once the steady thunder of newborn Humans cascading from ever-fertile bellies eased to a sprinkle every twenty years.

People would have had to face the idea of a static economy sooner or later; it was the Angli's gift to let us do it while there were still living oceans left.

But that's all beside the point.

When I got over the trauma of not being selected to go—no, I only *sound* like I'm crying—I was still worrying that little old question: Why, really, did the Angli leave that paradise planet they came from? *Why?*

"We want go see new places," Waefyel said. "We bored."

But he didn't say it right. Maybe telepaths transmit whether they want to or not.

"Waefyel—what *really* happened to those other people who were living on your planet?"

"They go away, maybe, or they die. I think they die."

That sounded sincere.

"Your people didn't kill them off, by any chance?"

"Oh, no! *NO!!*"

You can't fake shock like that—I think.

"So you just left, bringing your gods with you . . . What about the Angli that are still there, what'll they do with no gods?"

"No Angli stay, is all here. Up on moon."

"H'mm. Small race, aren't you?"

"Three, four million. Is enough."

"And your gods. Hey, those gods were really alive, weren't they?"

We were lying on a little beach on one of the Virgin Islands, where Waefyel had flown us. (If I could only live on hardtack, what journeys we could have made! I did try the stuff, but it tasted like dried galoshes.)

"Of course they live," he said. "They do things for people. All gods do."

"Ours don't," I said lazily. "Hey, do other peoples have live gods?"

"Yes." His big eye looked sad. "Except you. You first we find. No live gods here."

"Hey, you mean it . . . I thought gods were just an idea."

"Oh no, is real. Look out, you getting too hot."

"Yeah, thanks . . . Why did your gods want to leave that lovely planet?"

"Go with us."

"You mean a god has to go where its people go? . . . Hey, what happened to the other people's gods, the ones that died off? What happens to gods when their people die?"

"Usually—new word, see? Usually, gods go too. Lost in air, finish. Sometimes . . . not." His big eye was looking somber again. Not sad, just very serious. "We don't know why."

"Dead peoples' gods just evaporate. How sad. H'mm. But sometimes not, eh? What happens to a bunch of gods who live on with no people?"

"I don't know." He sat up. "Look, is too hot for you here. I listen your skin burning."

"Sorry. I didn't mean to fry audibly." But I picked it up. What? Just something. Time to change the subject, for Waefyel. Well, maybe it bored him. But I didn't think it was that. In my bones, I felt I was poking into something hidden. Something the Angli wanted hidden.

"I hope your gods will like the new planet you find. You'll be there, with the Humans, won't you?"

"Oh yes!" He smiled. "We find nice big one, lots of room. Lots of flowers." He touched a neck-chain of dandelion flowers I had twisted for him. (Yes, they have dandelions and crabgrass even on the Virgin Islands.)

"I bet our people will go back to the Stone Age," I said idly. (I didn't care if they went back to the Paleocene, if only I could have gone with them.) "Hey, maybe they'll start worshipping that old totem-animal of yours."

"Maybe." As though involuntarily, his eye took on a dreamy smile.

"And then when they get more advanced, they can worship that old fertility symbol. I guess they'll be in the mood. And work up to the lovelies. You know, that's neat! Here we don't have any gods of our own, and you provide us with a complete set, ready-to-go, carry-out gods! Why do you suppose we don't have gods of our own, Waefyel? Is something wrong with us? People *make* their gods, really, don't they?"

"I think so. Yes . . . What is wrong by you? We don't know. Maybe you have poison, maybe you kill gods!" He laughed and fussed at my hair—I had pretty hair then—with his tentacle tip. "But I don't think so . . . Some of the wise ones think you made a bad pattern of gods, some kind missing, see, so they couldn't go on and make more. A 'defective series,' that's right?"

"That's wrong, apparently . . . I wonder what we left out. Do you know?"

"No . . . but I think you got too many war gods. Not enough ones who take care."

"That sounds right." I was about falling asleep, there in the beauty with the lapping little waves on the pink sand, and this lovely friend beside me . . .

"I think we go inside now. Look Tee-Vee. I carry you."

"Oh, Waefyel." (Don't expect me to tell you about it, but we had something physical going between us. Especially then. It's not what you'd guess, either.)

Now there was a man staying at the hotel there. A serious older man, a sort of student. That evening we all got chatting, out on the terrace looking at the sunset. It *did* show the most lovely, weird green light. Beautiful infertility, drifting down. The uproar about that hadn't started yet. Anyway, this older man started talking about angels. Rather pointedly, too. Funny topic, I thought.

"Did you know that angels were the lowest order of divine beings?" he asked me. "If there was something to be done, a flaming sword to be brandished, somebody to be admonished, or a message delivered—particularly a message—they called in an angel. They were the workhorses and message-bearers."

"Yes," said Waefyel, unguardedly. I wonder what interest ancient myths about angels could possibly have for him. Probably he just enjoyed practicing his English, he did love that.

"Like gofers," I said. "The gofers of the gods."

So of course I had to explain gofers. (He *was* an older man.) Waefyel was delighted too. His first English pun, if that's what it is.

"How did angels get born?" I asked. "What about those little ones, cherubs, cherubim? Were they little angels?"

"No," said the man. "The connection of cherubs with infants is a late degradation. As to how angels got born, I wonder. I've never heard of an angel's mother or father."

"From the energy in the air," said Waefyel unexpectedly. "Elementals."

"Is there energy in the air?" I asked.

"You saw it. When gods dematerialize, a lot of it is around. Elementals," he repeated. And then suddenly frowned as if he were mad at himself, and shut up.

Next day we had to fly back. It was the twenty-third of August. The day after was the twenty-fourth. And even you must know what happened then:

They left.

Don't expect me to tell you a word about *that*, either.

Me just standing there, looking up at a vanishing point that reflected sunlight for one last instant . . . Me and a couple of million, no, more than that—just standing there with eyes streaming our hearts out, looking up at a sky that would be empty forever . . .

But at least I know, for all the good it does me, what had held me in its arms. Waefyel let out just enough so it had to be true. You get the picture, don't you? Or do I have to explain it?

I put it to Waefyel once, at the end.

"You're not an animal, like me, are you? You're something created out of energy, out of the minds of that race that died. You Angli are just pretending to be people."

"Smart little one."

"Like parasites. Oh, Waefyel!"

"No. Symbiotes—I know word. You good for us, we good for you."

"But you've trapped a million Humans to go with you and keep you alive!"

"They need us. They happy."

Surely you see. There they were, when that other race who had made them died off—a whole complete pantheon-of-pantheons, all those gods from earliest to last, from highest to the lowest "workhorses." As good as dead, doomed to live forever on an empty planet with no living energy to need them or support them.

So what did they do? I mean, what did the higher-ups, the really big gods, do? This whole evolution of orphaned, unemployed gods, doomed with no people?

Why, they ordered their faithful workhorses, their lowest order of functionaries, their *angeli*—(the sound of that name was just one of those cosmic coincidences, by the way; it meant nothing to them)—well, they ordered their angeli to build ships and *take* them somewhere. To find a race that needed gods and take them there!

And eventually they got here and found a people with no gods . . .

—And now some of our people will have gods again. And the gods will have people. Let them; I'm not jealous. All I want is one of the gofers back.

My gofer of the gods.

Our Resident Djinn

When God died, the Devil survived him awhile.

The obsequies were impressive, and not unduly long. Out of respect for his old Adversary, Satan ordered that the more flamboyant fires of Hell be banked, and the noisiest sinners muffled; he also decreed a half-holiday for senior staff—a purely arbitrary usage of antiquity, since Hell has neither night nor day.

As the last elegiac choirs of cherubim faded through the empyrean, so clear as to be heard even in Hell, Lucifer felt an odd disquiet in his brazen heart. It was almost as though some unaccountable new responsibility had fallen to him. Clearly, things were entering a strange new epoch.

Might it not be fitting, now that it was presumably possible, for him to pay his last respects in person?

But the flight upward would be a long one. He had come down express, but even so, morn had changed to noon, and noon to dewy eve, en route. He shuddered, causing a small thunderclap, as he recalled how his once-snowy pinions had changed to ebon bat-wings, his feet to taloned hooves, and his bright angelic features to the grim (but, he always considered, distinguished) features he now bore, as he fell. A long way . . . and he was older now.

Surely it would be only sensible to have a medical check-up first?

He whistled up a posse of work-goblins to scour the pits for viable physicians, and leant upon a forward battlement of his dread castle to wait.

High above the Purgatorial Plain, the view always soothed him. Here and there through the middle distance sparkled the flares of volcanic blow-holes, from which fiery rivers of blood and molten metal ran hissing to the Sea of Torment. Charred barracks and camps for the lower orders of fiends marked the ashy plain, while behind all towered the black abutments of the Mountains of Hell, each with its special horror. And looming above the center of the range he had had the fancy to install a great snow-clad peak, where he could arrange suitable punishments for those exceptional sinners who could endure heat. Its topmost spires were lost in the low-hanging gray clouds that scudded perpetually, mockingly, above the parching Plain.

In the foreground of this spectacular view yawned the Pit of Hell proper, whose seven levels had been besung by poets. From sentiment, Satan hadn't changed things there much of recent centuries. Down below the seventh level lay the fearful Gulf of Silence. Not even he knew what was in its deeps. Every now and then he would cause some especially vociferous evildoer to be flung down there, and listen attentively to the long-dwindling ululations. But none ever returned to tell of it, nor did anything else emerge.

Lucifer occasionally contemplated devising some chain of bodies by which the gulf might be plumbed, but he had as usual been kept too busy with the interminable adjudications and squabblings of the hierarchy of Hell.

Once, one of the modern breed of scientists, condemned to a short stay for excessive media exposure, had said that it might be a black hole in the making, since energy and matter here conformed to other laws; but he overestimated the Satanic attention-span, and was himself pitched in before he'd worked out half his theory. Remembering this, Lucifer leaned far out, to send his dark gaze into the darker depths. Might this be a gateway through which some new phenomena appropriate to this new age would come? But darkness met only darkness, with no change so far as he could tell. . . . Or, were there the faintest strange phosphorescent gleamings, as of something in slow stir, deep down there? He stared his hardest, still unable to be sure.

And the doctors were now arriving, a tatterdemalion band of butchers-turned-surgeons, of pricked pomposities and singed Feelgoods, all yapped and nipped on by the younger trolls. Lucifer turned and raked them with his terrible orbs, opening for the occasion his third one, which sees only fact. He thus detected one doctor whose qualifications were genuine—a sorry wight who had come under ecclesiastical displeasure for some forgotten crime, such as administering anaesthetic to women in childbirth. When Satan explained what was wanted, this man left off his groaning and agreed that a check-up was a sound idea. But he held up the stumps which were all that the Holy Office had left of his erring hands.

"You shall have them back—when I return safely," Satan told him; the flare of desperate hope in the man's eyes made the goblins snicker.

"The heart would be your problem," the doctor said. "But, er, Your Majesty—do you have one?"

"I do," snapped Satan. "Examine it instanter!"

So instruments were described, and devised by Hell's smiths and artisans, and the doctor went to work. Although he had a little difficulty in persuading the Lord of Hell to submit to a stress-test—several bystanding demons were inadvertently incinerated—everything proved out satisfactorily, and soon his mighty patient was pronounced fit for an extended upward flight.

"Your respiratory-vascular systems are as sound as a young tiger's," the doctor told Satan. "But even so, I can not guarantee against the effects of, er, psychic trauma. Stresses of, ah, supernatural origin, such—"

"You take care of the flapping, and I'll take care of the flaps," Satan replied, and waved them all back to their respective torments. Noting that some of his higher-ranking subordinates seemed to be evincing an undue cheer, he gave them all a short but pungent lecture on the folly of ambition in Hell. Then he strode to his tower for takeoff, the imps he had delegated to put up refreshments scampering in his wake with the pack.

Comfortably reassured and provisioned, Lucifer launched himself upward on his great black wings, and was soon riding the massive thermals of Hell, circling ever higher above his domains. Only he knew which of the tiny flecks of lesser darkness contained the promise of true light above.

As the smog thickened below him, and the faint glow of the sky slowly brightened around, he found himself in a sphere where there seemed neither up nor down, nor anything to mark his way. The thermals faded out. Disorienting; but his instincts guided him true and he knew that he would soon emerge.

But as his powerful wingbeats carried him higher, he could not help but wonder uneasily what his reception would be, and whether all that he assumed were so. That God was dead or at least seriously disabled, he knew; if only because he had been able to lay hands, or claws, upon the distraught messenger. The poor celestial was so overcome that he could only squeal helplessly as he was taken, and the Devil himself had been so surprised that instead of subjecting the messenger to agonies sure to wring the truth from him, he had contented himself with jerking out a fistful of wing-feathers before he let him go, still shrieking futilely for Divine Help. By this Satan was quite sure of the truth of his message, for had his Opponent yet lived, even a failed attempt on His minion would have brought pyrotechnic displays of His displeasure.

But what else went on up there?

Odd things had happened before. Take the whole business of

the Son and his fate. Flapping steadily, Satan shook his head; the metaphysics of all that had been too much for his pragmatic mind. The Father of a virgin's son? The crucifixion as a triumph? And the whole Resurrection hoopla—*Noli me tangere*, now-you-see-it-now-you-don't—either you're resurrected, or you're not, was Satan's opinion.

He respected the man Jesus as a sincere fanatic—he himself had made a tiring, good-faith effort at the Temptation; but the rest was all too much. To Satan, it smelt of the devices graybeards will use to conceal their impotence. Was something more in this line going on up there? Would he arrive to find some cockamamie Reincarnation, perhaps, in league with a borrowed deity? That Vishnu chap, for instance, had some vitality left. Omniscience can change to nulliscience, or omnisenility; he hoped he wasn't spending all this effort to meet with some metaphysical rodomontade. Almost, he turned back.

But then the sky cleared abruptly, and his misgivings vanished as he saw a familiar marker. He was passing it from below this time, but he knew what it read: ALL HOPE ABANDON YE WHO ENTER HERE. It was about when he fell past this that the last of his halo had gone skittering away lightless in a scorching blast from Hell. Death, what a day that had been!

Now he took a quick scan about, just to make sure that all was in order, and no guardians who hadn't got the Word were there to contend his way. All clear.

He continued mounting upwards under the cool sun of Heaven. It beamed from the bluest of blue skies, set with tiny pearled clouds. Far below, a faint smudge concealed his own immense dominions, but no sulfuric scent of them reached here to comfort his nose. How quickly he had come! Was he much stronger than he'd believed, or had Space itself shrunk? Who could say?

And yes, high under the celestial vault he could now make out a shining, a thickening island of something more than cloud. Why, Heaven itself was in view—he had already come halfway! It was definitely time for a snack.

A little cloudlet was passing him. "*Like to like in the empty air*," he told it, "*The Lord of Matter desires a chair*." A gesture, and the thing condensed gratifyingly into a sumptuous airborne couch. Things had changed, all right, he told himself. No simple black spell would function here if his Enemy still lived.

He found that the imps had packed a proper lunch, for once. A hearty sandwich of broiled liars' tongues (in which one of the smallest imps seemed to have become entrapped, so that he had to pluck it out and fling it away screeching. Little cannibals!) And a flask of raped virgins' tears, yes—and some pickled bikers' parts, a nice contemporary touch. He must remember to commend them on his return, he thought, munching pleasurably. Perhaps they'd like a plump politician all to themselves to torment? Gratitude was of course unheard-of in Hell; but a good administrator knows how to keep the help functioning.

Lifting the flask of tears, he reflected that he had indeed passed his point of no return: it was the sight of the Heavenly City that marked the limits of his banishment. Well, he would see it again now, the place he had so nearly come to rule, and where he had refused to serve. Not for an instant had he regretted his choice; but now an odd melancholy, almost a nostalgia, stole into his mood.

Away with it! He must be growing chilled, he'd forgotten how blessed cold it was up here. "*Fire! Your Prince commands you, glow! My resting-place alluming. Come warm me for an hour or so—but burn without consuming*." And at his cabalistic sign, a border of flame like Elmo's fire sprang out around the couch and himself, creating a cozy little inferno.

He finished his repast in a cheerier mood, then rose and grandly stretched his fiery form. As he turned he noticed that he'd left quite a mess; a wave of the hand abolished it. No need to act like an orc! And with a mighty wing-buffet to the air, he was on his way upward again, his eyes on the growing splendor above.

In what seemed a very short time, the flame-edged shadow of his dark wings fell upon the drawbridge leading to the Gates of the City. The bridge was down, the great gates stood ajar. No one was in sight.

As he hovered in for landing, a figure whom he recognized as Peter rose sleepily from the flowery greensward beside the gates.

"Avast!" cried Peter, rubbing his eyes. "Away with ye, black scum! What do ye here?—Oh, sorry," Peter interrupted himself. "For a moment I f-forgot." And the poor saint looked so woebegone that Satan checked his retort.

"Well, so you've come too—you might as well come in." But when Peter went to push the Gates wider, the task seemed so far beyond his strength that Lucifer gave him a hand, being careful not to scorch the beautiful pearl-work.

"Did you not receive my condolences?" he asked.

"Oh, yes—I meant to tell you, we *did* appreciate your note. And the lovely wrought flowers. Of course the wreath *was* a little warm"— here Peter glanced at a burn-mark on his palm —"we had to quench it a little first. But it's nice to know folks stick together at times like these."

The Devil chuckled deep in his throat. "Just thought I'd come up and see how you all were fixed." Then, as the full view of the Heavenly City opened to him, he halted.

"My word! It—it certainly has held up well! You've done a splendid job of maintenance, can't have been easy . . . It's been so long, but don't I see a few new features? Additions and enhancements?"

"Oh yes." Peter revived a bit. "One must keep up with the centuries, you know. And we get so many fine artists up here. Although, I must confess, some of the very recent stuff—ah well, I'm no art critic."

"I thought I recognized that Calder." Satan pointed to a vast luminous mobile. "But that one, frankly—" he indicated a giant cow's skull against a blue sky.

"An original O'Keeffe," Peter said, a trifle smugly. "She went right into production. . . . Would—would you care to have me show you about?"

"I would indeed," Satan replied. "But where are all your

people? I should have thought you'd be quite crowded with the Blessed by now."

"Oh, everyone's gone for the day. Uriel—he's so practical—he decided they had to do something to lift the atmosphere. So he and Rafe and the rest organized a picnic excursion to the Elysian Fields. Some of the old shades can still talk a bit, you know. It's very interesting. So they've all gone—that is, the ones who still have enough individuality left."

"Individuality? How do you mean?"

"Don't you find that? Oh well, it's that so many of ours seem to just melt away into grand abstraction, after a time. I expect it's the pure air, or something. And with all that singing, too. Don't yours? In an, ah, reverse sense, as it were?"

"No, I can't say they do. Mine stay all too identifiable. Although now you mention it I do seem to have noticed a rather shapeless vortex developing around one or two of my chaps. Fellow named Hinckel, or Hittle. Or was it Nickerson? Or Failwell?"

Peter nodded. "That's how it starts. And then more and more get sucked in till you get a kind of critical mass, and Blooie!—There's nothing left but a radiance."

"In this case it'd be more like a bad smell, I imagine," Lucifer commented. "But seriously, perhaps we have less merging because there's so many different ways to sin, but only one way to, ah, enter here?"

"That could be it!" exclaimed Peter; he seemed quite happy now. Peter loved a good theological argument, Satan remembered. "Although it has been said that evil is monotone. But, come, I must show you the new *son-et-lumière*. I never can pronounce that right. It's all computerized," he added with shy pride. "And that's our sports palace."

They were strolling by an impressive amphitheatre. Satan could see the scoreboard rising above the stands, but the format puzzled him—it seemed to show nothing but winners.

"Oh, it wouldn't do to have people lose," Peter told him. "The aim is to achieve a perfect draw at the highest possible score. You'd be surprised what thrilling games we have, when each team has to help the other avoid a win."

"I would indeed," Lucifer agreed politely. And then they fell silent, for they were entering the Avenue of the Blessed, the grand colonnade from which the risen spirits had their first view of the Divine Radiance. It was still radiant, and as they proceeded along, Lucifer was quite touched to see that the old barbaric Throne was still quite visible under the Renaissance splendors. Despite his foreknowledge, it gave him a jolt when he raised his gaze and perceived that Throne and dais were completely empty.

"Watch."

Peter whistled, and a passing dove alighted on his hand. The saint pressed what seemed to be a small set of buttons on the dove's breast. At once the radiance increased tenfold, in a great upspringing fan-work of colored lights, which seemed to elevate dais and all into a sunrise of coruscating brilliance, wheeling and changing as they watched, until the mind was quite bewildered. At the same time, music played, now sinking to a murmur, now rising in crescendo—a totally stunning effect.

"Marvellous!" the Devil murmured. "Bravo!"

"If only you could have seen it when—when—" But the poor saint broke down in weeping and could not continue. Satan turned away considerately, and found his own throat constricted. The nostalgia which had touched him earlier was back again, stronger than before. It all seemed such a shame. Why couldn't things have gone on for a respectable eternity?

Instead of asking the questions he had intended, having to do with the details of the Lord's demise and the complications of the Trinity, he found himself saying consolingly, "There, there, old friend. Always remember what a splendid career was his, starting from a simple nomadic desert deity."

"Y-yes, that's t-true," sobbed Peter. "You must forgive me. It's just that—ohhhh." And he wept again briefly.

"No need," said the Devil gruffly. "I assure you, I sympathize." Then seeing that the old saint seemed quite disoriented, he asked in gentle tones, "But tell me, what are you going to *do* with all of this?"

Peter gulped and blew his nose. "Well, at first we were just intending to maintain it as it is. After all, there is always the p-possibility that—the p-p-possibility—forgive me. Yes, maintain it as it is . . . b-but since then some of the higher-ups have had word that the space is going to be needed. We don't know what for. But after all, we have had the lion's share, so to speak, so perhaps it's fair. So we're having a kind of, of greensward sale, you might say.

"The Allah people have a bid in for the sound system—they do a lot of praying, and it seems they're having quite a revival." He nodded. "Yes, and they want some of the plantings, too. They *are* quite fond of flowers, I believe. And there's a Shinto sect who's asking for time, I think they're interested in the topiary. And of course the pavements, *that's* no problem. But all the rest—and the—oh, I don't *know* what we shall do, it all seems so horrid—and some of the cherubim are quite incapable of maintaining themselves in any other en-environment . . ." And he all but broke down again.

Satan noticed that, moved by the old saint's grief, he had absently clawed a divot from the flowery turf. He replaced it carefully, considering.

"It does seem a dreadful shame to have it all broken up," he said. "Let's see; I have some figures in my head . . . but how much is a cubit, in metric? No matter—I know it'll do. Look, my old friend, it happens that I have a lot of spare room in my foregrounds. Not that there's been any shortage of sinners. But do you recall the Doctrine of Infant Damnation? Well, I had to set up a vast sort of nursery area for *that*—and then, thank, ah, Fate, they discontinued it. So I have some very nice real estate quite vacant, not too hot at all, and the air has nothing wrong with it that a good set of scrubbers wouldn't fix. But the thing is, what with the current cost of energy and the ridiculously inflated prices of temptations, my cash-flow position isn't too good. I couldn't begin to pay you—"

"Oh, my goodness," Peter interrupted him, "The *price* isn't the problem at all. Why, we'd *give* it to someone who'd keep it all together!"

"Well, now, that was what I rather hoped. And I do have an abundance of labor, if they can keep their smudgy little hands where they belong." For an instant he looked quite fierce and his tail lashed. "What I'm getting at is that if your people agreed, we could ship this whole thing down and set it up very attractively, just as if it'd never been moved. Certain elements of the *view* outside might not be quite right; but don't I recall something about the Blessed regaling themselves by looking over the wall and watching the damned fry, wasn't it?"

"Oh yes, in primitive times—very primitive," said the saint hastily. "But this is really splendid! Do you actually mean you would? I'm just sure the Powers and Dominions would be *delighted*. They've been quite broken up about the sale. Oh, I can't tell you what this would mean!"

"And you could all come down for long visits, and check on our maintenance."

"Oh, yes—oh, I'm quite sure—"

"Of course," said the Devil thoughtfully, "there may be some of the newly Blessed who will be a bit confused by finding themselves headed downwards, to Hell."

"You don't mean those evangelist chaps? We aren't expecting them."

"*You* may not be," said Satan with relish. "No, I was thinking of the people you normally get. Perhaps if we made it clear that it's more of a museum—no, that wouldn't do either. Oh well, you'll think of something."

"Yes, I'm sure we will." Peter was almost happy now.

"By the way," Satan inquired as they turned away, and the far-off light show rolled to its finale, "what's that curious area near the Throne, where the light seems so—so—"

"I know what you mean," Peter responded. "Don't you recall? That was the Holy Virgin's place. And the Magdalene's.

But things there have been undergoing some very puzzling changes lately. I mean they *had* been, before—b-before—"

"There, there," said Satan. "Don't tear yourself apart, old comrade, after we've got one major problem solved. And I have a hunch what might be going on in the ladies' quarter—we've had a few problems ourselves . . .

"But to return to practical matters. Let's see," he added thoughtfully, "if all goes well, my boys could start as soon as you give the word. But don't you think someone should stay on permanent duty to handle admissions? And have you decided what to do about the Book—or have you automated that, too?"

"Oh goodness, no!" said the old saint emphatically. "Or rather, yes!—we tried it. Now that almost everyone has numbers it seemed quite promising. So we had one installed for testing—just a few million names at first. And there *were* a few little—is 'bugs' the word?—to unravel, things that would have been simple for any mere angel. Such as a person having more than one Social Security number. Would you believe we found one saintly lady with seventeen? She'd been feeding half a township. And, conversely, numbers that were attached to more than one name—several writers and, ah, show-biz people had dozens. But we soon got those ironed out. And in the process we discovered that quite a number of our very youngest people seemed to be most adept at such devices. So we organized them into record-keeping squads. They did seem to be delighted to have an alternative to making music, you know. And things were wonderfully restful for me—for awhile." He smiled reminiscently.

"But I gather something happened?"

"Well, yes. . . . We began receiving the most surprising people. There seemed to be a rash of petty disasters on Earth, theatre fires and so on; and I recall we got the entire complement of the Takewara Japanese Girls' Volleyball Team. That was no great problem—but then we received the whole staff and inmates of a Women's Correctional Facility near Tehachapi,

California. And then—are you familiar with an institution called the Pentagon, in the United States?"

"I am." Satan licked his lips.

"Well, it seemed that our, ah, computer had somehow made contact with *its* personnel records, as well as other data, and the most extraordinary things began to go wrong. It turned out that our young geniuses had grown a bit, ah, restless. And the next thing we knew one of our most revered archdioceses was under congressional investigation. . . ." He sighed. "In the end we had to scrub the whole thing and go back to our old hand methods."

"I see," nodded Satan. "Well, I'm glad to know all this. I believe it might account for a period of confusion that plagued us, too."

"You did? Oh dear—yes, that might well be it. Our sincere apologies. . . . And now"—he waved toward the open Gates—"here come our returning picnickers. I do hope the outing cheered them!"

A radiant procession of the Blessed was advancing across the outer bridge, guided by corps of seraphs and Celestial Girl Scouts. Behind them could be glimpsed a wild confusion of wings, as swan boats, riding-gryphons, hippogriffs, and other work-creatures of the air disentangled themselves from their heavenly harnesses. In the rear towered the Archangelic Presences, Michael in the lead.

"They do seem a little more normal," Peter observed, as the strum of many harps began to tingle the air. "Now to communicate your wonderful offer. Oy! Sirs! Lord Michael, look who's here!"

The great angel turned his face toward them, and they saw his features change as he recognized the visitor.

"He came to pay his respects," Peter explained hastily. "And he's thought of the most marvellous plan—"

"I have heard of your plans before, sir," commented Michael stiffly. But the others gathered round, prepared to listen.

"It concerns the disposition of your—of all this wonderful creation." Satan gestured. "Peter tells me you're thinking of letting it go piecemeal, and the thought gives me much pain." As he went on to explain his proposal, he found that he felt quite strongly about it—so much so that he thought of another argument. "And after all," he wound up, "think of your future incoming clientele! They can't just be left to wander between the worlds, can they? Who knows where they'd end up?"

"That's a point, Mike," Raphael said. "I hear that Valhalla is resuming limited operations."

"H'mm," said the great archangel, no longer so hostile. "But still, what, when they enter and find the Throne—as it is?"

"Well, I do have a suggestion there, though it's more in my line than yours. Some of my younger succubi are splendid girls; if I clean them up they'd look really quite acceptable. I could have the best of them put it about among the Blessed, while they waited *outside*, of course, that He is on a difficult Creation job and got tied up. Such rumors spread fast and would satisfy people. In fact they'd be pleased with a little inside information, as it were. It's the not knowing. And afterward—well, maybe most of them will go abstract, or whatever. And perhaps some of your artists could contrive something with that *son et lumière* dingus—"

Some of the younger angels gasped at that, and Michael said haughtily, "As you say, that is more in your line than ours." But Uriel, the practical one, nodded. "Really, Mike, this might allay a great deal of natural anxiety."

"And perhaps—" murmured Gabriel, fingering his Trump, "I know I sound foolishly optimistic, but, well, perhaps. A Return? And *then* think how awful it would be if we'd—"

Michael nodded again, and sighed a grave assent. And so it was decided.

As they walked toward the Gates, Lucifer was reminded of something. "I couldn't help noticing," he remarked, shooting a glance at Peter, "that the area outside is remarkably lush and pretty. But the ground beyond your walls in my domain would be, I fear, quite dark and bare at best. Not favorable for photosynthesis. So what do you say if I order up a platoon of fire-elementals—they've been shockingly idle lately—and had them station themselves along the outer crevices in the wall? That would give quite enough light to grow things, especially if someone went round now and again to remind them forcefully of their duties. They haven't a brain amongst them, and it would be a nice suitable job. With a very attractive end-result. What do you say? Of course I wouldn't think of stationing any of my personnel in actual contact without your assent."

"Nicely put," remarked Raphael. "I think it's a very good idea; we certainly don't want the City just sitting on a blasted plain."

"So then we're agreed!" exclaimed Satan, feeling remarkably elated. He stepped to the gate, inhaling mightily. "I'll have the first work crews up here before you know it. And of course I'll be with them to oversee everything. . . . Do I take it that you'd like the walls carried down first, so there'll be an enclosure all set up and waiting for—for the more delicate artifacts? I imagine you can guard the perimeter yourselves for the short time required?"

"Oh, we will!" chorused a seraphic band.

"How do you plan to move whole walls?" Uriel asked curiously.

"Work-dragons. Under proper control they can cut out a portion at a time as neat as you please, and fly it down. Of course, getting it back up here would be a different story." Satan chuckled genially. "But even so, we could probably come up with something," he added, as he saw a shadow cross a couple of angelic visages. "Well!" He spread his huge black wings, stepping to the sill. "D'you know, it feels fine to have a project again! Maybe I could persuade you all to help, by selecting and gathering your favorite flower-seeds, for instance." Daring, he added confidingly, "You know what they say about the Devil and idle hands!"

It seemed to go down well; several older angels chuckled. And with a "Farewell, all!" he was off in a great leap through the pearly little clouds.

"I hope we've done the right thing," said Gabe, the worrier.

"Think of the alternative," Uriel observed. They all sighed. And as they turned to go back in, Raphael was heard to mutter, "All those Moslems mucking about with my Excury azaleas . . . I just hope those dragons are careful."

"They will be, I'm sure," said Peter.

Lucifer's great leap outward carried him to a part of the sky where the cloudlets were few. He was feeling remarkably well, and, reminding himself that the way home was all downhill, he decided it would be pleasant to make one last flight upward, to where he could view all Heaven from above. *His* Heaven now, he reflected as he soared. Had he been crazy, offering them all free refuge in his domain? There would be problems, of course. . . . Really, the times were growing so strange that he could scarcely trust his own motives. . . . But surely some solid evil would come of this. His old instincts for mischief were still strong.

"If you can't beat 'em and you can't join 'em—outlive 'em!" He chuckled in his old, nasty way, melting a small rainbow that had come too near.

He mounted steadily, until, seeing a solid-looking anvil cloud above, he zoomed up over it and landed on the rim.

Ah, yes—indeed a superb vista! The glorious golden glitter of the thoroughfares, the jeweled park, and the great profusion of splendid mansions, from large to small, in the residential sections.

He lost himself for a moment in the sheer magic of contemplation. Then he began recasting his earlier estimates, to make sure everything could be suitably installed, with enough terrain to set it off becomingly. He'd have to accommodate waiters at the Gate, too—Peter had told him there was quite a queue in times of war or natural disasters. . . . The idea of poor old Peter handling a computer bank distracted him by its comicality. But there was a warning in it too, in case he himself were ever tempted to automate.

Yes, there would be room enough and to spare, he concluded.

He owed that to that mathematician-wallah who had calculated and impressed exponential birth-rates on him. He had cleared his infant-reception area on the fellow's figures. . . . Maybe he'd have him sent a cup of water, no matter what his staff thought of that. They'd soon see his trip to Heaven hadn't made him soft!

"What are you doing in my nursery?"

The clear little voice behind him startled him so that he had to shoot out his pinions for balance as he whirled.

A naked girl-child stood staring at him, quite incuriously, Satan saw. What was this, one of the Blessed who'd lost her way home?

But no; she wore no halo—and needed none, for she was radiant all over. And the cold serenity of her smile, the icy chill in her light-gray eyes, told him that he looked on something quite other than any mere celestial spirit.

"You'll have to speak louder," the child said, although he hadn't spoken. "I'm nearly deaf. . . . You're one of my old dreams, aren't you? Have they told you you'll have to move? All this is to be mine, soon, you know. As soon as I'm completely deaf—and a few other things."

"My apologies, I didn't mean to intrude." Lucifer fairly shouted, so that the cloud began to resonate worryingly. "This is your nursery, you say?"

"Yes. But I'm growing very fast now. Am I not, Mother?" She glanced back at a figure so veiled and still that Satan had taken it for a peak of cloud.

"Yes, child, you are. But I've told you, you have to be deaf, yes, but there are also other things before you're ready."

The child was studying Satan.

"I know who you are," she said. "And who you're going to be. You're Murphy!" She giggled.

It was long since the Lord of Evil had been addressed so lightly. Yet he was sure that this was no supernal innocence that mocked him. Rather it must be something new in the line of demons. Another Kali? He shivered slightly, his tail, usually so jaunty, thrust out at an awkward, nervous angle. Kali had been relatively nothing compared to this, he felt.

"And I know what you're planning to do with that place." She pointed down. "That's neat . . . but Mother says I must get over liking neatness, too. I bet you don't know who I am."

"No, I certainly don't," said Lucifer. "But I gather you are—or think you are—one of the people for whom space is being made."

"Not one of the people," she giggled, then was suddenly and coldly mature. "I *am* the people. Tell him, Mother."

"Men used to call her 'Physis,' the veiled woman said. "Now it's 'Nature.' 'Mother Nature.'" She uttered a single-syllable laugh as cold as a gull's cry. "What it will be in the future we neither know nor care . . . she made you all, you see. In her dreams. It is when she can create consciously that she will take over."

The girl, abruptly a child again, made a *moue*. "All I've done so far is sleep and dream and grow," she said. "It's very *boring*."

Her eyes took on a look so pale and fixed that she appeared not only deaf but blind. As she scuffed her foot in discontent, a rift opened in the cloud, so near that Satan involuntarily put out an arm to steady her, forgetting the heat of his flesh. Her little breast came against him as she straightened. He was appalled to feel a coldness quenching his very bones—and something else, too.

"You—she has no heart-beat!" he exclaimed to the veiled figure.

"Naturally. She has no heart," the woman replied indifferently. "Only her dreams have hearts."

Satan shook his head, massaging his chilled shoulder. "Evidently things will be very different, in the new order to come," he managed to say.

The figure nodded silently. Satan felt he was getting into very deep waters, but he persisted still. This might be his only chance.

"And may one inquire your name, too, Ma'am?"

"I haven't a suitable one. Once men called my favor Tyche. Now I am called Chance. I too am powerful, but only in my dreams. I dreamt *her*. Perhaps later I will dream again." She stirred. "And now it is time for you to go."

"Of course." Satan bowed his most courtly bow, making his tail curl normally. "I count myself privileged. But may I inquire about one more happening which just could concern you?"

The women inclined her veiled head.

"In my, ah, humble realms there is a pit so deep that none know what lies within it. Yet recently I seemed to observe a stirring in its depths. Is it possible that one of your new order is arriving in my small province too?"

"I didn't dream that, Mother, I know," the child exclaimed.

"Arriving, you ask?" said the woman. "Manifesting would be the better word, since if this is what I think, he is everywhere. Yes, it is possible that this is some incarnation of Entropy, my lord and spouse. He has no need of incarnation, since he is immanent—but your realms would be a fitting place for it, if this be his whim."

"I see. . . . And, and could you tell me what I am to expect from him, if it be he?"

"Nothing new," she returned coldly. Satan didn't like the sound of this.

"Is it possible that he will wish to make use of my—my space as well?"

"Oh, no, Mother!" the child interrupted. "Why, I'd thought of moving your place to Earth, remember, Mother?"

"And you had best remember to think twice about that plan, if you wish any toys left to play with," her mother returned.

"But," said Satan desperately, "won't Your Majesty have need of some place and services like mine? Some source of final punishment for those who break your laws or commit crimes?"

"Oh, I made all that much too complicated last time," the child told him seriously. "When I have power it will all be simple. My laws will be unbreakable. And there will be only one crime, for which everyone must pay."

"By my tail," exclaimed Satan, impressed by the small being's air of command. "Unbreakable laws! That will be certainly a novelty. And only one crime, of which everyone is guilty. What could that be?"

"Being born." The child's icy eyes turned full on him, freezingly. Behind her the tall figure stirred significantly, reminding him that he had been dismissed.

He bowed again, but received no acknowledgement. The girl was murmuring something to her mother, who listened attentively. His very presence had been forgotten.

As he opened his wings and stepped off the cloud-edge, he thought he heard the child say, "Oh, I do hope that's Daddy coming! So I can meet him at last."

To which her mother seemed to reply, "You should get on well together, child. You have so much of him in you." Her tone was the bleakest Satan had ever heard.

To get away from them he made a great flap which bent the air to his pinions, and went hurtling, almost with his former speed, toward the familiar comfort below. Never had Hell seemed so truly homelike.

Ah, he thought, checking his speed slightly to avoid vaporizing the clouds, it would be good to smell real Hellfire again. And as for whatever might be coming, or thinking of coming, out of that doubly-damned pit, well, he'd see how it liked a few loads of lava. Better yet, divert a reliable volcano. And meanwhile he had his Heavenly affairs to see to.

As the first trace of brimstone reached his nostrils, his heart warmed, though his shoulder still ached. Thinking of which, it occurred to him that he had come through this whole effort in fine shape; that doctor was evidently a capable man. Why not surprise everyone and give him back his hands? He was no lackey of Rome, after all. Let's see—what was a suitable catch? Oh yes—and whirling downward in all his dark splendor, he muttered to himself: "*Hands in the sands of time, Pat and putter and play; Hands that committed crime—Return to him today.*"

There, that would teach those smart-ass goblins to be so sure they knew what the boss was going to do. And if any of them made the mistake of thinking that Heaven had softened him up, they'd soon learn their error.

Whether or not those frigid, Graecophile oneiromaniacs up there spoke truth, if they had indeed created him and all this cycle, Hell was still his, and his powers were still real.

. . . While they lasted, a cold echo wailed.

Morality Meat

Cold, drizzle. Dark coming on. Trucker Hagen is barrelling up the interstate in his eighteen-wheeler, trying to make time. He's bound for Bohemia Club North, and after Carlisle the road will degenerate to double-lane blacktop and twist up through the mountains. The north end of the interstate has only been finished this year; Hagen hopes they got as far as Carlisle.

Darker. He switches on his lights. A mile or so behind him another pair of lights comes on. That green Celica Supra is still hanging on his ass. But a glare on the road takes his mind off it: the drizzle is freezing in the dips. Yeah, and his brakes aren't all that good. He eases down a few clicks.

The lights behind him brighten briefly, then fade back again. Pacing him, all right. Hijackers, maybe, waiting to move in? . . . But the same thing had happened on other runs up here, he remembers. And nothing had come of it, nothing at all. Probably just part of the general Bohemia Club weirdness.

It has a funny atmosphere, that place, he muses. All men,

most of them old. Not fags, no way. But not a woman there. Not one. And the old men are dressed all alike, some kind of shorts and badges too—almost like a bunch of senile Boy Scouts. Not Scouts, though—the place stinks of money. Very big money, if Hagen is any judge. Has its own airport; he glimpsed several private jets. And some of the cars by the main lodge made his eyes pop. The kind of money that's so big it hides, Hagen thinks. Hides out on uncharted islands, or like here in the mountains behind God knows how much private club property. The unmarked gate, with its gatehouse and dog patrol, is ten kilometers out from the lodge. Rich old boys pretending to be kids again, camping out in a fake wilderness. Pathetic.

But they want their city luxuries—oh, yes. The Bohemia fridge modules that fill most of the trailer behind him are full of steaks, chops, roasts—*meat*, for God's sake. At forty bucks a pound. Since the droughts and grain diseases finished off most of the US's meat production, Hagen hasn't tasted anything resembling beef in five years. Vegburgers. Soya everything—and that one rotten little so-called steak he and Milly had for their anniversary; fifty whole dollars. Even poultry got wiped out by that epidemic, and decent fish is hard to find. Hagen hates fish. But those old boys have their beef regularly.

Hagen spends a minute purely loathing them. But then he remembers that the supply boss he delivers to is okay. If he's still there, chances are he'll bed Hagen down for the night in the help's compound. And maybe he'll even get a piece of real bacon with breakfast. That'd be a nice start for the rest of his deliveries up here in ski-lodge country.

Just then he hits the slick. A bad slick, very bad, running out on a curved bridge. Damn, real ice on that bridge. The clear air has momentarily fooled him. And now he sees the roadbed is graded wrong, it cants outward to a right-hand exit just beyond the bridge. Oh, Jesus. He gears down, down, braking all he dares.

The big rig is halfway round the curve when he feels the cab wheels start to follow that outward grade. Jesus, Jesus—can he possibly go with it and make the turn into the interchange road? Too sharp, no way. He's fighting to get her off that slide, to get back on the high inside of the curve. Too late—too late; the tonnage behind him is tracking the cab, with that sickening greasy feel of ice. And a big concrete divider is coming up dead ahead.

Panicking, he wrenches the wheel too hard, brakes screaming —and feels nightmares coming true.

The rig is going to jackknife over him.

There comes a forever minute of ghastliness—slow toppling, crashing, grinding—an impossible tilt. The wheel is in his gut, his forehead is wedged on the icy windshield. And then the beast behind him takes control of the cab, flinging it back and over and sideways, banging Hagen into blackness in a thunder of clanging and monstrous rips—

—They are down.

And Hagen is still alive.

From somewhere below he hears the crackle start. Fire! He gets one leg braced and heaves up at the cab door with all his might. Brokenness is all down his other side and arm. The door gives. In a pain beyond pain he crawls up and out onto the cab side, trying to see ground. The trailer has ridden partly up over the cab, split open, and from the broken fridge module a rack of cold slippery things is hanging around his head confusing everything. He bats at them, trying to see.

Light is coming from somewhere now—that following car, he thinks dimly. It's slowing. They have to see him. And the fire noises are getting louder—he has to get down out of there, *has to*.

As he pushes through the cold things, he gets a look at them in the stranger's headlights, and despite his agony he twists back for another look. He thinks he has gone crazy—but then he sees they have little curly ends. Tails—pig-tails. Frozen piglet carcasses, is all. He goes sliding, scrambling down the cab side, lunging for the big front wheel. He hits it, steadies himself, sees a clear path to the ground and falls down it, crumpling as he hits.

The broken oil-pan has sluiced all over his head, but he can move.

Through the oil he makes out the green Supra, stopped in the ring of firelight. Two men are getting out. Hagen crawls toward them, hitching his broken side along the ground. Why don't the men help pull him away? Don't they know that rig behind him is about to blow to kingdom come, don't they know they're in danger too? He writhes, crawls, trying and trying to call to them for help. They'll help him, when they understand; they have to.

Earlier that same day, in the city far behind, a young girl carrying a baby struggled through the crowds to the L9 bus-stop, on the unfamiliar uptown side. She's sixteen years old and her name is Maylene; a small, *zaftig*, very dark black girl who moves tiredly. It has been a hard day at the K-Mart complaints terminal, a long trip home to fix up the baby and get her here.

The bus as usual is very late. Maylene watches two L9s go by without stopping.

By the curb is a clutter of streetpeople's box homes. The authorities don't bother bringing the fire-engines around here much. Maylene feels sorry for the streetpeople, but she's afraid of them too. She hates to see them burned out. The last time there'd been an old woman back in one of the shelters who couldn't get out.

The wind is icy cold. Maylene moves further back, into the shelter of the Drug Fair entrance. A gilt light falls on her from a display for PainGone. The light puts gold tints around her soft hair, and on the head of her pale-skinned infant, whose thin baby hair she has painstakingly corn-rowed and tied with a yellow ribbon.

The Drug Fair assistant manager, coming out to disperse the waiters, catches a look at her, and looks again. Something in the light on her narrow shoulders, the hollows under her cheek-bones that came from trying to feed two on wages that barely sustain one, maybe the very large brown eyes that seem to be seeing a crazy hope invisible to the others, jogs his memory. His Aisle Nine Christmas creche display has to be finished tonight.

At that moment an L9 arrives. It's crowded, but the driver stops. Maylene squeezes aboard, last as usual. She has the right notes in her cold hand. The baby, small as it is, weighs her down; she braces both legs, leaning against a seat-corner. She'll have to watch carefully, she tells herself; she's never been this way before. Into white territory. Is that good? Maylene can't tell, but closes her eyes an instant in a silent prayer for guidance. And luck. Then she has a feeling she shouldn't petition the greatness of a male God for a trivial thing like her luck. Maybe His mother will understand better, she thinks, and changes her prayer.

The woman whose seat she's leaning on suddenly jumps up and ducks away through the aisle. A black lady sitting by the window reaches for Maylene's arm and gently pulls her down into the empty seat before the man beside them can take it. The seat feels warm. Involuntarily Maylene sighs, smiles with the comfort.

"How old's she?" The lady is smiling at Maylene's baby, who opens her own huge eyes and smiles her unearthly smile.

"Two months." Maylene hopes the lady won't go on. As if catching the thought—or perhaps just too tired—the lady sits back up and rides to her stop with no more than a "Good luck, dear."

Now they were coming into an odd part of the city—one of the clean-looking little industrial parks with low office buildings, that sprang up after the bulldozers knocked down people's homes. What they called slum-clearance. Maylene unfolded the paper clenched in her hand and peered out. 7005 . . . 7100 . . . the next block would be it, 7205.

Yes, there's the sign, gold on white like an expensive candy-box. The Center is on the ground floor of one of the little office buildings, with a big car park at the side. It is about half full.

Just as Maylene gets out and starts towards the Center's doors, there's a snarl of truck gears and a man's voice cursing. A huge truck comes backing out of the car park and turns heedlessly across the walk. Maylene glances across the cars and sees his trouble: a big fat pipe runs from the second storey of 7205 to the small manufacturing plant next door, with a sign saying CAUTION, 13 FEET 7 INCHES. Steam, or something, Maylene thinks absently, all her mind on what lies ahead.

Holding her baby close against the wind, she scurries up the pathway. The double-doors say in gold script, "Come in! Come in! Welcome! For Blessed are they that give Life." And then, in the lower corner, "RIGHT-TO-LIFE ADOPTION CENTER NO. 7."

Maylene stops, her baby held so tightly that it murmurs. She *can't* go in. But there's another woman coming behind her. This gives Maylene strength to pull open the door and hold it for the other, a gray-haired, drawn-faced, white woman lugging a large, angry-looking infant wearing an engineer's cap. Behind her Maylene sees other figures converging on the Center. Most carry babies, but there's a childless couple—no, two. People looking to adopt babies? Maylene sighs and goes on in, wondering if one of those couples will take her baby away.

She's in a warm, bright room, facing a plastic-padded counter, behind which white-clad nurses are coming and going. But she has time only to notice that the walls are papered with pictures of little animals in dresses—mice, maybe—and that there's a row of empty high-chairs by the counter, before a nurse is beside her and the other mother.

"You've come in the wrong side, my dears." The nurse—she's white, like everyone Maylene can see here—urges them back. "Unless you'd like to adopt another pretty little baby?"

No smiles from Maylene and the other. The child in the cap lets out a loud squall.

The door marked "Baby Reception" is next to the one they'd come in. Inside is also warm and bright, with another padded counter. The walls are papered with foreign-looking flowers.

Several mothers are ahead of Maylene, talking about their babies to the nurses behind the counter. Each place at the counter has little side-walls for privacy, like in a bank. The nurses seem kindly and patient. But Maylene is wondering if her little one will be expected to eat sitting in one of those high-chairs. She had always eaten in Maylene's arms; Maylene could never have afforded a high-chair in any event. Will her baby be frightened, or cold?

Her baby—oh, how she dreads to give her up. She's the only thing Maylene has ever had all to herself; the love between them is like a living current. She doesn't dare even think about the days ahead, alone . . .

Whoever had given it to her she will never know. One of her brothers had found out where she lived, and suddenly he showed up at her room one night with bottles and what seemed at least a dozen wild young men; one or two of them looked white. He'd forced the drink down her, holding her neck and nose until she gagged it in. After that she recalled less and less, and finally nothing . . . but only came to in the morning alone and naked and sick, in a torn-up room.

She'd used no precautions, of course. She had no men friends and wanted none, and no one wanted her. She hadn't been quite a virgin; there'd been that terrible afternoon with her uncle when she was eight. And of course she knew what it meant when she started throwing up.

But quite soon she discovered that she very much wanted this baby. Even before she was born Maylene felt she knew her. The birth wasn't too bad, and after that their weeks together had given her all the joy she'd ever really known.

But then she started fainting at work, and the doctor at K-Mart laid down the law. She couldn't buy the baby's supplements and feed herself, too. And she might harm her child.

"People who adopt children take the very best care of them," the doctor told her. "They want them so much."

So here she is, feeling like death.

Suddenly these thoughts are sent flying—a white girl waiting behind Maylene stamps past her up to the counter, dumps her baby on it, and bursts out loudly, "To hell with this! You made me have him. Take him! He's yours." She whirls and heads for the doors.

"Oh—but. Oh, Miss—Missus—you can't! You have to sign a release!" A nurse darts around the end of the counter to intercept the girl.

But the girl is big, and determined. "Release?" she mimicks. "Hell!" She slams out the doors.

An older nurse in the background is calling at an intercom: "Doctor Gridley? Oh, Doctor Gridley!" From outside comes the racket of a car starting roughly. It accelerates away.

A tall man in doctor's whites comes out through a door in the back wall. "Another dumper?"

"I'm afraid so, doctor. We were a little crowded here for a few minutes."

"Well, just stick an 'X' on an orange label and I'll double-check it." He sighs. "Damn."

Meanwhile the baby left on the counter hasn't made a sound. Now it begins to gurgle softly and turns its face toward Maylene. Something is wrong with it, she sees. Dreadfully wrong. It seems to have no upper lip, and there's what looks like part of another mouth, or face, merged into its cheek. And its legs and one arm are all short and twisted, too, and it's wearing a smeared bandage-thing instead of a little jacket. But it gurgles and slobbers happily enough while a nurse bundles a baby-blanket around it and lays it in a crib-cart. She ties a big orange label on the cart handle, and holds it up for the older nurse to mark.

"Doctor won't have to do much checking on this one," the nurse smirks. The older woman, who seems to be the Head here, shakes her head crossly at the girl.

Maylene sees that all the newly-filled crib-carts have colored labels tied on them. Some have big letters: "CS," "DF," "S," "BF." Nurses are starting to wheel them into the back room.

The girl ahead of her turns away sharply, bumping Maylene. Oh-h-h—it's her turn.

She slowly steps up to the counter, but her arms won't loosen.

Unable to do anything at all, she stares mutely up into the face of the head nurse.

She looks down at Maylene's delicate little figure with its buttoned bodice, and understanding comes. "I bet your baby is breast-fed."

"Uh? Oh, yes," whispers Maylene. "What will . . ."

"Not to worry. We have two grand wet-nurses here." The nurse turns to the back. "Oh, Mrs. Jackson! Are you free?"

"Coming!"

Mrs. Jackson is a large, gloriously endowed, Indian-red, warmly-smiling lady. In no time Maylene finds herself releasing her precious armload into the other's friendly, capacious grasp. Mrs. Jackson's bodice falls open and the little corn-rowed head burrows greedily into the source of all good things.

"I . . . I didn't have much milk . . ."

"Poor little creature," Mrs. Jackson croons impartially.

"We just slip a warm bottle to her one day when she's feeding, and she'll learn so fast you wouldn't believe it," the head nurse tells Maylene. "Now, dear, there's only this little paper to sign, right here. You take my pen."

As Maylene goes out, numb, empty-armed, several pairs of hopeful parents are crowding in across the way. An idea comes to her: if she can just find a spot to wait out of the wind, maybe she'll see who takes her baby. She can see that bright yellow bow a long way away.

The six middle-aged people coming up the Center pathway are clearly not prospective parents, although they turn to the Adoptions door. They are, in fact, the Right-to-Life Committee, or rather one of those few remnants of the Right-to-Life movement whose interest in other people's babies had persisted after their births had been legally enforced. Their visit is expected.

They come shivering into the bright room, hugging coats about them and exclaiming about the cold, to find six easy-chairs ranged invitingly along the lefthand wall. Head Nurse Tilley hurries out through the small crowd around the counter to welcome them. They can see the high-chairs, now occupied, and several white plastic baby-baskets on the counter, almost hidden by three sets of excited parents-to-be. Occasional glimpses of waving pink toes appear from the baskets; the future parents coo.

The Committee comprises four women and two men, who seem well acquainted with Nurse Tilley. When they're settled down, and a nurse's aide has offered hot coffee, cocoa or tea, Nurse Tilley produces her accounts file and presents it on a lapboard for the group's accountant, Mrs. Pillbee, to examine. The other members turn beaming smiles on the infants and the adoptions in progress.

In the high-chairs are picture-pretty babies, all dressed in the Center's white teddy-suits with different-coloured bows on their baby forelocks. Three are clearly white, one dark, and there's an enchanting brunette in a gorgeous cornflower-blue hair-bow who is so pale it's impossible to be sure of its race.

"Just to think," says Mrs. Dunthorne, the Committee's leader, "if it hadn't been for our work, all these lovely, lovable little people would have been *murdered*. Murdered in the womb by unnatural mothers!" Her voice becomes choked, she dabs at her eyes with a scrap of lace. "A Constitutional Amendment," she says reverently. "To think that the terrible crime of abortion is forbidden forever now! Oh, we owe so much to you, Mr. Seymour. No one could have fought harder against those cold, heartless people."

She sneezes, and gets up to take a closer look at the babies in the baskets. A moment later she's joined by the lady who was sitting on Mr. Seymour's other side.

"If *only* he'd have it cleaned," Mrs. Dunthorne whispers to her friend. She is referring to Mr. Seymour's trenchcoat, from which flows a powerful odor of formaldehyde. Her friend nods, also dabbing her nose. "I expect he's not too well off."

"But is he going to spend the winter in it? I mean, no one

could be a nobler soul—Oh, you cunning wee thing," Mrs. Dunthorne says hastily as a nurse goes by.

Head Nurse Tilley is also glancing curiously at Mr. Seymour. She has long known him as the flaming figure of outrage who produced trimester fetuses in bottles at legislative hearings, and thrust them full at the TV cameras so the little faces and fingers showed, demanding to know who in the audience could kill or deliberately tear apart this "beautiful little person?"

The TV had not, however, shown the last Alabama ratification hearing, when Mr. Seymour had manipulated his bottles with so much emotion that one broke in his pocket, and he had bolted for the corridor crying, "Get this *thing* off me!"

Mrs. Dunthorne and others had surrounded him at once and no one ever mentioned the episode. But it is becoming clear that someone—perhaps their new male member, Mr. George?—must tactfully raise the question of coat-cleaning.

Mr. George, at the moment, is questioning Nurse Tilley. He seems to have more interest in figures and details than Mrs. Pillbee. Nurse Tilley is all smiles; she has never been sure how far the Committee was clued into the Center's total operations—the operations that made the Center possible—so she played it safe. These people might still be under the illusion that the trickle of adoptions and voluntary contributions could do it all.

"That's right," she says. "All one hundred and thirty-four infants cleared for adoption have found parents since your last visit. Plus six in long-term hospital care. I'm happy to say we even found a home for one mild case of Down's syndrome. The mother had been told that hers would be a Down's baby, and when she found she couldn't obtain an abortion, she made several attempts to self-abort, and then refused to eat until her life was threatened so she had to be forcibly fed. But the child survived all this and came to us. The adoptive father is a child psychologist who believes Down's babies can be greatly helped."

Murmurs of gratification.

"Oh, my," Mrs. Dunthorne exclaims, "Mr. Seymour, we

simply *must* get more publicity for the work our Centers are doing! Wouldn't that help you, my dear?"

Nurse Tilley assents a trifle dubiously, as Mr. George breaks in.

"Now tell me, Nurse. You show the adoption rate of babies that are cleared. But I don't see your total intake, your holding of babies both cleared and uncleared."

Nurse Tilley smiles harder. "Oh, that figure can be reconstructed for any day, even any hour you choose." She shuffles papers expertly. "But frankly we haven't found it useful, because, among other things, times vary so wildly. It can happen that a baby comes in, gets checked, and goes out adopted in two hours, while another one with a case of the sniffles is held for two weeks. And if a baby is suspected of a communicable childhood disease, it can mean holding quarantine for a large group. You know how *some* mothers are about vaccinations . . ." Her tone is pointed and there are responsive sighs, as if she had held up a cue card saying "Black Welfare Mothers."

"And weekends—the labs are closed, you see, but people come anyway; even the time of day makes a difference—" She chats on automatically, trying to dispel the image behind her eyes that haunts her life—the vision of babies, babies, babies inexorably being born, unrelentingly flooding down over Center Seven and the rest. Sometimes she felt she would drown in surplus babies, babies at first individual, tragic, then finally only figures. Figures which bore no relation to the hundred and thirty-four she had cited to the Committee. Numbers which her job depended on obscuring from the prying eyes of the Mr. Georges.

"—and people holding responsible jobs tend to come in to adopt quite late in the day, even at night. We never close. So our population fluctuates." Big smile. She hopes it will quiet Mr. George. But he has one more question.

"Do I understand that you keep them all on these premises?"

"Oh, yes. We have plenty of room back there, and luckily we've been able to obtain some holding space upstairs too. Of course, we have a full pediatric staff, a cook, and two wet-nurses for infants that need weaning. Excuse me, is something wrong, Miss Fowler?"

While she was speaking, several couples have made their selections, checked in at the legal desk, and gone. But one couple is upset. The woman's voice is loud, touched with hysteria. "But there *must be one*, Nurse. We called."

The nurse at the counter explains. "They had their hearts set on a fair-haired baby with blue eyes."

"Everyone in our family," the woman cried, "*everyone* has golden hair and blue eyes. Show them, Hugo!" Rather sheepishly, the man pulls off his fur cap, revealing a crest of ruddy gold. His eyes, like the woman's, are bright blue.

"I know this is a darling baby"— the woman gestures at a basket—"but her eyes are hazel. It's no use, Hugo. Let's get out of here."

"Oh wait, please," says Nurse Tilley. "I see we must let you in on our little secret. First, please, can I count on you to keep something *really* confidential?"

Puzzled, the couple nod.

"Very well. Miss Fowler, would you bring in the blue-ticket basket in the reserved—" her voice drops to a murmur. Miss Fowler nods and goes. While they wait, Nurse Tilley explains.

"You see, my dears, there's such an unthinking demand for blond, blue-eyed babies that if we displayed them normally, the others who may be lovelier and better in their own right wouldn't be looked at. And people would even quarrel over them—dreadful. So we reserve these few for people like you, with a special need. By the way, the baby I have in mind is a girl. Does that make a difference?"

"Oh, no! Oh—that's what we—"

Smiling, Nurse Tilley holds a finger to her lips and they fall silent.

In a moment Miss Fowler comes back in, carrying a white baby-basket. Nurse Tilley glances over and nods her head, Yes. The basket is placed before the waiting blond couple. Miss

Fowler opens a dimity flap to display the infant. The Committee, staring frankly, see them both gasp a long breath, and then explode together in almost incoherent expressions of delight. Miss Dunthorne and Mrs. Pillbee edge closer to look.

In the Center's white blanket lies a peaches-and-cream baby; her forelock is true yellow gold, tied with a little green bow, and her large eyes look up with the deepest gentian-blue gaze the ladies have ever seen. In the gaze is a beguiling hint of curiosity, and she smiles with great sweetness.

"She's just been fed, she doesn't feel too active," Nurse Tilley tells the enraptured future parents. The brilliant blue gaze hides as the baby's eyelids droop. She yawns like a kitten, then looks up again at the huge faces pressing lovingly toward her.

Nurse Tilley continues smiling automatically as the papers are filled out, the deliriously happy adopters dropping pens in their reluctance to free hands of their treasure. The nurse's work over the years has taught her much about infant development, and she has carefully observed this angelic-looking child. What she has been watching is a trace of—call it slowness. Perhaps it will wear off. But in her heart of hearts, Nurse Tilley has a prevision. That wonderful blue, blue, faintly questioning stare, that smile, will exert their magic through the first years. And motor development will probably be okay. But by the time she's about ten the smile will begin to lose its charm, and the little problems with reading and math will begin to loom larger. With puberty, the reactions will begin to change from exasperation to tragedy. And then . . . Nurse Tilley's vision ends in the unchanging light of an institutional day-room, where a graying blonde woman will look up from the picture magazine with that same bright blank wondering smile. And the peaches-and-cream forehead will wrinkle as she wonders why the kind people who'd taught her to say "Mummy" and "Daddy" don't come around any more . . .

Nurse Tilley shakes herself. She could be wrong—she has to be wrong. And the couple had asked for a blue-eyed blond. Which was what they had, no more, no less. From outside comes the quiet starting of a big, expensive car. Nurse Tilley has checked enough to know that money at least will be no problem here.

"Do you have many like that hidden away back there?" one of the ladies is asking.

"Oh, no—just when we get an unusual type someone might ask for. Oh! Oh, Mister George! We don't go back there, if you please."

But the quiet Mr. George has quietly vanished through the doors to the back room, with Nurse Tilley in hot pursuit.

She has him back in a moment.

"I should have explained. We do try to keep conditions as near sterile as possible. Of course they're not truly sterile, but for instance we wear different shoes from our counter ones. And feeding is just over. If one baby gets frightened of a stranger you could have the whole place yelling and losing their dinners. And the doctors are doing their rounds. If you'd care to watch, I should have opened this for you—"

She draws back a vertical blind to reveal a big plate-glass viewport in the back wall. Long lines of crib-carts can be seen, extending to the distance. "Here are some paper shoe-covers, if you'd be so good."

As the group gets shod and shuffles to the glass, Mr. George says drily, "That fellow in the red cap and bloody sheet doesn't look very sterile to me."

"No, he doesn't. And I'm going back there right now to find out what's going on. If you'll excuse me—" She leaves the party clustered around the viewport.

Through it they can see Doctor Gridley and his two colleagues working down a line of cribs quite near. The babies' temperatures are being taken. Mrs. Pillbee turns away, slightly pink around the nose. In the middle distance Nurse Tilley has intercepted the strange figure, a man in workman's clothes covered with a blood-stained sheet worn like a cape. He's holding one forearm with the other. Doctor Gridley goes over to speak to Nurse Tilley. He gestures to the man's feet, and the watching group sees the man is in his stockings. In a moment or two Nurse Tilley, smiling, comes back out to them.

"An emergency," she explains. "Really life or death. One of the workmen in the plant next door got his hand caught under a blade and nearly severed it. Bleeding terribly, of course. They made a tourniquet and took him to the back door here because they knew we had a doctor. He even had the sense to kick off his boots before he came in. Poor fellow. There's a good chance he'll keep the use of his fingers because the doctor got to it so quickly. But if he'd had to wait for an ambulance he might well have died from loss of blood. I can assure you, Mr. George, that this sort of thing doesn't happen often! Well! Is there anything else you'd like to look over?"

"Lots of black kids over on the far side there," remarks Mr. George, still peering. "I suppose you quarantine them?"

"Oh, my goodness, no. That's just pure chance tonight. See, there're whites among them if you look."

Eyes followed Mr. George's gaze to the right side of the big room, where crib after crib holds a small black head; several of them wear colored bows. The back wall of the room turns into an offset, where a medical station might be, and the group of crib-carts is lined up as if awaiting treatment.

A medico carrying a trayful of little syringes is at the line.

"What's he going to do?" asked Mrs. Pillbee. "Vaccinations?"

"No, I think not, that's usually done individually. I think that's the evening shot. Vitamins, and an infant tranquilizer. One of our worries is that a restless baby might start the whole roomful howling just before bedtime." She glances at her watch. "I think that's what's going on now—he's putting them to sleep."

"What does DF mean?" another of the ladies asks. Nurse Tilley frowns.

"DF . . . DF . . . D'you know I can't remember! I know BF means 'Breast-Feed', and CS means 'Cleared for Show' and an orange tag means all data missing—the mother just dropped it and ran away. DF . . . must be something to do with vaccinations."

"Are there really that many black families wanting to adopt a baby?" asks a lady who hasn't spoken before.

"Looks like it!" Nurse Tilley laughs. "Of course, they may all give out suddenly. But we absolutely discourage cross-racial adoptions," she adds soberly. "It's not fair to the child. One thing about black adoption, you see much more of parents who already have two, three, even four kids adopting another, or even two. With whites it's your childless couples who adopt. Anything more? No?"

Coats and scarves are retrieved.

"Of course, you can always go over and watch the receiving side, but frankly, I'd advise against it. Here you've seen the happy endings of a few little stories, but at the input you get a steady diet of depressing scenes. Of course you might be interested in the unobtrusive methods we have for keeping new babies quarantined, and I'm very proud of the staff over there, they do a wonderfully sympathetic job at high speed. If one dawdles about sympathizing *too* much, you know, people break down and lose their resolution to do the right thing. Takes quite a knack. I'm proud of those girls. But there doesn't seem much point in your depressing yourselves after you've seen how well most things turn out, does there?"

The Committee couldn't agree with her more.

Outside, the wind has grown even colder. Maylene can't find a sheltered spot where she can see the doorway well enough.

The plant next door is working on night shift, but when Maylene goes close to it her view is blocked by two big trucks. Finally a Burger King trailer pulls out, and Maylene stands by a warm vent from which she can keep watch on the Adoptions door. She's right under that pipe from the plant to the Center, it should shed some heat.

But just as she's getting warm, a guard comes and shouts at her. She can't hear what he's saying because of a rumbling, scratching sound in the pipe overheard, more like a conveyor belt than steam. But his gestures are unmistakable—he wants her away from there. Maybe he thinks she's a streetwoman. But she has to go. And anyway, the vent and the rubbish smell bad. So she just keeps walking fast, to and fro in front of the Center.

As she's about to freeze, a girl's voice calls softly, "You watching the door?"

"Uh—yes."

"Not there. Round here. They come out the side." The girl ducks back into the car park and Maylene follows to the shelter of an old van. From here she can clearly see the side door; it has a light over it. At that moment a couple come out with a baby in a plastic shell-basket. Maylene gets a good look at the baby's head. No bow.

"You fix a ribbon on your baby?"

"Yeah. Red, with some gold stuff in it."

"Mine's yellow."

"I wonder, do they take them off?"

"Don't say it."

They have to step back for a white couple coming out with a baby in one of the shell-like plastic baskets; the Center must give them away. The baby has pale straw-colored hair. The woman is carrying him, and as they go round the van, Maylene hears her say, "That's *weather*, darling. This is *cold weather*. Oh you'll get to love it, you'll have a little sled—Oh, Charles, isn't he adorable? Just *exactly* what we dreamed of."

The man halts to look. "Yeah, yeah," he says happily. "Sure is . . . we better get him in the car before we freeze his little nuts off."

"Charles!" she giggles.

A weary-looking older white woman comes walking slowly around the corner from the main door. She halts by the van's driver's side and starts fumbling with keys. Then she sees them.

"Oh—I'm so s-sorry—" And then she's crying openly, leaning her head on the van. Uncertainly, the girls go around to her.

"Oh, I'm sorry . . . D-don't mind me, it's j-just a mistake, it's all a terrible mistake." She's crying so hard, silently, that her body shakes the van.

"Ma'am, you shouldn't drive like this," says Maylene's new acquaintance, whose name is Neola. "Is there something we can do for you?"

"N-no." The woman's head swings from side to side, despairingly. "A mistake—look at me! My periods stopped four years ago. I thought I was through with all that, I thought there wasn't any danger, and we didn't take any—and then the doctor took another test and told me the baby was defective. *Bad* defective. And it would cost like thirty thousand dollars so it could even walk. We don't have any thirty thousand dollars, all we have is just the money for our girl's college. And so I decided to have an abortion, but they said that was illegal now. I had to *h-have* it. And it tore me all up inside, when you're older, you're not flexible like a girl." She lifts her head and stares at them despairingly, adding in a low voice, "When you looked at her from a certain angle she didn't look defective, you know. Just for a second she'd look really pretty. Like she might have been if I hadn't been so *old*. Oh-h-h . . . oh dear, I didn't mean to dump my troubles on you, you probably have enough. When I was in the hospital first there was a little girl who'd been raped by four men including her own father—and they wouldn't help her. I heard later she tried somewhere illegal and died. *That's* trouble, I shouldn't boo-hoo."

She looks around disorientedly, then at the keys in her hand. "My dears, I have to take this junk-pile out. Where can you stand? You're watching the door, right?"

"Yeah. Oh, we'll find a place."

"Easier said. It's colder'n a bitch." Hearing her own words she laughs jeeringly.

But there just is no shelter. The cars beyond the van are all knee-high compacts, except one truck at the far end.

"We'll go down there."

"Where you can't see the door. Oh, *dear*." The woman looks

across the mid-lane to the row of cars opposite. "Could you see the door from there, I wonder?"

Suddenly they all jump as a horn taps melodiously right opposite. A car door opens, and a formidably chic, young, pale-skinned black woman leans out.

"You watching for your kids?" Her accent is markedly "white."

"Yes." Maylene is intimidated by this spectacular creature.

"So am I. I was going to ask if you want to sit in here with me where it's warm. You can see perfectly."

"Oh, yes thank you."

"Well that solves the problem," says the white mother of the defective child, getting laboriously into the van.

She drives away, and Maylene and her new acquaintance climb timidly into the warm velour interior of the fanciest car they've ever been in.

The light-skinned woman says, "Only one problem. If I see someone with my son I'm going to follow them. That's why I have the car facing out. You may have to get out in kind of a hurry—but there'll be time. I won't kidnap you."

"Follow them?" Maylene asks, surprised.

"Yes. I want to see who they are and where and how they live. Oh, I'm not going to make trouble or anything. They'll never know I know—but I want to keep track as long as I can."

"Oh, I wish I'd thought of that," said Maylene wistfully. "But of course I don't have a car."

"Hmm . . ." The strange young woman is evidently turning this over in her mind, trying to figure some way to help, but there seems no way. "A taxi, maybe?"

Maylene laughs. The stranger picks up her real leather purse. "Look—"

"Oh, I couldn't, I just couldn't," Maylene protests.

Reluctantly, the young woman puts the purse away. "Did you bring your baby in?"

"Yes . . . and she's, uh, breast-fed—"

"Oh, well," the other says relievedly, "I hate to tell you, but she won't be coming out today. They wean them first."

"Have you been waiting long?" asks Neola.

"Six hours. I don't know why. It's crazy, but I have this hunch . . ."

"Did you put a ribbon or something so you can be sure?"

"Yes. A big blue headband."

"Mine's red and gold, and hers is yellow," said Neola. "We were wondering, do they take them off?"

The girl sighs. "Yes. That's another trouble. I guess they leave them on if they're going to show them right away, but they probably come off tonight. The first day must be the only time you really have a chance, unless you get close enough to see its face. I s'pose that's all my hunch is, really—just a last chance."

There's a silence in the warm car. Several couples come out with baskets, but none of the babies wears a bow.

"God, you hear some stories," the pale woman says reflectively.

"Yeah."

"Are you one of the tragic ones? Don't mind my asking, I'm kind of a reporter. I'm going to do a piece on this, believe it."

"No," says Maylene sadly, "I just couldn't feed us both. I'm a K-Mart Company trainee, and they take so much out of the pay they said we'd get."

"Me too," says Neola. "Only I'm at an airline, learning computerized reservations. They say, when you get good and are due for your full salary, they fire you and hire other trainees because it's cheaper and the new girls are almost as good because they try so hard, see?"

"Sweethearts," the reporter girl says acidly. She pulls out a notebook and asks them for some facts and numbers. Maylene notices that her attention never totally leaves that door.

"Why did you have to give up your baby?" she asks daringly when the strange girl puts her pad away.

"I didn't exactly *have* to. I wanted to because I hate his

damned father. I thought he was my *friend*, see, not to marry, but like a real deep friendship that would last . . . and he's great, politically." She notices their blank expressions. "I mean, he seemed to be all for women, and ERA, and real equality, etcetera, etcetera. Yak-yak. One afternoon I happened to pick up the extension while he was chatting with a man chum, and I learned a whole lot in a big hurry. Among other points his advice was, always keep your women pregnant: 'a little bit pregnant.' Notice that 'women,' too. Plural. He wasn't just talking macho, he meant it, he was giving real advice to a pal on how to live. Anyway I went home and soaked a couple of pillows crying. And then I tried the abortion route, I guess you know all about that . . ." She sighs. "I'd imagined we could sort of raise the baby together, you know—Oh, I didn't expect him to do housework, we weren't living together. But I thought he'd be—like—*there*. Now it seems he has kids all over town he's never seen. The great revolutionary. Keep 'em barefoot and pregnant." She laughs the strangest, hardest laugh Maylene has ever heard.

"Oh," say the other two girls together, not understanding much except the pain.

"But you could keep your baby?" Maylene asks.

"Correction. *His* baby. *His* little pregnancy. You know how he did it? He punches pinholes in his condoms. And I thought he was so nice and considerate, wearing them. Because my doctor says the pill is bad for my heart. Pinholes! And I think once he pinholed some girl's diaphragm. No, I don't want the pinhole baby, thank you."

Maylene can sort of not quite almost understand.

At that moment the front seat fairly leaps under them as the strange girl jerks upright to see better.

"It's him! It's him! They've got my baby!"

Across the street, a light tan couple are laughing over a white baby basket out of which sticks a little head with a big blue bow.

The girl is quietly turning the motor on.

"Listen kids, I'm sorry but this is as far as we go. Oh God, they're getting into that Mercedes. Look, here's what you do. Go straight *in* that side door and look around hard and fast at the babies on show. Then sit down as if you're expecting somebody. Make up a name, say anything—Mrs. Howard Jellicoe. Tell 'em she told you to wait. Get it? They'll let you stay long enough to be sure if your babies are going to be shown tonight. If not—I hate to say it—I'm afraid you've had it. It's getting late. Of course, you could always try tracking them legally, claim there's an inheritance or something."

The girls are out now. She pulls the brake off. Down the row, a silver-colored car is quietly backing out towards them.

"Goodbye, kids. Good luck. Remember, walk straight in!"

The silver car is pulling out of the far exit. Their temporary benefactrix accelerates smoothly after it.

"You know," says Neola, "I don't think she hates that baby so bad."

Maylene nods. Their own plight strikes home on a blast of icy wind.

"I'm scared," Maylene says.

"So'm I. But we're together, the worst they can do is tell us to leave. We aren't breaking any law. Come on now. Come on."

They go up to the Adoptions door and enter. The same mice Maylene had seen hours ago are still frisking on the walls. In her panic, she forgets all about Mrs. Howard Jellicoe. But Nurse Tilley, guessing their trouble and knowing how cold it is outside, lets them stay quite a long while, and even look through the window to the back.

The long lines of cribs bewilder and discourage them. Just as they're about to turn away, they see a nurse pick up something from the floor by the cribs—a full plastic bag.

"That poor man from the plant must have dropped this," they hear her say, holding it up. "But whatever *is* it?"

One of the doctor-looking men comes over and looks.

"Pigtails!" He snorts. "Piggy-wigs' tails!" He shakes his head and goes away.

"Yech," says the nurse, going to a side door.

After one last despairing look, Maylene and Neola turn away. It's clear that no red or yellow ribbons are waiting to be shown this night.

Hagen lies sprawled at the feet of the two strange men who are looking silently at his crashed truck.

"Help!" With his good hand he paws a leg, tries to pull himself up. The crackling noises behind him sound bad. What's the matter with these guys? he wonders foggily. Don't they know they're in danger? When that tank blows—

"Help!" he moans. "Danger . . . fire! Pull me back! Please, help . . ."

The man whose leg he clutches neither helps nor resists, but says something to his companion that Hagen can't hear.

Then Hagen has an idea. These men must be hijackers, watching their target going up in smoke.

With tremendous effort he tells them, "Meat. Only meat. Don't die for meat." He coughs, agonized.

By his face on the ground is something peculiar. A bloody, white pig's tail with thread hanging out of the frozen end where it had been knocked off.

Some kind of blurry realization grabs the back of Hagen's neck with a giant hand. Vomit shoots out of his mouth and nose onto the strange man's shoes.

The shoes back away—Oh, God, are they leaving him? Oh, no—

"Listen," he gasps with all his fading strength. "I know where the safe is. The safe—*money*. Help me and I'll show you. After it blows. But for Christ's sake *get me out of here now!*"

At last the man above him bends down.

"Okay. We'll help you, but you have to look over here." He snaps his fingers beyond Hagen's ear. "Try."

Too confused to wonder, in very bad pain, Hagen turns his head towards the man's snapping fingers. He never sees the crowbar as it swings down and ends his life.

Alive, Hagen would have recognized what had happened to

his head. He had seen skulls crushed in just such a pattern before. No doctor who'd ever worked on truckers would hesitate a minute over the cause of the gulch in Hagen's skull now: roll-bar impact.

He has barely slumped in death before the strange men begin hauling his body up over the bottom of the truck and jamming it into the cab.

Hup—Hup—Slam—and they're off the truck, legging it for the Celica Supra yet managing to avoid the gushing oil. Cool types.

The Supra backs across the bridge like a rocket, just as—

Whomp! The whole crumpled nine-axle rig leaps at the sky and collapses in a sea of blue and red flames.

But instead of heading out of there, the Supra pulls over, headlights off, and waits while the flames roar orange and yellow, sending a stench down the cold wet wind. Presently they're only isolated pyres around the great tangled skeleton. No other cars come by.

As soon as they can, the Supra moves back to the wreck and the men get out with handlights. The stink is now ferocious. One man begins walking methodically around the wreckage, looking carefully at certain things on the ground. The other goes up to the charred cab, handkerchiefs wound around his hands against the heat, and satisfies himself that the contents of Hagen's metal-jacketed pad of invoices for his coming deliveries are charred into black powder. He sweeps his torch around to make sure that any papers which Hagen might have stashed in niches in the cab are beyond recognition. Neither man makes any effort to search for the safe.

Suddenly the man on the ground grunts and holds up part of a freezer module on which can be read the letters "BOHEMIA CL." It's a freakish accident caused by melting ice-lumps. It might interest prying eyes.

Prying eyes are very much disliked by aging oligarchs, who consider it none of the public's business what they choose to do or eat. It was to prevent just such a one-in-a-million mishap that men like those in the Supra are employed to escort certain sensitive loads. Their job is to remove any potentially embarrassing leads to the Bohemia Club.

So the printed board, and another discovered fragment go swiftly into some still-active flames, along with a few organic bits and pieces which survived the blast in recognizable form.

Soon they're satisfied. They return to the Supra, obliterating the footsteps behind them with scraps of insulation, which go in the Supra's trunk.

As the driver gets in, there comes a flash over the low hills in the highway ahead. It's the lights of a police patrol car, appearing and disappearing in the dips at a dawdling pace. It will accelerate when the driver spots the wreck's glow.

Briefly, the men squint ahead. They won't need lights. The moon's now showing through ragged, racing clouds, light enough to get them to that wooded side turning they can wait in till the cop goes by. Then they can ease back onto the interstate, and hit the Supra's speed. Their employers must be promptly informed that the expected supplies won't be arriving, and have to be reordered.

The car gets into motion while the man beside the driver is still closing his door. The floor-light shows an overlooked lump of muck on his heel.

"Hold it." The lump is rapidly knocked off—unburned wet sawdust around something that curls shiny yellow, as if it were nasty life. The man hits it to the ground outside with his torch, and takes a closer look. It's only a muddy tag-end of yellow cloth. Nothing at all. Cursing himself for getting jittery, he slams the car door. Next instant they're gone.

Nothing at all. Except of course to a *zaftig* little girl who'd prayed to God's mother for luck. She was right to pray so; her official God has long been growing increasingly gerontomorphic. From the smooth-faced idealistic young God who had driven the money-changers from the Temple, He has become a heavy-browed, bull-necked deity, more concerned with the effects of currency rates on national economies in the light of the IMF's commitments, and His diplomatic and territorial relations with other similar gods; in short, a more civilized version of His own Father.

And He has become quite deaf, especially to the higher, softer voices of women and children. It is a millennium now since He has heard a bird sing, and sparrows have been falling unheeded for a very long time indeed.

His Mother, of course, can hear such voices, and is often thereby greatly moved. But, like all female deities when the Bull Gods take over, She has almost no powers left. Small things like Maylene's luck she can sometimes help with. And who shall say that it wasn't luck which, by improbable stages, moved a torn, bloodied, yellow ribbon from the meat-packing plant rubbish pile where Maylene might see it, to a burning truck hundreds of miles away, thereby retaining, in Maylene's huge brown eyes, the wholly unrealistic light of hope?

All This and Heaven Too

There is a tale that is recounted to young children, as the family gathers round the Heat-O'Stat on a chilly night. When one of the boys has displayed too firm an intention to have his cake and eat it too, he is apt to be told: "Remember the crown prince's wedding night!"

Here is the story. To appreciate it, we need to set the stage.

We have first a small nation named Ecologia-Bella, which is perfectly charming. All the men are hardy and handsome and considerate, all the women are talented and delightful and exactly five feet three inches tall, which was determined (by popular vote) to be the ideal height for love. This populace is not all of one race, but is of the same culture; a satisfying place has been made available for everyone, and all preventable misfortune is disallowed.

The scenery of Ecologia-Bella is sumptuous, running from snow-capped mountains through rich forests and lakes and flower-strewn meadows to long tropic beaches of pink-white sand with a wondrous coral reef to play in.

Ecologia-Bella has industries, which are by design highly labor-intensive (which is why places can be found for all). Most of the women make exquisite embroidered gossamer wool cloths, which are so much valued in other countries that everyone who even pretends to be rich or tasteful must have one. And they are paid for in gold. International fashion-setters have their favorite designers, and pounce on everything that comes from their looms. And the women of Ecologia prudently change the colorings and styles every year or so, that no one may collect them all.

The men of Ecologia-Bella grow woodlots, which they cut in rotation to make the finest, acid-free, beautifully watermarked paper, much sought after by wealthy letter-writers, and primarily used for documents of state and the recorded sayings of titled nonentities so cherished by other governments. For this paper, payment is in pure silver. And when a woodlot is to be cut, rattlers and clappers are installed in it to discourage birds and small animals from nesting there until all is safe again.

For those men and women who don't choose to weave or make paper, a wealth of other occupations is open, such as making music in the streets, sweeping chimneys, raising sheep, composting the trash, and running the government. For these tasks they are paid in fresh nutritious food and small change.

All this requires energy, which Ecologia-Bella has in plenty. Its rivers cascade from the heights, and the less scenic of these falls have been harnessed for clean electric power. Some of the electricity is used to extract hydrogen from the sea-water; the hydrogen is then mixed with a finely-powdered metal, which forms a non-explosive hydride. The hydride flows, so it can be pumped through pipelines or canned and trucked to filling stations all over the country, much as we do with petroleum products. When a traveler has exhausted the hydrogen from his container of hydride, he returns the spent metal powder for a new box and drives away, emitting only pure water-vapor from his hydrogen-powered vehicle, while the metal powder is returned to the plant for recharging.

The cost of this whole operation is very low, since the chief ingredients—sea-water and electricity—are in bountiful supply; and hydrogen power is used for every need. All the plumes of white smoke puffing from factories or locomotives are composed, like summer clouds, of clean water particles, since the burning, or oxidation, of hydrogen has water as its sole by-product. A traffic snarl in Ecologia-Bella smells like a sweet spring day, and flowers and shade trees grow lushly on the highway verges. Children playing in the cities' streets absorb no carbon monoxide or lead, but only moisture which makes their hair curl and keeps down various viruses.

Turning now to the darker side, Ecologia-Bella has of course an Integrated Armed Force, which wears white-and-gold uniforms with plumes on Sundays. On work-days they wear highly efficient camouflage, and practice maneuvers with their violently lethal equipment, which they have purchased with the silver and gold. Typically, they buy only a prototype or two of each item, which they promptly copy with improvements. Every soldier knows not only how to read the instructions on his gunship or whatever, but how to write them if necessary. As a fighting force they are formidable beyond all proportion to their numbers; their individual strength is as the strength of ten because their heads are well-furnished and their hearts are pure.

There is an aspect of interest in Ecologia-Bella's method of manufacturing some of their war machines and other mechanical devices. It is well known that many teen-age youths love nothing better than to take apart and reassemble some form of locomotion. Thus, at high-school age, instead of allowing this energy to go to waste in the restructuring of jeeps, vans, and motorcycles, all the boys and girls who wish to are introduced to the task of assembling, say, an attack plane or a tank, after classes. And great is the pride of the young artisans when their own bomber rolls out of the hangar and takes to the air.

This does of course result in some rather odd names for deadly machinery, but the sight of "Wildflower Junior High" painted on his rocket-launcher serves to remind the operator what he is preparing to fight for.

This same youthful interest is also harnessed in the fabrication of the I.A.F.'s computers and telecommunications equipment. And many are the youngsters' innovations that are judged worthy of incorporation in standard models.

All this unwelcome military activity is forced upon Ecologia-Bella by the character of its neighboring nations, in particular the large state beyond its mountainous side, Pluvio-Acida.

Pluvio-Acida's landscape is said to be low and hilly, but no one has seen it for many generations because of the peculiar opacity of the air. It is also rumored to have once had topsoil and live trees, but the ground is now so eroded and churned up by people digging holes to mine whatever the previous hole-diggers didn't find, that, except for stretches of pavement cracked by subsidence, to step upon open ground is to fall into a kind of dry sludge scented with hydrogen sulphide.

The Pluvio-Acidans, like all sensible people, use fossil fuels, i.e., petroleum, for energy, with the usual results. They have a rich but limited fauna consisting of brown rats, cockroaches, and two kinds of house-fly, and a species of crabgrass still grows wild.

The very rich, of which Pluvio-Acida has many, landscape their sludgy holdings with cleverly-made plastic trees and grass, producing a mildly pleasing effect. The other class, the poor, or proletariat, of whom the nation has far more, look at the landscapes of the rich on state TV, which also tells them what to spend their wages on.

Pluvio-Acida enjoys a very high rate of employment of able-bodied males between twenty and thirty-five; the current figure is 105 percent. (The extra percentage points were caused by some census takers' failing to distinguish certain workers from robots.) The unemployed cause no problem, since on the average day they cannot be seen. All these workers toil like mad in smelters, machine-shops, mines, forges, rolling-mills, chemical plants, and so on, and the national product is extremely gross.

The typical breakfast of a Pluvio-Acida worker consists of a sugar do-nut dunked in raw alcohol; for lunch they omit the do-nut. The birthrate is high, but overpopulation is kept down by a series of unavoidable industrial accidents, called Oops, which are believed to be totally unrelated to the births of a great many children with three legs, six fingers, spina bifida, or open-skull.

Pluvio-Acida has a heavy schedule of exports. Its smelters and forges, etc., export melts, ingots, pig-iron, chunks, groockers, and slurp; these are paid for in diamond tiaras, blood, and organs for transplant to those who can afford them.

Its armed forces are strong, if unorthodox; there is a small cadre of technicians who can operate the complex war-machines and a large mass of those who can't, who are issued Kalashnikovs. Their hearts not being very pure, their individual strength is not that of ten. But unfortunately there are eleven of them for every Ecologia-Bella soldier.

Pluvio-Acida has a flourishing nuclear industry, despite its having occasioned a good many Oops. And in the most desolate corner of the least-enlightened province, mushroom-shaped clouds can occasionally be seen to arise.

That is as far as it goes, however, for the Pluvio-Acidan Information Transmission Service, or P.I.T.S., which is as ubiquitous as the house-flies, has reported some curious cloud formations rising from a barren islet off the Ecologia-Bella coast, always under strict security and particularly when the jet-stream blows south. (To the south is the land of Numbia, whose inhabitants have been through so much they don't care whether they are radioactive or not.) These clouds are studied by experts, and the dread word "fusion" is whispered about. So Pluvio-Acida's Deep Strategic Thinkers are playing it safe.

However, if P.I.T.S. had been a little more thorough, they might have found that the islet has been leased by a Mr. and Mrs. Fusion, makers of ceremonial fireworks, who are using it to work up their ever-more-splendid secret surprise programs for the royal festivities of Ecologia-Bella; the island is safe from the prying eyes of their competitors, for the fireworks business is a cut-throat one.

But it is now time for our story.

We start with a handsome young crown prince in the nation of Pluvio-Acida, where royalty is determined by a simple count of wealth. And as he attains the age of eighteen, just next door the royal rulers of Ecologia-Bella perish, and their beautiful fifteen-year-old daughter is crowned queen.

Amoretta, the little queen, is orphaned by a typical Ecologia-Bella accident. Her parents, having been married fourteen years and being very much in love, decide to go for a ride in the royal swan-boat. This boat—really a sort of sea-going double bed—is drawn by seventeen tame white swans, who put their necks in gold harnesses to obtain corn from a pan in front, and thus propel the royal barge.

As the couple reach the far end of the lake they are fondly talking over the events of their life together, and wondering how fourteen years could have gone by, and assuring each other that they are totally unchanged—which they are. And presently, noting that they have reached the most private part of the lagoon, it comes to them to celebrate their anniversary and their love in the most natural way.

Which they do.

And then the swans, who have always wondered about people, get the idea too, and begin with great splashings and chasing to help them celebrate. And some beavers on the bank, affected by the general outbreak of love, join in with even more rocking and tail-whacks. And somehow, in the midst of this riot of love, the boat is pushed, or pulled, over the low falls at the end of the lake, and overturned. And alas, when the royal couple go under, they are so warmly embraced that they neglect to swim.

When Amoretta is told of the tragedy she is overcome with grief, for she loves her parents, as does all the population of Ecologia-Bella; even her infant brother Truhart, who is as yet incommunicado, begins to weep.

The grounds-keeper, in a fit of tearful revenge, determines

that no such thing will ever occur again; he carts all the cobs, or male swans—save one—to the veterinary's. From whence they return honking soprano. The solitary intact cob he encloses in a golden pen so built that lady swans may go in, but he can not go out.

The grounds-keeper's wife says that this is cruel because swans mate for life; but after a little observation she is compelled to admit that so long as the ladies are allowed regular visits to the golden pen, they seem perfectly happy with their soprano spouses. And they raise fine cygnets without the usual territorial strife.

The deaths of Queen Rhapsodia and King Uxor come in due course to the ears of the rulers of Pluvio-Acida, who are of course the richest couple in that land. They have two sons. The eldest, Crown Prince Adolesco, is a throwback to some nobler stock—a handsome, blue-eyed, virile young man with a face as open as springtime, and—which is what panics his parents—a heart full of lofty ideals. He is often heard to utter the most unthinkable criticisms of the land he is to rule, and to intimate that there might come a time when changes would be made. The Pluvio-Acida Stock Exchange average falls fifteen points when Adolesco's father catches a head-cold.

The younger brother, Prince Slimoldi, is quite a different cut of sludge; squat and vaguely fungoid, with a face like a ferret and a mind to match. He stands in Pluvio-Acidan eyes for a fine young man, and much the better of the two. It is not, however, clear what should or could be done about this; the elder brother seems to bear a charmed life, and none of the irresolute efforts at changing the succession have worked. His horse sees and jumps trip-wires; he gives the cyanide-laced soup to a beggar; and the hired sharp-shooter has an off week.

As our story opens, we find the young crown prince in a traveling mood. Two points motivate him to travel to Ecologia-Bella.

Firstly, he became aware of a steadily increasing traffic of eligible—or self-declared eligible—royal bachelors in that direction. News of a beautiful virgin heiress to an attractive throne is getting about. Dowager queens escort their immature male offspring across Pluvio-Acida, heading for Ecologia-Bella. Doddering noblemen tighten their corset-stays and set out upon the matrimonial road. Among the throng Adolesco notes several apparently suitable candidates: the bold young king of a rich, if frozen northern country; the handsome heir to a tropical paradise in the south; and the suave, fatherly monarch of an eastern empire, who knows how to make his harem sound attractive to western ears. . . . Adolesco frowns, currying his best cross-country hack, a great snow-white gelding. What do these suitors have that he doesn't? How dare they come courting one who is his—*his*—own neighbor?

The second factor impelling him is parental. Our young prince has reached the age where the converse pressure is impinging on him. Holographs of stunning heiresses appear mysteriously upon his bureau. His parents give a grand party for the second and third richest couples, with their charming daughters. Scented letters, enclosing miniatures, float in from far-away courts. It begins to dawn on Adolesco that if he doesn't take a hand in this, his parents will have somehow got him committed to he knows not whom . . . And is it only by chance that no image of a maiden queen, said to be a darling vision, in her toy kingdom, has been produced?

He asks. And discovers that Ecologia-Bella not only is not taken seriously, it is positively disliked.

"That's where our people get all those communist ideas," his father growls. "Dreadfully ignorant people," his mother adds. "Why, they don't even understand capital gains." She rolls up her protruding eyes, a daunting sight.

Two weeks later, preceded by a courtly letter requesting to be received, young Adolesco sets off alone for Ecologia-Bella. (His horse is shipped by oxygenated container to the mountain border.)

Here he books passage for himself and his horse on the Ecologia-Bella Overnight Express through the mountain passes and tunnels, not unobserved by the Ecologia-Bella Observation Service, and disembarks to ride down through the fantastic forests and other charms, where he meets many mild but pleasing adventures.

He arrives at the palace on a beautiful and chilly spring evening, the white horse picking his way along the lakeside path. The sunset is casting a golden nimbus around horse and golden-haired rider—and seated at his pommel is the palace cook's littlest daughter, whom he had found trudging home through the chill.

At a grove of scarlet maples by the barge-landing his mount suddenly halts and stands stock-still; there is a silver figure among the rosy maple blooms. It is a young girl, so absorbed in feeding the baby swans that she doesn't hear his approach. He has a moment to observe her perfections—then she turns, startled, as the child calls her royal name.

"Oh," she cries, "I wanted to be alone! So many *people* have come."

He wheels to leave instanter, but in the business of setting the child down it seems he must dismount, and she has time to notice that he wears no spurs, unlike the Prince of Paradisio, and uses only a snaffle, not the cruel curb of the north.

So presently, with the cygnets full-fed, two golden-haired figures set out for the stables leading the great horse. The sunset intensifies its mellow splendor around them both.

. . . There really is no need for us to follow in detail the ensuing course of events. So let us briefly drop the curtain . . .

When it rises again, a few months later, there are revealed two beautiful young persons who are deliriously, enchantedly, calamitously, in love.

"He is different," says the young queen to her advisors. "He really wants to change things, and make peace and do good."

"She is intoxicating," the young prince writes to his best friend. "And the country is really a revelation. Why, if we were one nation, you could buy an estate here." (Ecologia-Bella prohibits the sale of land to other than third-generation nationals.) The prince is so taken with Ecologia-Bella, which embodies many of his more impractical ideals, that his first thought is to save it intact as a sort of Disneyland annex to Pluvio-Acida, changing nothing except perhaps some laws relating to outdoor advertising.

We have mentioned the queen's advisors. These constitute the Council of Ecologia-Bella, a small, poorly-paid, self-instituted group of older men and women, who come together now and then when some new factor or emergency threatens the stability of the country. It is clear that the present situation calls not only for watching, but perhaps for action.

So a lady whom the queen likes very much points out to her, "If you wed Prince Adolesco, our nation will become a part of Pluvio-Acida and subject to its laws. They will start mining and clear-cutting and dredging and drilling for oil all over Ecologia-Bella."

"Oh, no," replies Amoretta, dreamily but positively. "He swears he would change nothing. It will be mine to rule."

The lady looks at her and sees that there is no use discussing the changes that may take place in a man's resolves between eighteen and thirty.

"He will be your lawful king," she only observes. "How will you like being told what to do or not do?"

"Oh, I thought of that." Amoretta is braiding a flower into her yellow hair. "I wouldn't like it at all from King Boris or Prince Raoul. But my dear Adolesco is different. He truly loves me. I am sure he would never go against my wishes."

The lady sighs, and retires to report to the others that nothing can be done with sweet reason. The queen has been infected with a sweeter poison.

At the same time, Adolesco is having his troubles with his own parents and advisors. But they are not so severe. The idea of peacefully annexing their old irritant, Ecologia-Bella, has charms. And as the king's advisors point out, if this marriage is forbidden, only Mammon knows what wild idea the prince will have next. At least this may be expected to settle him down while keeping him near home—and occupy him with something other than tinkering with Pluvio-Acida's economy. And some of the nobility look out at their plastic trees and think that it might be pleasant to have an estate in Ecologia-Bella.

The advisors of the younger brother, Prince Slimoldi, draft up a cunning document which has the effect of giving Slimoldi certain powers over Pluvio-Acida—when Adolesco shall have inherited the kingdom—in the event that the new king devotes more than a certain percentage of time to the affairs of Ecologia-Bella. Such is the crown prince's bedazzlement with love, and so dense is this prose, that he signs it without demur.

Thus the way is clear for the grand Ecologia-Bella-cum-Pluvio-Acida nuptials. Out on their rocky islet, the Fusions envision a rocketry display unparalleled in history. And the people of Ecologia-Bella, seeing only the handsome, young, idealistic crown prince, and the radiant joy of their young queen, rejoice in the match.

But the Ecologia-Bella Council are not so easily contravened.

A plainly-dressed older man, of whom the queen has always been just a little in awe, comes to see her, bearing a large volume in which the laws of Ecologia-Bella are inscribed on the finest and most durable of that country's parchment.

"My dear," he begins, after accepting a cup of scented wine, "it may have escaped your notice that there are certain legal aspects to the marriage of our sovereign—namely, you."

She looks up with a face that would melt a stone lion; he hardens his heart.

"Oh, I know about that," she tells him. "The people must approve. Do you want me to call a referendum?"

"No need, no need." He waves the referendum away. "I am satisfied that the people, particularly the younger ones, have taken your plans to their hearts. But there is another consideration, which must be invoked in view of your youth."

"What's that? Do you wish me to wait till I'm old and wrinkled?"

"You may be only slightly wrinkled at, say, sixteen," smiles the councilor.

"*Sixteen?* That's a whole year away."

"Precisely." He opens the volume. " 'In the event that the ruler is less than sixteen years of age, the council is empowered to defer his or her nuptials to that date, unless some emergency dictate otherwise. . . . There is no, ah, emergency, is there, my dear?"

"Emergency—?"

"No, ah, royal heir in view?"

Little Queen Amoretta draws herself up to her full five-feet-three. "The Queen of Ecologia-Bella is not an animal!"

"Splendid," the councilor approves. But to himself he wonders; a royal bastard would of course create difficulties, but if that could be avoided, his experiences have indicated that there is nothing like a spell of unchecked intimacy to cool love's first ardors.

He clears his throat. "There is another point in our laws, my child. I'm sorry to have to tell you this. But our ancestors, who devised the code that has served us so well, were familiar with the course of love. They laid it down that if and when the marriage-match of a monarch would imperil the independence of Ecologia-Bella, the assent of the full council is required before it can take place. Moreover, the determination that the independence of Ecologia-Bella is in jeopardy is to be made, not by the monarch, or by popular vote, but by the full council itself.

"And it is my sad duty to tell you that the council has determined that this match of yours would indeed imperil the independence of your nation, and our recommendation is that it not take place."

"You mean that you can—you will—forbid my marrying Adolesco? Forbid me the joy of my life?" Her eyes blazing, the little queen actually stamps. "Never! Who passed this law? I'll change it!"

"Not so fast, my dear." The old councilor remains seated,

waving his hand soothingly. "Not so fast. I have not said we *will* forbid it. But you must accept the idea that we *can*. You are queen, but you may not change basic law."

Amoretta is pacing.

"I know!" she flings out. "I'll abdicate! That's it, I'll just abdicate. Then you can't forbid me doing anything!"

"Ah, my dear, assuming that the prince would still find himself able to wed a commoner—"

"He would! I'm sure of it," she declares, and then adds, for she is an honest girl, "I'm pretty sure." Her face is a trifle thoughtful.

"Yes. Assuming that, my dear, would the people of Ecologia-Bella let you? And we couldn't let you do anything which would cause such convulsions. Think. They have just lost your beloved parents. Your brother is but an infant. Will *you* now desert them—and for purely selfish ends?"

"Well . . . N-no."

"Spoken like a queen."

"Oh!" Amoretta collapses into her chair, suddenly more child than queen. "If I can't marry Adol—I'll die! . . . I'd *rather* die!"

"Do you mean that? Come, think."

She does think for a moment. Then, "Yes," she says slowly, surprising him a little. "I think I *would* rather die than never marry my love. There'd be nothing to live for, then . . . Are you 'empowered' to kill your queen?" she asks bitterly.

He doesn't take the bait, but merely says gently, "Very well, my dear. But first let us see what time can do. You will agree to set your nuptials for one year hence, when you will be sixteen?"

"On my birthday," she says firmly. "If I must."

. . . That next year passes in a whirl of pleasures—all pleasures save one, that is, for the little queen is serious. Adolesco, who has other resources, submits.

But to the council's dismayed eyes, the passage of time seems to do nothing to abate their monarch's virgin passion. Now and again the elderly councilor drops by to inquire formally.

"You still feel that you could not endure a life without young Adolesco, my dear?"

"I still do," she replies; and sometimes she smiles.

However, the year does accomplish something.

Various council members find occasion to consult with their queen on diverse problems, economic and social, of Ecologia-Bella; they are small, soluble problems, to be sure, but enlightening to Amoretta, who had always assumed that her state somehow ran itself. Now she perceives that there is a subtle ongoing process whereby a quiet push here, a tug-back there, a plan within a plan, are required to keep her nation on course. She is impressed by the length of foresight employed, the keen eye for socio-demographic changes, the seriousness with which any unusual manifestation—for instance, an outbreak of minimalist art among the weavers of a province—is viewed.

And, most enlightening of all, she is taken, heavily but inconspicuously guarded, on a state visit to Pluvio-Acida.

"Your brother is very . . . different from you," she says lovingly to Adolesco.

"Slimie's a nerd."

"I think he is worse than that. He is cruel. I see it in his eyes."

Then she sees something new in the eyes of her young lover—a flash of anger, gone as soon as perceived, but unmistakably there. It's all right for him to call his brother a nerd, but it's something else to have his family criticized by outsiders.

Amoretta says no more, but soothes the kitten-scratch with a kiss.

"I love you so!"

"And I you. Oh God—let's run away."

"Queens do not run away—nor kings," she adds hastily. "Besides, it's only a month now, my darling. Thirty little days!"

"Thirty eternities." His eyes devour her.

. . . And so at last the great day dawns, fair and explosive.

It is fair because Amoretta had been born on Midsummer's Eve. The explosions, heard faintly through the mountain passes, are caused by the Pluvio-Acida border guards on the far side, attempting to halt the hordes of their fellow citizens who have been encamped nearby, waiting for the moment when Pluvio-Acida and Ecologia-Bella would become one. In the vanguard is a cortège of Pluvio-Acidan nobility, checkbooks clasped, determined to have first choice of Ecologia-Bellan real estate.

The sunrise detonations are also augmented by the popping of an air gun in the palace park (air guns being the only ballistic weapon allowed out of Armed Force hands). Prince Adolesco, dressed for the chase, is popping away at a congregation of fat stags and several plump pheasants, who are crowding about him in expectation of treats. The air-gun pellets, being of local manufacture, annoy them only slightly.

"Damn and bedevil them!" the prince cries out in anger to the sky, and follows this with far stronger imprecations at a particularly obese deer who is trying to get its nose in his pocket. Then he hastily modulates down again as Amoretta and a group of special friends come in sight, taking a farewell sunrise stroll. The prince had hoped to work off far stronger tensions by stronger means.

The queen runs to him. "What's wrong, my darling? Are you hurt?"

"Why in—why won't they run? Move, you godlost bird! Fly away! These animals, they're hopeless cowards, Amy, that's what they are! Why *won't* they run?"

"Never mind, darling Adol—we'll train one to run! Fast as lightning!"

The prince utters a groan of complex frustration and flings the air gun far. Recovering himself, he salutes the company, kisses his beloved's hand and stalks away.

Amoretta gazes after him, smiling fondly. A senior lady among her friends observes that smile, and feels her heart chill, for it seals Amoretta's fate. It is not the mere open radiance of an infatuated girl; there is in it a new element which the year past has developed—the undauntable spark of the maternal drive. Amoretta knows her lover now; she is aware of so much that many think her heedless. But instead of dimming her passion, this has done just the opposite. Adolesco has become in part her son, of whom all is forgiven. She sees his faults and counts them as nothing, with a mother's unshakable conviction that he will outgrow them under her care.

The lady sighs at the dilemma: this misdirection of the flooding drive to mother things might have been aborted had Amoretta had a real babe to coddle; but it is too late now.

Yes, alas; we see that even in Ecologia-Bella a girl may take to her too-motherly heart some scapegrace, who will usurp the place of her later, rightful children. Not that Adolesco is a scapegrace; he is only very young and formless, and the shape into which he will later crystallize may not be so attractive.

But we must return to his wedding day.

The noon-hours are occupied by a more-or-less ceremonial brunch, attended by Prince Adolesco's parents, the rulers of Pluvio-Acida. They arrive in the morning in their royal jet-liner, which is of course conventionally fueled. A respectable crowd is assembled to view the arrival of King Puerco Volante, Queen Porcellana, and Prince Slimoldi, although there is a good deal of discreet sneezing and holding of noses.

Queen Porcellana reciprocates.

"What is this terrible smell?" she demands of Adolesco, who has bounded up the ramp to meet them. "It's like poison gas. My God! Do you suppose—?"

"Cool it, mother dear. It's only fresh air. Affects some people like that at first."

The queen sniffs. "No wonder I see people wearing nose-masks. It's those dreadful trees. The first thing you must do is have them all cut down. I've been told they cause pollution."

And by the time King Puerco Volante and his family reach the palace where little Queen Amoretta is awaiting them, they are so overcome by oxygen fumes that they say nothing worth relating.

Their participation at the brunch is cut short by Queen Porcellana's feeling faint, and they gratefully retire to the royal guest suite.

Shortly the rest of the party retires too, to rest and prepare for the festivities ahead. The wedding is scheduled for the early evening, that having been the hour of Amoretta's birth, but the summer sun is still high.

And now the elder councilor pays his last visits.

He finds the little queen *en déshabille*, dreamily perfecting a bridesmaid's wreath of flowers.

"My dear," he says with great solemnity, "are you ready for the hour when your wishes—all of them—come true?"

She starts to reply gaily, then checks; this is no ordinary conversation. "Yes . . . I mean, yes."

"Then you will come with me. That hour is very near." He unfolds a great gauzy veiling cloak he has carried on his arm.

She stares at him for a moment, then snatches up her mirror and brush and begins to work feverishly. "Oh, but my—and my nose—wait!"

"No need for that. It will all be attended to." He nods toward an elder lady and the ladies' maid, who have silently entered behind him and started to select things from her closets and dressing-table, and place them in a great plain bag. "You will meet all these again shortly. Now put this on—that's right, it must cover your face—and come with me. Speak to no one. We must hope that you pass unrecognized."

She follows him out and through the back ways of the palace, which she knows well, but where so many strangers have been coming and going on unexplained errands that one more is scarcely remarked. In a small courtyard is a long, low, inconspicuous auto with a driver in mufti, into which he hands her. When they are settled and moving, he clears his throat and speaks:

"Now, my dear. You must learn that there is a certain hour, loosely speaking, which is out of history and is not timed on Ecologia-Bella's clocks. I put this metaphorically, to convey that actions taken or deeds done during this hour do not count. They have no official existence. And that hour is the time just before a royal ceremony of marriage, where we are now."

"But what—!" she asks, for during the past weeks she has become ever more puzzled. She has been told that she cannot, she will not marry Adolesco, yet every sign seems to say that she will. She has not been so foolish as to hope—and yet she has, a little. But what she has been vaguely expecting is something more official, or even catastrophic, not this strange speech.

"I know—I'm being kidnapped!"

The councilor holds up his hand.

"No. Permit me to continue. The reason for the existence of this absent hour is that Ecologia-Bella's scientists long ago determined that the parades, speeches, hours of formalities and convivialities, and the other turmoil of a long wedding day are not conducive to the happiest outcome, that night, for the newly wedded pair. Both will be exhausted, keyed up, over-fed, over-speechified, and who knows what, when they are finally left alone in a glare of public attention. Do you follow me?"

"Oh, yes! In fact—"

His hand goes up again.

"So it has been arranged for them to be alone, whilst they are fresh, in an hour which does not exist, in a place which is in no guide-book, to do whatever their hearts desire, in total privacy, as befits one of the most tender moments of their lives. Where I am taking you, the queenly and maidenly scruples which you have upheld so well may be relaxed, for this is an old tradition. All details have long been worked out. You have nothing to fret about, nothing whatever to do save what you wish, and trust us to place you before the altar in plenty of time. The populace will have had their ceremonial parades and viewings, and all things proper done, as they were when your maiden mother took this path before you. Do you still follow me?"

"Oh, yes! Oh, yes indeed! How wonderful! But—"

"But in your case, my dear," he goes on firmly, "there is a difference. I have said that *all* your wishes will come true. You have seen how you will have your heart's desire, your Adolesco, at the best hour of his life. But you have also wished to die if you cannot marry him. That, my dear, is still true. You may not and will not. And therefore this will be not only the happiest hour of your life, but the last.

"When the time arrives you will be given two vials to drink, one bitter and one sweet. The first one will see to it that your time of happiness is indeed totally happy, without any of the little physical tensions and drawbacks that often minimize a maiden's first experience of physical love. That is the bitter cup. The sweet one will ensure that after your total mortal fulfillment, a slight and painless chill will come over your body. That will be all you feel before you faint away. But that faint is fatal; you, Queen Amoretta, will never awaken. To put it bluntly, after your love-tryst you will die. Are you still prepared?"

"Yes." The little queen lifts her chin, her sweet lips set.

"Good. Then there is one small thing you must do. Your prince, having seen you die in his arms, would naturally be inconsolable, distraught, and quite unready for certain things he must do. Therefore, at some point during the, ah, proceedings, you must tell him—and convince him!—that you are your own double. That the queen found herself unable to overcome her scruples and sent you, her double, instead—as indeed, is both parties' right. You can see the need for this, and your ingenuity will know how to do it, I think?"

"Oh, yes—but will he never know? Will he marry someone else? Oh, that—no, no!"

"Calm yourself. The deception is just for an hour. And he will marry nobody—unless it be many years hence, back in Pluvio-Acida. And he will very soon know that the tale of a double is poppycock; that he spent this hour with the Queen herself."

"Very well. Is that all? Now I must think . . . Why, are we going to the cathedral?"

The wedding is to take place before the grand altar of the Goddess of Restrained Fertility, one of the great architectural ornaments of the capital.

"Yes, but to a part of it that few know of."

"I suppose my body will lie in state," the little queen says bravely.

"Yes, for a day. In the Cathedral of the All."

"Then will you see, please, that Donna does my hair?"

"Certainly." The elder pulls out his jot-pad and carefully notes this. There was silence for a block or two.

"My poor people," the queen muses at length. "I do think they liked me, don't you? And I tried to do little things . . . but I was so young."

"More than liked. They will have to get to know the sterling qualities of your brother before their grief abates. . . . And now it is my official injunction to you to think only of the joy immediately ahead. Think how you will soon feel when your prince appears with open arms and you are free to respond."

"Ohhh. Yes." And she thinks of nothing else, until they draw up at the rear of the cathedral, beside an inconspicuous old service door. Getting out of the car behind them are the elder lady, and the maid, with the bag.

"This is Lady Verdant, my dear. I believe you know her. She will take care of everything, and be within sound of your call at every moment."

With that, the councilor departs.

A suitable time later he knocks at the prince's door.

"Oh, come in."

He enters to find the prince drying off from his seventh shower of the day in a pair of shorts emblazoned with the arms of Pluvio-Acida. He is fretfully trying to sharpen the ceremonial sword which his parents brought him, along with the other necessary accoutrements of the wedding. He is also glancing frequently at an ormolu clock which he suspects of having stopped, so slowly does the afternoon pass for him.

"This thing will *not* take an edge," he exclaims. "Absolute tinware. That's another thing I love about Ecologia-Bella—all your stuff is such fine quality. I wish I knew what you do to your work-force."

"Perhaps it's what we don't do," the councilor smiles. "And

now, my dear young Prince, you are about to participate in an old Ecologia-Bella custom which I fancy will please you more than anything on earth."

"Oh, god, do I have to get dressed?"

"Absolutely not." The councilor shakes out another great gauzy robe. "Oh, perhaps you might take a nice-looking dressing gown—that gold one over there will do." He motions to the valet who is entering behind him. "And a pair of slippers. Old stones are cold."

"And that's not the only thing that is," mutters the prince, but his curiosity is roused, particularly when the valet selects a bottle of scent and a brush among the items he is putting in a bag.

"I think your complaints in that quarter will soon cease," beams the councilor, helping him into the all-disguising cloak. "Now just come with me and try to look unnoticeable."

There follows a repetition of the backstairs journey, the auto, and the councilor's explanation, omitting that part specific to Queen Amoretta.

The prince's response is everything the councilor could wish.

"What a wonderful country!" Adolesco exclaims over and over, nervously crossing his legs. "What an enlightened land!—You really mean this? She'll be there? It's not some joke?"

"On my honor. Why, look—" he picks up a flower Amoretta had caught in her veiling. "She has just made this trip before you."

"Oh my god! What a country!" The prince clutches the blossom as if it were the keys to Heaven, and recrosses his legs.

From the sunny afternoon in the parking area, they enter the inconspicuous door of the cathedral, and find themselves in a cool, dim, ancient corridor. On its left wall are tall marble abutments, which form the rear of the massive pedestal of the Goddess' great seated statue. In a recess is a sliding panel, which has been pushed aside to reveal a polished walnut door under a softly glowing lamp. The councilor motions Adolesco to stop.

"Inside that door is an apartment, furnished with all things desirable to lovers. There are several rooms; your valet will be in a back chamber, ready to dress you later for the official ceremony, for which you will be called in ample time.

"In the first room you come to is a bed. And in the bed will be a young, virgin queen, who has never seen the nude body of a living man. Nor has hers been seen by male eyes, nor touched by a male hand—not even a doctor's since her birth. And, mark well, she is also a queen, of a long line of sovereign blood. Your behavior will require your utmost sensitivity. I know you have it; I have closely watched your talent for avoiding anger or alarm in a blooded horse. This is not to imply that the queen is an animal, yet we all are animals in our basic emotions, and the same sensitivity runs through all, does it not?

"I leave you now. Compose yourself, and knock. If there be no answer—no answer—enter. But if the answer be 'No,' you must on no account dare to enter; call me and I will get you hence. But I doubt this mischance will occur. Now goodbye. May you have all the happiness your love deserves."

The councilor takes the disguising cloak and leaves him.

Adolesco inhales deeply, and approaches the charmed door. When he knocks, it sounds to him like gunfire, though his hand had been as gentle as he could make it. Involuntarily he holds his breath, listening. No sound, certainly no voice, comes from behind the door.

His throat full of panic, he turns the latch and opens it.

The room that meets his gaze is a blur of soft light and color. He looks blindly round once till his gaze is stopped at a great silken bed.

The silk is pulled taut over what he can clearly trace as a young girl's small body, and over the held-up top edge, under a mass of gold hair, are the two largest eyes he has ever seen in his life, seeking his.

Their eyes lock together. Tentatively he takes a step forward . . . then another . . . "Amy—?"

—But it is needless to follow in detail the drama that has played as long as the human race, though seldom at such intensity.

Enough to report that all goes well, very well—even the storm toward the end, when Amoretta confesses to being her own double.

"It all happened at the last minute—the poor little queen was so torn up between her idea of propriety and her love for you that she got sick—I mean, really sick. And she knew she couldn't go through with it right, she wouldn't be any good for you. But she couldn't bear the idea of calling out 'No' and having you turn away all disappointed. So she called on me—in fact, maybe I suggested it. I'm not so strict on this virginity business as she is—I mean, I'm a virgin—I mean, I *was*—" She laughs enchantingly, so like a jollier Amoretta that his heart twinges.

(In fact, Amoretta, little mischief, is thoroughly enjoying her role.)

"But I kept on just for her, see, because we should be alike. I've always taken my job very seriously, I study her. You'd be surprised at some of the things I've done! Big long ceremonials of course—and some close work, too. Nobody's ever suspected. I went with her to your country in fact—did you ever suspect when I was with you on the stand reviewing the Pluvio-Acida Army, Navy, Air Force, and what-all?"

"That was *you?*" The storm has long since melted away.

"It certainly was. She knew it would take forever, see, and I like military shows much better than she does. My, you have a huge Armed Force. And oh, my, you were so handsome!"

"And you were very beautiful . . . But do you mean you've been around the palace? Why haven't I met you?"

"Oh, you have. It was a tremendous thrill for me. But you never gave me another glance, no one does. I have different hair and eyes and all, and a piece of pink tape on my jaw that changes my whole face. Oh, and a bit of padding here and there. I call it my Uniform 'B.' When I'm being her it's Uniform 'A.'"

His eyes go over her, caressingly, astounded. "But you're so alike . . . it's unbelievable.—Look here, how do I know you two won't play more tricks on me?"

"Oh, we *couldn't*. Not now. But I'll tell you a secret—look!"

Unself-consciously she rolls over to show him her peach-bloom bottom. "See that great brown spot on my left, uh—" Suddenly remembering who he is and what's been happening, she blushes rosy all over the peaches and makes to hide.

He holds her firmly, laughing and peering. "You mean this teeny little beauty-spot I can barely see?"

"Well, yes. But the queen is *perfect*, see. That's my mark. So you can always tell."

"That might present a problem at an official function."

And between giggles and struggling they are soon entwined in the classic reconciliation. The whole thing now seems to the prince rather more titillating than disappointing. What excessively healthy young man can be truly insulted by having a beautiful extra virgin to initiate on his wedding day? Nothing is amiss that a splendid Ecologia-Bella seafood salad won't cure, and that has thoughtfully been provided.

So he is asleep, and she nearly so, when she feels the final, fatal chill gently taking her. She has strength only to whisper a goodbye, but it is too faint to wake him. Not until the councilor is standing over him with the dressing-gown does Adolesco come groggily to his feet—and he might have been hustled away without knowing anything is amiss did he not stoop to kiss her farewell.

Then the coolness of her flesh and the stillness of her body strikes him to full, frightened wakefulness.

"Oh my god—what—Help!"

"Help is here. We have always been afraid of this," the councilor tells him, pulling him back so that two white-coated strangers may get at her.

"She has a heart condition. But these are our best cardiologists, they will do everything possible. Now you have other matters to concern you. Come, leave this charming lady to her doctors—you have a queen to marry!"

So the prince reluctantly finds himself in another chamber, being bathed and dressed in his most beautiful crimson uniform, and when he would have returned to the bedroom he finds it locked against him. But a long mirror that shows him splendid in scarlet and gold lightens his mood, and since, after all, he can do nothing, and this is a different story, he turns his rising spirits to his duties immediately ahead.

He is, it seems, a trifle late.

"You must hurry now," says the councilor, guiding him to a winding passageway. "Just follow this, quickly—there will be people at the end to tell you what to do."

And now our single tale becomes complex, for it takes place in three arenas at once. Let us look first at what has been happening outside the cathedral:

The wedding parade from the palace is splendid beyond compare. Leading off is the first band, and never has music been gayer or more stimulating, never have uniforms glittered and instruments gleamed so brightly in a summer's sinking sun.

Behind their marching band comes a phalanx of the people of Ecologia-Bella, all in their national dress, which runs heavily to snowy ruffles and bright silks and braid, and is wonderfully becoming to everyone. These are the winners of the contests which have been held all year—contests of tree-felling, tapestry-broidering, chess-matches, gymnastics, welding, flower-growing, chimney-sweeping, computer-building, and everything-imaginable-contest winners, all prancing gaily along tossing flowers, together with some that have won no contests at all, but are merely beloved.

And then comes a splendid float, signifying everything noble and free and delightful, in a wondrous confection of so many flowers that their perfume pervades the whole air.

After it begins the long line of carriages, all beflagged, each drawn by matched teams of different breeds of horses, shining sorrel and ivory and ebony and spotted and red. The first carriages convey parties of visiting notables, and elder folk—and never have horses strode so stirringly, never have harness and head-plumes so sparkled and tossed. At this point comes a steam-calliope drawn by ponies, to keep up the beat, and right behind is the royal marching band from Pluvio-Acida, braying out their country's anthem—which is mercifully no more than briefly audible, by reason of the steam-calliope.

Following their band come two coaches of the royal family of Pluvio-Acida, nervously clutching the handholds of this unfamiliar vehicle, between perfunctory waves at the crowds.

And then comes—Ahh!—the first of the bridal party's carriages, in scarlet and gold, carrying the young nobles who will serve as Prince Adolesco's ushers. And behind them, in pastel colors, come three open victorias like huge floral bouquets of Queen Amoretta's bridesmaids and special friends. And finally, finally, passes a great white-and-gold landau like a wedding-cake, in which, totally veiled in gossamer and flowers, sits the queen. (Or so it is believed, for Amoretta really does have a double.) She is accompanied only by her senior maid of honor and a beribboned nurse holding an equally beribboned Prince Truhart, and she waves warmly, but not frivolously, to the adoring crowd, since this is a solemn day.

And behind her comes the cause of it all, a magnificently handsome prince upon a tall snow-white horse, who curvets and prances like Bucephalus. The Prince's handsomeness is sensed rather than seen, because the plumes of his dress-uniform casque are so gorgeous that only glimpses of his face can be seen. But his heroic figure and horsemanship are ample proofs of royalty.

Behind him comes a mounted contingent of the Palace Guard in gold and white and more plumes, their magnificent horses keeping step. After them follows a final band, whose tootling and booming pace the horses. The last element is a large troop of the prize-winning animals raised this year, with their proud and largely juvenile owners, all led by a great black bull.

And the whole is followed by a melodious rabble of street-singers, jugglers, and stilt dancers; while the end is brought up by a highly functional squad of debris-collecting trucks in white-and-gold.

And from start to finish of the line of march, at the sides of the way are people releasing (and handing out) balloons, and white doves who have been trained to circle becomingly before heading for their cotes, and others passing out floral streamers and whistle-pipes and confetti—and also a sprinkling of dress-uniformed police men and women, whose main task is to retrieve mislaid children who have temporarily joined one of the bands.

And inasmuch as the prince is from where he unfortunately is, the crowd contains more than a sprinkling of emphatically non-uniformed palace guards, who happily have no cause that day to display their special talents.

The parade ends in front of the cathedral, where there is a fine grassy square onto which the popular elements of the parade disperse and find their places in a reasonably orderly way, while the carriage passengers draw up to disembark on the cathedral's main steps to enter the huge nave, which is already well filled.

The bridal party proper disappears around the corner to debouch at the official side door, which opens into a large corridor of antechambers and retiring rooms, where a procession may prepare and form up.

And here we leave them for a moment.

In the main hall, the organ, a famous beauty, has been softly playing various celebratory bits. Now it voices several grand chords, and all fall still. Into the silence rises the music of a single flute from overhead—a delicately enchanting yet solemn solo, symbolizing the tenderness and depth of the impending event. The flautist is world-class; even the Pluvio-Acidan contingent cease rustling and complaining to listen.

Following this, according to Ecologia-Bella custom, a veiled priestess of the Goddess of Restrained Fertility advances to the flower-flanked altar, and beautifully chants a prayer for all the appropriate blessings, and in only their appropriate number. As she completes her chant, the archbishop of all Ecologia-Bella advances to her place before the altar.

But at that moment the priestess notices that a certain small green light amid the flowers has not come on, signifying a delay. With long experience in ceremonial matters, she adds a prepared coda to the prayer proper, plus a moment of silent meditation, and the light is on. She turns and is walking away—when there occurs an extraordinary event for whose inception we must return to the royal bridal party itself.

We left them entering the corridor of antechambers which are at the side separated from the nave by a heavy baize double door.

The various parties vanish into their respective retiring-rooms to effect those inevitable small repairs and recuperations required after a long, tiring ride. The royalty of Pluvio-Acida are offered light refreshments, which the Puerco Volantes have never been known to refuse, and restoratives are presented in the chambers of the gentlemen ushers and the bridesmaids and friends of the queen.

But the figures of Queen Amoretta and Prince Adolesco quickly disappear into separate royal apartments where they may be alone. These are set in this side of the pedestal of the great goddess-statue, where, unknown to most, they communicate privately to the even more private apartment on the far side, which we have already met.

Thus, when the young lady who has ridden in the queen's carriage enters the queen's retiring-room, she is quickly relieved of the royal crown and robe and veiling, and turned loose to mingle and enjoy herself among the other bridesmaids, who are unaware of the substitution. And a secret door is opened, and a small, cold figure is carried in. Lady Verdant alone remains, to attire the recently so-vividly alive little body in the irony of her wedding clothes.

Next door, a happier exchange is being made. The temporary prince enters, gratefully relieving himself of the overly plumose casque and Adolesco's sword and other accoutrements. He is in fact a handsome blond groom from the royal stables, who has thoroughly enjoyed himself—save for the feathers—on the prince's splendid white horse.

As he reverts to groomhood, there enters in haste Adolesco himself from the secret corridor, who still has barely presence of mind to thank his impersonator, and they might have got into a discussion of the gelding's off rear pastern problem, but for an elderly man—whom neither the prince nor many others have ever seen before, or since—who hurriedly enters and grasps the prince's arm.

"Quick! You are late! Your queen stands alone before the altar, the archbishop is waiting!"

The unknown functionary hustles the prince into the main corridor, which to his eyes looks ominously deserted, and they rush to the great baize doors. The prince's escort takes a peek out.

"Hurry! She is becoming impatient! Oh, Heaven—she is turning away. This is no time for explanations, young man—Are you strong enough to carry her?"

"Yes! But—"

"Then dash out there, pick her up and carry her back to the altar and *marry her*," the elder exhorts him. "Go!"

And such is the profound disorientation of the young prince, after a day fraught with emotional events, in which he has obeyed strange commands with even stranger outcomes—that he dashes forthwith out the baize doors into the cathedral aisle, where a veiled girl is walking away—picks her up bodily and carries her back to the altar, where the archbishop, being a trifle near-sighted, automatically begins to intone the wedding service. And any remarks by the lady are drowned out by the choir overhead, who burst incontinently into song.

The congregation is frozen dumb with shock. But at the first moment of relative quiet from the choir, the priestess throws off her veil and cries, "Release me this instant, you imbecile! I am not your queen!"

And indeed, all see that she could not be, for she is as beautiful as Sheba, and as black.

This moment of cosmic embarrassment is ended by the arrival of a posse headed by the council and Prince Slimoldi, who between them manage to get Adolesco back behind the baize doors, having urged the audience to remain calm.

The antechamber events which then begin to ensue can be

imagined, for the discovery of the queen's body is imminent, but we must pause a moment to inquire how this bit of what can only be called buffoonery comes about on tragedy's *eve*.

First, the identity of the elder who gave Adolesco the idiotic commands is never satisfactorily resolved, and he has disappeared. The more Machiavellian-minded suggest that he may have been one of Prince Slimoldi's advisors. Others take the view that he was simply an over-age cathedral retainer whose wits had been overcome by excitement so that he misinterpreted matters. The populace in general tend to believe that Adolesco was temporarily deranged by the news of his queen's death, and, ignorant of the country's customs, saw what he thought was his lost love waiting.

Whatever the explanation, the episode effectively quenched the gathering glow of the young prince's charisma in Ecologia-Bella. To have reacted to the death of his beloved by rushing out and attempting to wed the priestess, simply couldn't be seen in any very favorable light. The Ecologia-Bellans relate it with guffaws and giggles between their sighs.

But is this not an outcome which the more foresighted members of the council may have wished? Is there not an element of danger to a small country whose people begin to sentimentalize the ruler of a neighboring, hostile state? And, finally, is not the removal of latent dangers the council's business?

Thus there are those who surmise, on the rule of *Cui Bono?* that the council itself may not have been so *very* surprised by the prince's actions; it simply went off better than their hopes. Even the kindest of Ecologia-Bellans agree that a youth who could behave so isn't ideally suited to be their king.

But we must return now to the antechambers of the cathedral, where word is starting to run that something dreadful has happened to the queen. As the members of the procession emerge to form in line, a white-coated man stations himself beside the queen's door, and from outside come the unmistakable sounds of an ambulance arriving.

"The queen is gravely ill. The wedding is . . . postponed."

"Vehicles are coming to convey you back to the palace, or wherever you may wish to go," the councilor tells them. Attendants materialize, ready to help.

But the prince pushes his way into the chamber where his queen's body lies. One look at the idle equipment dismays him.

"Why aren't you *doing* something?" he demands of the doctors with Lady Verdant. "Revive her, damn you! Let me by—I will!"

He is restrained, but not before his fingers have brushed the stony coldness that convinces more than words. He stares down, heart-stricken.

But one wild hope remains. There has been too much confusion today.

"Leave me alone with her for five minutes! I demand it as my right."

"Very well, Your Majesty," replies the Lady Verdant, motioning the others from the room. But as she turns to follow, she says to him quietly and sadly, "Do not concern yourself with moles, or beauty-spots or such, my poor young prince. I removed the one you saw, as I put it on. You see, the queen conceived her tale of a double to protect a little of her modesty. It was the queen herself you were with."

He looks at her in silence, his last hope gone. He has, he realizes, loved Amoretta very much, and never more than now. . . .

Let us leave him to the few moments' privacy allowed to royalty and grief.

When they are over, the councilor comes in. He has a proposal.

"I won't intrude on you with my condolences. Death has touched me too. But there remain practical matters. I imagine you would prefer to spend some time now in your homeland—you will appreciate that at the moment your, ah, image here is rather mixed."

When the Prince frowns at him uncomprehendingly, the old man adds, "Ms. Victoria Ntutu."

"*Who?*"

"The priestess you, ah, partially wedded."

"Ohhh." He clasps his hand to his forehead. "What shall I *do?* I don't want the family—"

"Listen. The Ecologia-Bella International Overnight Express will be departing shortly. I remembered that you enjoyed your trip in her, and I have taken the liberty of having the royal coach attached to the first section. If you give the word, I will convey you privately to it. Your things will meet you there. By tomorrow noon you will be at your capital, having had a long night and morning of peace and calm. What do you say?"

The prince's assent is never in doubt.

So that is where young Prince Adolesco spends his wedding night, and it is as soothing and pleasant as—under the circumstances—can be. And curiously, this is his last night as prince.

By a chance which not even the Ecologia-Bella Council could have improved on, his mother, Queen Porcellana, is now actually quite ill from an excess of oxygen combined with the deprivation of certain food additives one can become quite dependent on. She demands to leave this dreadful place at once.

So King Puerco Volante orders up the royal jet, undeterred by the fact that the weather has broken at the queen's death, and storms are in the mountains. Moreover, the pilot has been celebrating a little prematurely.

When the mountain passes turn out to be raging vortices of thunder and gales, the pilot retains the sense to rise high above the ranges. But when a massive cloud-to-cloud lightning bolt strikes the plane and takes out the electrical systems, he cannot recall in time which of the six hundred and eighty-five switches will solve matters—and orders the party to bail out.

And alas, it is discovered too late that the last surviving family of porcupines in Pluvio-Acida, escapees from the local zoo, have been nesting in the royal parachutes. The multiply-punctured silk ruptures above two thousand meters. And poor King Puerco Volante belies his name: he can in no way *volar*, nor can Queen Porcellana or Prince Slimoldi.

So Adolesco arrives refreshed in his capital to find himself the King of Pluvio-Acida, and for the next years has a great deal to do.

Thus when a youngster grasps at too much, and is told to "Remember the crown prince's wedding," he may reply, "Yes—but he ended up king!"

To which may be given such answer as seems appropriate.

There is a coda to our story, which no man alive today in Ecologia-Bella may know:

A few days after the tragic death of Queen Amoretta, in an ancient, rambling, stone-and-mortar nunnery high up in the wooded mountains, a brown-haired girl opens her brown eyes and speaks for the first time, slow and soft.

"Am . . . I . . . alive?"

The old man who is bending over her says, "You are. Queen Amoretta is not."

"How . . . sad."

"Yes and no. Would you take something to drink? You've been unconscious for several days."

"Yes. . . . An accident?" She is more alert.

"No. A rare new hypothermic drug we are testing for certain conditions. Including difficult rescues."

"Oh . . ." She smiles, and soon has soup to occupy her.

And we can fill in the tale from here on. Sister Inconnue, as she is called until she shall choose her name, gradually regains all her memories. Meanwhile she has been studying. They have started her on the knowledge of all the flora and fauna of Ecologia-Bella. The nuns are a teaching order, and its best pupils finish at universities all over the world, before returning to enrich their country.

"It all seems like a dream," she says to the councilor on one of his periodic visits. "Very sad and rather silly. But why?" she asks earnestly. "Please tell me, just why? Couldn't you have done it, well, differently?"

"No way," says the Lady Verdant, and bites her embroidery-thread.

"You see, my dear," the councilor explains, "after very earnest thought by the full council, we came to two conclusions. The first was that a small country as vulnerable as ours simply cannot afford a beautiful young virgin queen. You saw what was already arriving at the palace; there would have been no end to it. Jealousies, conflicts, all sorts of involvements. And sooner or later, the country's freedom would have been imperiled. That isn't true for your brother, he can't bring home a ruler. The international succession laws are archaic, of course; a crime. But we can't change that.

"One other—and equally important—discovery was that somewhere under those golden curls was a brain, which it would have been a sin to destroy, and a shame to waste upon the symbolic activities of queenship. This way, if you study hard, you can make yourself perhaps into a councilor of Ecologia-Bella, and that, as you may have noticed—"

"Is the real power in what I thought was my land," she says mischievously.

"Exactly. A dangerous system, but the best we have found."

"I see . . ." She looks away reflectively. "I wonder. Maybe, when I am old and very wise . . . would it surprise you if I proposed another?"

Yanqui Doodle

Of course they have to visit a hospital. To show they care. But which hospital? Not a big base hospital, but not a front-line station either—Congressional Armed Service Committee members are too precious to go where real iron is flying. Not to mention the value of the half-dozen generals escorting the fact-finding tour of the Bodéguan front.

A perfect hospital is found. The town of San Izquierda, just inside the Bodéguan border, has finally been liberated by American troops after the Libras had nibbled at it several times, and each time been run out by the Guévaristas. After the sixth loss the GIs were sent in to take it conclusively—what was left of it. Now the front has rolled forward twenty-five or fifty kilometers—depending on whose maps you used—and a big mansion formerly owned by one of the dictator's pals has been converted into an Intermediate Rehab Unit. The patients are a mix of GIs who would go back on duty, with some whose condition was bad enough to invalid them back to base, or even home.

So now the cavalcade is driving toward San Izzy, trying to make time. This is the last event of the senators' day, and they've been delayed at Hona Base. There was an obstacle course demonstration by US field instructors, and a parade of Libra troops in training, and speeches. That caused the trouble; even General Sternhagen had been moved to say more than a few words.

Senator Biller, the ranking committee member, sits in the rear of the stretch Mercedes with two American flags on the fenders. Behind him come two new '98 Caddies with the rest of the committee and some more generals, similarly beflagged. All the other escort vehicles bear twin flags, one American, the other the official Libra flag, which had been somewhat hastily designed and is not everywhere recognized with confidence.

The senator sits between General Schehl and the interpreter. She is a neat and sultry-looking young lady, whose grasp of such fundamental phrases as "founding fathers" is, Senator Biller feels, a trifle shaky. He is wishing he could give her a short course in American—er, United States—history.

He is also musing on the Libra troops he had spoken with after their parade. The Freedom Fighters. The average Freedom Fighter had a distressing tendency to look like any fifteen-year-old greaser embracing an M-18.

"What did the Guévaristas do to you?" he had asked one youth. "Why are you here?" The youth looks at the ground, then into space. "Guéyas very bad," he says to the interpreter, who amplifies, "Much oppression."

Biller persists. "What did they do to you? How did they oppress you?" The boy says something angry. "They wanted to recruit him for the Army," the interpreter explains.

"But you're in the Army now," Biller says against his better judgment.

"Gué army very bad!" The interpreter smiles ravishingly. "Here is more better."

Looking around at Hona's substantial barracks, the lad's new uniform and boots, the slight but perceptible bulge under his belt, Senator Biller can believe it.

The boy adds something, scuffing his toe.

"Only he is worried about his Ma-ma," the interpreter goes on. This is something Biller can relate to. He pats the boy's shoulder comfortingly and smiles.

"He is afraid she will sell his motorcycle," the interpreter finishes.

Several Libras are listening to the exchange. Senator Biller looks round at their young faces and tells them what fine young men they are, what a good thing they are doing evicting Marxist-Leninism and saving their country for Democracy—all of which the interpreter seems to shorten unduly.

Then there is a bark, and all come smartly to attention, faces blank. The senator moves on.

Meanwhile his colleagues, some of whom can speak Spanish, are likewise mingling with the troops, forming invaluable first-hand impressions of the state of the minds and hearts of the people to whose aid their country had sent her armed might and the blood of her sons. Afterwards Senator Moverman exclaims, "Fine brave boys! To think they'd be fighting Soviet gunships bare-handed if we hadn't sent them aid!"

Another legislator inquires as to whether they had captured many Cubans. A look of intense wariness comes over his informants' faces. "Fidelistas very bad. Very bad soldier." It turns out that they mean "Very dangerous."

"Where are they? Can we see some of the Cubans you captured?"

There is a quick confab, and somebody says "Fidelisto!" and laughs in a private way that gives Senator Biller grave qualms about the Geneva Conventions. A traitorous thought crosses his mind, about other boy-men in other uniforms, sent abroad to die for Soviet geopolitik. He shrugs it away. War is evil. Lying down under Communist tyranny is worse.

It is at this point that old Senator Longmast indicates his desire to address the assembled Libra and US troops, and gets into his brief explanation of What They Were Fighting For that so terminally delays them. When he is reminded that they have a hospital to visit, he says, "We owe it to them," and goes on.

Now the party is trying to make up lost time on the San Izquierda road, which features a plethora of potholes and other obstacles. At the moment they have come onto a herd of scraggly cattle trapped between the steep banks of the mountain road.

The cars stop, the party gets out to stretch. Below them is a superb view of San Izquierda in the evening sun, nestled around its almost-intact cathedral. Shadowy mountain ridges, forested by pines, stretch away on either hand. Senator Biller reaches for his camera, as do others.

They are at a small crossroads. On the other road a rusty country bus has also stopped, is letting out people. The scene is very peaceful. Tropical birds are making exotic evening sounds. There is only the far-off rumble of heavy trucks on another road; a convoy, probably.

Beside the senator there looms up what seems to be a self-propelled great load of sticks. It turns out to be on the head of a small old woman. Biller reflects that only weeks ago she and the town had been under the iron boots of the Guévaristas. He catches her curious eye on him and grins broadly, saying "Libertad!"

"Si! Si!" Her face lights up with a toothy grin. Life is good; only that morning she had sold her twelve-year-old daughter to three *Yanquis* for pesos four hundred, about twenty dollars.

Senator Biller steels himself against the impulse to tell his driver to help her with her load. (They're used to it, this is the way they live.) He turns to his snapshots of the town below.

Ahead, the cattle are dispersing. The party is getting back into their cars. On the side road the bus has started up too.

"See—hospital!" the driver throws back over his shoulder, waving at a large building set in a garden just in view several kilometers ahead and below.

* * *

In that same hospital, Pfc Donald Still had come back to life some two weeks before. The last thing he remembered was hearing his patrol leader yell and finding himself falling with an unbelievable pain on the inside of his thigh. He also remembered thinking that the path behind the ridge they were following was a natural site for mines, but he was too exhilarated to object. They were in hot pursuit of a bunch of Gués who were running and dodging just behind the spine of the ridge. The trees cleared out ahead. Don popped another BZ, looking forward to getting himself some good bursts.

Now he was flat on his back, feeling terrible, with a heavy wrapped-up leg. Steel rails on the bed, Above him afternoon sun filtered through ornate windows in a high dome. Mostly silence all around, no shots, no footsteps running. This was no battle-aid station. The choppers must have carried them all the way back to wherever this was. He felt that a lot of time had passed here: dreams of struggles, dreams of himself shouting.

His mouth and eyes were painfully dry, his head hurt, he felt weak and fluttery inside and his leg ached horribly. Automatically he reached for a Maintenance pill. But his pill kit wasn't there. He was in hospital PJs, no pockets, no pills, nada.

"Hey! Hello!"

A dizzyingly beautiful girl's face swam in front of him. No, on second look she wasn't so gorgeous, only cute and very clean.

"Where am I? What's with my leg?"

She produced a clipboard. "You're in San Izquierda Intermediate Rehab Fifteen. Your leg is okay, you'll be walking tomorrow when the cast comes off. You were lucky, you just lost a lot of blood." She smiled meaningfully. "*Very* lucky."

"I need an M."

"Oh-oh." She frowned. "Wel-l-l. Tomorrow you start detox."

"But this is still today!" He tried to smile over sudden panic.

"Wel-l-l. You're just making it harder for yourself."

"But it's today. You said. *Please*."

Without saying anything she turned away and came back with

the precious yellow tab. He managed to clutch it and dry-swallowed. She tut-tutted at him.

"We've got to stop that pill-seeking behavior, soldier," she said cutely.

In spite of himself he grinned at her, or rather at the blessed tide of relief that would come through his veins in a minute.

"Make the most of it, soldier," she told him and went away.

He loathed people who called him 'soldier' but he wasn't about to antagonize his supply. The M was working already, he could feel the first faint glow, the all-rightness, stealing over him. Without Ms, who could make this war? Nobody he knew of.

"Hey, what happened to the others? To my unit?" he asked when she passed by later. "Jack Errin, Benjy?"

"Your friends? I'm afraid I don't know. You were brought in alone. I did hear you were an only survivor. I'm afraid your friends were casualties, soldier. Or maybe they weren't badly hurt."

Friends, he thought. Yes, he'd liked Jack in a far-off sort of way, and Benjy was a good guy. But didn't she know that in this war you don't have pals? When you're on Ms you don't need 'em, when you're on BZs you don't remember the word.

"What do you mean about detox tomorrow? What are they going to do to me?"

"Because you're going home, soldier. *Home*—I told you you were lucky. Why do you think you're in an Intermediate Unit?"

He had no idea.

"Because we can't let you boys go home full of that awful stuff, can we? So you have to get two-three weeks of detox. It won't be so bad. Think about going home."

He lay back, his head spinning. Through his body the gentle glow of the M was taking away all worries. Tomorrow was a long way off.

But think about going home? He didn't particularly want to. Home wasn't much since Geri had split. But to tell the truth he could hardly remember her. It had been one of those draft-notice marriages anyway, and so far as he knew he hadn't left a child. Her letters had been short and almost illegible, starting with a hot sort of personal pornography, and ending last fall with the "I guess we better think this all over" one. She'd been staying with his folks in San Diego. Not much of a life for her. He guessed she was really divorcing his mother. He chuckled to himself.

So now where should he go? Back to San D. first, then he'd see. Something would turn up. No point in worrying now. In fact, he couldn't worry if he tried.

He remembered the week they had first issued the Ms. What a change. All the guys who were muttering about going AWOL just quit. They'd often wondered what was in them. Not cocaine, nothing he'd ever heard of. Miracles of modern science.

No, wait—the first thing they issued was the BZs. He'd been given some specially, when someone had noticed him firing his M–18 in the air instead of at the Gués in front of them. What the hell, a lot of the others were doing that, too. The boys they killed had been so young, and they shot so badly. He'd expected the Commie Gués to be ten feet high and mean. Not baby-faced twelve-year-olds. Of course those same twelve-year-olds had been laying mines that blew unlucky grunts apart, but . . . but . . . looking straight at one and blowing his guts out was somehow different. They ran away fast enough, wasn't that what counted?

But the Army saw things differently. Kill! Kill! His training . . . so he found himself being given some red capsules and instructed to take one when he was in a shooting situation. BZs—Battle Zones—they had removed all his reservations about blowing anybody away, made it exhilarating. In fact, they had removed all his reservations about anything. But luckily your memory of what you'd done behind BZs wasn't too good. They had swept through several little hamlets, putting the flamers to it all, and there were flash-memories of other things—patch-views of female flesh, lots of screaming and one that bothered him a lot—he didn't want to think about that now.

So then had come the green Sleeper tabs, and after that there weren't any more dreams. Trouble was, men started nodding over their rifles on patrol. So then there was the general issue of Ms. For Maintenance. It made an ideal combo.

But detox? Detox before going home? Nobody had said a word to them about that. He'd always assumed they had some other magic potion, that there'd be some kind of gentle end. Well, it would all be okay. It had to, he thought, drifting off. Nobody'd do anything so brutal.

He woke up with somebody pushing a tray at him. "Soft diet."

Trying to eat the stuff he didn't feel so good. The M was wearing off. Probably they hadn't given him enough while he'd been here, his blood levels were low.

A different nurse was on duty, an older, dark-haired woman. She brought him an M when asked, without comment.

"You're starting detox tomorrow, you know," she told him. But she seemed nicer, more like she was worried for him.

"What's so big about that? Is it bad?"

"Well-l-l . . . you've been on this stuff how long? A year?"

"Around that."

"We're just starting to get long-timers like you."

"What happens?" he persisted.

She frowned. "Detoxification is always hard. You have to get your body making the chemicals again itself. The only way is to go cold; tapering off is like cutting a dog's tail off an inch at a time to be kind. But some people take it like a breeze. Most do. Hold the thought."

He wasn't worried. But still he wondered. "I thought they'd have something for us. I mean, they put us on it."

"You mean you were ordered to take the stuff?"

"Oh, no . . . but strongly suggested. Because . . . because there were things . . ." He wanted to stop talking and enjoy the M's good feeling.

"Well, there is Slobactin. That helps. You'll be given some."

"Thank you," he said dreamily. She went away.

He lay back, looking vaguely around. The room seemed to have been part of a mansion—a ballroom, maybe. Only a few other beds were in here. Too far to talk. A bed was rolled in with a lot of fuss going on around it—a new arrival fresh from the operating room, he made out. This was some kind of way-station. By craning his head he could see metal-grilled doorways, apparently leading into corridors the Army had built on. Two muscular-looking male techs or orderlies sat behind desks, keeping an eye on things. It was very peaceful; the first time in a long time he had heard no firing.

Bedtime came, and the cute little blonde nurse came in to douse the lights and distribute pills. The yellow-and-pink cap she gave him was all wrong.

"Nurse, I want my Army sleep pill. My ND." "ND" was for No Dreams.

"This is just as effective," she said serenely.

He doubted it strongly. "I want my regular ND. I'm entitled to it, it's still today."

"You're not entitled to any particular medication, soldier. You're entitled to have us make you well, that's what we're doing."

Her voice had a nasty edge, her smile was pure plastic.

"But it's not fair! The NDs are for—for special reasons." He couldn't tell her about the dreams. "—Please. Can I have mine tonight? It's still today."

"You have your sleeping pill. Now calm down and go to sleep, you're disturbing the other patients."

"I'll keep everybody awake if you don't give me the right one!"

"Don't try it, soldier." She smiled toward the grille where the two big orderlies were watching him alertly. She went away.

He lay back, fuming. He'd meant that the dreams made him yell. Well, they'd find out.

"You get on *her* shit list, you dead," said the soldier in the next bed, separated from him by a tiled plant-stand.

"But she said—"

"You dead," the man repeated.

To his surprise, he did drift off, and dreamt only innocuous fantasies about his old dog.

He woke in the night, feeling a knife grinding him under his ribs. His old ulcer pain. He'd almost forgotten, he hadn't had that since his first ND tab. And there was another trouble, an itch under his leg-cast. A roach or something must have somehow gotten under it and was struggling about. He banged at it futilely, and finally called.

Miss Plastic approached with a flashlight.

"Shshsh! What is it, soldier?"

"My ulcer hurts. I need some antacid."

She made a note on the clipboard. "I'll tell the doctor about it. Maybe he'll prescribe you some in the morning."

"In the morning? Christ, I need it right now, I feel like my stomach's boring through.

"Sorry, I can't prescribe medication. But I'll have the doctor look at you first thing, I promise." Cutie-doll smile.

"But antacid isn't a prescription drug, a medication! Christ, you can buy Maalox or Mylanta over the counter by the gallon. You must have some here. I *hurt*."

"Anything other than your meals is a medication, soldier." She turned the flash off.

"Wait! Do you mean this shit?"

"Don't swear at me."

"Well, wait one minute—there's bugs under my bandage. A bug. I can feel it crawling around."

Expertly she slipped back the sheet and explored the top of the cast with the light.

"No bugs. You calm down, the bugs will go away."

"But I can feel them! They itch! Can't you at least cut that stuff so I can scratch? You said it comes off tomorrow." No use, he could see that. "Isn't there something you could squirt under it? Some bug killer?" he asked weakly.

"Sorry, soldier. There are no insects, nothing, under that bandage. It's all in your head. Now, are we going to be good and go to sleep—or are you going to cause trouble? There are men here a lot sicker than you are, you know."

He looked up at her in the dim light, living proof that a cute girl five feet three inches high could be a monster.

"If you'd give me my ND I could sleep. It's not tomorrow yet!" His voice was high with anguish. She didn't reply, just clicked the flash off and went away.

He saw her checking the inhabitants of the other beds on her way out. Two men came awake at this, screamed briefly and thrashed about. Didn't she know being wakened like that could be bad news in the combat zone, didn't she know *anything?*

"Take it easy, soldier," he heard her say. Then she was gone.

He lay back and felt the supposedly nonexistent bugs scratching like mad. One bastard's legs were in the tender place back of his knee. Goddamn. He made a determined effort to break the cast on the bedrails, got nowhere. Then he recalled something.

In a story he'd read, "insects" like this were a feature of going off drugs cold turkey. Victims were driven crazy, tore themselves bloody. The doper's DTs. Was *this* what detoxification was going to be like? Oh, Christ, oh Christ.

He tried to relax, but there was no more possibility of sleep. And his ulcer was really hurting now, gnawing deep. Going without antacids could be dangerous, his old doc had said. Your stomach could perforate. He almost hoped his would, that would be a lesson for Miss Plastic. Medications! . . . God, he could see the inside of a US drugstore, all those good things laid out ready to your hand. Mylanta, Maalox, Alternagel, Tums—in his civilian days he'd been a good customer for all that. But the ND-tabs had stopped the pain. He'd have to get hold of more the minute he was turned loose. But what if they only issued them in the combat zone? Well, he'd get back there by hook or crook. Back to combat? Why not? If he was comfortable and could sleep there. How long would this damn detox take? Two, three weeks had they said? Could he endure it?

He rolled, rolled, tossed, trying to find a position where the pain was better and the bugs were quieter . . . some time toward morning he must have lost consciousness.

Detox started officially right after breakfast, when two strange orderlies descended on his bed, checked the rails, and started rolling him toward one of the closed-off corridors. He'd been enjoying a nap at last, almost didn't wake up in time to size up his surroundings. As they relocked the grille he sat up and saw that he was in a wing the Army must have added on—plain plywood walls, low ceilings, all the way down, with doors opening off each side to a blank wall at the far end. First came a second grille, strong steelwork, and polished in the middle as though hundreds of hands had gripped it. As they went through, he saw that the first door bore a hand-lettered sign: Quiet Room. The door had a small wire-reinforced glass window in it. And there was sound coming from it—a faint, pallid mewling or keening, like an animal far away. Then they were passing closed, featureless doors, 205, 207. At 209 the orderlies stopped, opened up, and pushed him in.

209 was about four meters square, with a screened, barred, frosted window. There was a bed already in it. The orderlies wrestled it around to take out.

Don said, "They told me I was going to walk today. They're supposed to take the cast off. Where's the doctor?"

"Don't know anything about that," one of them grunted, opening the door.

He started to panic. It seemed to him that once he was shut in here they would just forget him, let him starve and die, immobilized in the heavy cast.

"Where's a *doctor?* Would you tell them I need a doctor? I have ulcers, see," he added idiotically to their backs as they went out. The door closed.

At that he dragged himself up and by tremendous effort managed to get one leg over the guard-rails. Then he saw that the reason the cast was so immovable was that somebody had strapped it to the bed-rails, top and bottom. Must have been done when he dozed off. By straining to his limit he got the top buckle undone, but no way could he reach his ankle. Panting, he lay back. His hands were shaking like leaves in a wind.

"I'm not functioning," he thought. God how he needed an M. Was it possible that only ten days ago he had been a competent combatant, leaping up mountainsides?

He looked around. The room contained a straight chair, a small set of drawers on wheels, and a lidless toilet. No means of calling for help.

That gave him an idea. Legitimate need.

He called tentatively, "Nurse!" No response, nothing. There was nobody out there. He raised his voice as loud as he could. "Nurse! Nurse! *Help!*"

Almost instantly there were footsteps and the door opened. Miss Plastic.

"Nurse, I have to go to the can. Why isn't this cast off? You said I'd walk today. Where's the doctor? Does he know about my ulcer?"

She stared at him unsmiling. "We don't holler like that, soldier. It upsets other patients. You have to think of the others here."

"Well, how can I get help?"

"Someone looks in every fifteen minutes, around the clock. You can tell them what you need."

They went through the bedpan routine; she restrapped the buckle he'd opened and departed.

The morning dragged on. As she'd said, every quarter-hour the door opened and a face looked in. Often it was the dark-haired nurse, but he didn't bother her except to ask once if the cast would really be removed. "Yes. Soon, now. Doctor is making rounds."

The invisible insects had quieted down to where he could forget them, but in their place came a growing horde of aches and discomforts, everywhere. Bruises he dimly remembered from combat time hurt. Was all this what the Ms had been hiding from him? He groaned, trying to get comfortable. Did they even *have* a doctor in this crazy place?

At noon came the doctor, and with him Miss Plastic, carrying his lunch. She put the tray down on the bureau, out of his reach. The doctor was old, about Don's father's age. He was a grunter. He tackled the cast with an electric saw. Miss Plastic kept having to hand him things; it did Don good to see her obeying orders, sweet as peaches.

"You were very lucky, son, (grunt) very lucky. Hm'm. I think I'll take these stitches out now, but (grunt) no walking for three days, hear?"

"I can get to that toilet, can't I?"

"Hm'm'm. Very well, yes, to the toilet—but *only* there and back, understand? Mm'm. Meals in bed."

"Yes sir."

"And nurse, you keep an eye on him to see he stays put."

"We always do, sir."

"That's right (grunt). We put a pin in that bone, son, so you won't have a short leg. We don't want it wiggling around, (grunt) we want it to heal tight. Keep it just as quiet as you can."

"Yes sir."

"M'm'm . . . say, that looks good. Mind if I steal a bite?"

Without waiting for a reply the doctor plucked a small something off the tray, nodded, and went out. As they were leaving, Don called, "Nurse, I can't reach my lunch."

"Someone will be right in."

He lay and watched it getting cold. Food here was godawful enough when hot. In desperation, he crawled up on his good knee and then got that leg to the ground and leaned just far enough to grab the tray and pull it across himself as he collapsed. God, he was weak!

Just as he got settled the door opened and a strange red-headed nurse came in.

"My, we *are* impatient, aren't we?"

"I didn't step on the leg," he said defensively.

"Good." She looked at him seriously. "You'll have to live the rest of your life with whatever you do to yourself now. The doctor went to a lot of trouble. Follow his orders."

Somehow this got through to him. This nurse was someone in authority, he felt. He realized he'd been acting childishly. Long ago he'd been known for his patience and good temper. What had happened to him? Was all this the drugs? Or the effect of being without them? He no longer felt at all hungry, now that he'd gotten the tray. In fact he felt sick. And he was trembling and sweating.

"Nurse, I feel pretty terrible. They said you had something that helps. May I have some? Something-bactin, I think."

"Slobactin. Yes, you'll be getting some with your regular medication."

"And I forgot to tell the doctor, I have ulcers. They've been acting up. Can I have some antacid?"

She made a note on her clipboard. "Yes, I'll tell the doctor as soon as he comes off rounds. Anything else?"

She was straightening his bedclothes. As she patted the under-sheet she suddenly frowned disapprovingly, but said nothing more before departing.

He fell into a sweaty sleep, forgetting his lunch, from which he was wakened by a man saying "Roll. Roll over here."

"Huh?"

It was one of the two big orderlies. He was dumping something into the bed, something heavy that felt both cold and warm.

"Roll over to the edge so I can spread this."

Groggily he complied, finally made out that the man was working a rubber sheet onto the mattress under the regular sheet. When he rolled back the bed felt clammy and hard on his bruises.

As the man left, Don began to feel scared. Did these precautions mean that he was going to be sick in some ghastly uncontrolled way? Well, he was starting to feel much more nauseated. And, goddamn, nothing to york into here, except the untouched lunch tray with its weak white plastic flatware. The orderly had put it back on top of him. He hoped it wouldn't come to that, tried deep breathing that hurt his ribs.

At the next door-check he asked for a sick-basin, and to have the tray taken away. It was little Miss Plastic. She checked the uneaten food.

"It's starting, eh, soldier? You're slow—you must have been on that stuff a long time."

"A year."

"My, my . . . soldier, how *could* you do that to your body?"

How could he begin to tell her, assuming she really wanted to know? Instead he asked her a question.

"Nurse, have you ever had ulcers?"

She laughed. Then she said with a smug little lift of her chin, "I've never used a day of sick leave in my life." The implication was strong: those people who got sick did it to themselves.

"Try it sometime," he said through suddenly chattering teeth.

"No thanks!" Merrily she exited, taking the tray but forgetting his basin.

That afternoon was bad. The itching started again, and he scratched his arms bloody. Miss Plastic caught the blood on the sheet, looked at his nails, and clucked. "Marie hasn't been here."

Shortly an orderly came in, leading a small mestizo girl in a pink smock.

"Manicure time."

The girl grabbed his hand in a surprisingly firm small grip, and was already cutting. Cutting right down to the quick, he saw. When he protested, the man came and stood over him. "Routine procedure, fella." Don subsided, and the orderly produced a movie magazine and sat in the chair. The cutting went quickly; Don realized he would be helpless to ease himself, and tried to save out one finger. "No, no!" Marie said.

"Yes! Leave it, please."

The orderly put down his magazine and loomed over him again. "I said it's routine procedure. She does them all. Every one . . . you want to make trouble, fella?"

Looking up at him, Don decided he didn't. The girl finished with a filing job, and then, to his amazement, pulled back the sheet and tackled his toenails with a dog-clipper.

"Oh, no!"

"Oh, yes!" she said mockingly. The orderly watched impassively as he let her begin, then returned to his gaudy magazine. "You could infect yourself, fella," he observed.

When the job was finished Don felt like a declawed cat, or a defanged wolf. God, the lengths they went to to render him helpless!

And more. Just after they left, Miss Plastic came in with a mestizo porter carrying what Don recognized with wonder as his duffel bag from main camp. One of the Army's eerie efficiencies. The duffel was plonked down and the little nurse swiftly opened it and started to unpack it onto the floor. Searching. His hunting knife went first into a big plastic bag she had. Then his cigarettes, and then she opened his shaving roll.

"You can keep these." She pulled out toothpaste and brush, and then resealed the kit and dumped it into her bag.

"Hey, are you going to take that away? I need those things."

"No metal or glass," she said firmly. "No liquids. And no heavy plastic."

Don was a fairly neat packer; he had put a clean uniform and his fresh laundry into plastic bags. Those got dumped, and the bags confiscated.

"Why those?"

"No bags. Patients have been known to try to do themselves harm."

"With a *Baggie?*"

She didn't answer. He guessed she meant you could smother yourself with one. Ugh—what a way to go. A tremor of fear ran over him. Did people here really get that desperate?

"That reminds me—where's my watch?"

"At the desk. With your dogtags. You get them back when you leave."

He felt nakeder than ever, but nausea was rising in him again and he couldn't protest. This time she brought him a basin, and watched him as he retched up liquid. Then she crammed his remaining stuff back into the eviscerated duffel, zipped it up, and left with her bag of booty.

He lay back, sweating and shaking. There was a peculiar sourceless pain in his legs; no position eased it. The itching started again, and rubbing with his denuded fingers only made it worse. Finally in desperation he managed to get out of bed and grab his toothbrush from the windowsill. Scratching with that gave him some help, but it soon became bloody and he knew if somebody saw that it would be taken away. There was no water in his room other than the can, so he sucked the toothbrush clean, sick with disgust at the taste of his own blood.

The endless hours passed so; finally came medication-time. With the vitamin-like pills came two small brownish tablets—the drug-deprival medicine?—and a tiny paper cup containing Maalox. So Redhead hadn't forgotten. He gulped it hungrily, and took the pills, dreaming of the beautiful yellow M-tabs he needed so.

Dinner came and went untasted, and then the night settled in. To his exasperation, they wouldn't switch off the ceiling light. He tossed and turned, finally ending with the small pillow over his eyes.

And then the deprivation really started on him. The random pains that had bothered him turned ten times worse, savage stabbings in his arms, legs, guts. His head throbbed. His mouth and eyes were painfully dry. And the skin-itch he had thought intolerable migrated into the interior of his joints where he couldn't get at it. He had visions of armies of rustling termites marching with their little tickling legs, through his capillaries and finally into the marrow of his bones. The only relief was to jerk the joint, but then it came back worse a moment later, so he had to jerk again. He tried to relax, but there was no respite from the beastly internal tickling and no hope of sleep. The light glared down on him, he was twisted and contorted and jerking in a pool of sweat, the rubber under him sticking everywhere. There was an interval he didn't remember clearly, which brought the two orderlies in to put him back to bed. At another point the heat was so bad that he got out and grabbed up the chair to push it through the screen and break the glass of the closed window. His weakness was appalling; even so he managed a strong jab with the chair-legs. But this was no ordinary screen; the chair bounced back on him without leaving a dent in the wire. Weeping with frustration he tried again, with the same result, and finally staggered back into the bed to shiver and sweat. His nose itched and ran unceasingly. Nothing to wipe it on but his pajamas.

Only one part of the night he remembered: toward morning he must have fallen into a doze, and the nightmares began. The worst was a static image of the inside of a hut. A woman lay on the floor by his feet; he didn't want to look at her. But in front of his eyes a cloudy red-and-tan bundle hung in midair. He particularly didn't want to look at this; it seemed to him that if he saw it clearly he would die. He jerked himself awake, trembling and quivering all over his body.

Daylight brought some relief, but not much. He was weeping continuously now and retching. He had given up trying to keep himself clean; the bed was sodden. His bones had turned to termite-ridden Jell-O, and the pains gnawed and jabbed him. Once he thought that the worst was over, but soon the excruciating bone-deep tickling began again, and he lay jerking helplessly, unable to rest.

Time passed in a torture-ridden blur. Strange people looked in on him, spoke meaninglessly and did unhelpful things. Several times he became aware that he was raving and shouting, but had no idea what he said, or to whom. Medications came, and he promptly threw them up. Meals came and went; sometimes he upset the tray in his bed.

The vomiting began to give way to uncontrollable diarrhea. At first he tried to get out of bed and make it to the can, but he was so weak that soon he failed and lay in his filth on the floor until the next room-check.

The windows darkened, and night brought with it all symptoms intensified. At one point he became aware that his wrists and ankles were tied to the bed-rails, and roared in protest until his dry throat gave out. There was an IV stand by the bed; a face scolded him for tearing the needle out.

Only toward morning did he fall into an exhausted doze, and the nightmares came again. He was with the patrol, rushing a bunch of Gués. The man next to him fell, screaming. He was holding a flamer to a thatched roof, the roof caught and roared up. And always there was the terrifying static scene of the interior of the hut, and the supine woman. By now he made out that she was wounded in the belly. He tried not to look at the ambiguous bundle hanging before his eyes, but it had more details: a bright point was sticking up from it, and something ran up to it from below. Also it moved and cried. He woke screaming to see the windows lightening, and experience the strange momentary relief that dawn seemed to bring.

Days and nights, how many he didn't know, passed so. The IV apparatus came again, and the tying-up. He was too weak to protest.

Finally came the afternoon when he realized that the horrible internal tickling had given way to plain pain, which was far more bearable. When medication came next he was able to keep it down, and to drink a glass of water, which stayed down too. But his mood had changed; from anger and bewilderment he was in the grip of a terrible bleakness and despair. Every train of thought ended in horror and death. His body might be somewhat detoxified now, he thought, but his mind was not. If this was reality, he desperately needed the magic tabs which would keep it at a distance. Images of them floated in his mind; his need was so great that he had hallucinations they were somewhere in his room—surely in his duffel bag. Three times he crawled out of bed and searched, finding, of course, nothing. He wept. Behind the tears, an iron resolve formed; he would get hold of some somehow, get back on the regime which made life bearable, even pleasant. The tabs were everywhere at the front, distributed freely. That was where he belonged, not home. What was home compared to that relief?

That night he fell into a really deep sleep, and with it came a jumble of new nightmares. Himself firing directly into the face of a little mestizo boy, watching the boy's head explode. The platoon awakened at night by a rush of Gués toward the ammo cache. And again, that static hut interior, where he was standing by the wounded woman. He saw her wounds clearly now: her whole belly was opened, the skin and fat folded back from emptiness like a heavy fruit-rind. She writhed feebly. Knife-work, that. And, inexorably, the amorphous bundle before his face cleared, became—Oh, no!—a bleeding newborn baby, skewered on a long machete blade. The lower part of the blade was clear now, there was a hand gripping the handle. Whose hand? Not his—Oh yes, *his*, he could feel the balance shift as its gruesome burden wriggled, moved its legs. A desperate squalling sound came from it.

He tore himself awake by sheer willpower, lay gasping as the windows paled. And in the growing light he knew—this was no nightmare, this was a memory. *He had done that thing. He* had gutted the parturient woman, skewered her baby on his knife. What came next he did not know—the deed itself was quite enough. Under the Battle Zone tablets he had become a savage beast, seeing the enemy everywhere, even in the unborn. *He* had done this. And god knew what else. The sleeper-tabs had kept it from breaking through. God, how he needed one!

As day grew, a kind of sanity came back to him. For the first time in days he could think. He thought about what life would be like, remembering this deed. Impossible. His soul was one huge flinch. He could not help hearing the cries, seeing more details, smelling the stink of guts. No. He wanted only surcease, wanted to die.

To die—taking these horrors with him, forever finished. Yes. Every hour he remained alive he would be tortured by those scenes in his mind, by the utter shame and sickening remorse. Afraid of what else he might remember. He couldn't go on like this. To go home, bearing this living memory in him like a cancer? Never. He would die here, he would manage somehow.

The resolve seemed to ease him a little. But when he drifted to sleep again, the memory came back, and with it the brief touch of bloody little hands pawing at his, as he drove the machete in. He screamed and woke.

Some time later the little blonde nurse stuck her head in. "You're better!" she observed brightly. "All right, today you get corridor privileges. Up and out!"

He could barely make it; she had to assist him and let him lean along the wall crab-fashion as she took him out in the corridor. He blinked; he had forgotten that the world held more than that room of torment.

"You better practice so you can make mealtimes. You'll get your meals up in the day room now, no more service in bed." Somehow they had arrived at the grille ending the corridor. He held on and peered through it blearily.

"They unlock this when meals are served," she told him. "Someone will call you."

The mention of meals set him retching again, but nothing came out. She came along as he crab-walked back to Number 209. "Practice!" she repeated cheerily. When they got back inside he struggled for the can, but failed to make it. When the spasm was over, Miss Plastic helped him back to bed. From somewhere she produced a mop.

"This is the last time. From now on you'll be expected to keep your room clean. The mop can stay in the corner here for a while." Expertly she wrung it out in the can, washed her hands in the tank, and flushed. It came to him that the scene had been repeated over and over before this.

He didn't see how he could make that trip again, let alone eat anything, but at chow time the biggest orderly stuck his head in and ordered him out. He staggered into the corridor, found it filled with what seemed hundreds of people. The man coming out of 207 was bandaged all over his head and shoulders, only three black holes showing for eyes and mouth. Bemused, Don fumbled along the wall with the crowd to the open grille, found a big dolly stacked with trays. A man beside him said, "Look for your name." Seeing Don's helplessness, he asked, "What's your name?"

"Still."

"Smith?"

"No . . . Still."

The stranger pounced on a shelf. "Here it is. Take it and sit down at that table and eat, or they'll take it away."

"Thanks."

Shakily Don carried the tray over to an empty seat. Soup had sploshed all over. In spite of his illness, he managed to hoist a bowl of it and drink some. Surprisingly, it tasted good. He finished it. On all the trays the flatware was the same wobbly white plastic, like a cheap airline's. No metal.

When he got up to go, someone pulled his sleeve.

"Take your tray back or they'll get your ass."

"Oh, thanks." He hoisted up the iron-heavy tray, grateful for the strange camaraderie of this hell-hole. These others had been subject to Miss Plastic and her bully-boys, they knew the drill. He noticed a couple of men who kept rhythmically jerking their knees, tapping their feet. He knew what they were feeling—that ghastly unstoppable tickle. Did it ever go away for good?

When he got back to Number 209 the nice dark-haired nurse was making up his bed with clean sheets.

"Oh, thank you." He collapsed in the chair.

"And here are some clean PJs." He realized he'd been going around in sweaty shit-stained ones. God, he must stink.

"You can get clean ones any time from the laundry room. It's opposite the showers, down by the day room."

"Showers?"

"That's right. But you have to tell the nurse you're going in."

"Great. Thank you . . . the trouble is, I'm so weak. *Weak.* I can't believe only a few days ago I was in combat."

"That's the effect of amphetamine withdrawal, honey. You have to pay a price for being Superman for a while."

"How long does it last?"

"Until you exercise it away. That's the only cure, keeping active."

"But it seems to be worse every day. Weaker and weaker. I'm afraid I'll die here."

"Don't say that, honey. Nobody ever died from detox and they never will. You'll just get healthier and healthier." Earnestly looking at him, she went on. "You're perfectly safe here. Don't be afraid."

Something in her tone struck him. You don't talk about dying here, he thought. They're afraid of suicides. That's what she means by safe. I can't get away. He chuckled painfully. 'Safe' to him had meant something quite different, well-secured perimeters, safety from Guévarista attack.

"Where are the Gués now? I don't know anything."

"The war's going well, I hear. The front's quite a ways farther than when you came in."

"I've got to get back."

"Oh, no you don't. The war's over for you, honey!" She bundled up the old sheets and prepared to leave.

"Thank you very much," he called after her. But a qualm had smitten him in the pit of the stomach. *She meant it*. No more, for him, the easy world of combat with the little yellow pill-cases full. What would he do at home? Roam the night streets, looking for black-market Ms? No way. He had to get back. Back at the front was everything he needed, including the neat way to die.

Depression and nausea washed over him deeper as he got into bed. The images of the dying woman, the tortured baby came again. He couldn't go on like this. Couldn't. Hatred of himself was like a poisonous fog in his head. It lasted all afternoon.

That night when he got to the tray-dolly he found that someone had made a mistake. A real metal knife lay gleaming on the tray that held butter and catsup, just above his own.

Nobody was watching. It was the work of an instant to get that beautiful knife into his pajama leg, stuck into the bandage.

He made himself pretend to eat, to wait until others were

leaving. Then he hobbled back to 209 with his prize. Relief. The way out. But that would be at night; where to hide it meanwhile?

He found the perfect place—a loose piece of molding in the upper window edge. All but the very end slid neatly inside. Then he took it out again—it was much too dull, it needed sharpening. The window-screen might do.

Between room-checks he honed it carefully. It took a decent edge. He tested it on his wrist, leaving a thin red line that oozed a red drop at one end. Okay. He put the knife back in its hidey-hole and lay in the bed, studying his wrists and memorizing where the best cuts would be . . . a peaceful death, bleeding. You just got cold. Pity he couldn't hang his arms over the edge of the bed to drain, but room-checkers would spot that. They wouldn't spot blood under him in the bed until much too late. . . . He'd have to cut deep, get the arteries flowing well. That would hurt—but not so much as the stuff in his head. *That* would never hurt him again.

Some commotion was going on in the corridor, but he took no notice. Not his concern. Never again, his concern . . . The noise was from the next room, where the bandaged man was. Someone had told Don that he was a cook, burned by a stove-fire. He was due for a lot of plastic surgery after detox. Now he seemed to be just outside Don's door, yelling at somebody. "Leave my room alone!" It didn't seem to do any good. Doors banged.

Presently Don's own door opened, and Miss Plastic marched in, followed by the two big blond orderlies. Don had named them in his mind, Hans *und* Klaus.

"Get up and sit in the chair, please."

"Chair? Why?"

"Just get up and let us at your bed. This is routine."

As he went to the chair, Hans intercepted him and gave him a quick but efficient body-search, patting all down his pajama legs. Then he seized Don's hand, turned it over, and grunted. He held it out to show the nurse the cut wrist. She nodded, grimly. The search intensified.

Klaus was stripping the bed thoroughly. Sheets, rubber, pillowcase, all went on the floor. Then he expertly flipped over the mattress to expose the springs and searched all around the bottom and the bed-rails.

Don had got it by now. They were looking for the knife. *His* precious knife. Thank god he had resisted his first impulse to hide it under the spring-bars.

Klaus had been circling the room, checking the baseboards. When he came to the set of drawers, he and the nurse took it apart, looking at the bottoms of every drawer, the bottom of the chest. Then he turned to check thoroughly around the toilet and in the tank, while Miss Plastic put the drawers back in. Hans was heaping bedding and pillow on the bed.

"Now sit on the bed, please." Dumbly he obeyed. They went over the chair. Then Klaus and Hans went back to the baseboards, while the nurse dumped out his duffel bag.

Hans was circling the room now, looking higher and higher. A quick probe of the doorjamb, the electric outlet—and then he was at the window. Don sat rigid, not daring to breathe or look, while Hans's hands ran around the lower sills. Klaus was stuffing his things back into the duffel, Miss Plastic had gone to the door, frowning and tapping her foot.

"All right." They seemed about to leave. Don's heart thudded with relief—but suddenly Hans turned back and ran his hand along the top of the window molding. Oh, no!—a rustle, and, damn it, god damn it—he was drawing out the knife from its hiding place, looking at it curiously, testing the edge Don had put on it.

Miss Plastic and Klaus were advancing on him with a canvas thing.

"Just slip your arms in here."

"What is it?"

"A tux," Hans said, and giggled. They had his hands drawn halfway down the sleeves before he could react. But when his hands found no cuffs, he realized what it was—they were putting a straitjacket on him!

"No! *No!*"

"Come on, soldier, relax. You're due for a night in the Quiet Room."

"What? I haven't done anything, you can't—"

Much too late he started to struggle. He was on the bed now, face down, with Hans on top of him and Klaus tightening the long straitjacket sleeves around his body. He kicked, kicked, could connect with nothing. Then Klaus was kneeling on his legs, pulling up a heavy zipper.

In seconds he was being hustled out into the corridor, helpless. Even so, his training enabled him to swing them, to get one hearty kick aimed at Klaus' crotch. But at the last minute he held it—he couldn't win here, god knew what nasty revenges they would wreak on him if he broke Klaus' balls.

His first impressions of the Quiet Room were heat, and the stink of disinfectant. There was no window, only the small heavy glass insert in the door. There was a can with no seat. A bare mattress lay on the floor skew-wise. That was all.

They dumped him on the mattress, and then came the final indignity—they pulled off his pajama pants. He was protesting and crying out, and he could hear how his voice sounded muted. The Quiet Room was efficiently soundproofed. The faint keening he had heard near here might have been someone yelling his lungs out.

"How long? How long?" he beseeched.

"We'll see," said Miss Plastic crisply, and they marched out. The door slammed to with a heavy thud.

He got up behind them, to press his face against the glass in the door. It was one-way. Behind his own reflection he could make out only the blur of a ceiling light. In despair, he let himself fall back on the mattress. But there was no relaxing—under the straitjacket the invisible insects were starting their scratching again.

That night he could not, would not remember.

He tried things, nearly breaking his teeth. He located a rough edge on the toilet and backed up to it, sawing the canvas against it. But he accomplished only the smoothing of the metal edge; the damn jacket wasn't normal canvas but some super-stuff. He spent an hour leaning against the door with his face to the glass. Once a head loomed up outside. He shouted "Help!" with all his might. The head went away.

The diarrhea came back, he tried to make the can but fouled himself. The insect-itching was beyond belief, he could not lie down but paced, paced, paced the tiny hot room.

Finally weakness felled him, he crawled to the mattress and lay curled in a crazy ball, jerking. And on, hour after torment-filled hour . . .

Sometime during the eternity the door opened and the dark-haired nurse came in. She had a glass of water for him, and a cool wet cloth with which she mopped his face. It felt unbelievably good.

"How . . . longer?"

She frowned. "Soon, now. I'll speak to somebody."

"What is this . . . bad-cop-good-cop routine?"

She didn't get it, just shook her head No.

"Look, I'm not yelling . . . any more . . . I'll be . . . good."

Gently she said, "Here's something a patient told me, he said it helps. Find some place on your body that doesn't hurt—maybe your left ear, maybe a hand, your tongue, maybe. Anything that isn't hurting—you concentrate on that. Think *only* about this place that isn't hurting. *Think* about it. I was told it really helps."

She went away.

He tried her recommendation. Maybe it helped.

When the light in the door-window was changing, Hans and Klaus came in. They boosted him up and untied the jacket. His arms were so stiff he could barely pull them free.

All dirty and naked as he was, he was led back through the empty corridor and pushed onto the bed. He was careful to say nothing, not to resist in any way. He had done some thinking.

The point was, to get out of here. Ending his life here was just plain impossible, they'd convinced him of that. He was terminally 'safe,' all right.

So he had to get out their way. He had to go along. Grin, pretend to be getting better, stand everything. No asking, even for Maalox. No arguing about gradual detoxification. Even smile at Miss Plastic . . .

Could he do it? Oh Christ, oh Christ, for even a quarter of an M-tab! He was so weak, so weak. Could he do all that cold, keep it up?

He had to.

After all, they thought he was headed home, they couldn't keep him here forever. And he guessed they were overcrowded —there'd been a lot of beds visible through the grille, in the big domed room he'd waked up in. Probably they were eager to mark him 'cured' and get shut of him. Probably they were eager to see that their savage system worked, that he was successfully 'detoxed.'

He smiled grimly, lying in his dirt and shame. He'd be playing to an audience that wanted to believe.

So he tried. Almost falling with weakness, he carried his trays to the table, made himself eat, spoke friendly to the guys beside him, and didn't tell anybody when he got back to his room and threw it all up. The world spinning around him with dizziness, he paced the corridor, swinging his arms. "For exercise." The dark-haired nurse smiled at him. When Miss Plastic stuck her head in on her fifteen-minute checks, he made himself smile and greet her. Once he even apologized for giving her so much trouble. She smiled and said, "That's what we're here for, soldier." In his mind's eye he held a picture of what she'd be here for if he had a chance, and grinned back. He made a try at keeping his room clean, used the mop when a check was due.

But the trouble was, he wasn't getting any better, inside. The nights were hells of nightmare memories. And he grew, not stronger but weaker; the weakness was like an iron yoke on his shoulders, and every effort left him dizzy and gasping. He hid this as well as he could, blaming his occasional falls on the loose hospital slippers. One day he made it to the showers, and nearly drowned himself fainting in the stall. He found the linen-room and clean pajamas, but it took him half an hour to get them on, leaning against the shelves, the room almost blacked out. Weaker day by day.

What was the plan—that his body must relearn to make the substances, as somebody had told him? What if his body wouldn't, what if he was too far gone? He didn't know much about his internal workings, nor care, but he did know that individuals varied greatly. What if he were one who didn't recover, whose adrenaline gland or whatever had died? He felt he was running on a shrinking energy-supply, like an exhausted battery, each day less. He became genuinely frightened that he couldn't keep up the deception, that he would be stuck here with his unbearable memories forever.

But, miraculously, it worked. They were overcrowded in the detox wing. In less than a week he found himself ordered to move again, this time to a corridor with chairs in it, with open access to the space between the grilles, the 'day room.' At the far end of the corridor were normal double doors, giving onto a green gardeny-looking place. His room was no bigger; but he had a table, and the window, though screened, had clear glass and curtains. He went to it, looked out on a wall and a tangled garden. And the glass could be opened by a screw-handle through the screens! He made his trembling arms turn them wide, sank down on the chair to pant in the fresh air. Oh, god! For a moment he actually felt better.

On his second day there he was given 'Grounds privilege.' Hans came and unlocked the end doors and pointed out the path around the untended garden. "Take walks! Three a day." He went back in.

For a few minutes he couldn't believe it. Air! Openness! He buried his face in an overblown big red rose flower. Perfume of wine, perfume of freedom . . .

Tentatively, slowly, he walked out along the path. An

eight-foot chain-wire fence topped by triple barbed wire ran beside him. Nothing he could climb. The fence enclosed the garden and a piece of wild country with trees just outside it.

Just then a twinge of dysentery struck him. He pushed through the garden hedge toward a small grove of pines. They'd run the fence outside this. He could see why—the grove was edged with a shoulder-high growth of thorn-bushes. He fought his way through these to a tiny clearing in the center. Here he stopped, warned by a familiar smell. It took him an instant to locate the cause, under the blanket of pine needles.

For sure, the fencing team hadn't bothered to check out this grove. A dead GI lay among the needles, his M–18 by his outstretched hand. The hand was almost gone to bone; the body was weirdly shrunken and desiccated under its shell of body-armor. He must have been killed when they finally took San Izquierda. But Don stopped not to think of this—with a strangled cry he flung himself down beside the dead man, his hand clawing at the inside pocket of the rigid vest.

And—oh, god in heaven!—it was there!

Incredulous, he drew out the small yellow case, opened it with fingers all but out of control. It was—full! Oh, precious, precious—he stared at the rows of Ms, the slot of BZs, the line of Sleepers. Here, in his hand. Carefully, carefully, he drew out an M and closed the box, before swallowing it. What incredible luck, come to save him just as he was at his last strength!

Then his body made its needs felt again, and he hastily dropped his pants. Squatting there, he saw that the dead man had been on the same mission—his armor pants were down. Somebody had seen him, or was waiting there; the corpse's lowest parts were blown away, gray fragments of pelvis sticking out of the long-dead meat. Big black tarry puddle, mess, so old that the flies were almost gone. Death finished up quickly down here. But leaving him the priceless pack in his hands, the first faint glow stealing through his veins.

Where to hide it?

Under his leg bandage. Then he rose and made his way carefully back to the path, around to the door. On his way he noticed that the big link fence had a set of gates, chained and padlocked.

He knocked on the glass and Hans presently let him back in, locking up behind him.

"Great walk," he babbled at Hans. "Makes you feel better already."

In his room he took careful thought. Here they didn't do the fifteen-minute check, but no telling when someone would come in. Finally he took the pills out of the case, and hid them by ones and twos, in the hems of the curtain, under the edge of the electric outlet, in a crack around the back of the can, and other nooks. He wouldn't forget where they were, not he! At suppertime he slipped the empty box, twisted out of recognition, into the waste can that came with the trays.

Dinner that night was a time of glory. The weakness had faded to a mild fatigue, all pains were gone; the M was affecting him the way it used to, giving a rosy glow of alertness, all trouble far away. He talked to people, asked them questions and listened to the answers, even helped one of the zombies from the detox corridor to find his tray. The man grunted at him; looking closely at his eyes, Don saw the redness left by BZs not quite gone. His arm was in a heavy sling, sticking out from his side. "It'll get better," Don told him gently. "You just have to put up with the shit." The man grunted again.

Seeing Miss Plastic, Don saluted her cheerfully and told her that the garden walk had really set him up. Better be careful, he warned himself. I'm acting drunk. He toned down his grin.

She frowned. "If you're going to be going outside, soldier, you'd better wear some clothes."

"Clothes?"

"In the laundry room you'll find fatigues. That's what they're there for."

Better and better. On his way back to his room he collected a set that seemed to have all its buttons and parts. The laundry here was done by rock-crusher, he thought merrily, glowing with all-rightness.

That night he had his Sleeper, and slept for the first time, sweetly, without dreams. Whatever the war had brought was far away and somebody else's story.

His last thought was that he must be systematic, ration the pills. They had to get him back to the front. He knew now that he was hooked; with the tabs he was normal, without them he was a sick shadow. And the front was where they were. It wouldn't be hard to break away and head there; not many people went AWOL *to* the fighting. And with a little fast talking, any unit would take him in.

The next days passed like floating flowers. Again and again he had to caution himself not to act too euphoric, but no one seemed to see anything odd. Even the dark-haired nurse accepted his story of what the garden and the flowers had done for him, and smiled tenderly.

Then came the morning when everybody but he seemed to know he'd be leaving the next day, with four or five other guys who had been detoxed.

That afternoon he found out something else, too. Had he miscalculated or forgotten? Whichever, he could locate no more Ms. Search as he would, there were none. The NDs and the BZs were okay, but no Maintenance. What the hell, he'd been without before, he could make it.

But as the hours dragged by and the insects began to show up again, his resolve weakened. He fingered a red BZ. They were supposed to be for when you were in actual contact with the enemy. But here, far from the front, what could they do to him? He couldn't recall any bad effects, except a burst of strength. . . .

A nonexistent termite column crawled under his waistband, he writhed to scratch it. A minute later he had to do it again. Oh, god, not this . . . if he watched himself carefully, didn't let anyone look too closely at his eyes, it'd be all right.

He popped the BZ.

. . . As he'd thought, nothing happened except that he felt more alert and the bugs faded out. Colors seemed lighter and brighter, too. Hell, BZs are only some kind of super pep-pill, he thought. But he'd gotten sloppy; he was standing right in front of the window, where any stranger could look in and see him. Perfect target. He backed away, pulling the curtains to.

His mind drifted to his last day of combat. Hill Number Thirteen-forty-seven, that's what they were taking. Down here they called mountains 'hills.' The front was well ahead of there by now, people said. But where was the enemy now?

He glanced worriedly around, opened a chink in the curtains and peered out. Nothing moving out there. Nothing in the corridor, either. Or, wait—his ears seemed to have sharpened—there were some footsteps up at the far end in the day room. Little tapping steps.

As he listened, they grew clearer, sharper. Heading his way now!

And he could catch a faint jangling sound. Aha, that would be the big key-ring Miss Plastic wore on her wrist.

Enemy sounds, coming along the wall. Coming for him?

Automatically he flexed his hands, fingered the callus on the outer edges of his palms. Had they grown soft? Did someone think they could take him, now? He sidled to the door, listening hard.

The footsteps were alone.

The little blonde nurse comes on duty early again that afternoon. She takes extra duty a lot, partly because there is nothing to do in San Izquierda, but mostly because of a nagging sense of responsibility. Twice, coming back, she has found doors open that should have been locked. People are so sloppy. Right now, for instance, both the orderlies are out on lunch break together, quite contrary to orders. She looks round the day room; no hard cases here. But are the garden doors locked? The orderlies have grown specially careless about that, now that so many patients have Grounds privilege.

She decides to check them before she does the detox ward.

She straps on her official key-ring, and starts down the empty corridor, tap-tap-tap.

As she passes one of the last doors, it opens silently and a shadowy face looks out, right into hers.

To cover her start, she smiles brightly and starts to say, "Hello, soldier."

They are the last sounds she ever utters.

She never knew what struck her throat, smashing the delicate larynx and crushing her vocal cords. She had no idea that the human hand could strike such a blow as the Army's sentry chop, no idea that she could be rendered voiceless before she had a chance to scream.

Bent over with pain, she feels herself being dragged into the room. Her clothes are being yanked up. She beats futilely at inhumanly strong hands. A voice says thickly, "You know I'm going to kill you afterwards?"

And then a smashing blow hits her face, breaking teeth, and another.

"You won't be a cute corpse."

The orderly he called Hans had given him the idea with his bed-search. Now Don heaves up the mattress, and flattens the little corpse on the sagging springs. No blood on him, no blood anywhere. He pulls the mattress back—there's scarcely a discernible mound. To disguise it he makes up the bed tight and neat. Anyone looking in would see a nice clean empty room, soldier.

Now to fix up a few little things, collect his pills and go. He has taken charge of the key-ring first thing; there are two padlock-type keys on it.

The corridor is empty, Hans and Klaus are nowhere to be seen. The garden door is locked, but the first key he tries opens it smoothly. He slips out, locks up behind him. In a moment he is forcing his way into the little pine grove.

Nothing has changed, except a few more pine needles on the corpse's face. His first thought had been the gun and ammo—but wait, he'll need ident. He grabs the dead man's dogtags. Its chain slices through the poor hollow shell of neck. Isidore West—he is Isidore West now. Isidore for San Izzy. West hadn't been carrying any papers, only a crumpled snapshot of a girl. Well, he'll be welcome wherever he turns up.

Maybe the body-armor would be a good idea too. Reluctantly he slides the dead man out of his jerkin, but can't bring himself to touch the fouled breeches. He shakes a big black beetle out of the vest, and gets it on under his fatigues, the usual way. Ammo belts on top.

Okay, now out the gate, the M-18 stuck into the loose fatigue legs. At the last minute he picks up two grenades West had been carrying, and hooks them on his belt.

The second key opens the fence-gate padlock, and he exits neatly before anyone comes out to the garden. Good; he doesn't want any more hassles, although he now has a neat place to stow any bodies. He resnaps the chain and lock behind him.

Outside is a gravel road. A sign points to San Izquierda, it carries a silhouette of a bus. Good. Transport is what he needs, and GIs can ride free on buses.

But he wishes he had a map. The front must be somewhere to the north—he can identify that by the sun—but where and how far? He recalls the company's maps, with their neatly-drawn lines and estimates of Gué position and strength, even his own company marked in. Somewhere up in the States men are sitting in peaceful rooms, drawing such lines. Numbering hills. Moving little tin soldiers over the terrain, as word comes to them.

He is one little soldier out of place, but the mapmakers won't know that. He and Isidore West.

Chuffing behind him. He whirls, but it is only the San Izquierda bus, on its way out from the town. It stops beside him, right on cue, and a girl gets out. For a flash, he thinks it's the girl who chopped his nails. But no matter now; he hops in and hobbles back the aisle, still concealing the gun. The BZ feels like it's running low. He sits down on the back seat, fishes out another and swallows.

The bus holds only a few passengers: three women with babies, a few very old women and men, two or three children, baskets of chickens and a pig with a rope on its hinder legs.

He waits till the hospital is well behind them before slipping out the gun. It needs cleaning badly, but it's functional. Cradling it in one arm, he makes his way up to the driver.

"Where are the Guévaristas now?" he asks in his painful Spanish.

"Nada, nada." The driver seems amused.

"But where is the fighting?" Don persists. "I am lost." As he says it he realizes he's saying he has perished, so he tries again. "*Me equivocado*—I've made a mistake. *Dondé*—where are they? *Mís amigos* are there. I must go to my friends."

"Ah!" The driver gestures grandly ahead. "*Al norte*—far, *muy léjos*, very far."

"Ah," he says in his turn, "*gracias*. I go with you to the north. I do not want to go back to San Izquierda."

"Si."

He turns and heads back to his seat, nearly falling over the pig.

At the next stop an old woman with chickens gets off and a boy on crutches swings himself on. He is minus one foot, the leg ends in a dirty sock strapped up. He looks a very young sixteen. As he sits down Don sees that he is wearing Gué uniform pants under his smock, and his one boot is a Gué combat issue. A wounded veteran, apparently, left behind when the front moved on. The boy casts him a sharp look, then turns his head away.

Don flinches, takes out another BZ. But it doesn't work fast enough to prevent him from thinking of those easy-living men up home in their war rooms, drawing lines on maps, moving their tin soldiers.

The bus keeps chuffing northward, now and then stopping to let people off. Going home after a day in San Izquierda. Here and there in the woods are tucked little Maya-style *casitas*, each with its tiny corn-and-melon-and-bean plot. Almost all have a papaya tree leaning close to the roof.

The bus passes a hamlet. Here almost all the houses have been burned and gutted, but two old men get off. The boy with one foot is still aboard, talking to a middle-aged woman. His tone sounds angry.

Don can't help staring at him, feeling adrenalin pump a little. Had this lad been one of those who had ambushed B Company, back before Hill Thirteen-forty-seven? A lot of his comrades bought it then. It was well inside Bodégua, but no one knew how far. The border was mushy here, it supposedly followed a mountain ridge that divided and divided again. *It's their country*, a voice had kept saying in Don's head. Just as the pants that boy was wearing were the official uniform of their army. However unsavory their government, it was theirs. Not his, to invade and shoot up their sons. But this was the *enemy*, a limb of International Atheist Red Communism. He didn't look much like the enemy, or a limb of anything now.

The boy laughs sharply at something the woman is saying, and turns to glance at Don. "*Yanqui*," he says under his breath, or seems to say—the bus is making so much noise it's hard to be sure. "*Yanqui* assassin." He looks hard at Don, meeting his eyes, then suddenly seems to see something that changes his mood. He slumps in his seat, saying something to the woman. She gathers her baskets, gets off at the next stop.

It comes to Don that his eyes must be reddening from the BZs and the boy had seen that and knew that Don was a berserker. They knew about BZs, all right.

The bus has turned off the main road, and seems to be circling back toward San Izquierda. He'll have to get off and start looking for a ride north.

Suddenly the boy cocks his head to listen. The bus stops, and Don can hear it too now—the heavy rumble of six-by-sixes. In a moment it comes in sight on the road they'd left—a long convoy of camouflage-painted trucks and weapons-carriers. GIs were crowded in the trucks, hanging their legs out over the tailgates.

That would be replacements and supplies headed for the front. That's the kind of ride he wants to catch. And that must be the main road to the front, too. He'll get out here and go back and wait.

Just as he's making his way up to the doors, there comes another sound. The crippled boy gives a peculiar whistle. Then Don hears it—under the convoy's noise and the bus's engine is a steady slapping beat—a chopper. Probably guarding the convoy. But wait a minute—the sound isn't right. He twists to stare out the back window and catches a glimpse.

No mistaking—the ugly square end of a Krasny 16, guns sticking out. A Gué fireship, out after the convoy.

Meanwhile guns have opened up ahead, from something he can't see. The fireship slides neatly sideways, out of sight over the ridge. All sounds cease.

For a second Don has a double flash; BZs sometimes do that to you. It's so peaceful here, in an ordinary bus on a quiet country road, the pines rustling in the soft wind. He feels disastrously out of place. And then the sun flashes on copter blades beyond the ridge, and there's the racket of guns and thuds out of view to the right. The people in the bus come to life in a general stampede for the doors. They know a bus could be a target, they'd rather take their chances by ones and twos in the brush. The pig screams.

But the driver resists. He shouts "San Izquierda! San Izquierda!" and the bus starts fast. People are pounding on the doors, yelling at him to stop. Don is beside him now, he grabs the emergency brake, but it has no effect. He gets his foot down on the brake, the driver pushes him and tries to punch him away. Don punches back. The bus wobbles to a stop. The doors open, and people pour out, including the boy on crutches. At the last minute, the driver yells something and dives for the door after them, leaving Don alone in the bus.

Panting, he sits down in the driver's seat to consider. Now he really has transport—he can turn this thing around and follow the convoy till the petrol gives out.

There's a crossroad just ahead. But as he looks, it fills up, first with cattle, then with a bunch of civilian-looking cars, obviously waiting for the cows to clear. Clean, expensive-looking cars with fender flags on them. Even the escort jeeps are shiny clean, with little flags too. Obviously it's some kind of high-level party touring here. They seem unaware of the Gué fireship behind him. Senior-looking civilians, shining generals, and a woman have gotten out, are staring around at the scenery, looking at San Izquierda which must be right below them. To Don's amazement, several of the men produce cameras and start to take photos. *Tourists*, by god, Don thinks.

And then corrects himself. These aren't tourists—these are some of the easy-living men he'd dreamed of, the ones sitting in front of big terrain maps, drawing lines, while their aides move little soldiers and flags around.

These are the men who sent him here.

Without thinking, he has popped another BZ.

Without thinking, he has started the bus. Automatically, he unhooks the two grenades and arms them. Meticulously, he breaks out the front window with his gun-butt, then reverses the gun to point out.

The men ahead are getting into their cars, all bunched together.

Good.

A raging fury he has never experienced roars through his body. Do those men know, can they guess, that the little figures they move around are real live men and boys, boys who bleed?

The front, the Guévaristas, fade far away. His foot slams down on the accelerator, the old bus churns forward. Faster, faster yet. Don is half-crouched now, his rifle through the empty windscreen. Standing on the gas, steering with one elbow, he takes aim. Faster yet the bus surges forward, dead toward them. The grenades tick. The first burst comes from his rifle, finding targets. Then another. Screams.

—And Don Still, standing on the gas on his glory ride, fires fires, fires—his enemy in his sights at last.

Come Live with Me

I have known fire.

Four seasons ago the land grew dry, and a hideous hot wind came over the upstream trees. Then came ill-smelling clouds, lit from below by a baleful red glare. The water falling over the rocks into my pool grew warm. And then the fearful fire itself appeared, first in the treetops and then running through the forest below. Crackling and roaring, it leaped my stream, and blazed down both banks to the crashes of falling trees.

I was terrified. I flattened myself to the stream-bed, looking up through the water at the vortex of flame above. Would it grow hot enough to kill me? I could not know, but only cowered. Some of my familiars had taken refuge with me. I perceived that several of them had been injured, but I let them remain, though their pain burned me.

After what seemed an eternity of terror, the glare lessened. I sensed that it was raining. Thunder and light-bolts were added to the uproar. But this was good—it damped the flames. Monstrous billows of hissing whiteness arose from the land. Only pockets of fire remained.

When night was over, cautiously I took stock. The only damages I could sense were nine fully wilted leaf-pads, and the heat-death of my newly-forming blossom stalk.

Next day, when the ground was cool enough, I sent two familiars out to scout the fire's path. It was then I found what has been my overpowering worry since—upstream, between me and my only neighbor, a burnt tree had fallen across the stream, blocking the flow of our mating-packets.

Since then, desperate, I have tried every means to dislodge it and let the packets through. But my pond-dwelling familiars are too weak to move the log. And it is almost at the edge of my control over them; I cannot get them to combine their efforts, or pursue any course persistently. It is now three seasons that I have been cut off, my blossoms futile, their egg-cases heavy and urgent with pressure. My anthers are distended and painful. Three seasons of desuetude! I am nearly frantic. My thoughts are disordered by worry and panic, my control over the familiars is erratic. I can only hope that some flood or other natural event will dislodge the downed tree, but this does not seem likely. In gloomy moments I feel it was futile to have survived the fire only to rot in this living death.

But this night has come a new fire, quite different. It is in the sky. Through the eyes of a flying familiar I watch it grow quickly into a line of descending flame, cleaving the dark sky until it disappears into the horizon trees with a splash of flame. An instant later comes a rolling thunder quite unlike a natural storm. The stream bank jars slightly. Will this be followed by ground-fire raging through the woods?

I send the familiar to look. Yes, there is a ring of flames on the ground, but it is still small. A rock or pod-like thing lies at its center. From this pod my familiar sees a ring of white foaming stuff issue onto the fires, damping them, as I had seen rain do, but more powerfully.

For a time all is still. I am about to release the familiar to resume its food-hunting, when it registers movement at the pod or rock. It is opening! Light shines briefly from within it, a moving thing comes out. What can it be? It is large, much larger than any of my familiars, and carries itself peculiarly upright.

I reach out, though I think it is much too far away.

To my surprise, the thing or creature seems to respond. It starts to move, still upright, in my direction. I intensify my call.

But my familiar has become too hungry and restive to control. I let it fly away and summon another.

When I can see again, I perceive that the creature—it is definitely an animal—has reached the edge of the stream and started moving along it toward me. Contact grows clearer every moment. This animal is vividly alive and complex in new ways. I concentrate on deciphering its lures, its pheromones. Again I am surprised: it holds patterns of long-term yearnings, as I do; there is something it longs for as I long to be freed of the log-barrier.

As I become able to sense the world from within its strange mind, I am suddenly thrilled by the realization that here is the possible familiar who could help me. It is tall and strong; its forelimbs are clever. I resolve to seize it carefully and well. This is no crude *dasmit*, to be taken by simple food-smells. I must research its needs, evolve simulacra, deal teasingly . . .

As I am thinking this, a tendril of awareness from the pod alerts me. The pod has opened again, and another similar creature has come out. I can spare only a minimum of attention for this one, just enough to know that it is also of this strange complex kind. And now my familiar hears it vociferate. Meaningless to me, but I record it: "Kevin! Come in, Kevin. Kevin, where are you?"

Enough sense of direction comes through for me to perceive that the second creature is calling to the first. And the first one has a name, "Kevin." I have never met this before, except with the *florain*. But this is not a need-tied *florain* name like "Kevin-food-giver" or "Kevin-lost," but stable and specific, detached from any situation. As I ponder this, I perceive that the second creature is holding up a small object with a long spike on it, to which it is speaking. "Kevin! Kevin, come in, George here. *Kevin!*"

It starts moving, heading toward the unburnt woods. I see that it will meet with the first animal if this goes on. I do not want this. I block the behavior.

But when I do this, a wave of hostile emotion, of rejection, strikes me like a physical blow. My awareness is made to fall away from contact. What? Has this creature sensed me and deliberately ejected my consciousness? This has never happened before.

"Get out of my mind!" it vociferates loudly. And, as I attempt to re-enter, a barrier springs up within it, a clamorous repetitive noise which actually hurts me as I come against it. I withdraw my tendril to await a better chance, and concentrate on "Kevin" who is still coming upstream toward my home.

As their braking fires die down, George sees Kevin spontaneously unstrap himself and start preparing to go out upon the new planet. He is overjoyed. Ever since Clare's death, three planets back, Kevin has been a zombie, docilely doing whatever George or June told him to, but no more. This is their second landing on this planet. A day ago, if George had told him to measure all the rocks in a straight line north, Kevin would be at it still, rounding the curve of the planet, unquestioningly measuring rocks. But now he seems to have made a great stride toward healing, has recaptured some motivation toward his old duties which he loved so much. Normally it was he who would have been first man out.

George glances at June to see her eyes shining, a finger to her lips to warn him not to speak. Dear, officious little June—as if he would!

In silence they watch Kevin put on his brush-suit, select the gear he needs. Maybe—maybe they have done the right thing in not returning to Base.

According to regs they should have returned, of course, after the loss of Clare in that tornado, and the incapacitation of Kevin, so near the start of this FES. But FES—First Exploration and Sampling—is relatively easy work. Two mated couples are normally assigned to each mission, but more to promote sanity and serendipity than for any work need. George and June, the senior couple, can easily do Clare and Kevin's work as well as their own, if they go a little slower. So they have decided against a return to Base, for Kevin's sake. FES work was the love of Kevin's life, next to Clare, and if he is to recover, surely the presence of new worlds will do more to help and stimulate him than the dubious ministrations of Base Therapy. But as the weeks drag by, with Kevin totally silent and withdrawn, they have begun to doubt their decision. Now it looks as if the gamble is paying off at last.

His standard Temperate Forest World gear in hand, Kevin goes silently to the lock. His slow, mute progress is a far cry from the Kevin of old, who would have been peering out every port, exchanging excited guesses with Clare, and impatient for June's air tests to finish. But a far cry also from the Kevin who had sat slumped and unseeing through their last seven landings.

June signals A-OK on air. "Perfect. Oxy nice and high."

George opens the port lock and lets down the ramp into the burned-out clearing in the dark night outside. All but the last embers have been quenched by the ship's foam. They watch Kevin march stolidly downramp, both thinking how acutely he must be missing Clare's light step beside him—Clare who is now only a cold body in their refrigeration chamber.

"I'll be out as soon as I secure ship," George calls to him. Kevin will need an aide, if only to help lug samples. George doesn't intend to interfere with him in any way; that he has even gone out now is enough.

Almost inaudibly, Kevin mumbles "Good."

When George does go down the ramp into the fresh, delightful air of this unknown place, Kevin is nowhere to be seen. As they had noted from the ship, this landing-place much resembles their previous base on the opposite side of this world. It seems to be a one-continent world, geologically quiescent, in which the same ecological matrix has spread everywhere. George recognizes several types of trees they have met before.

Kevin has left a trail through the ring of ashes on the downhill side. They are near the headwaters of a large river basin; it is standard operating procedure to select the main stream and work up and down it. Kevin has probably headed straight down to find the stream before moving up.

George follows, wishing he had asked Kevin to activate his beeper. The woods are dense and dark. He halloos a few times to Kevin before turning on his light to pick up the trail.

As he does so, an odd sensation brushes him—almost as though a feather had swept over his mind. He disregards it as he scans for signs of Kevin's passage. They are difficult; Kevin has the habits of a scout. The fact that George catches no gleams of Kevin's headlamp means nothing; the younger man has fantastic night vision, and is much given to dark night-walks. But George's pace is so slow that he gives it over, and unslings his caller.

"Kevin, I'm lost. Come in!"

No immediate answer. He resumes walking in the direction Kevin should have gone. As he does so, the feathery touch comes again. This time he recognizes it. His mind has been brushed by a scanning telepath. George has been on Alkab Nine, with its dominant race of powerful and bad-tempered telepaths, and he hasn't forgotten the lessons he learned there. He turns up his caller's volume.

"Kevin, come in! This is George. We have a problem. Please respond now."

No answer. George resumes walking and has an instant of confusion. When it leaves him, he discovers that he has turned ninety degrees away from his previous course and is moving parallel to where the stream must lie and in a downstream direction.

He shakes his head, sweeping his thoughts in the way he'd

learned to do, and resumes his chosen course downhill. What is interfering with him? Such a high order of telepathy should imply great powers, yet the planet has revealed no sign of civilization or of inhabitation by intelligent life.

A moment later the check is repeated, and he is moving off course again. Angry now, he jams his thoughts and shouts loudly, "Get out of my mind!"

Determinedly keeping his mind closed, he corrects his course again, and sets up a cacomnemonic. This time he senses that the entity has withdrawn. A few strides more and his caller beeps.

"George?" It's Kevin's voice, but languid and neutral.

"Where are you, Kevin?"

"Down by the river. I'm going upstream."

"Kevin, wait for me. And turn around and walk back a few yards."

An unidentifiable sound from the caller. Then Kevin says clearly, "George, I don't want to."

Forgetting his intention not to interfere with the other man, George demands, "What do you mean, you don't want to? Have you found something?"

"No . . . but there's something interesting upstream. I'm going to it."

"I'll tell you what's upstream, Kevin. There's a calling telepath there. I think it's got hold of you. Kevin, this is an order. Turn around and walk back toward me!"

Again the caller makes an odd sound, and then suddenly gives its disconnect-chirp.

"Kevin!" George roars, hoping his unaided voice will carry. "*Kevin!*"

No response from the still forest. Only a few small wildlife noises, of which he was marginally aware, have ceased.

George is silent for a moment, debating what to do. Then he calls June in the ship and tells her what's happened. As he's speaking, the caller jangles and Kevin's voice cuts in.

"George . . . Clare is here. I've seen her."

"You've seen no such thing," George shouts at the caller. But Kevin is gone again.

"Damn, damn," George says to June. "It must have taken an image from Kevin's mind. Oh, by the gods, this is some sophisticated beast. Do I dare to go after him alone?"

"If we only knew what its range is," June's voice says.

"Or how many there are."

"Yes . . . George, the walls of this ship seem to stop it penetrating. Is there some kind of helmet we could try?"

"Junie, you're a genius. I was going to work on that before this mission. But it seemed so unlikely, I mean, we've never found more than one race. I'm coming back to the ship now and we'll see if we can contrive something."

I let my consciousness ride along with "Kevin" as he makes his way along the stream-side animal trails toward me. I am becoming increasingly aware that this will be the most difficult task of my life, calling for more skill than I perhaps have. I am a young being, not fully developed. Far downriver, I know, lives a cluster of others like me, but far older and wiser. I, and my mating partner upstream, are the only successful results of a massive egg-transfer effort of several seasons ago, with the goal of colonizing the whole stream. They used flying familiars to carry the embryos in their pouches and claws. It was very wasteful; the familiars, when they got beyond clear range, tended to drop the eggs on land or in unsuitable places. And since we are symbiotes, our own embryos had to go with the young host-plants, to inoculate them. In only our two cases did the drop go right.

Now, looking through Kevin's eyes, I can see small stands of our host-plant here and there in the stream. To him, the multi-petalled, fragrant flowers are very beautiful. But to me, seeing them growing there empty and incomplete, mere brainless vegetation, the sight is sad. It is up to me and my neighbor now to produce enough of our own eggs to float down and lodge amongst them and penetrate. But all our efforts have come to nothing, because of this horrible log, which prevents his pollen-packets from floating down to my eggs, and his fertilized eggs from breaking free. I have two familiars reliable enough to carry my pollen to him, but until that log is removed his eggs are trapped. Hungry fishes are eating our precious germ-plasm. I *must* achieve control over Kevin. Even if he cannot remove the log, he can carry my mate's fertilized eggs past it, and my pollen up to him, far better than the familiars.

What must I do?

First, I must bind Kevin strongly to me, so he can resist the efforts of the other creature to separate us. (Back behind us, I can still sense "George's" thoughts angrily directed to searching us out.) And I must make use of Kevin's strongest drive, to reclaim this "Clare" whom he has lost. I have images from his mind, and at a turning in the path I show him an impression of her. It is shadowy and soon gone, but it works—he cries out "Clare!" and breaks into a run until he passes the turn and finds nothing.

But when he comes into my cave she must be there, close up. Can I do it? I concentrate on his memories of eyes, hair, skin-texture, the movements of her limbs. These involuntary memories disturb Kevin, but there's no help for it, I must know. I decide to have her perch on the ledge for a few moments before vanishing into the winding tunnels behind the cave. The light in the cave is dim, and flickering because it comes through the waterfall which pours down outside. Maybe, with luck . . .

But can I make her speak? She must at least say his name. And something more—perhaps "Wait." I have heard George say this. Can I convert it to her tones? I find memories of her speaking and concentrate . . .

But then a new thought strikes me. I must motivate him to leave the cave and continue upstream to where the log is, to move it. So the simulacrum must say something of this. I could of course put a task-image in his mind, as I do with the familiars, but it will take strong motivation to get him to leave that place where he believes he has found her. Only her words can do that.

I see that I must know more of Kevin's language. I decide to spend the time of our journey upstream learning this.

As we travel along, I become conscious of a sensation of pleasure, of rightness. This, somehow, is part of the right life for me. Here in this creature are faculties I have found no use for. Why, for instance, do I possess the appreciation of verbal speech when my usual body has no breath nor throat nor lips to speak with? Why do I understand vision, with only the remote, erratic eyes of my familiars to see through? I have often pondered this strangeness. Now here is this creature who has speech and eyes, and hearing, and purposeful mobility. Is it somehow my destined familiar, a super-familiar who will stay with me long after the log is moved, stay with me always?

But I sense that Kevin is no mere familiar to fulfill practical needs. He is in some sense an alternate self. Yet I am tied to my host-plant, to my cave; I cannot go freely with him. Could he be destined as another host? But this is impossible. There is no way I could penetrate. How, what to do? How I wish that we could go together to consult the Wise Ones, far out of range downriver!

As I am thinking this, I feel Kevin hesitate and stop. He has come to the rocks below the falls, where the path swings wide. I could send him a direct command, but instead I let him glimpse the figure of Clare, high up among the streamside rocks. The figure beckons to him and then slips away toward the falls. In an instant he is springing after her, only to see her at pool's edge, by the falls—then stepping along the ledge which leads behind the curtain of water.

"Clare!"

And he is after her, into my cave, so quickly that I have barely time to arrange a view of her seated on the ledge, smiling at him. Now I must concentrate all my skill at making her respond to him, rising and welcoming his embrace, then gently breaking away to say, "Later. Wait. The stream must be unblocked above us!" Then she is to leave him and disappear back into the dark depths of the cave. He of course will follow, but will find only the narrow upstream exit to the cave. I will place in his mind an image of the downed tree just out of sight, as I got it from my familiars. And a sense of the wrongness of the blockaded collection of pollen-packets and egg-pods, the helpless prey of fishes below. He will not comprehend, but with luck he should do as she suggested.

Meanwhile, outside, George and June have lifted off in the ship, under slow, quiet impeller power, and are following Kevin's path upstream. Presently June says, "Look, there's rapids. And a waterfall. See, the path detours around."

"Right." He swings the ship to follow. "Juneo, don't you sense something ecologically weird about this? The flora and fauna are all about the same as we saw on our first landing, but here suddenly is a telepathic being or beings of some kind."

"You mean, how could it have evolved here?"

"Yes. On Alkab Nine, for instance, only the dominant race had really strong telepathy, but several of the lower animals were weakly telepathic. Where a trait appears in a dominant race, there're always signs of it on the way up, so to speak. Like Human technology—several of our animal species use tools of a crude sort. And the same with speech. But this trait appears saltatively, as if it dropped from the skies."

"Hah!" says June. "Speaking of which, look way up there on the hill. Do you see what I think I'm seeing?"

"By the gods, I do." George leaps for the scope. "Juneo, you've got good eyes. Well, this adds a new dimension to the puzzle. But whatever this is, it was a long time ago, and our immediate task is Kevin. Hello, the stream's blocked just above us."

"Only a tree down," says June. "I think this area was burned-over a few seasons back. But look on beyond, just coming into sight. Do you see that big pond full of water-lilies? Maybe our telepath lives there. At any rate, it's about as far as

Kevin could get in the time we've been following him. Maybe we should go down and see."

"My feeling too. But if that thing—or things—is there, how do we keep from being caught by it? Do you know any cacomnemonics?"

"Any *whats?*"

"Fancy name for a powerful nonsense jingle that keeps running through your mind whether you want it to or not. I had to learn some for Alkab Nine. They create such a mental noise a telepath can't get a hold on you."

"No."

"Of course, you can't do much thinking while you're repeating one, but you can do simple things, like grabbing Kevin. Here's an old one: '*A pink trip ticket for a ten-cent fare—a blue trip ticket for an eight-cent fare—punch, punch in the presence of the passen-jare.*' I forget the start."

"A pink trip ticket for a what?" June frowns.

"Wait, here's a simpler one. Dreamed up by an old fiction writer.* '*Tension, apprehension and dissension have begun.*' "

"I think I could do that one."

"Good. Now, the second you sense anything—*anything*—impinging on your thoughts, start repeating it. This thing touches very delicately—I'll probably sense it first, and I'll start off aloud; you join right in. There'll be no time to spare. It had me walking in the wrong direction before I knew anything was there. Wait—I'll set the lines on the ship's caller, so all we have to do is click on and sing along with it. Remember, it must be going on *in your mind*. Now let's get those mesh hoods we dreamed up on our heads and try a sortie."

While he has been speaking, he sets the ship down gently on the hillside above the pond, which lies in a basin in a meadow. The only feature on the shoreline is a large boulder on their side.

When they open the lock, the sweet perfume of the pond's flowering lilies fills the cabin.

*Alfred Bester, *The Demolished Man*.

"Could that be a sleep-gas?" June asks.

"No, I don't think so. There were a lot of them around in the place we lost Kevin, and I got no symptoms . . . All right, let's go."

They go down the ramp, but have only made a few yards towards the lily-pool when George grabs June's arm. "Start repeating—it's here! *Tension, apprehension and dissension have begun* . . . come on!"

She looks at him blurrily, and with obvious effort begins repeating the jingle. As she goes on, her voice clears. "Whew," she interrupts herself, "Was that it? But so light, so nothing! *Tension, apprehension and dissension have begun! Tension, apprehension and dissension*—George, I can't *think!*"

"I know, I've had more practice. Listen, you go back to the ship—don't stop repeating—and monitor me by radio. I'll at least try to spot Kevin. *Tension, apprehension and dissension have begun*—"

He starts down toward the pool, while she returns to the ship, her lips moving. Once inside, she goes to the view-port and sees George on the flat shore, staring around. Then he starts around the verge. As he disappears behind the boulder, June turns the outside caller up to full volume. George reappears, making an arm signal: Nothing. June takes her eyes off him long enough to glance up and down the stream. Then she turns down the caller and shouts to George. "Come back! I see Kevin back downstream. We must have passed him!"

He returns aboard, saying, "A telepath is there, all right. But no sign of Kevin unless he's been dragged underwater. No tracks along the shore."

June points him to the scope. He takes off the metal mesh hood and looks. "That's our boy. He seems to be dragging out a log. Let's move the ship back downstream, and make a run for him."

The ship whispers past Kevin some distance uphill. He doesn't look up, but seems completely absorbed in clearing the stream. The main log comes free, upsetting him into the water.

When he regains his footing, he sees George and June issuing from the ship, starting to run toward him. Without hesitation, Kevin springs up on the bank and starts to run downstream, toward the falls. He avoids the detour-trail and dashes among the tall rocks where the falls start, George and June in pursuit.

"Kevin, Kevin—come back! We're your friends!"

But he races on, his feet skidding on the treacherous footing. To his side the stream has fallen away into a deep gorge. He disappears behind a big boulder.

When George comes around the boulder he finds Kevin turned back to confront him, the edge of the gorge just behind him. George slows.

"Kevin, please! Come back to us!"

But Kevin only backs up, dangerously near the verge. George can see his wet footgear slip as he steps.

"No," Kevin shouts above the water's roar. "Leave me alone, George. You go back!"

At this moment June rounds the boulder to join them. Kevin waves his arms protestingly, and the gesture turns into a desperate scramble for balance. George lunges at him, but Kevin twists away—and before their horrified eyes he teeters on the brink.

"*Kevin!*"

Kevin gives a grunt and suddenly his footing gives way. He goes over backward, his flailing legs vanishing last. In a sudden silence they hear a sound like a heavy fruit breaking.

Trembling, they crawl to the edge and look down. It's a sheer fall onto rocks that jut from the swirling water. Kevin's body cannot be seen.

"We d-drove him to his d-death," whispers June.

"I know. We should go down and find him."

Shakenly they make their way down to a ledge beside the falls. The falls plunge into a deep pool, with water-lilies growing around the edge. No sign of Kevin.

"Look, there's a cave behind the falls. D-do you suppose he could have washed in there?"

"Try . . . don't slip."

They make their way precariously along the ledge where it runs behind the falls. It broadens as they get behind the curtain of water. In the cave the water is almost still, except for a peculiar disturbance at the far end, where the ledge slants down into the water.

"Ohhh!"

Kevin's head and one arm have thrust out of water by the ledge, among the lily pads. As they stare, an animal resembling a large earthly beaver appears by his neck. It has its teeth sunk in Kevin's shirt and is tugging his body up onto the ledge.

"George, is it going to *eat* him?"

George takes a step forward, then checks. A particularly large, strong lily-stalk is by Kevin's body, slowly bending toward his head. George's metallic hood has fallen back on his shoulders, but he makes no move to cover himself. "No more interfering," he says thickly.

The "beaver" has got Kevin's body balanced on the ledge. They can see watery blood streaming from the battered head. Now the animal, as if satisfied, sits down on the far side of the ledge and begins to groom itself. The tall water lily stalk has bent far over, level with Kevin's head. Its petals come to rest on his ear. They see that it is not a flower stalk, but a large terminal leaf-bud.

The petal-like leaves begin to open, to curl back against Kevin's cheek. In the silence of the cave, drama is unfolding.

The inmost leaves open now, revealing something that is no normal plant—an ivory-colored ball-like object apparently growing into the plant's meristem tissue at its growth-point. As they stare at it, it begins to rock, at first slowly, then faster and faster, as though it were trying to loosen itself. Underneath it, they can see tendrils binding it to the plant. They seem to be long, perhaps growing, tubes down to the plant's aquatic roots and branchings. As they watch, first one comes loose, then others, and the tips writhe across Kevin's head to his dreadful wounds.

The tips work through his blood-streaming hair in the dim and pulsing light. First one, then others seem to disappear inside the lip of the largest wound.

June clutches George's arm spasmodically, but he remains still.

"Wait, June. He's dead."

Now the ball-like body, drawn by its tendrils, is dragging free of the plant, onto Kevin's neck. The bleeding slows, diminishes to drops.

"It's shrinking, George. It's going *into him!*"

"Maybe."

But the alien object is unmistakably shrinking, as though it were draining itself through its tendrils into the fissures of Kevin's skull.

June, staring wide-eyed, absently pushes down her own hood.

"Why, it's talking to us, George. Telling us not—not to interfere."

George nods.

For moments that seem like hours they watch the grotesque process. Mysterious, slow, the plant is acting on their dead friend. Then they see that a difference has come over Kevin, as though blood has returned to his pale face. Suddenly an eyelid flutters—or does it? Yes—the lid trembles again. And now the other. Very slightly, his whole body stirs, and his head shifts sideways, carrying the husk of the strange parasite. His mouth works silently.

Then he stirs again, and to their amazement the dead lips move purposefully. "You're George," he says faintly. "And you're June. I'm Kevin. Hello." His eyes are open, staring at them.

"T-take it easy, Kevin," George manages. "You've had a bad fall."

"Yes." There is a pause, then Kevin says more strongly, "I'm okay now, I think. Hey, I can read your minds! Hold still, let me look—"

The two watchers suddenly feel a presence in their own heads. To George, it is far stronger, cruder, than the feather-touches he had experienced before. Perhaps the groping of a new telepath discovering its own powers? This must be Kevin, learning from his alien parasite. So the transfer is not only one-way.

Kevin is frowning. "I'm Kevin *and* someone else. But what's there? Who are you in my head?"

Then, as they stare, his mouth contorts, and he answers himself in a creaky uncertain voice quite different from Kevin's own.

"I . . . have . . . no name . . . yet. I am with you . . . now. You will not . . . die. You will . . . give me a name . . . when you are ready. I am . . . right for your body."

"Kevin?" asks June fearfully, "Are you still there? Are you all right?"

"Yes, I am," says Kevin's normal voice. He stirs and manages to come to a sitting position; but his face is clenched with pain.

"Be careful," they tell him.

"I'm okay I think, except I have this fierce headache. Hey, telepath, symbiote, or whatever, can you fix my head? It hurts."

"Yes, I think so," comes the strange voice from Kevin's mouth. "And it is . . . our head now while I am with you. I have been healing the damage. Now I will . . . try to cancel pain." The parasite's speech is becoming clearer, easier.

For a moment or two, nothing. Then Kevin's face relaxes, his mouth spreads to a grin. "Hey, that's wonderful. Thanks . . . is anything else wrong with me?" Experimentally he wiggles legs and feet and arms and hands, lifts one arm as though to feel his head and pulls it down again. "No—no, eh?" he asks. "Better not yet," he answers himself. "Well," he says in Kevin's voice, "I seem to be all present. I guess my head took the brunt of it, didn't it?" He turns to the others, the alien husk hanging free behind his ear.

"So, what now? I can see you're fairly well stunned," he says in a voice so like the old cheery Kevin that George and June can only shake their heads in wonder.

"You—you were brought back from death," June tells him.

"That big plant did it." She points to the stalk, now slowly righting itself. What had been the leaf-bud hangs open and blown. "Or rather, something that was in the plant did it. It seems to have moved into you."

"With its powers of telepathy," George says.

"Hm'm'm. So, what are your plans for us, friend plant? Or should I say, ex-plant? Do you intend to take me over?"

"Not so far . . . as I know," the alien voice responds. "I am a very young being. I saw that I could be of help, and also gain your powers of sight and speech and moving about. For the present, I must remain with you, that is all I know."

"Would you move into another body if we could find one you like?"

"Oh, yes. And somewhere, I believe, we have proper bodies of our own. But only the Wise Ones know that. It was my plan, before your . . . fall . . . to go with you somehow to consult them."

It takes time for all this to be explained, and all are agreeing to the idea of visiting the Old Ones when Kevin exclaims loudly, "Hey! Friend telepath, are there any more like you right around here?"

"Only one, my neighbor and mating partner, upstream from here. Perhaps you have seen his pool."

Kevin says intently, "We have—another body on the ship. It was my mate. She was killed by a blow like mine. We have kept her body cold so it hasn't changed. Do you think your mating-partner could or would do for her what you did for me? Does your partner want vision and mobility too?"

June gasps.

"Yes indeed," the creaky voice answers him. "But as to whether it can be done, we can only try."

"Then come on!" Kevin exclaims. He makes to jump up, but staggers and clutches the cave-wall for support. "I—I guess I can't lead the way, but could you two put her on the folding trolley and get her down to that pond? You know where it is, could we do that?"

"Oh yes, the ground is quite level."

"Then I'll crawl after you upriver and meet you there. Friend, can you guide me and help me a little?"

"I think so . . ."

"Hey," says Kevin, "how do you like that for a name—Friend? You've certainly done a friendly thing, reviving me. And if we could only revive Clare—ooops, I better not get too excited."

"Take it easy, Kevin. We'll go first and get her."

"Great. Then I'll get started. George, June—see you at the pond. What's the best way out of here, Friend?"

"Back through the tunnels. There is an exit—you remember, you found it when you were searching for Clare's image." Friend's voice has become far more fluent.

George starts to say something about Kevin resting longer, but June cuts him off. "This is the most important thing in his life, George. I believe Friend will keep him from harming himself. You can, can't you, Friend? Put him to sleep, or something."

"Yes."

"Don't you dare," Kevin growls, already making wavering progress to the back of the cave. They follow, feeling their way, until a gleam of light ahead shows the crack that gives on the outer world. When they emerge, the ship is in plain sight high on the hillside.

"George, June, thanks a million if this turns out to be—to be a wild idea." Kevin chokes up. "And . . . listen, be careful with her, won't you? Oh, hell, I know you will. Okay, off you go."

They turn up toward the ship, while Kevin starts painfully along the streamside trails. Looking back, they find it strange to see only a single figure; "Friend" has so impressed their minds as a separate being.

"I'm glad I actually felt that telepath at the pond," George says. "Otherwise this would strike me as crazier than it does."

When they reach the ship and open the refrigeration chamber, they find Clare's body covered with frost.

"Oh, now this strikes *me* as crazy," June cries. "It looks so *hopeless*, doesn't it?"

"We promised," George reminds her. "He'll be waiting for us . . . What I'm worried about is the effect on Kevin when it fails."

"I know . . . Maybe Friend can help him."

George grunts. They set to unfolding the trolley and carefully easing the stiff, icy body up onto it.

The trolley is the old-fashioned type with a single large center wheel which enables two people to carry a heavy load over rough terrain. As they start down the hillside, more frost accumulates on Clare. The alien telepath gives them a brush, but doesn't molest them further. "Friend must have contacted it," June guesses.

They reach the pool-side, near the big boulder.

"Better put her in the shade so she won't thaw unevenly."

June is gazing down at the white marble figure—all white, clothes and all, except for a pinkish stain on the head. "We're being crazy, George," she whispers. "Aren't we?"

"I don't know. We're in the realm of the unknown now."

"Yes. Oh, there they—he—is. Oh, he's stumbling. Better go help him."

"Right." But when George attempts to start down the trail away from the pond he finds his legs won't move. "Damn! It's got me. Get out, you—let me go help my friend come here. *Your* friend is with him, he needs help. Let me go! *Tension, apprehension and dissension*—" He shakes his head, his legs, and finally sets off at a wobbling pace which grows more determined as he goes.

June watches him meet up with Kevin and take the younger man's arm across his shoulders. She has inspected the banks of the pool and selected a small beach down which to push the trolley. They can easily slide Clare's body off at the water's edge . . . but is the plant or whatever's housing Friend's mating partner within reach of this spot?

"Are you near here?" she calls. "We have something for you to do."

As if in answer the surface lily-pads part, and a big leaf-bud pushes just above water. It looks larger and stronger than Friend's plant-host.

"Wait, please. Wait for the others to come." It seems to grasp her message; there is no further motion.

When Kevin and his invisible passenger arrive he gives a cry and bends over Clare. "How *can* it revive her with all this ice?"

"The surface frost is coming loose," says George. "We better get her down onto the ground soon, before there's so much thawing we might break her flesh."

With great care, the three of them tilt the trolley and gentle the corpse down onto the smooth, muddy shore.

"Friend, can your friend reach her head from here? Kevin, look at her head so Friend can see the wounds."

"It is good," says Friend's voice.

"I don't know, but this could be important. Friend, Human beings—that's what we are, Humans—"

"H-humanss?"

"Yes. Well, we come in two types. Male, like me and Kevin, and female like June and Clare. It has to do with our reproduction. Do you have different types too?"

"No. Each of us makes both pollen and eggs."

"Good. Then we don't have to worry about compatibility."

"Oh, George, honestly! We're trying to save her life! What difference does it make if a brain-symbiote is technically male or female?"

"Just a possible factor," George says stubbornly.

"It may be," says Friend's voice, "that our proper hosts were of two types."

"Your proper hosts—?"

"Only the Wise Ones know that."

"It strikes me," says George, "that no matter how this turns out a visit to your Wise Ones is a high priority."

"Oh, yes."

"She's warming!" Kevin exclaims. "And we haven't told your mate here what we want. Will you now, Friend?"

"Certainly. Although much of it has already been passed. Do not talk, please."

In the silence on the sunny, muddy bank, George and June have time to realize anew what an insane venture this is. But one look at Kevin's wildly intent face keeps them quiet.

As the two telepaths commune, the watchers see the strange bud-stalk elongating and bending to rest beside Clare's head. Something, perhaps the chill of her body, makes it withdraw a little.

"He says, this will be slow," Friend reports.

"Right."

"Can your mate go back to his plant if—if he has to?" June asks.

"Oh yes. Slowly . . . now we must wait very quietly."

And there in the sunshine and flower-scent the eerie scene repeats itself. The bud-stalk's outer leaves fold back, this time revealing a golden ball or knob, which begins to rock itself free of its plant structures. Presently golden tentacles, or tendrils, come out onto Clare's cheeks, crawl toward the gash in her skull. The tips disappear within it.

"That was what happened to you," June whispers to Kevin. "It was all we could do not to interfere."

"Sshsh!"

But the process seems to have stopped.

"Cold—it is too cold," Friend's voice says. "All we can do is wait."

Kevin gives a cry of despair and flings himself down beside Clare's body, clasping her to him. Then he pulls back and tears her stiff clothes from her, exposing her lovely body to the sun. And pulls off his own wet garments so that he can hold her against his naked front, while his hands caress and chafe her back. June goes down in the mud beside Clare's legs to massage them.

After what seems an eternity has passed so, they see that the tendrils have begun moving again, swelling and pulsing regularly.

Suddenly Kevin gives another cry. "Her arm moved! It's working!"

"Possible," says Friend.

But then nothing happens for a long while. Kevin and June are joined by George, each trying to bring life to the cold flesh without doing harm. The sun brightens. The golden shell of the telepath has visibly shrunk. Is the tension of life coming slowly into the slack face? They cannot tell—until at last one eyelid flutters.

"Clare! Clare—are you there?"

The other eyelid flutters open, her chest rises slightly and falls again.

"K-Kevin?" The voice is as faint as a feather's fall.

"Yes, I'm here—oh, my darling, darling girl—"

"Wha . . . happened?"

"A branch hit you in the tornado. Lie still, darling, rest and get stronger."

Her eyes close. George and June gaze at each other, overcome by miracle.

"My mate is communicating with her," Friend's voice says.

Presently her eyes open again, and a new voice speaks through her mouth. "So . . . good . . . to see clearly," says the strange telepath. "I see what . . . you mean."

"Yes," says Friend's voice. "Do you not feel the rightness?"

"Oh yes." Clare's eyes look round wonderingly as the alien in her head takes in the wonders of direct vision. Experimentally, one of her hands rises and falls. But Clare's body is too weak for more. Soon the eyelids close, the limbs relax.

"She is sleeping," says Friend.

"We must get her back to the ship," says George. "Is your mate ready to travel?"

"Oh, yes."

They lift her again upon the trolley—astonishing to feel the warmth of life where an hour ago there had been only ice—and cover her with June's parka. Her wounds have bled a little, but are now visibly closing as the empty golden skin hanging from them drops away.

"It's healing her!" Kevin exclaims.

"Yes, as I did to you," Friend's voice tells him. "But the cold made everything difficult. Luckily my mate is very strong."

"Look," says June as they push the trolley up the trail, "your friend must have a name too. Do you have something you call him or her, or would perhaps 'Mate' do? It has good connotations in our speech."

" 'Mate'? Yes, I think Mate will do very well."

"As we go along," George says, "you two, look in my mind and I will concentrate on what our ship does, where we come from, and what we normally do. That will save time when we come to plan our course now. Because of course, finding you has changed everything."

And so we do this. I don't know how it is for the partner I now call Mate, but for me, with Kevin's mind helping me to understand, the revelation that these Humans come from another world, that the bright points in the night sky are suns like our own, only very far away, and that these Humans have been going from world to world, exploring, soon begins to seem natural. And that finding us has "changed everything" because they must now return to their home base to report the finding of another intelligent life-form is clear to me. But along with this comes the hint of another puzzle which is soon revealed more vividly.

At their ship, June and George prepare nourishment which I understand we take in through our mouths. Kevin takes a shell of hot "soup," and sits beside Clare, where he begins to feed her alternately with himself. As he does so, I feel our face forming into an expression so personal and tender that I experience a need to withdraw my attention. This surprises me; it must be a response developed when I was bound to some other life-form, which my empathy with Kevin has reactivated.

This empathy is growing fast. I begin to understand that these Humans do not necessarily reject the intrusion of another mind, but they have also under certain circumstances a deep need for privacy. I ponder this problem.

Meanwhile Clare is asking Mate, "Can you taste how good this soup is? How it gives us strength?" "Oh, yes," comes Mate's still unaccustomed verbal response. "How did you eat, when you were with the plant?" Clare asks sleepily. Mate replies that his roots took in simple solutions and transferred them to his leaves, which released to him a more complex solution which felt something like this "soup." "Ahh," says Clare, and abruptly dozes off above the container of soup that Kevin is putting to her lips. I think back briefly and find that the memory of my previous plant-bound existence is fast fading. But an idea comes.

"Mate," I ask through Kevin's mouth, "do you think that the abilities we used with the plants are still open to us?"

"You mean—" Mate takes me up; I see he has got the idea from my mind, but I want Kevin to hear it in words.

"Yes," I say, "I mean the ability to turn off our consciousness and go into deep sleep when long periods of no activity lay ahead? It has occurred to me that our Human hosts may need to be alone together at times."

"We can try," Mate says.

"Yes, but not now," interposes June. "That's a beautiful thought—Kevin, do you understand what Friend means?—but there's quite a period of activity coming up ahead, now Clare's through eating."

"I get your point and I thank you for it, Friend," says Kevin. "If you're going to lift ship, let me strap Clare in." As he bends over her he lets our lips brush her face. It feels—extraordinary. Plants had no such emotions. Are we perhaps returning to some earlier mode of feeling? But what, if anything, came before our plant-bound lives? I cannot know . . . but why do I feel there was *something?*

The question is soon answered, or rather, added to a much larger one.

June and George take the ship off the ground very smoothly and gently, but before I can begin to grasp the marvels of flight, I see they are heading not downstream to the Elders, but up the hillside. Ahead and below is a strange formation I have sometimes glimpsed through the eyes of flying familiars. It is as though a huge great broken eggshell had been overgrown with vines and bushes. Our ship circles slowly, then lands beside it.

"What's here?" Kevin asks.

"Come out and see, if you're strong enough."

"Lead on."

As we come out of the ship the outer wall of the thing towers above us, and we can see gleams of bright, hard stuff between the leaves. Clare and Mate have stayed behind. I hear his voice call from her sleeping mouth, "Be careful! Much pain and badness is here!"

"I sense it too," I tell them. "But I think it is in the past."

George and June are attacking the vines with another of their astonishing tools—a hand-held cylinder which spouts flame. For a moment I fear the fire, but then I see they have it well controlled. Soon they have cleared what seems to have been an entrance up in the shiny wall. It is thick, like the entrance to our ship; the walls of this thing are strong. It must have taken great force to crush them so. Around the cleared area are many unknown markings.

George and June help Kevin clamber up to the entrance-place. We all look in. The vines are not so thick inside. We can see it was once a great closed container now broken open, with innumerable projecting angles, cables and strange objects scattered about.

"It's a ship, all right," Kevin says. "Badly wrecked. Do you know anything about this, Friend?

The sight has triggered some impersonal memory in the deeps of my mind, but it will not come clear. I tell him so. "Maybe the Elders—"

"Yes, that's what we thought," says George. "We wanted to make sure first."

I am receiving strong impressions of badness here, of fire and pain and confusion, but it is all long ago.

"Look down there." June points. "They didn't all get away."

Down the inside of the wrecked "ship" some white things can be made out, sticks and globes, with tatters of fabric.

"Bones," says George. "Let's leave this for the experts. We can take holos."

They take out more equipment—the number of tools these people have is amazing, this is apparently a tool for visual memory!—and they point it here and there, sometimes clearing the leaves to let in light.

"A lot of charring," George says. "Friend, I have a hunch. Assuming these people were your ancestors—"

"Wha—?" I let Kevin's mouth fall open in startlement.

"Yes. Or rather, the survivors were. After the crash they were burned, and burning. So those who could ran for the stream to quench themselves. But their bodies were too badly injured—"

"—So they transferred to the first large life-forms they could see," June takes him up, "the lilies. And it turned out there weren't any other better animals or plants . . . how does that sound to you?"

I am too astonished to respond.

"Maybe the Wise Ones have preserved some legend," George says. "Let's go to them now."

I return to our ship with my thoughts in a whirl, and have trouble framing a coherent account for Mate. He seems to take it more calmly than I. Speaking softly, so as not to rouse Clare, he asks the other two, "Are you inferring that we were always double life-forms?"

"A host and a—a symbiote. I don't think you're parasites."

"Could you form any idea of what those, ah, hosts, looked like?"

"Not really. Only that they were large and strong, with big brain-cases. And I think I recall something that could be smaller forelimbs, don't you, June?"

"I g-guess so." June, like me, seems to be more affected by the emotional or tragic aspects of this unknown drama.

"The current must have carried the plants, or their eggs, pretty far downstream before they got stabilized," George observed.

"Maybe that's why they are endeavoring to restart a colony up here," I hazard.

"Sounds likely . . . Whew!" George and June are preparing to drive the ship up. "Well, that lays out our next job pretty well!"

"What is that?"

"Why, to find out where these people came from, where their natural hosts are, and take you all back," June answers for him.

"Really? You would do that?" Mate and I ask together.

"It's our duty. Regulations regarding lost or stranded star-travellers," George says matter-of-factly. "Only we're going to have to get some detective work done, unless the Elders have preserved the data. If we aren't that lucky, somebody back at Base is going to have to sort through a mountain of star-charts. Assuming your system is known. If it isn't—we mount a search."

Mate and I are purely astounded.

"Kevin," I say slowly, "you're going to have to teach me some expressions for total bewilderment."

"And gratitude," adds Mate.

"Oh, yes."

The ship lifts off.

Clare stirs, and Mate takes advantage of her wakefulness to look out. I have Kevin's eyes riveted to the view-ports. We are seeing at last the world we had glimpsed through the eyes of our familiars—*the* world, as far as we then knew. Our lives . . . now it is so small!

The stream descends, becomes a broad river. And very soon we are over what June calls an "estuary," a flat region of winding, slow-flowing streams and swamps. Here and there are stands of water-lilies, but they seem too small to be the colony we seek. On the horizon is a broad, level line of light which Kevin recognizes as a huge body of water into which the river runs—a "sea."

And now we come to a much larger aggregation of water-plants, in a pond with many signs of animal activities around the shore.

"This looks right," I tell Kevin. "The Elders would have many familiars."

"Yes," says Mate, "See those birds watching us. And . . . even through the walls of this ship I can sense a center of mental activity."

"I see a good landing-place down to the right," says George. "But now, how do we approach the Elders? It strikes me that we're walking bare-ass naked up to a pretty strong fortress of telepaths. What if they're hostile?"

"Oh, they would not be hostile," I say. But George's words worry me. I recall my first reactions to Kevin: a creature to be used. Mate voices my concern.

"They might see us only as potential familiars," he says through Clare's mouth. "Especially if they have some task they want done, as Friend and I wanted the log moved."

"H'mm," says George.

"What about the language?" June puts in. "How could you learn their language if you were carried upstream as eggs?"

"The plant embryos were inoculated with our eggs, which instinctively made contact with the plant. We were kept with them long enough for them to teach us a little. I believe we can speak mentally, as Mate and I used to when conditions were right."

"Well, if you say so," says George. "But I vote we make up more of those hoods before we open any doors."

"Yes," Mate says. "When your ship is opened there is bound to be a rush of inquiry."

And so they set the ship to circle, while George and June cut hoods out of a piece of metal-mesh fabric, which they fit over our heads. Then they put their own on, and lower the ship onto the landing site George has selected, near a large stand of water-lilies. I can see plant-shoots emerging from the water.

When they open the port for Kevin and me to leave, I sense the excited inrush Mate had warned of. The hoods are only partially effective, but the incoming mental tendrils are disorganized and chaotic, we have no trouble with them.

"Close up after me," Kevin says, and takes us out upon the ramp.

Almost at once we are assaulted by a mind-wrenching blast. I feel Kevin stagger. Desperately I send out to them, "Wait! I am one of you. I have much to share with you. But you must be quiet and let me transmit."

The mental blast doesn't slacken. To my horror, I perceive how right Mate was—these beings aren't interested in anything we have to tell them, they wish only to gain control of us for some purpose of their own.

"Wait! Wait!" I plead, but I feel my mind disrupted under the barrage. Worse yet, Kevin is starting to go down the ramp, they have evidently captured him. "Help!" I cry aloud.

I recall little of what followed, only that a voice is beside us repeating *"Tension, apprehension and dissension have begun,"* and I feel Kevin being jerked backward. From the port a voice calls "Kevin! Turn back! Come back to me!"

This seems to penetrate his trance. He turns and sees Clare at the port. At the same moment, a wave of calming strength comes to me from Mate.

Somehow, with George's help we manage to stagger back up the ramp and fall in the port. George closes up behind us, and the fearful assault is cut off.

June has lifted off the ship before we stop trembling.

"Well, so much for that," says George when we are out of range and can remove the hoods. "They don't act much like elder or wiser beings."

"I have a theory," June says. "Look down below, do you see what looks like the remains of a plant-colony a way upstream from that mob?"

We see it. Most if not all of the lilies are dead and rotting.

"I think there's salt in the water so near the sea. And it does something to the plants. Could that be the original colony of Elders and their young went farther downstream before they rooted? That would account for their drive to get back upstream. Oh, if only we could find one of those Old Ones still alive, I bet we could talk to it! And it could tell the others, when they're in a mood to listen."

"There is one still alive," I say, peering at the old colony. On its edge is a very large lily, not flourishing, but definitely alive.

We go down near it, and cautiously open the ship. A far-off mental clamor is still discernible, but it isn't dangerous. The old lily has lifted its small bud.

When Kevin and I go out I can feel gentle thought-tendrils seeking my mind, nothing like the crude assault earlier.

"Are you one of the Old Ones?" I query it.

"Yes. Not one of the first, but I am the last who remembers the first. Where are you from, and what is this strange host?"

I open my mind to him, including the discovery of the wrecked ship.

"Ah yes . . . I was beginning to think it was all a dream . . . They told me of our beginnings, but so much is lost."

"These star-travellers intend to find our home planet and take us there. But it will take time to search, they say. We tried to tell the others, but they attempted to capture us."

"Yes. They are becoming like animals. I can perhaps tell them later, through my friend downstream, if he still lives. I fear your deliverance will come too late for me, but I am glad to have heard your news."

"Did the First Ones tell you anything of the world we came from?"

A gray mist is over his thoughts. "Oh, so much is lost . . . Wait, they did teach us a verse—" Here he draws himself farther out of water, and to my amazement begins to rustle his leaflets in a strange, sounding way. I had not been aware that our plant-bodies could make sound.

"Listen." And he sends out a series of chords and notes that rhyme. "They thought a verse would last after speech had become garbled."

"But what does it mean?"

"Why, young one, that is the speech of your ancestors. I will translate. The first line"—and he rustles again—"means, 'Three lights in line in a black sky: red, yellow, and white.'"

"Wait!" Kevin interposes. "We should take a record of this. George, June! Bring a recorder!"

More equipment! When all is set up, the old being goes through the verse again. "'Around the yellow light moves a world. In the direction of sunrise, a great red light with three others.'" Then come numbers, in a sort of rhyming sequence: "—nothing, four, five," he finishes.

"Those could be coordinates," George whispers. "But on their own system, of course. Ask him if they knew of other worlds."

"Oh, yes," comes the mental reply. "You say these beings call themselves Humans? It may just be that I have heard that name once."

"Then there's a chance they're on our charts," comments George when I pass this on.

"Ask him if he could give another sample of their language, with a translation," says June. "Maybe something like 'we are stranded here and need help to return to our home.' We could play it for your hosts when we find them."

Gravely, he does this.

We ask him a few more questions. But he is tiring fast. He sends to me, and Mate: "You are fortunate beyond thinking, young ones. You will go among the great races of the stars when I am dead in the mud of a wild planet, never to see our home."

I am close to weeping, and I see Clare and Mate are equally touched.

"Is there anything we can do for you before we go?"

"Ah, thank you, but no. I have my familiars, who watch the stars rise."

"Could you come in my head and go with us?" June asks impulsively.

"I thank you gratefully, Human female. But I am too old to make another transfer. And, in any event, no one could transfer into that bony shell unless it was ruptured. But your generosity warms my roots."

"Whew!" says George, as we get in the ship, "I guess that saved me from having to slice your head open, my little warm-heart!"

—And so it ends. I am in a starship, setting out with aliens on a quest for my home. In one long day I have changed from a water-plant to a creature whose home is among the unknown stars, whose forebears came here in their own ship of space. We may not find our home in my lifetime. Yet the Humans have said that Mate and I may live among them, earning great prestige as healers. I hope that we find our home and our proper hosts—oh, how I hope it! But the alternative is not unbearable, and Mate is with me. We may have young and found a settlement among these strangers, wearing who knows what bodies.

Now I am going to ask for the use of one of their "recorders," so that I set down all these events while they are fresh in mind. Of course, it will have to be in Human speech—I know no other verbal tongue. And who knows where this record will end up? As a legend of adventure on our own planet, or stored among Humans to relate the birth of our colony there?

My only regret is that I did not ask the Old One the name of our race. So I must begin it, "Day One in the history of an unknown people."

Last Night and Every Night

He was not unimaginative. As he waited for the cow to come out, he could appreciate the dark slash he made in the pool of streetlight, the sleek pale highlight of his hair. Night, rain, empty city street, background traffic drone—like an old flick. Where in hell was the cow?

She came out then, hesitating at the lobby entrance of the expensive apartment building. A twat-head, he thought. Staring around, touching things. He gave a quick glance left and right. No one. He threw his cigarette away and started toward her across the wet street.

She was very young, he saw now, and small. Shorter than he. And what the hell was she wearing, some kind of nightdress? He slowed down as he neared her. Easy. This was so easy. How many had he done? A hundred? A thousand, more like. Bring 'em in smiling. A professional, he was.

She lifted her head to stare at him. Big stupid wet eyes, short upper lip, pointy little pimples under the thin dress. Chicken meat. Anna ought to put out at least fifteen for this one.

He had his special face on. Boyish, uncertain. Let her look deep into his blue eyes under that sincere hair. No need to pay attention to what he said or what she said. The same old shit. Trying to hold back at first, trying to put him down—and then sniveling it all out, plop, plop. Like, evicted. Like, you too? Like, they threw her out. Like, no one would speak to her. Like, where are we going?

They were walking along beside the silent buildings now, he making the noises at intervals and wondering idly how Anna and Honky always knew. Servants probably, he decided. Places like these have lots of servants. It was time for the pitch.

"Look," he said, "you have to get indoors. It's all right for me, but you—" He gestured at her damp dress.

"My purse," she whispered at her empty hands. What a cow.

"These friends," he said. "Good people," he said.

"Oh, like this?" she said. "I couldn't . . ."

He stopped paying attention again, letting it drone on. Night, rain in the empty street. Background traffic hum. Why was it always so empty? The cow had fallen silent, goggling at him. He made himself pat at her soft little arm. She flinched.

Anger flamed up his neck, although he knew it was his own bad timing. What did she mean spooking on him? He looked at her more closely behind his clean eyes, letting his hand fall empty, pathetic. Maybe I *will* see you later, cow, he thought. Maybe I'll take the trouble to watch you in Anna's special room with the one-way mirror. I'll be floating and you'll be screaming. Like that Cuban girl, like the others.

The Cuban girl, he thought suddenly. When was that? Something confusing here. My head. He shook it, and saw her looking at his distress. Softness oozing at him—the anger licked back in a hot silent roar.

"If you really think so," she was saying.

Sick with rage, he said ever so gently, "I'm sure it's all right."

Sure as hell she was no virgin, Anna couldn't bitch, he had a right to something once in a while. So what if one wasn't smiling? Just don't mark her up. He let their eyes meet in the way cows loved. A smile trembled between them.

"Hel-lo," he murmured softly. Softly his arms came up, not touching her. The street was silent. Gently he braced both hands on the wet stone behind her, trapping her between his arms, letting her melt toward him. Tenderly he smiled his hatred, wondering where he would hurt her first. Those tits, yes, and then a boot up, sweet . . . He shifted his weight slightly, the bitch-stink thick in his nostrils. Her lips brushed his softly, and suddenly—

—he was jumping under a hail of water on his back, deafened by tire-scream. He whirled, confused, cursing, slapping his legs, hearing the cow's gasping giggles. The car—where in hell had it come from?—slowed to park in the next block.

"Come on," he said, grabbing her arm. She spooked again. He let go and made himself speak gently.

"You're wet, you have to get indoors."

His anger was splintered now; it wouldn't hold him up. Get on with it. Wearily he formed his boyish grin, feeling it wrench his cheekbones.

"You're shivering," she said and suddenly took his hand. He let her. Which way was Anna's? There. They sloshed on.

"Is it far?"

"No."

What the hell was wrong with him? Mechanically, he made himself picture her in Anna's room, mechanically he said something that made her smile. At last they turned between the big gates into the porte cochere.

"Here? Your friends?"

"That's right," he told her, feathering his knuckles on the chimes. She was gaping around at the portico. Honky opened up.

"Even'n, Mistuh Chick. Even'n, ma'am." Rich warmth of Honky's jive voice. "Oh, my! You step right in, ma'am. I'll call Miss Anna."

Still staring, the twat was got inside to drip on the carpets under the twinkling chandelier, to bug her eyes at Anna swirling down the grand stairs, to receive the enfolding handclasp that was almost a motherly hug.

Behind the two women's backs Honky was giving him the fist. He returned a spitting gesture. The cow was going, "But, but, oh how kind of you," as Anna led her up the stairs.

He knew what was beyond those stairs—the closed doors, the soundproofing. He had been up there a lot. He could go up any time. That was part of the deal.

The cow turned and waved at him.

"I'll be around," he called. Why did they get that look? God, he was sick of that look. The whole damn place looked peculiar, too, just for a minute. Like . . . was it daylight? He frowned and focused on Anna's retreating figure. Behind her skirt Anna made a fist and then five fingers, twice.

"Fifteen," he told Honky. "She's smiling."

"You saw the boss," Honky said, peeling off two bills. Then he added a card. "Here. Next."

"Up against the wall, father," he said, looking at the card. It was the other side of town. "It's raining."

"It's always raining. Get your ass over there."

"I think I've got a cold," he said, but he turned and marched out.

The man who had been sitting in a deep armchair beyond the planter got up as the door clicked.

"Not much left there," he commented.

"Not much left of any of us," said Honky. He wheeled on the man. "Why do you do this to us? Why don't you let us die dead? Stop the game. Stop it!"

"Sorry." The man picked up his raincoat. "You know we're short of personnel. You realize the rate is three hundred deaths per year in this city alone? And every last one of them has to be met, you can't leave them milling about on the streets. A lot of them we can take care of with relatives or friends, but what do we do with the people who don't have anybody? You want a flipping band of cherubim caroling from door to door?" He struggled into his coat.

"You make us like dogs. Zombies!" groaned Honky.

"On the contrary," said the man, pulling on his rubbers. "We're just letting you go on doing what you did in life. What's unfair about that? You three were pretty good as hustling friendless women, so we're making use of your skills. With certain—ah—necessary modifications, of course. If it's any comfort to you, these bits of your personalities won't hold together too long. Chick, now. I'll have to be finding a replacement for him soon, I fear. He wasn't much to begin with. But it all helps, it all helps. Anna's fairly intact so far. So are you." He started for the door.

Honky grabbed his shoulder.

"Let us go," he pleaded. "Let us die!"

"Sorry," said the man again, shrugging him off.

"Goddamn you!"

"It's not policy," the man said. Shining faintly, he went out.

Backward, Turn Backward

It's the day.

Both days.

In the big double bed lies a naked old woman, clasping a naked old man in her shrunken, leathery arms. It's eleven in the morning.

"Any minute now," he says in his hollow voice.

"I still think it was a half-hour later," she objects.

"What does it matter? We're comfortable here. Oh, my darling girl, it'll be weird. Not knowing where I work or what we've been doing. Do you realize we won't even know our friends?"

Her once-sweet giggle is an old woman's cackle now. "But we'll have each other. And Fred's going to drop over soon, to help us out . . . poor Fred; he's had his."

"Yeah . . . hey, do you s'pose we could catch a convoy going to the beach?" She looks down at her age-ruined body. "I don't even have a bathing suit any more!"

"So buy one." He pulls one arm loose and holds it shakily up to look at. Impossibly thin and knotted, with what had been his muscles hanging like jelly-bags from the bone. "My god . . . do you really believe this, sweetheart?"

"You're the scientist. But yes, I'd say I abso-posilutely do. Oh, my love, my love!"

"I'll see you as I never did."

Almost imperceptibly she flinches. "You saw me."

"Well, I was aware of this ravishing Queen-of-the-Prom type, flashing around with all the money boys. But I never really *looked* at you; I mean, what was the use? You were too busy being popular. By the way, did you have any girlfriends?"

"Girls?" She seems to be gazing into an unpleasing distance. "Oh, I had . . . cordial relations with, with other girls like me. And I was aware of you, too, love, only you seemed so beyond everything. And cold." She laughs again, more deeply.

"And I had acne." He too laughs. "Lord, what acne I had."

"Yes, I guess," she admits.

"I bought some acne medicine Wednesday. The clerk really eyeballed me."

Her laughter has ended in a faint mewing noise. "Oh! Oh, I think it's starting! Oh——forgot——" Her hand goes to her mouth and she pulls out her false teeth, drops them.

"Hold tight," he mumbles.

They slump unconscious.

Just fifty-five years earlier, the members of St. Andrews Junior College senior class file into a curious, tunnel-like structure and begin taking off their clothes.

Along both walls are plain padded bunks, single and double, upholstered in a metallic-looking substance. There are knobs and dials in the headboards, and beside each is a locker for clothes and a white towelling robe hanging over a mirror.

Diane and Jeffrey pick out a double bunk at the far end, and start to strip.

Back by the entrance, Don Pascal sits down on a single bunk and carefully adjusts the readouts on his bunk-head before he takes off his old jogging shoes. As usual, he is alone. It isn't that people actively dislike Don, it's just they don't seem to notice he's around. His steady four-point average and his truly horrible acne don't help much, either. Sneakers done, he strips off the rest of his stuff, bundles it into the locker and lies down straight as a mummy, gazing at the ceiling. He is smiling to himself.

The heavy vault door at the entrance swings shut with an ominous clang.

Diane's head pops out of her jumper, she stares at the naked youth beside her. "Oh! . . . I guess I *am* a little scared, Jeff."

"Nothing to get spooked over, people have done it a zillion times. Good god, you're beautiful. What I can't figure out is why you chose me, I mean, we barely know each other." He has a nice grin.

"Oh, Jeff . . . well, I've always liked you."

He squints at her. "Come off it, Princess."

"Oh, all right. I guess I didn't want anyone who . . . who knows me better to see me—afterward. *You* won't care."

"Aha. Keeping up the old image, eh? You think they won't love you if they see what you'll look like when you get old."

"Oh, stop. That's not fair. You know it, people can't help associating it in their minds whenever they look at you later. I could have a terrible scar or be blind or something."

"Okay, okay. No one remembers anything anyway, but I guess you're not one to risk that they might be wrong. Hey, we better set our dials. What are you taking, the usual four weeks?"

"I sort of hate to, the prom's the week after."

"Fuck the prom, this is serious business . . ." He was fixing his lapse-time to four. "When are you going to hit for? I mean, how old?"

"Seventy-five."

"Not for me." He turns a dial to fifty. "I want to have time to enjoy what I make."

"What you *make?*"

"Yeah. Do you think I'm just going to loaf around gawking at the marvels of the future, or chase tail? I've been doing a lot of work on leveraged commodity futures, and index options. The data I get should make me ve-ry verrry reech. So rich that pretty ladies like you will jump all over me."

"That's clever." She looks at him with a sudden appraising glint in her beautiful eyes. "Yes . . . but how can you bring back this data? If you won't remember anything, and you can't bring back anything but your bare body. . . ."

"I know. And writing on your skin's no good, the ink or whatever stays behind. You'll arrive without that lipstick, by the way . . . But I figure a certain kind of scar could get through, like if I get a really sharp scalpel and bury a thread under my skin, like embroidery-writing, just the bare vital figures and dates—the thread couldn't get pulled out without leaving a scar. Even if it takes a microscope to trace it."

"H'mmm—"

A computer voice speaks. "Four minutes."

Admiration lights her huge, soft eyes. "I wish I were as far-sighted as you!"

He looks her over, unwillingly starting to react to her beauty, so near. "You never even took a business course, did you? Feckless child!" he laughs a bit thickly. "Counting on some man supporting you for life."

She turns her eyes away and murmurs mischievously, "Well, there are some who seem to think it's not such a bad idea . . . but I did think I'd look in back papers and memorize the name of a Derby winner—if they still have Derbies."

"No good. You won't remember. And one winner wouldn't do you much good, after taxes. Get at least a dozen and implant them my way."

She lifts one arm and looks at the flawless, creamy skin. "And go around with horses' names all over me!" she laughs. "Still, there *are* plastic surgeons . . . thanks, Jeff, you may have given me an idea."

"Three minutes," the voice says.

"Oh . . . Jeff, can you stand the idea of being sixty, seventy, *eighty*—with no being young to look forward to!" She herself can't really imagine being eighty; but she had seen her favorite aunt grow wrinkled and stooped and jowly and complaining. Not to be stuck with just that, with no magical vacation in youth ahead to buoy her. No way.

"Two minutes."

She clutches his arm against herself. "Oh, Jeff, I—I—it's——"

He starts to embrace her, and jerks back. "Watch it, watch it—I don't want this thing to catch me in an embarrassing condition."

"Oh, I'm sorry . . . tell me, Jeff, where do you think you'll be when you wake up?"

"Well . . . I'll know it's coming, so I'll lie down somewhere. In my private penthouse gym, if things go as I plan. With my butler standing by with a tray of snacks and drinks, and three or four fantastic young things—like you—soothing my brow and holding my slippers. . . . While down below the chauffeur polishes my Mercedes, or maybe my Alfa Romeo—and my personal pilot studies some maps. And in the corner is a well-concealed safe holding lots of Bahamian CDs. That sort of thing . . . how about you?"

Her eyes gaze beyond him. "Well, it's summer—so I'll be, say, in Hyannisport. In a dreamy bedroom—flowers and white wicker furniture and apricot silk walls. —And on the dressing table will be a photo of a lovely-looking man and two—maybe three—great kids, the youngest is a baby . . . The sound of the surf and trees rustling outside. In the dressing room, my maid is laying out my new outfit to host our little party on the yacht tonight. Keys to the cars, and to the townhouse—house—s-se—ohhh, it's happening, oh—"

"See you in a month, kid—" Jeff's voice fades on a high note, and his head lolls back. She has passed out.

The tunnel lights dim as the power-drain hits. The young bodies are all still, but a strangeness is on them, a creeping of change, like motion. The hum of power rises. Around them the great energy-field pulses and strengthens; in a space which is time, an unimaginable scanning probe goes out on mysterious tropisms, seeking identities in far-off presents. Maximum identity of configuration, no less than the person, him or her self, in time ahead.

When a connection is made, there would come a lightning-swift transmutation, a reorientation—at the end of which their young selves would occupy the space-time niches in which their older bodies were found; and, nature being symmetrical, their older selves would find themselves back here.

And the exchange would remain in place until the preset return was reached.

It is not, of course, true time-travel. Merely the closest that anyone has come to it yet. You can only travel one way, and only to yourself. And you can bring nothing forward or back with you, not even memory. It was for this reason that the military had let the technology slip away from their control. What profit could come of a spy who could recall nothing, and bring no notes? What use in sending a battalion of unarmed naked men into the future?

So it had filtered out, first to the ultra-rich, then to the merely rich but privileged, and finally, by the time of Diane and Jeffrey and Don, it had come to the point where pricey boarding schools offered it to their senior classes as an extra attraction.

Back in the tunnel, the lights brighten. The throb of power dies, the air loses its strangeness.

On the bunk where Diane and Jeff had lain, a bald man of fifty with a thick gray mustache opens his eyes. He finds that the body against his is that of an old, raddled woman. As tactfully as possible, he draws away. Diane opens her eyes.

"Huh-hello," she quavers. "Who are you?"—She pushes herself upright, makes for the robe hanging near. As she pulls it away from the mirror, she stares blindly at her image. "*Oh my god—!*" She's even more disoriented than he is.

"Jeffrey Bowe." With forced calm he too gets up and gets his robe. "It's happened, all right. Ouch, my back. I feel horrible . . . I'm sorry, but I can't remember your name, either."

"I'm Diane Pascal. Diane Fortnum, I was. Di Fortnum . . . were we close friends?"

"No, just friendly," he starts to say, but she's no longer listening.

"Wait! Where's Don!" Looking around wildly at the crowded tunnel, her white hair flying. "Where's Donny? Donny Pascal?"

"God, I don't know. Down there somewhere. Who wants him?"

"He's my husband, my love, my life—" She gets herself under control. "He must be here somewhere, we were in the same class. I better get to the door, before he—look, Jeff, I'm sorry but this is terribly important."

She hobbles off barefoot at top speed, pushing through the throng of old men and women who are milling about uncertainly. He hears her calling Don's name in a cracked voice.

On the bunks a few people are struggling feebly or lying still, evidently too sick to get up. Jeff sees medical teams and stretcher-bearers making their way to them. The vault doors are open.

The P.A. system crackles and a girl's voice comes on. "All of you who can walk should now leave the chamber. Transport is waiting for you outside."

She goes on to tell them that unless they have made private arrangements, they will be driven back to the school dorms. "Remember that you are still technically students at Saint Andrews, you are entitled to meals and living privileges here in your regular rooms. For those who wish to stay here, we have arranged a series of lectures and short courses. We've found that a brushup on elementary math and some languages are most popular. Sign up when you get to the dorms. There is a staff member to help you.

"There is also a temporary medical station set up in Dorm A, and we urge that each of you report for a basic check-up, and to get any medicines that you take regularly. For those of you who find themselves seriously ill, a geriatric specialist has been laid on at the regular infirmary. If you are incapacitated, you will be taken there, and from there to whatever medical facilities you need.

"None of this will affect your return to your school-age selves at your designated time."

Jeff feels both real and unreal at once.

As he moves along with the crowd going out, someone starts to weep loudly. It's a young girl kneeling on her bunk, clasping a robe against her. Jeff can't recall her name, Jeanne Something.

"Nothing happened!" she wails. "I've been left behind! Oooh—what's wrong?"

An attendant gets to her. "Take it easy, honey. Take it easy. You'll get another chance."

"But *why?* What happened?"

"What age did you set it for?"

"Ei-eighty-five."

"Well, I'm sorry, but the reason the probe didn't pick you up was because you aren't there. That means you are dead by then. I'm sorry, sweetie, but eighty-five is *old*. Come in again with the next group Monday, and set it earlier."

"I'll be dead by eighty-five?" she says wonderingly.

"Uh-huh. Look, you could get killed in an accident tomorrow, you know that. It's all in the averages. Upper class and upper-middle live longer as a rule, but there're always a few who miss."

A boy has joined them. "I missed too. At eighty, goddamn it. You're sure we get another crack at it?"

"That's right."

"What if I miss again? Do I get another?"

"If necessary. As many as you need."

"Hell. Oh, well, what's the difference?"

"Please clear the area. Please clear the area," says the P.A. voice.

As Jeff moves on he can hear Jeanne still saying to nobody in particular, "I'll be dead . . . at eighty-five, I'll be dead . . ."

Jeff passes the vault doors and sees the robed figure he recognizes as the remains of Diane, locked in the embrace of another robed scarecrow with wild white hair, oblivious to the world.

He frowns, puzzled and repelled. This aged passion corresponds to nothing in his conceptual world. He grunts disgustedly, fingering his mustache. Well, he can only hope that his younger self, somewhere ahead in the mists of the future, is having better luck.

Fifty-five years into that future, Diane is just opening her beautiful young eyes.

There is someone lying beside her, she senses, but she does not turn to look yet.

She can see only part of a dim bedroom, Venetian blinds are down. But even in the gloom she sees at once that this is no bedroom in Hyannisport, or anywhere like it. Not that it is ugly—it's tidy, in a kind of motel way. The walls are indeed apricot-color, but paint; the drapes and blinds white. But there are no ferns, no elegant wicker furniture, no huge mirrors. There is a plain dressing table, straight out of Sears Roebuck, as are the bench, the lighting-fixture, everything she can see. One small bottle of perfume sits on the table, but no photographs. The pale carpet is worn; the room speaks long-term habitation.

Icy dismay, a wrongness too deep for expression, is growing around her heart.

She listens; instead of the sea and leaves, a window air-conditioner whirs.

If she lies perfectly still, refusing to exist here, perhaps all this will somehow go away, give place to what should be. *Must* be. She closes her eyes, her ears.

But a voice speaks. A young man's voice, the kind that always seems on the verge of breaking back to boyhood.

"My god . . . you're so beautiful."

She will not, will not answer, will not acknowledge this reality.

A hand touches her, a hand that trembles, timidly caressing her flank.

"Diane—Diane Fortnum! What are you doing here with me, I wonder?"

Despite herself she whispers "Who—who are you?"

"Don. Don Pascal. We were in the same class."

"Don . . . Pascal? *Don Pascal?*" Astoundment, horror, strengthen her voice.

"That's right. Don Pascal, the nerd. In bed with Diane Fortnum, the queen of the senior class, queen of everything. Every man's dream . . . and yet we must know each other fairly, fairly *intimately*, wouldn't you say? Diane, if I may, do you even recall me?"

"Well, I sort of . . . yes."

"I know. Queens don't know nerds. And I had such terrible acne. Terrible. You better know that before you turn around and look."

"I—I'm not going to turn around. This is some kind of mistake. I don't belong here. It'll change back in a minute, it *has* to. I know it will—" She's started to shake.

"No," he says gently, "Diane Fortnum doesn't belong here. But I'm seriously afraid that this is where you were. These things don't make mistakes . . . but you can wait if you want to, of course."

There is a silence. Diane lies with closed eyes, unmoving except for the waves of shaking that come over her. Her skin feels the cotton-dacron of the plain sheets. The air-conditioner gives a brief chatter, then settles down again.

Just as the situation is becoming untenable, there comes a faint animal sound and a tug on the sheet under her breast. Her eyes fly open—to meet the round green gaze of a big black cat. He is standing up to inspect her, with his paws on the edge of the bed, ready to jump up.

She has always liked cats, especially black ones. This one extends his muzzle toward her, sniffing, and then draws back as if puzzled. She checks her impulse to speak to it. The cat studies her a moment longer, then, apparently not finding what it expected or wanted, it turns away and stalks to the bench, showing itself to be a big neutered male. It leaps lightly up to the seat and settles with paws tucked under, still watching her critically.

"Looks like someone else thinks you belong here," Don says and adds quickly, "I don't mean to be cruel, you know . . . Oh, my, my, your back is so god-awful lovely . . . don't I ever get to see your front?"

Diane stares despairingly at the cat. Under the air-conditioner's hum she can hear his heavy purr. The steady reality of this place is soaking into her, Hyannisport and yachts are fading fast away.

With a gut-wrenching sob she turns over toward Don and buries her face in the pillow. Another sob—another—and it all comes out in a howl of woe, like an animal. His arms go round her, she is crying into his neck.

"There, there, let it out. Tell god what you think of him. Life's dirty tricks. Let it out, honey, pound on me if you want."

His hand caresses her back with sympathy, with authority.

When the spasm spends itself and the shaking dies to shivering, she mops her eyes on the sheet and looks up to see him. The awful acne. "Oh! Don't touch me!" She gives another howl, looking around the nondescript, unglamorous room. A plain seersucker robe lies over the foot of the bed. She scrambles up and puts it on. "Ick. But this *can't* be true. And I'm sorry, but you're hideous. And touching me." Tears start streaming down her face again.

"It's pretty bad, isn't it?" He touches his own face experimentally. "They must have something to cure acne now. I'll go find it." He too gets up, sees some underwear laid out, and starts putting it on.

"And this room," she sobs. "Th-this hideous cheap place, I hate it. Hate, hate, hate it. There's *got* to be a mistake!"

"You know something?" He sits on the edge of the bed to put socks on. "If you weren't so angelic-looking you'd strike me as a self-centered, materialistic, greedy, rude little shit. As it is"—he shakes the sock at her—"you're a distractingly beautiful, rude, greedy little shit. And I've had about enough. You thought you'd wake up in the White House as the First Lady, is that it? You're already rich, I know that much about you. Your father is a millionaire stockbroker in Chicago. But you wanted to be rich-rich-rich. Old money too. Right? You'd be Mrs. Fabulous. Well, you didn't make it. And this room isn't hideous. Now look what you've done to puss-cat!"

Offended by the uproar, the cat is stalking out, tail rigid.

"And what do you think you've done to me? Waking up with a snotty piece of tail who goes into hysterics because I'm so repulsive to her. I'm a human being, you know—or has the thought crossed your mind that there *are* other human beings?"

She's in better control now. "Yes," she says formally. "I *am* sorry. I apologize . . . but I still think there's been a mistake. Maybe I was visiting here, you know?"

"And the time caught up with us? Well, maybe. But I want you out of here just as badly as you want out. If we can't find out where you belong, maybe we can find a hotel that conforms to your standards and you can wait it out there. *If* we have the money, that is. Indications are that whoever lives here isn't exactly rolling in it."

"Um."

"I better explore. There'll be a bank-book somewhere." He gets his feet into too-wide slippers and stands up, casting her a long, hard look. The plain little robe looks neat on her, her face is all innocent sadness. But he shakes his head deliberately, No.

Suddenly she says "What's that?" and points to the headboard. Hanging there is a taped-on envelope. He bends over and reads aloud:

"READ THIS BEFORE YOU LEAVE THE ROOM. BOTH OF YOU.

"We must have left that for ourselves," he says.

"You may have." But her voice lacks conviction; the printed letters look like her own script.

"Yeah, well—" He detaches the envelope and turns it over

curiously. It's a good, apricot-tinted stationery with embossed lettering on the back. "91225 Ridgeway Place, Arlington, Virginia. 22206. Enclave 47.' That must be here. But 'Enclave 47?' . . . things have changed, kid."

He opens it. "This looks like my scrawl. I'll read it to you, okay? Better sit down. Here goes.

" 'To our younger selves, greetings! We know you won't remember anything of your lives since school, since it hasn't happened yet in your reality. You won't even know where you are. So we've tried to answer the most vital questions.

" 'You are in your own beloved home. The house you've lived in for thirty years. It's all free and clear, the mortgages are paid.

" 'You have been married for thirty-five years.' "

Di is making a half-strangled sound, her eyes enormous. Suddenly she gasps and bursts out. "But it doesn't say my name! You may have written this to your wife, but she's *somebody else!* It doesn't say me."

He looks at her, looks down at the letter, and sighs. "You're making a great try, kid. But, I'm sorry, I think you better look at this stationery. Up top, there—" He hands her the apricot sheet.

Embossed at the top is the address again, and above it, quite clearly, is the embossed name: Diane Pascal.

She stares at it, makes an indescribable small sound, and drops the paper into her lap, blinks, picks it up again unbelievingly and stares at it. Her breathing is ragged, but she's not crying. She drops the thing again and stares slowly round the room, her expression so bleak and forlorn that he can't help but pity her. Greedy—selfish—shallow—crazy—she's still a human being in pain. The pain of lost dreams.

He gets up and goes over to embrace her shoulder. But she shudders away from his touch, sits like a statue. He remembers his acne.

"Chin up, kid. It's only for four weeks. You can make it."

Slowly she says as if to herself, "This . . . is . . . my . . . future? This? Oh, but how *can* it be? I was so sure, everything was going fine—"

His anger returns. "Just what is so terrible about this? You have a home and a husband, and you're not in an old people's home or starving, and I have a hunch a lot of people are. And when we wrote this you sure didn't seem to be ashamed of your name. H'mmm?"

"But . . ." she says vaguely.

"It's *middle class*, is that it? And you were upper. But even that wasn't good enough, you planned to be upper-upper-upper. To marry into the golden life. Well, you missed. I don't know why, as you say, you seemed to have it all working . . . I heard you were even staying virgin, to—to present the most desirable package."

She nods minimally.

"Well, we'll discuss that when we come to it."

She casts him a look of scorching scorn. But he has his temper in hand, he only laughs.

"We certainly won't come to that!" she snaps. "I see now. This is a *possible* future. As that thing said, it isn't reality yet. Well, it won't be! I'll change it, I'll do something differently—"

"You won't remember anything."

"I'll remember enough! I *will!*"

He frowns at her. Is she really psycho?

"This upper-upper business really meant something to you, didn't it?" He muses. "The golden realms of the gods, his-and-her Lear jets, designer everything, houses everywhere, staffs of servants; utter invulnerability. You thought you had a ticket to it. You were going around with boys from that world, you had them dazzled."

As she still sits silently, he sees her sway. Her face is dead white.

"Wait a minute, honey. Come over and lie down. You're in some sort of shock. Here—" He sees a carafe. "Drink some water."

She accepts his help passively. Then, noticing she's still holding the letter, she wrenches away and starts to rip it up.

But he's too quick for her. "No-no, baby. This must be

important, we thought it was important enough to write. You lie there quietly, and I'll read it to you. Okay?"

She shrugs. Her color is a little better.

"Okay: '—thirty-five years.' That'd be about twenty years from now, by the way. 'But the point is, for all these years we have loved each other deeply. Deeply. Every year more. A profound love that you never knew about. We discovered it. Most people haven't experienced it, we think.' "

He glances at her. She seems to be taking it in, she's staring at him puzzledly.

" 'You first started living together more as a matter of convenience. That was in what's called the Great James Depression, although poor old President James really had nothing to do with it. It was worse than the one in the early 1930s, people say. Partly because of the violence—but you'll get all that later. Di had lost her job, but Don was kept on by TCK, the mammoth pharmaceuticals concern. (Don, I'll tell you about your work on a separate page, you're on a month's paid leave now.) . . . Anyway, he found her on the streets and took her home. It was a tough pull supporting two on his pay, but you made it. Later he got her a lab job with TCK.

" 'After things started getting a little better, we realized that what had grown up between us was serious. We haven't been separated for more than a few days ever since. We just got married for practical reasons, it made it easier to get in this enclave.

" 'You have no children. Due to an old illness, Di's tubes are blocked. We decided adoption wouldn't be satisfying, and we've never regretted this.

" 'Di retired five years ago, after working in various technical jobs and in doctor's offices. She came to enjoy her work and took courses. Don has his MD, but he only practiced for a short time before going with TCK as a biochemical researcher. He's a senior consultant now, goes in once a week.

" 'We are old now, very old. Di's eyesight is failing, and Don is a caricature of a man. We have looked forward to this month of youth for many, many years. More than you can probably understand. Try to make it memorable. Maybe you think you don't much like each other now; Di says to remember what a snotty little shit she was. And Don was a social zero with a repellent skin condition. Certainly we were and will always be *different* from each other. But our differences turned out to complement each other, and we have been through a lot together. You will go through the riots and near-starvation and save each other's lives. You will despair. (You must look through the book by Hawkins on current history we've laid out for you on the kitchen table.) But our differences paled in comparison to our loyalty to each other. Our love. By now we are almost one person. Neither of us could be happy for a moment if the other was in pain, nor totally unhappy if the other was in sunshine. It's one of the greatest riches life can bestow. But you can't really understand this now. We couldn't, at first we thought it was almost a trap, such love. It seems incredible that you'll recall none of this, which hasn't happened yet in your reality—but maybe some of the glow will come through.' "

He pauses to glance at Di, his own face slightly puzzled. She seems composed enough, staring at the ceiling.

" 'Now Di will take over the rest of this letter, which is just practical information on where things are and how to live in this era. And who your friends are. The best of them, Freddy Tillum, will come over this afternoon and help you out a lot. He'll call first. To you he may seem just a garrulous old nobody, but we beg of you—we plead—do not hurt or offend him in any way. He has meant—means—more to us than we can say; not least, he saved our lives once. Now before I turn this over to Di, a warning: DO NOT GO OUTSIDE THE HOUSE UNTIL YOU HAVE FINISHED READING THIS AND TALKED WITH FRED. WE MEAN THIS.'

"Whew, I'm hoarse." He takes a drink of water. "Over to you, Di, when you're up to it . . . It must be pretty weird, writing to yourself, I mixed the pronouns all up. And I can't say it's a model of expository prose." He is shuffling through the remaining pages. "You did yours with headings, much better organized. Oh, here's an item—the cat's name is Henry. Henry Cat, or *Henri Quatre*. Cute. He's six . . ."

When Diane says nothing, but continues to lie still, Don goes around and lies down on the far side of the bed, carefully kicking off his slippers first.

"A lot to take in," he says gently. "The Great Depression . . . riots . . . near-starvation . . . despair . . ." His voice changes slightly. "Love."

Her eyes are still roving the ceiling. Suddenly she makes a sort of grunt and moves to point at the headboard.

Hanging there is a small object, which had been behind the letter. He gets it down. It turns out to be a tube wrapped in a note: "This will cure Don's acne in a day or two."

"Eureka!" He opens it and starts dabbing his face and neck, chuckling. Even Di smiles faintly. He gets up and goes to the mirror to complete the job.

"I'm so hungry," he says. "Something like milk would do us both good. Do you suppose you could help find it? Even in the future, milk has to be in an icebox, wouldn't you say?"

She seems to come to some decision. "All right. I . . . I guess things aren't going to change by themselves. Acting as if it's real for a while won't make it more so, do you think?" In fact she's starved, the milk sounds too good, even in her despair.

"No, I don't think so," he says seriously, relieved at her signs of sanity. "I think you're stuck here for four weeks. With, or preferably without, me," he adds in a cold tone.

She glances sharply at him. He catches the look and wonders if this is her first experience of being rejected by a male. But he says only, "We better be careful and not touch much till we know more."

She gets up, and they go out of the bedroom to find themselves in what seems to be a living room. Over in the corner it changes to kitcheny-looking things, including a large square yellow shape that ought to be a fridge. Beside it is a sink with a drainbasket full of eating-ware and glasses.

The refrigerator door has no sign of a handle.

Don squints along the shiny surface, sees nothing. Then he chuckles, stands back, and says loudly, "Icebox, open!"

Silently the door swings wide, light comes on inside.

There isn't too much inside, but Di spots what has to be a container of milk.

"How did you know to do that?" she asks him, pouring. "You want a big glass, right?"

"Right, thanks."

"How *did* you?"

He shrugs. "I don't know . . . we're in the future."

"A future," she says softly but firmly.

"I suppose in your version the butler brings us the stuff, with, say, caviar sandwiches?"

"Don't."

"Listen. You've put me through hell, Di. You can't expect me not to get a couple of laughs out of it."

"There's Henry's dish." She holds it up to rinse, but there's no faucet.

"Hot water, on," she tries. A stream gushes down. "Off! Off!" Hot water off!" It quits. "There's probably some means of controlling volume," Don offers. "We better be careful what we say around here or we'll have a slapstick comedy, everything turning itself on."

Just as she is pouring milk for the cat, who has rejoined them warily, a chime begins to sound.

"Oh, Christ, we should have finished reading your part of that letter. Is that a phone or a doorbell?" He is tracking the chime. "It comes from here . . . this box? But how do I answer it?" He twiddles something. "Hello? Hello?"

"Hello there," a voice responds from a wall grille. "This is Fred Tillum. Are you there, Don or Di?"

"Yeah, Don here, but I don't know how to use this thing."

"Just talk at it the way you're doing. It's supposed to be

convenient, but it makes for very little privacy." The voice is old, but unmistakably genial. "I hear by your voice that you've changed."

"We certainly have. We haven't finished reading the notes we left ourselves, but we got to you. Hello, Fred."

"Hel*lo* Don. I can't wait to see you as a teenager!"

"Better you look at Di. She's incredible . . . I'm incredible too, but the other way. I have acne. Or maybe leprosy."

Fred laughs. "Do you still want me to drop by? The bus gets there at three—I'm in Enclave 55."

"I most certainly do. As for Di—well, you'll see. She's so sick at the idea she married me and lives here that she can't really talk. She's made up her mind that this is an alternate future."

"*Di* isn't happy? But—"

"I know, I know. And frankly, the way she is now I'd just as soon have an alternative. Maybe you can help straighten us out."

"Oh, dear," Fred says slowly. "I don't know what I can do. But I'll try . . . until a little after three, then. Your gatehouse will call you. You tell them my name and to let me in."

"That's another thing we need to know about, Fred. What in hell has been going on?"

"Oh, it's a long, sad story. Till three, then. —And you better not go outside today. Do you have enough food? I could bring some."

"I think we're okay. Di's checking . . . yeah, we'll do. Thanks a lot, though. I can see we're really into a new world."

"You are indeed! Well, bye-bye."

"Bye. . . . Now, how do I hang up?" He twiddles at it again, and presently there's a click and a dial tone. "What'd I do?"

"And how do we call out?" asks Di.

"We read your letter. You did the practical stuff, remember?"

As they go back to get the letter, Di says musingly, "I read a story once . . . where a mouse did something differently, some tiny thing, I forget what. Changed its mind about eating some cheese. And it changed the future of the whole world."

Don sighs. "Are there mice in your dorm?"

"Some girls say so."

"Better start feeding'em."

"Oh, but it doesn't have to be mice. You don't get it—"

"I get it," he says somberly. "I read you one hundred percent."

They haven't quite finished reading when the phone chimes again. When Di produces the bedroom extension, a burly-sounding male asks them if they're expecting a visitor, and if so, what's the name?

"Uh, Fred. Frederick, I guess, uh—"

"Tillum," Don puts in. "From Enclave 55."

"Check. This is Captain Jordan. I understand you two changed today. We'll need temporary IDs on you as soon as possible."

"Yes, our notes say that. But we're so tired, and we aren't going out of the house. Could we come tomorrow?"

"You're not going out tonight? I have your word?"

"Oh, yes, Captain Jordan."

Don adds his assent.

"Then first thing in the morning will do. Can you be here at seven A.M.? Do you have tricycles?"

"The notes say yes."

"Then remember, you use them in the roadways, never on the walks. Is there a map of the enclave in your home?"

"I saw one back of the door," says Don. "But we haven't looked at it."

"Good. Look for Eastgate guard office . . . you'll notice Southgate is the main ingress and egress, Westgate is near the first-aid and hospital complex, and the shopping district. Northgate is sealed."

"Why is that, Captain?"

"Too many gangs of arsonists out there, and nobody was using it. So we voted to seal it off for the time being."

"I see. Thank you. We'll be there at seven if we don't get too lost."

"Good." He cuts off.

"What a nuisance," Di says.

"Yeah, in your rightful world, doubtless the cops come to *you*. —No, now, don't get mad. Can you ride a tricycle?"

"If I could at seventy-five, I can now."

"Me too. What's those?"

"The old IDs that were in the letter. Can you believe those photos were me—and you? Like a nightmare." She pulls hers back, but he stops her hand.

"Oh, now, you aren't so bad. Different stages of life. For the stage we were—are—in, you look pretty good."

She makes a revolted noise, thrusting them away.

A different chime sounds.

"Oh-oh. Which did you say is the front door?"

"Over there."

Fred turns out to be a dapper, white-goateed old man, chatty and relaxed. And to their surprise, black, dark black. Even Don had somehow surmised that the enclaves were white, or largely so.

"My, oh my!" Fred exclaims. "Let me look at you! No wonder people kept staring at me when I changed . . . youth, youth—who was it said that youth is wasted on the young? . . . But it's more than just youth, Di—you're a stunningly beautiful girl. Let me look. Oh, my." He advances on her. "May I?"

Before she can duck he has taken her face gently in both big hands. He turns it to the light, gazes for an instant and kisses her lightly on the forehead. "Oh, my! I hope I didn't shock you," he adds, smiling. And sits down, his knees cracking audibly, on an ottoman by the sofa.

"If you knew how many times I've done that," he tells them. "Come to think of it, we've even slept in the same bed. When you were sharing my place, we gave Di half the bed and Don and I took turns on the floor." He laughs merrily. "You don't remember a bit of all that, do you?"

"Not a shred."

"Yes, that's the way it is." Then looking more closely at Don, he says, "You look fine too. But I could recommend something for that, er, condition."

"Yeah—I find I bought myself a tube. I've already started using it."

"Fine, fine—It'll do its job by Wednesday."

"I can't wait."

"But meanwhile you have all the rest—straight, strong body, clear eyes, quickness, smarts. *No pain*. Di, you can see all right now, can't you?"

She nods.

"Oh, *good*. Really, you make me regret I took mine ten years ago. But I was overcautious—shorter black life expectancy, all the rest, I thought sixty-five was about all I could be fairly sure of . . . Well, I can enjoy yours vicariously. And now, most important, what can I do for you?"

Don says slowly, "I'm still digesting all the political-social stuff. I guess Di is too. . . . All the decent people locked up in enclaves with the Army guarding them, and the streets turned over to the mob . . . I guess I thought that if this country ever came to something like class apartheid, it'd be the other way around. . . ."

"Ah, yes. But you see, that would have been impossible. Unsocialized, unskilled people existed in gangs and old buildings everywhere in the cities. Especially the generations just growing up, who were babies in our youth. By ten they were in child gangs. All unskilled, illiterate, with no stake in what we thought of as *the* society, our society; no way of making a living by legal means. . . . Plus of course the Mafia types. You see it all started gradually, an enclave here and there, private guard armies. Industries and utilities had their enclaves when we were in school, remember?

"By the time the public schools virtually broke down, and mobs started attacking buses and trains—mass robberies and hostage-holding, for ransom, you know—and daily bombings—there was no other solution but to secure those who begged to be secured. Especially the old . . . remember, even in our youth there were parts of cities you couldn't walk or drive through in broad daylight? Parks. Oh, my."

"How did they choose?" Don asked curiously.

"Simple, at first. If you wanted it, and could pay, and had a job or some other means of support, and no police record, no drugs or alcohol problem, you were eligible for an enclave. Groups formed—for example, your 47 is all TCK workers and their families. Things are a bit more sophisticated now, there's some kind of psychological assessment . . . and not all what you call 'decent' people are in enclaves. There's some living out in loose groupings in the calmer parts of the cities, mostly the young and adventurous. A few ideological saints, too. People who try to help with the kids. No one knows how long they last." He shook his gray head sadly. "Cruel, cruel . . ."

"How do you mean, cruel?" Di asks. "Criminals and bombers. . . . " She shudders.

"Cruel as nature. You see, the brutal fact is, we've locked them out to starve. Or prey on each other, cannibalism—we know that's started. A city produces no food, and the intake and allocation is all in our hands. We've set up certain basic food-distributing points, but it's a question how many of the really needy can get to them—or get home safely. Old people, the sick, young mothers with babies. They're out there too. Would you believe these women are still pouring out babies? Babies who, if they live, won't have a chance of getting educated, will have no skills, no means—let alone desire—to fit into a peaceful middle-class life. We're allowing a monster to develop."

"God," said Don. "What's ahead?"

"Maybe worse. The local population seems to be diminishing, especially in young males. For a while people thought that was great, that they'd just killed themselves off. But now reports are coming in. It's the same everywhere—armed gangs are spreading out from the cities into the countryside, attacking any isolated settlements or farms. Basically for food. They have some women with them.

"We foresee self-perpetuating nomadic bands of raiders, who

descend on a place, suck it dry, and then move on. Naturally the country is arming too, but they can't really defend themselves without turning into fortresses. And the farms—all agricultural fields and herds are indefensible and vulnerable. The effort to grow food for the cities is going to need a whole new army to defend it. In my more pessimistic moments I foresee war without end. The barbarians in the outskirts of Rome . . . and drugs, by the way, are woven right into their lives. Our former civilization is a frail network infested and riddled through with mobile savages, predatory barbarians with their own values and culture. Sheer anarchy doesn't last long, you know. Strong men arise . . .

"We're rather like the inhabitants of ancient Britain, who lived in daily fear of the onslaught of Vikings, Danes, Goths. Life becomes a question of just holding on; nothing new, no advancement is possible. —Well! I do seem to be speechifying. It's so long since I've had a chance to speak to a new audience! My apologies . . .

"By the way, did your letter tell you this enclave has been attacked in force three times?"

"No! What happened?"

"It was in the days when the National Guard was still in charge. Fifteen years or so back. They breached the walls with regular siege-engines, and just poured in, looting and raping and killing and burning. Somehow they were driven back or killed. After the third one—it was happening elsewhere—the regular Army took over. The President is still Commander in Chief, but last election a general, General Packwood, came in. On the theme of protecting civilization. . . . Needless to say, our foreign policy is in shambles. No one really knows what's going on, but what we hear from abroad would indicate that they have their troubles. The military is in power in Mexico, too, and in a great many other states. Canada'll be next."

"Je-sus," says Don softly. Di just stares at Fred as if she couldn't believe. Don thinks of something.

"How about the upper-upper class?" he asked. "The ultra-rich?"

"Same thing—enclaves for some. But I hear a great many of them have private islands where they are virtual rulers, with their own private armies and air defense. Of course, these have a food problem too. But they manage; they buy up boatloads of fresh produce from out-of-the-way places—and I guess they eat a lot of fish. Little by little, though, money is losing its value, and a sort of barter economy is setting in . . . of course, it's already set in, outside. . . . May I?"

Expertly, he causes the sink to deliver a glass of water.

Di seems to come to herself momentarily. "May we—may I—get you something? Cupboard A, open!" Despite herself she grins with satisfaction as an upper door swings wide. Inside are bottles. She takes one down.

"Some wine, Mr. Tillum? This seems to be a Riesling. Let's all have some."

"Great idea." Don plucks three wineglasses out of the drainer. "Do we have some nuts or crackers, Di?"

She has already produced a can of nuts.

"Oh, no, no," Fred protests. "The wine is just fine. But I happen to know that those nuts were one of Di's treasures." He laughs.

"To luck," says Don, raising his glass. "I gather we'll need it."

"To luck." They drink. The Riesling is quite good.

Fred sighs. "And it's a wound I can't conceal," he says, "that so many of these savages are black. Ironical, that three-quarters, seven-eighths white genes—even fifteen-sixteenths—makes a black person. Africa would disown us!" He chuckles. "Not their fault, of course; the earlier generations of whites who turned them loose illiterate and property-less didn't have the foresight or the will to cope. It could have been done then for a fraction of any state's welfare budget today—or rather, yesterday; welfare is gone now of course. Blacks *wanted* to embrace your culture then.

"And in our youth it still would have been possible, by a massive, intensive effort with the kids. But raising one child is a whole-time job—I mean education and all. And it has to start with the mother. No good, after you have a child brain-damaged by malnutrition or drugs in the womb. Re-raising a child takes one-on-one work. Who would do it? The white kids were already problem enough. . . ." He gives a short laugh with a bitterness they hadn't heard before. "Well—enough of that. Oh—" He reaches for an inside pocket.

"Look!" They see three pink pasteboards.

"Tickets for the big Kennedy Center bash! You left them with me. It's a gala, a smorgasbord, with the best singers and ballet of today."

"Fantastic," says Don. "Just great. Hey, we had sense!"

"Lovely," says Di abstractedly. "But . . . what on earth—"

"What do you *wear*, huh?" laughs Don.

"Not to worry," Fred assures her. "It's dress-as-dress-can. There'll be people there in work clothes." Di shudders faintly. "However," Fred goes on seriously, "Di told me to tell you she *has* a dress she got specially for you. It seems it suits both ages . . . such technicologies!"

"I'd love it," she says resolutely.

"Now," Fred goes on, "you might prefer to go by yourselves. You won't offend me, believe it. The only thing is, I can introduce you to many of your friends. I tell you what—I'll take a different bus, and you can join me in the lobby if you care to. For as long as you like or don't like. I have to come over here on the three o'clock anyway, to take one of your buses; 47 voted to run transport to it but 55 voted No. All they'll run convoys for is sports, pox on them. I doubt I'd have joined 55, except that they jumped me up the waiting list because they needed a gynecologist. That's what I am. So I moved in fast. That's when you stayed with me, before my poor housemate had three friends sharing the sofa with him."

"Fred," says Don, "we go all together and no more idiocy. If Di doesn't want it she can go by herself or stay home."

Di's training comes to her rescue. "Oh, my goodness, of course not. We'll all go together, Fred!" She smiles ravishingly.

Fred gets up creakily, beaming down at them. "That's settled then. You will be my guests at dinner there beforehand; the buses leave here in daylight, around five-thirty. I have a friend to see over here, and then I'll be with you about five. Oh—the date is a week away; that's good for you because you'll find you're very tired the first day or so. The change takes energy. . . . Now, is there really nothing I can do for you?"

"I was wondering," Don says, "do you think it'd be all right for us to look out the front door—and the back too—under your supervision? The letter said not to *go* out till we get our IDs, but I wanted to check for a newspaper. Seems we get one delivered."

"Sure thing. It'll be at the back, the carriers come the alley route, but you'll want to see the front view first."

"Oh, great." They troop to the front door. "Be my guests," says Fred, and opens it wide.

Outside is summer sunshine on a green, tree-filled suburban community. They see their house is one of a block of pink-tinted masonry row-houses. Across the wide sidewalks and roadway is a similar row, tinted green. The configurations of the houses and windows are subtly different from those of their day, as if there is some new construction method. Their little front yard is unfenced, like all the others. But it has a fine great maple tree, against which is leaning a tricycle.

"The gate office gave me that," Fred points. "They keep a supply for guests."

Three people on tricycles are humming down the roadway from the left. The boxes in the rear of the cycles seem loaded down.

"They've been shopping at Westgate," Fred says. The cyclists, two older women and an old man, wave at them. They wave back. A large golden retriever gallops up behind, tail wagging.

"Looks like an easy way to go," Don says.

"It is. Well, now for the back and your paper—and I must hop to catch my bus. There's a lady I want to look in on before I go. She had a difficult time of it. Twins," he explains, seeing their puzzled faces.

He leads the way back through the house. "Yes, people come

over to the 55 clinic to see me sometimes," he tells them. "No reason, though, Ted Enkerly here is a fine doctor. . . . Maybe they think I have a trace of witch-doctor magic." He makes a witch-doctor face and waves his hands, looking for an instant quite frightening.

The back door gives onto a short flight of steps down into a pretty little walled garden with a shed against one wall. The newspaper is lying on the bottom step. As Don retrieves it, Fred tells Di, "Your cycles are in the shed, I believe. You'll find there's a tunnel between the buildings on that side, if you want to go out the front. Or you can just go out the alley, everyone does. See, there's the door."

"It's unbolted," says Don, restraining his desire to look at the news.

"That's right," Fred says. "I guess you'll take a day or two to get used to unlocked doors. One of the beauties of enclave life."

"That's lovely," says Di, looking around a trifle nervously.

"And now farewell!" Fred hurries back to the front door and lets himself out before they can get their goodbyes in order. But he turns back to give them a card.

"My number. Call any time you need anything, day or night. I mean it. Now, duck back in as soon as I'm gone, right?"

"Right . . . oh, thank you so much," they say together, watching him wheel his machine into the roadway and hop nimbly on.

"Bye-bye!"

"Bye!"

"It's nice out there," says Don wistfully as they go obediently back inside. "I'll be glad when we get those ID-whatevers."

"Do you know, I think I saw peas ready, in that garden," Di tells him. "And baby carrots."

"My god, you actually know something use—I mean, something about gardening?" Don says with wonder. "And does that mean you know how to *cook* them?"

"A few things only," Di says firmly. "And I do *not* know how to run a dishwasher."

"Of course, of course," Don says agreeably. He opens the newspaper.

"I'm going to look in the closets," says Di.

"Checking for that dress, eh?" He grins. "My god—this little thing is called the *Washington Post!*"

The dress turns out quite acceptable, a gauzy, glittery kaftan, with a matching muff for a purse. The slippers are too wide, but stay on. And she sees Don has a dinner jacket, hanging in a plastic bag. A black tie, slightly greenish, hangs over the crossbar. The rest of their wardrobes seem to be an assortment of tee shirts and slacks, in nice colors. There are a couple of pairs of rubber thongs, with a note on top:

"Di dear—it occurs to me my feet may have changed a lot. I have bad arthritis. But you can always use these . . . P.S. Look in your bedside table drawer if you haven't already—preferably when you're alone. And destroy this note."

She backs out of the closet with it crumpled in her hand, and goes into the kitchen where the garbage is supposed to be.

Don has fallen fast asleep into his paper, looking most uncomfortable on the sofa-end. She herself feels suddenly very tired indeed.

But she disposes of the note, and goes back to the bedroom, to the bed-table. The drawer sticks just a little, and then pops open, revealing an envelope lying on top, addressed to herself. As she picks it up wonderingly her eye is caught by something shiny below. She pushes aside a couple of hankies and sees what it is—a handgun. Somewhat smaller than a forty-five, she judges, staring mesmerized. It has a very short barrel. She knows enough to see that it's a revolver, and the visible chambers are loaded. H'mmm! Does Don have one too?

She closes the drawer, and, holding the letter, goes around to his side to look. In his drawer she finds no gun, but a large black spray-device on a canister, marked with unknown chemical designations and the words, *U.S. Army*. She closes the drawer.

As she sits down to read her letter, a stray humanitarian

impulse strikes her. Don is going to be miserably stiff if he stays in there. She pockets the letter, gets up to go to him.

"Wake up, Don. You'll get stiff, sleeping like that. Come and lie down properly. I'm going to."

He looks so helpless, and then smiles so gratefully . . . Panicked, she hardens her heart. "But don't get any ideas."

He barely wakens as she leads him back to the bed and pushes him down. Even his effort to kick off his slippers fails. "Thanks," he mumbles, nosing into the pillow. She leaves him so and goes back to her side, still wearing the spartan little robe, and lies down as near the edge as possible. She waits till she's sure Don is dead to the world, then pulls out the letter and opens it. It's all in her handwriting:

> To myself—as I was:
>
> I know you, girl. I know what I was like at nineteen. If I hadn't been so good-looking others would have seen it too—a selfish, rich, greedy, ambitious, cold-hearted dope. You've set your sights on what you want from life, and you believe you have the equipment to make it.
>
> So what went wrong? What really happened? If you want to know, read on. Don made me leave that gap in our account of the time before we came together. He thought you couldn't take it. I think you can—and you'd better. You won't remember it of course. But maybe something will sink in and change you a little.
>
> You got back just before the prom. (God, the word seems like something from another world!) And also that same week came news that you were accepted at Yale. You were on air. Glowing. At the prom you must have been a dazzling creature.
>
> Three men—boys, I mean—proposed marriage to you that night.
>
> I took seriously only two of them: Wally Blair, heir to the Blair fortune, and Bill Armitage . . . William

Armitage III. Wally was sweet and cheery and roly-poly and loved me to distraction. But he was only about half as rich as Bill, who was tall and dark and good-looking if you granted that his eyes were a trifle close together; and he had beautiful formal manners. He already had millions in his own right, and he was heir to a big chunk of the old Hunt empire. He kept a low profile; I only by accident found out that he came and went from school in his mother's private seven-sixty-seven. And he was going to Yale, too.

I didn't hesitate long. You won't.

The general idea, pending full family conferences, was that we'd get married around Labor Day. That was to be low-profile, too. I was just discovering how the very rich lived, their fear of display attracting kidnappers.

He seemed really dazzled by me. And he was sexually hungry. (The news that I was a virgin went down very well with all the Armitages.) It didn't seem appropriate for me to hold out for the remaining weeks. I stayed later and later at his place, and finally moved in. (God, I remember frantically buying new nighties and underthings, hoping he'd approve!)

Then came a few strange weeks. Bill showed a kind of cold, crazy rapture—which as the days passed became more cold and less rapturous. But always polite. I know now what the trouble was—I was an abominable sex partner, a lump, with the idea that just flopping limply back and accepting him was all there was to it. Orgasm? No way. I masturbated afterward. Maybe he did too. He was almost totally inexperienced, and, I know now, shy. *And* full of his own superiority. Probably a different, older woman could have helped him. Not Miss Prom Queen.

And then, about a month after I moved in, you'll get the telegram. I had been only vaguely aware of the Big Crash—remember our father was—is—heavily into stocks? Anyway, it all went blooie at once, total wipe-out, not a cent left. And Father shot Mother and himself dead. Yea.

I had to go back to St. Louis for a week, and Bill went home while I was away. To consult The Family, I now know.

So the night I returned he had this lovely present waiting for me—a complete set of Mark Cross luggage. And he took me out to eat at Miro's. I was still shaken, and he was very tense. We should have been glad to be together again, but it was not a successful meal. At one point Debra Barringer, a dumpy, freckled, undistinguished girl stopped by our table and treated us to two separate and quite different looks of pity. This woman's father had gone short through the whole collapsing stock market, and could leave his daughter millions for every freckle. I thought she was inexpertly trying to offer condolences on my loss, but she knew what was ahead for me, and I had no inkling.

When we got home, he said to me, "I'm sure you realize we must have a talk, now things have changed."

"Changed?" I was groping around, poor innocent, I was afraid the scandal of my parents' deaths was what he meant.

"In the present circumstances, don't you agree that it would be very inappropriate—unwise—for us to marry?"

What could I say? What will you say? I tried to kid myself he meant marry *just then* or something. No. He meant the marriage was off, off, off. Still not believing my ears, I muttered something and had the sense to keep still. Because, you see, what he was talking about was simply the *money*. God knows, Daddy's few millions wouldn't even pay their aviation fuel bills. But he *had* them. The difference between a few millions and zero is the difference between being marginally eligible and not. I might as well have caught AIDS, or dropped off the planet. He seemed pleased that I acted so sensibly—I was merely stunned—and he certainly expected me to agree with him. Rules of the game. In fact, he was feeling quite sorry for himself to have his fiancée snatched away.

He said, hoping for my approval, "Since you'll be moving, I thought the luggage might come in handy. It will, won't it?"

I assured him it would. He was much relieved. The correct gift for the girl you're throwing out.

"And it occurred to me that you might be a bit, er, financially, er, embarrassed for a time, so I took the liberty of booking a room for you at the Martha Washington, for a month. I mean" —he actually blushed— "it's all paid for. You aren't offended?"

You will assure him you aren't. The Martha is, or was, an old middle-class women's hotel, full of broke young models and senile ladies.

"Ahhh," he sighed. "Thank you!"

And then he wanted to make love.

To say goodbye, see? I let him. And in the morning I packed up all my new clothes in the beautiful luggage and he called a cab. He seemed anxious to forget or omit nothing. At the very last moment he stuffed five twenty-dollar bills in my purse, apologizing like mad, so I'd have cash. (Later on how I resented having to pay that huge cab fare—I was hungry!)

My first and just about my only thought was modeling. By the grace of fate the fall showing season was on and they needed people; they gave me work and some training. And they actually kept me on through the Christmas rush. But then . . .

On the evening they lay you off, you'll drop into a singles bar with the intention of getting drunk for the first time in your life. We never drink to speak of.

Over in one of the booths will be a beautifully dressed,

nice-looking older man, watching everything. I didn't really notice him until the waiter brought me his invitation. I joined him, and before I could stop myself I was telling him about being fired and penniless. It wasn't an unusual tale those days.

He was all sympathy, and his voice was very nice, with only a hint of Mediterranean accent. His name was Nikko.

It wasn't a week before I moved in with Nikko. His love-making was a revelation, literally a revelation to me. He brought out feelings I'd never dreamed of. In a short time he had me hypnotized, totally sexualized.

That was his business, you see. He was training me. Nikko was a high-class pimp.

I thought I was in heaven, when I wasn't too woozy to think.

And then came the night when we visited one of his "dear old friends" in his hotel room. I think Nikko put something in my drink. At any rate, he suddenly excused himself, leaving me there. He just said, "Be nice to Ted for my sake, carissima, will you? I'll be waiting for you."

For a few more weeks he kept up the act, and then one night at his place, when the phone rang, he said to me: "Carissima, I feel very unwell. You can go over by yourself, can't you? You know the game."

Well, I protested, but he had me. One night when I objected too hard he turned like a flash and gave me a black eye. And shortly he, I guess, sold me to another pimp. He had a new girl to train, see?

My dear, even now I can't go into the next months or years . . . Skip to the stage when I was actually whoring, working the streets, soliciting passersby—with a great case of clap. And my looks were against me here, they didn't appeal so much to street trade. I wasn't a success, though I tried—you'll try—because the man I was working for then was tough about money. You had to make at least so much or you got no meals.

Of course I tried to run away. But where was I to go? And when I did try, this guy caught me. He beat me over the kidneys with his belt.

Somewhere along the line I got turned on to cocaine, but I was too broke to get really addicted.

All I was really thinking about was how to kill myself. You'll find even that isn't easy with absolutely no money. Or privacy. Then for quite long spells I'd think I was simply in a long nightmare. And then I'd come to and the suicide planning would start again. I didn't have a friend, only the few callous-jealous acquaintances hookers have. No, that's wrong, a few hookers have really good friends among the others, who try to look out for them. Not me.

Di lays down the letter, shivering. This woman, her older self, is telling her what will happen to her, what has already happened to the writer. From Prom Queen to street hooker, diseased and suicidal. It's too horrible to believe—and yet she has to believe it. "*No*," she gasps soundlessly, afraid of waking Don. "No, it *can't*—I can't—" This *has* to be some hideous alternate future.

And yet it is so solid, this is a real voice, her own voice, speaking to her across the years. What can she do? Somehow she will have to change things, to do something which will make *this* future impossible. But how, if she will forget all about it? Soon, very soon, she will be back in real time, she'll go glowing to that Prom and enchant Bill Armitage—and the whole horrible scenario will unroll from there . . . in a mere matter of months, she'll be determined to kill herself, that's how bad it will be.

No; whatever she does, she must do it now, while she still remembers the truth . . . The image of that gun in the drawer comes to her mind's eye. Her older self had placed it there. *Why?*

She shakes herself, and picks the letter up.

At this moment comes a weight on her knee; she looks down and sees Henry Cat looking up at her.

"Oh, Puss, Puss," she whispers despairingly. The cat jumps up beside her, settles itself fastidiously, and begins to purr. She gives a tiny sob, and with one hand stroking Henry, she begins again to read:

Are you still reading, Di? *You better*. Get a clear picture. For about three years, that will be you, my poor little fool. That is what happens to fools. See it, feel it in your body and soul. Sick, helpless, starving, utterly degraded. I think it was the price of overweening ambition, my dear. To have neglected reality, to have cast your fate in with a merciless man who happened to be rich. William Armitage III and his gift of luggage. —If there was a word for spitting in disgust I'd write it here.

And you had no skills. You had learned nothing. You *had* nothing but your body. That's what I mean by "fool." Think on it.

Well. And then came the night of nights. I was out in the rain—I remember that rain because I'd put heavy makeup on to cover two black eyes and some other bruises. A figure came down the rainy street, I moved to intercept him, without looking or caring. I never looked at the johns.

And the next thing I knew this voice was saying, "Diane! Diane Fortnum! Oh, my god—" Someone had recognized me, my deepest horror.

I tried to run. But I was staggering, and I fell. The man picked me up. I don't remember much after that except being in a cab, and then being half-pushed, half-carried up some stairs, somewhere.

Di, it was Don Pascal who had picked me off the streets and carried me to his home.

He fed me, and cleaned me up, and got me cured of clap—god be thanked I didn't have AIDS—and he got me into a private detox ward for a week or so.

I was like in a daze. I'd scream at night, for hours, I guess. And he'd be there, stroking me and sort of singing to me. "Di, my little Di," he'd croon. "It's all right now honey, it's all right . . ."

That was what we were concealing when we wrote about starting to live together.

I couldn't believe it. One minute I'd be down on my knees thanking him, and then would come this weird return of my schoolgirl values, and I'd see him as Don the nerd, and curse. Why couldn't it have been somebody else, anybody else, who rescued me? I raved against him, as though he'd kidnapped me away from some party.

And then as sanity returned I'd see him differently again, as the strong, sweet, highly intelligent man he is. (He was a doctor, then, too.) And that's the way I've seen him from then on, because that's what he is. The one great fact of my life is that he loves me, and I love him, more than I can say or you can understand, and we're together.

Only a man like that would have rescued you, would have known what to do or how to do it.

I think for a while he had some idea of looking up Bill Armitage and damaging him severely. I persuaded him to forget that. I told him the only bit of wisdom I'd gleaned from the entire affair—that Bill was acting perfectly reasonably from his own subhuman lights. Scott Fitzgerald said it—"the rich are different." And the very rich are differenter still. They may become infatuated with a poor girl, but that's as far as it goes. Marriage is business. And *money marries money*. I had simply removed myself from the ranks of the marriageable, and he expected me to know it as a matter of course.

All right, Di. Now you know the unbreakable strength of the bond that will tie you to Don, and fate willing, him to you. He's like the Chinese; they believe that if you save someone's life you're responsible for them forever. And, Di, it's *love*, which you have never known. By the way, it seems he had had this feeling about me, which he never expressed, from way back in school.

It hurts me terribly to know that you have all this to go through. But if there's any way of remembering it, let alone changing it, no one has ever found out how.

My poor young creature, your older self sends her love to you from safe beyond the dreadful seas that you must cross.

Diane Pascal, age 75.

And below, in a larger, emotional hand:

Di—For god's sake try to make him happy now. Try to love him. He is a wonderful man, and you owe him your life, your joy, everything.

As she puts the letter back in the drawer she realizes Don has waked.

"What's that?"

"Oh—just some notes I wrote to myself. Woman stuff."

"Um." But he lets it pass. "Are you all right?"

"Why, sure . . . Henry's here."

"Well you better throw him out and get some sleep or you'll be dead in the morning. Can't you sleep, honey?"

"Don't call me that," she mutters between clenched teeth, so low he doesn't hear. She stretches out, and carefully deposits Henry on the floor. She finds she is very tired. Don's breathing changes; he's already back asleep. But just as she's drifting off too, she feels a movement. Don's arm, as if from long habit, is gently touching her arm. Curious, she lets him. His hand finds her hand, and clasps it with such a feeling of warmth and love that her resolve melts. Is this how their older selves slept? She clasps the hand back lightly, he gives a sigh, and they go to sleep so.

Her last thought is of the gun in the drawer. She doesn't mention it to Don, then or ever.

The days pass dreamlike. They go for their IDs, and watch a tech sergeant carefully compare the new thumbprints with the old. They match. And they learn to ride their tricycles. Strangers wave at them in passing; they wave back, but don't dare stop.

The Westgate market malls turn out to be well-stocked and cheerful. When Di and Don go in to get some pants that fit better, they find what they need—and are also shown a thick catalog full of interesting and exotic items they can order. Apparently shops in all the enclaves are like this—a small basic inventory plus a big special-order book. Di has discovered no shorts in the home, and after an inquiry to Fred about conventions, she picks out a playsuit that fits her with the belt cinched in. Apparently her older self has given up shorts; too many varicose veins, she guesses grimly.

They pay with an Enclave 47 credit card from the letter. The note attached said simply, "Try not to go over $300, dears."

All the store people stare at them openly, smiling and saying things like, "Enjoy yourselves, kids."

Enjoy themselves?

Well, the Kennedy gala turns out to be quite fun, a medley from before their own times to the present. Some of the new music is a bit bewildering, but there are two stunning new sopranos who sing a kind of mock-battle of high notes, and a boy dancer from Enclave 72 who would be great in any age. The Kennedy itself is changed and rebuilt; arsonists had got at it in the early days.

And there is talk. Fred introduces them to an assortment of people, young and old, who are "their friends." "I knew you by Di's dress," a Linda Somebody laughs. "But Di never looked like *this* in it. Wait till I tell her. Oh, wait, we *must* have holos. Freddie, have you taken any?" When Fred admits he hasn't she scolds him, and before they know it they have a date to have their pictures taken. More people join in, and it soon becomes a party.

"Must have something worthy of wearing that gown for. But we'll bring the food! You two just get yourselves ready and we'll do all the rest. Marly, can I blackmail you into making one of those fantastic banana puddings?" Marly assents—others volunteer various dishes—and a red-haired man winds the whole thing up by promising to bring a lambchop for Henry Cat.

"How has Henry taken it?" someone asks.

"Well, he's condescended to sit on our laps now," Don tells them, "but I'd say he misses his rightful owners. He keeps sniffing us in this puzzled way."

Others are talking sports. It seems an eighty-year-old former world tennis champion is just about to have his young weeks, and he's challenged the current Wimbledon winner. He had made the first switch when he was in peak of condition, and trained hard.

"It's going to be one great game," the redhead says. "And it'll settle for good all those arguments about could Boris have beaten him in his prime. Now we'll see!"

"Did you hear the Cleveland Opera company is going to switch all together, and put on operas fifty years from now—with their voices right at perfection?"

"Oh, my—but maybe they won't *have* opera in fifty years."

"Then they'll show them how."

Everyone laughs, but it seems to Don and Di that a momentary pall comes over the bright gathering . . . fifty years from now; who knows?

"Oh, look, Di—there's your dress!" A woman she knows only as Clara is pointing to one side, where a gilded stairway curves upward to the boxes. Isolated for a moment, the stranger coming down pauses and turns back to speak to the man behind her, giving them all a good view. She is indeed wearing what looks superficially like Di's gown—a swirl of twinkling blue.

But Di can plainly see that it is *not* the same—the fabric flows and drapes from expert cutting and daring fitting, the decoration is not mere sequins, but an intricate embroidery of mingled pearls and tiny beads. The cloth itself is a more subtle shade and texture. It might as well be labelled "designer's original"; beside it her own finery is clearly off the racks.

"See?" says Clara, satisfied. "I *told* you that was a good buy. There it is on the Enclave 19 crowd!"

"Y-yes," Di manages to say. Rage is filling her throat. She wants to rip off the wretched cheap copy and flee out of there. Because she *knows* the woman wearing that dress: it's Debra Barringer, the first person who will let her know that she no longer matters.

The man she is laughing with is Wally Blair. Panicked lest she see more and worse, Di turns her back and hides behind Fred, and the five-minute curtain call chimes. There is a flurry of last-minute sherbets, and they are heading for their seats.

"Don't forget—Thursday at six!" Linda calls to them.

"Righto—I'll put a bowtie on Henry," Don laughs.

The beautiful arias and the dance finale change Di's mood. But as they come out into the summer night, they find Bus 47 temporarily blocked by a bigger, shinier, newer bus with "19—Watergate" on its side. Glancing in, Di sees that the seats are different, too—more like lounges.

Di seizes Don's arm to hurry him on to their own 47—but to her surprise he releases himself and hands her over to Fred, saying "Excuse me, honey, I've just seen something" —dashes back and leaps up the steps into 19, among the incoming crowd.

"Lift your feet," they hear him say loudly to the fancy-uniformed driver. "Lift up, I say—hurry! There's a snake under there I want. Out of the way, please!"

At these words, the driver not only lifts his feet but climbs onto his seat, peering fearfully at the floor. "A snake! A snake!" the passengers are exclaiming, trying to go both forward and back together.

"That's right, make room! Don't scare it!" And Don dives down among the driving pedals and gears. There's a flurry of action punctuated by Don's calls for more room, which the passengers are frantically trying to give him.

He emerges with a black-and-orange snake-body thrashing

around his arm. He seems to have hold of it just behind the head; it is opening its jaws and darting its tongue about.

"Does anybody have a spare pocketbook?" Don calls out. No one replies, they are all too busy getting as far away from him as possible. Don shakes his head, trying to soothe the snake by stroking it with his free hand, and climbs out of the bus to return to 47 with his prize.

"You're not bringing that thing in here!" Linda tells him forcefully, barring the entrance.

"Oh yes, I must. —Didn't you see in the *Post* that this specimen had escaped from the zoo? They'll come right over and get it as soon as I call them."

"What is it?" Linda's husband asks dubiously.

"A young yellow-backed python. It's not poisonous."

"How did it get in that bus?"

"Lord knows. Probably came down Rock Creek. The paper said someone left two cages open. The zoo now only has one left, so this is very valuable to them." He raises his voice. "Can anybody spare a pocketbook to keep it in for the trip home? It won't chew up anything."

Clara speaks up. "If George can put my stuff in his pockets you can borrow mine."

"Good, good." He goes back to where George is stuffing his pockets, complaining, "What in god's name do you carry all this stuff for, Clare?"

After a bit of wrestling Don gets the frightened python off his arm and into the bag. "I'll have to hold this shut. Di, honey, where are you? A million thanks, Clara—if there's a reward I'll see you get it."

"Oh, super!"

"Good luck. Their notion of a reward may be a pair of free tickets, you know."

"Oh well, everybody's broke these days," Linda says cheerfully.

"Not *everybody*," Di whispers bitterly to herself. The image of the true form of "her" dress on the golden stair still chafes her.

The buses pull out, attended by the Army vehicles of their guards. Is it Di's imagination, or is Bus 19 more heavily guarded?

She is twisting about, trying to count, when she glimpses a black football-shaped object flying out of the crowd. It hits the ground just in front of 47 and disappears under it.

She is too surprised to react. But others have seen it too—there is shouting, the crackle of intercoms, people running. With a tremendous jolt their bus accelerates faster than any normal bus could. The driver shouts "Made it!" and the rear window is suddenly full of an explosion. Di sees a squad of security men racing up the side alley, firing as they go.

"Somebody just tried to bomb us!" the man called George exclaims excitedly. "That was close, you know? If our driver had tried to slow down or avoid it, we'd be evaporating right now!"

"And the squad cars let us through," Clara puts in. "Oh, Mr. Driver, well done!"

"Well done! Well done!" others echo.

"So they're still at it," George says disgustedly, settling back in his seat.

"Yeah. Just the other day, did I tell you—" another man puts in, and the talk changes to close calls others have had.

Clara turns around to Di and asks in a whisper, "Did you tell Don? —I mean, about the Westgate sniper?" she adds, seeing Di's blank look. "Oh that's right; you don't remember a thing. Well, you had a close one, believe me!"

They all seem to take it so casually, Di thinks. Even sort of boasting. She is reminded of old biddies comparing notes on their latest horrifying operation. And, as she keeps finding out, all of these people do have some pretty dreadful tales to tell. The survivors, that's what they are. And me too, I suppose, if I could remember. Me and Don.

When they reach Southgate, and disembark to tricycle home, Di finds she is really weary. Even tucking up her gown is an effort. Don hears her sigh, and glances over, smiling. "Me too. Oh for beddy-bye. Hey, do you know any of those old songs we used to sing on hikes? I've got to do something or I'll fall asleep pedalling."

They waver homewards to a chorus of "Oh, we're ninety-nine miles from home, we're ninety-eight miles from home—" Other couples join in softly, and the summer night street is filled with fading song and laughter as each party goes its different way. They barely remember to wave at Fred, who is still in the bus that will carry him on to 55.

The time passes dreamily, here in this impossible future. The next day they take a picnic lunch to the zoo—a convoy runs there every week—and eat on the lawn by the great new aviary. A large number of animals have been saved from the hungry mobs; there are fascinating stories put up by each cage of how the zoo people had escaped bearing tiger cubs, or wildebeeste babies, or a great ape dressed in human clothes. Now these refugees are mature and bearing young of their own, and the zoo is nearly back to its old self. There is also a horrifying photo of a gang hacking an elephant to death, knee-deep in flesh and gore.

They become friends with the Southgate military detachment, and Captain McEvoy takes them up in the watchtower where the ravaged city outside the walls can be seen. The streets are nearly empty in daylight, and there is, of course, no normal traffic; gasoline supply systems have long since broken down.

Other enclaves are visible in the distance; the air is clearer than it used to be. For the first time they realize how thick their walls are: there is a roadway on top, protected by battlements and firing ports, and another vehicle track halfway down, for quick access of troops to any part of the wall. The structure must be over sixty feet high and nearly twice that in width at the base.

"It's like a medieval castle," says Di. "Where's the boiling oil?"

"We have worse than that, unfortunately." He points to a hose system coiled to one side. "That stuff is lethal, and too heavy for wind to disperse." Di shivers.

Out in the emptiness of Florida Avenue a rusty armored

vehicle is progressing at walking pace, accompanied by a loose gang of rifle-carrying men.

"That belongs to some local gang-leader," McEvoy tells them. They watch as the men systematically search every habitable-looking building along the way. They emerge from one with three captives—a screaming girl and two battered youths.

"Oh, Captain McEvoy—can't you *do* something?"

He shakes his head sadly. "We used to try, now and then. But we just lost some good men. And another gang who'd been hanging around waiting for a chance damn near broke into the enclave while we were out . . . And when we did rescue a few people they turned out to be a problem—they were part of a ghoul gang, they had human carcasses hung up to smoke in their den. No enclave would take them . . . Frankly, anybody who's survived this long out there you don't really want." He grimaces. "I know it sounds heartless . . ."

Di and Don sigh wordlessly, watching the gang of raiders move slowly away. *I was one of those out there*, Di thinks.

"I know, I know," McEvoy says. "You think that probably this or that lot being roughed up may be all right—that you have a duty to try, right? Well, I've tried. But my duty is to keep this enclave secure, and that's job enough for my men. Just seeing that the food-distribution goes okay. Would you believe they set traps for us? Last month they set a young boy on fire, to lure my men off."

Don and Di shiver, climbing down the narrow steel steps; it's dark because of the bulletproof shielding on the tower, only pierced here and there with firing breaks.

"I guess all we can do is keep our minds off it," Don says. "And be thankful for men like Captain McEvoy."

"So horrible," Di murmurs.

"Yeah. Think about the party tonight."

It is an unfortunate remark; he is surprised by the peculiar grunt she gives, as though she'd been poked in the diaphragm.

But Don says nothing more, and they emerge into cheerful summer sunlight.

As they pedal home, she's still silent. He puts it down to McEvoy's account. And of course it is that, partly. But only partly; the truth is she is still galled by the vision of the bright, exclusive world on the golden stairs, the world from which she is forever excluded—the world which was briefly open to her, the life she so nearly made. Oh, had she braved the invisible barrier, gone up and spoken, say, to Wally, she would have been temporarily received with smiles and friendly greetings. Temporarily—until the lamentable facts of her situation were made clear. Then would come, not rudeness, but an imperceptible pulling-away—the invitation omitted, the overtures unreturned. The silence of doors closing. The unspoken hopes that she wouldn't presume, wouldn't make a nuisance of herself. Would realize that any basis for friendship no longer existed. It had gone where her father's millions went. Leaving her to be happy—they benevolently hoped—on another plane of life. The plane of fairly good copies of the right dress, of the simple joys of returning a snake (ugh) to the zoo, or overfeeding an unregistered, mixed-breed black street-cat. Of simple concerns other than the serious question of whether it isn't just a *bit*, you know, something, to hang the El Greco sketch in the guest bathroom. Or whether the salmon-fishing in Norway has gone downhill. Where, above all, the concern as to whether one can *afford* something simply doesn't exist . . .

Money, of course, is it. If *her* father had gone short in the market, she would be on that golden stair, greeted with genuine gladness. She would not be cycling to her two-bedroom rowhouse with a formerly very unpopular man whose acne is just healing up, would not be worrying whether her Sears Roebuck sofa pillows need cleaning—for a party of pleasant nobodies. But it is deeper than that. The sofa pillows are actually quite attractive; she doesn't really crave to go ballooning in Patagonia or sit in the owners' boxes in Louisville. No. What stabs her in the gut is the feeling—more than the feeling, the absolute knowledge that she is *excluded*. That there are people she can never meet, let alone have as friends; places into which she can never enter. *Excluded*. Condemned to copies, to second-best. Not regarded as fully human. *Not wanted*, by people no better, in absolute terms, than herself. To be on the outside, absolutely, irrevocably, forever. That's what's intolerable.

And this is her future. Her one and only life. Unbearable thought.

Or—wait—is it? She *isn't* yet Mrs. Don Pascal. In a few days she'll be back as herself, Diane Fortnum, with the prom ahead. This nasty future isn't sealed, isn't absolute—it may be just one of a perhaps infinite number of possible futures. Maybe it is even *probable*, if every small detail rolls off as it's now set. But she can change it. She can, she must, do something to make this sickening scenario not only less probable, but *impossible*. . . . She is thinking so hard that she nearly cycles past their path.

The party that night is really quite fun. And the wretched "nobodies," when she is with them, are in fact very pleasant, friendly people, with amazing life adventures to tell. And worst of all, when they have gone, and she and Don flop down on the sofa and banish Henry to his chop-bone, the house itself seems really agreeable and homey; it's amazing, she thinks, what a good selection one can make from Sears Roebuck . . .

The next moment, her good mood reverts and she realizes that she is coming to feel at home in this second-rate life. She finds her face wearing a contented smile. Good god, is this really what she would settle for? Are her values slipping from her control, is she no more than an animal, content with a stomach full of food, a pat on the head and fresh straw in her stall?

She wipes off the smile. No. She must not, will not give up and slump into mediocrity. She is still herself, Diane Fortnum; not to be excluded, worthy of the best.

The image of the gun in her bedside drawer floats before her.

With it she *can* control the future. If there is no alternative, she can still force one. To give up is worse than to die . . . to settle for exclusion *is*, in truth, to die, to be no longer herself . . .

Don calls to her as he comes out of the kitchen, bearing two glasses of warm milk. He knows she likes this, it sends her to healthy sleep.

She gets up to follow him, feeling torn in two. And Don—that's another part of the problem. The acne vanished as promised, revealing him to be, if not stunningly handsome, at least a very pleasant-faced young man with a well-cut, aquiline nose. And his eyes are unarguably beautiful—almost too long-lashed, compassionate, sparkling for a man. It is an intelligent face, and one which is very hard to dislike.

She has always despised girls who were susceptible to male looks. Who "fell in love." If the truth be told, love has never really figured in her scheme of things—at least in the sense of *her* loving some man. Love was something that moved men, that gave her control. She really believes herself to be incapable of passionate love, and certainly the awkward advances of the boys she had known never gave her any trouble in retaining her virginity. Just as certainly, she does not in any sense *love* Don now; but she has to admit that he is pleasant to be with. He has a talent for friendliness, companionableness, which his physical blemishes had made it hard for the world to discover . . .

As she peels off the well-photographed dress she begins to notice how the word "pleasant" is coming to infest her thoughts. The house is pleasant, the life is pleasant. —Damn pleasantness! "Pleasantness" is another word for mediocrity, she thinks, savagely, and an old saying comes to her: *The good is the enemy of the best*.

When she thanks Don courteously for the milk, something in her tone makes him look at her oddly, but he says nothing. They lie down to sleep on their usual strictly divided sides of the bed.

Only, when his sleeping hand gropes for hers in the darkness, she quietly evades it.

But there is no denying that the bed itself seems to be becoming narrower, really too narrow for two people to sleep in without touching.

There comes a day, at the start of their third week, when Fred goes with them on Enclave 47's periodic convoy to the beach. This is a grand event, including optional use of some little sailboats, and water skis, and a barbecue-cum-clambake—and it requires borrowing several Army units from other enclaves to keep it all secure. The weather is perfect. Despite the fact that they have to stay within the security perimeter, there is a sense of freedom and space which everyone has missed without clearly realizing it, and the result is an exhilarating good time for all—even the troops, who are given free time in rotation. Riding home in the slightly damp and sandy bus, under a full moon on the empty freeways, they alternately sing and doze, and no bombs or other attacks mar the day.

That night they both nearly fall asleep undressing, and Di hears Don's breathing change to sleep before he has taken up his usual distance. She lies back, looking at his flawless face so near hers on the pillow, and her head imperceptibly slips closer . . . so close that his breath stirs the curls on her cheek. His long lashes lift drowsily; they gaze into each other's eyes, more than half asleep, and without either willing, their faces draw together. Lightly, almost playfully, they kiss . . .

It is Don who suddenly draws back. He looks at her confusedly, and then says "Do you really mean this, Di?"

When she doesn't answer at once, he bursts out, "Don't play with me, girl, for god's sake."

She can only murmur, "Oh, Don, you *are* nice . . ." and tentatively kisses him again. He really jerks away.

"Look. I know you're keeping yourself virgin for Mr. Zillionaire Right. I positively don't want to get mixed up with this—with you—and get hurt. It could be I love you."

She can't help herself. Looking into his beautiful angry eyes, so near, feeling the warmth of his body under their shared blanket: "But, Don . . . if we don't recall any of this . . . maybe it doesn't count?"

He breathes hard, shakes her a little, staring into her face. "You little—you little teaser. All right. Tell me: Yes, or No? Do you want this? If you don't, I'll go sleep somewhere else, no hard feelings. But I am *not* your brother or your girlfriend, kid. I'm a man who loves you and wants you. *Now*. But you've got to say it, Di. I won't take any more 'Oh Don' and fudging around."

Unexpectedly his eyes crinkle as if he's going to weep. He shakes his head impatiently. "What'll it be? Yes or No?"

"I . . . I'm a little afraid . . ."

"I'll be gentle. Come on—Yes or No?"

So low she can hardly hear herself: ". . . Yes . . ."

"What?"

"—Yes. Oh, Don—"

"Of your own free will?"

"Yes. Oh, damn you. Yes!"

At that he draws a long sigh, puts out his hand and delicately strokes her face. Another gentle kiss. More stroking, light as flowers moving down her. Presently her body grows hot as fire under his hand. But still he makes no move, until she says tearfully, "Oh, yes, Don—Don, please—" Then, gently, gently, he helps her peel out of her robe, and takes her naked body to his.

Now she dreads the onset of the fevered pawings and maulings she had known from other boys, but here was nothing like that. "Let it ripen," he whispers, with his hands under her buttocks, only slowly pulling her legs apart so that their genitals touch. "Let it ripen." And he makes her move her hips, searching for him, only now and then guiding her. "Please," she whispers, afraid it will go bad, will tear and hurt her. But still he makes her search and arch, until they both are love-wet and he is trembling with the effort to control. Only when she has it right, and is pushing against obstruction does he whisper, "Yes! Now!"—and hold her hips up strongly to his thrust—and he is finally in her deep, with almost no pain, but with a great sigh of relief. "Yes! . . . Yes! . . . This is the way it was meant to be—darling, my darling Di." He holds her still a moment, then says "Try moving a little, I'll follow how you feel."

She tries, with a little pain sharpening a pleasure she'd never felt before. But soon he can contain himself no longer. Gasping, with two long thrusts he comes, and then lies still, clasping her tight to him.

"Di, I'm sorry I couldn't bring you with me. But next time we'll do something different and you'll come too. Oh, my darling—was it any good for you? Do you hurt much?"

She tries to say Yes and No together, and they babble what first-time lovers do, until sleep takes them both in a bed that is no longer too narrow at all.

Some time before dawn she hears the toilet flush, and when he comes back he makes her get up and go, too. Then, crouching over her, he says "Di, now you must do what I tell you, right? I'll stay right here and I want you to stimulate yourself—never mind telling me you don't—do it exactly as if you were alone, hear? But stop just before you come. Can you do that?"

"Oh, b-but—"

He takes her hand and puts it to her vulva. "None of that. If you're too embarrassed, pretend I'm another woman and you're showing me how. Now. Do it!"

So she does, and when she tries to hurry and gets tense he makes her relax, and just as the first big contractions start he pushes her hand away and takes over so skillfully she can't believe it. And when there's no stopping he thrusts into her again without releasing her clitors, and confused waves of orgasms sweep through them together . . .

It is not until some time later, when they are at the icebox drinking milk, that she clearly realizes two things: First, that Don is a lover whose like she could never meet again, and, secondly, that they had inadvertently pushed Henry Cat out of the bed and he is now sulking at them from under the coffee table.

So they placate Henry and take him and the milk back to bed. And the first gray light of dawn is in the window, so Don gets up to draw the blinds and also turn the phone chime off. But Di can't go to sleep until she has told Don what she has realized about him. Which she does, about fifteen times, and they both collapse to unconsciousness till mid-afternoon.

The days still pass dreamily yet now with frightening speed. Fred is with them a lot, but never too much; he seems to sense what has happened. And then next week he brings something to them which is indeed a trifle frightening. It starts with a serious private phone call to Don.

They've just been out cycling, so Di takes the opportunity for a nice long shower. Afterwards, when she's in her plain robe—which she has long ago decided is quite smart—Don sits her down for a talk.

"Di, you know I never read you all of that note I wrote myself about my work at TCK. Well, something has come up with one of Fred's patients that involves it. The thing is, I'm one of the doctors who is on the board that hands out what are called the Means of Self-Deliverance. Suicide pills in English. Actually it's a set. Suicide is legal now, you know, and people who have justifiable reasons can be issued one of those sets and do it with a doctor in attendance. Fred isn't on that board, because he's a gynecological specialist. One of the quite justifiable reasons is terminal illness, particularly a painful one.

"So Fred has a former patient who's a widow, and has just been diagnosed as liver cancer. And she wants to go—who wouldn't? But she detests the Enclave 55 medico who's on the board, and wants to do it through Fred and me. You see, you and I were quite good friends of theirs while we were living with Fred, before 47 opened. We kind of drifted apart afterwards, but Fred says the friendship is still strong on her side. And also on ours, though of course we won't recall her now. She's named Marie Alvarez. Fred said Alvarez was a delightful guy—he did that lithograph over there that you keep remarking on. He went, from the same damn thing, about eight years back, and Marie never really got over it.

"Now she's asked Fred to ask me to get her a set of pills and let her die here, if it wouldn't be too much trouble. She thought that it wouldn't be so emotional for us, since we'd see her as a stranger now. What's your reaction, honey? The death itself is perfectly peaceful, there's a strong fast-acting soporific so you just go to sleep first and then anywhere from fifteen minutes to an hour later you stop breathing. But Marie, he says, *is* an emotional type. She may do a bit of crying and hugging first. Would that throw you?"

"Oh, poor thing, poor thing," Di says with a compassion in her voice that has only recently come to her. "Of course it wouldn't throw me. Tell her Yes of course, from me—wait—*if* it can be quite soon. I don't want to, to complicate our, our, oh, hell—the days further along."

"That fits exactly, honey. She wants to do it as soon as possible. . . . I could get the stuff tomorrow morning, it's my day to go over there, and she can come here that afternoon or evening or whenever's okay with you. Fred will bring her and stand by, get the wagon, and so on. Does that suit?"

"Suits . . . my god, what a funny world this is. Setting up dates for suicide. Do you suppose we s-serve anything? Suicide snacks?" Her voice is a little shaky; Don looks at her carefully.

"Watch it, darling. These are some powerful emotions we're dealing with here. You can be joking and all of a sudden you're in hysterics. How are you on nightmares? I wonder if this is such a bright idea . . ."

"No, it's really okay. I know what you mean. But seriously, I don't think a glass of light wine would be a bad idea if it doesn't upset the—the medicine."

"Good enough. I'll call Fred." He hugs her; she hugs back lingeringly, and he goes to call Fred and take his shower.

That night he says to her, "Something's bothering you. Tell."

"Well, it's nothing really . . . or maybe it is. It's just—it's just our bed."

"*Bed?*" Then he gets it. "Oh, for god's sake, no. The lady is *not* entitled to pass out on our bed. She gets the sofa. We can go in the garden or huddle in the bedroom if it's raining. I'll stay with her until she is unconscious. But no bed. If I have to, I'll tell her the couch makes a better position."

"Oh-h, thank you."

"Yeah, I'll pass a word to Fred about it too."

"M-maybe people will have special temporary guest-suicide-rooms—"

She finds his hand gently over mouth. "What did I warn you about?"

"Oh yes. Right."

"And we'll look at the evening newscast tonight for sure." He chuckles. "I'm starting to get a little embarrassed when people ask us about something that was on it and it turns out we haven't seen one for a week."

She laughs the melodious little snort that Don finds so contagious.

They miss the evening newscast again.

Next day everything goes neatly. Even the problem of the papers which Don must present to TCK, and which are now at Marie's enclave, gets unscrambled; Fred persuades the morning bus-driver to hand them to Don, who then continues on to the TCK bastion. He returns with a small sealed package.

"I don't know," he tells Di, "this looking nineteen can be awkward. Maybe I should have started a beard first thing. Ms. Dickey refused to recognize me and called me a kid playing games."

"Never!" Di strokes his smooth cheeks. "Oh lord—get that package away from Henry! We've got to lock it up, he'll keep after it till he gets it open."

They secure the death-pills and then decide to go to the big enclave swimming pool until Fred and his patient arrive on the three o'clock.

The evening's events unroll as planned. Marie solves the

problem of introductions by simply clutching Diane and starting to hug her and sob, as predicted, and Di hugs her back. She turns out to be an attractive woman in whom the effects of grief and age and illness haven't quenched a glowing charm. As Don takes charge, Marie turns the hugging on him—but not too much. She is clearly as eager to get this over with as they are.

In a moment it is time for goodbyes. Marie is a woman of taste. Sitting on the couch, with Don holding the package, she waves farewell to Di and Fred—waving them out, with only, "Good luck, my dears. *Buena suerte*." And they leave her so.

Di and Fred are waiting in the little back garden when Don comes out, gently closing the door behind him. He nods at them gravely as he makes for the wine. He holds up his glass. "To a very good person." They join him.

Their neighbor to the south is inspecting her carrots. Don remembers to tell her not to be alarmed if she hears the first-aid wagon in about three hours. "It's one of Fred's patients, Ellie. She wanted to say goodbye over here."

Ellie's eyebrows go up. "I must say I think that's generous of you," she says a trifle tartly. "We did that once and it was not such a good experience."

"But those look like wonderfully good carrots," Fred puts in. "What variety do you plant?"

And the talk turns to normal matters as Ellie goes in.

But some time during the wait, during the occasional grave silences, as Di's eyes absently travel over and over the shabby brickwork of the little garden with its garbage cans housed in their shed, over the low wooden fence where she can see the posts and wall-tops and oddments of a dozen similar little gardens all down the block—while she is hearing absently the far-off sounds of a patio-party where someone is having a bit too much to drink, and the music is decidedly unmelodious—some time as she notices that Fred does need a clean handkerchief, and Don retells his encounter with Ms. Dickey . . . an unwelcome voice whispers in her ear that *this* is it, that this is *all there ever will be*, for her forever—and Diane becomes absolutely certain why her older self had left that gun in the drawer. For her to use. In whatever way would hurt Don least, of course. No . . . not "would." *Will* hurt him least . . . because she is certain, now, how she can and will change that future. Only one way is certain: it cannot happen if she isn't there.

Can she do it?

She can. She will.

A tremendous peacefulness comes over Diane then, and stays with her through every hour of the next few days as they rush by. In their bed, peacefully she admits that this is not only sex, but love, true love; that Don is not just a lover, but The Beloved. Peacefully she fixes up their little home and admits that, yes, it needs a coat of paint, but it is their own beloved home. Peacefully she chats with Fred, and laughs at the jokes, and, in short, is for once in her life simply happy.

No thoughts of golden staircases, no hatreds of exclusion can disturb her; the word "forever" has lost its sting. Because she knows how she will solve everything.

She recalls how, when she made the first change, back in the school's time jumper, there seemed to be an interval at first when she could have roused herself and delayed the oncoming change. And that's what she will do this time. She will see Don go safely off to sleep, unknowing, and in that final moment she will resist long enough to carry the gun to her head and fire. He will remember nothing; mysterious as these things are, she guesses that with luck he will awaken and never know anything of this life, know only that a snobby, pretty girl with whom he was barely acquainted has died. There will be no pathetic derelict for him to bring home from the streets. He may well love someone, sometime, but it will not be her. And with his gift for love, that replacement-love may well be deeper and more loving yet. And she herself will have known real love, for all these unreal weeks, without ever going through the hell her older self had known . . . Yes; all is solved. She is at peace.

If only the time didn't fly by so!

On the last morning she does sniffle a little. Don reproaches her.

"You'd think we were never going to see each other again, sweetie. Remember, we have our whole lives still to go. And tonight we'll be in this bed together. Only a little older, that's all. You want we should have it twice over, I suppose. Well, so do I, but nothing can take this from us. Memory is forever—and we've been lucky in ours, lucky to have lived when we could actually have some of the best part over again. Chin up, woman!"

"Oh, my darling, my dear . . ."

"And my darling too . . . tonight let's give Henry some cod-liver oil, his coat looks rusty."

"Yes. We should." (And what about Henry? She hasn't solved that. But cats must take their chances. If reality has a pull to reassemble itself, as somebody said, Henry has a good chance to be taken care of by someone.)

But god, how the time goes!

They are still in their robes, eating a late breakfast, when eleven chimes.

"Oh, leave the coffee-pot, Di. Our older selves can clean it." Don is drawing her toward the bedroom.

"Should we leave a note or something?"

"What for? We'll *remember* this, fluff-head."

"Of course, how silly of me." She hops into bed on her regular side, and opens the bed-table drawer, ostensibly to get out a Kleenex.

"Do you think we should take off our robes?"

"It seems to be the custom to change naked. Maybe there's something about getting the atoms of the clothes mixed up with your skin or something."

"Oh god, no. Well, off with them."

As she pitches the robe over the foot-rail Don grabs her for one last embrace. And the minutes—the minutes are flying. She hugs him with all her strength. Then suddenly she remembers something.

"Don—would you think I was crazy if I asked you something?"

"Probably . . . what is it?"

"Well, I have this horror of—of seeing your face change. All of you. Of having you see me. Would you think I was gaga if we went to sleep back to back, the way we did the other night? It felt so comfortable too. Did I tell you—"

"Yeah," he says, "I remember. Premature babies live longer if you brace a pad against their backs. Okay. I have to admit you have a point about not wanting to see it. Wait one minute, though—" He kisses her soundly. "Right, roll."

They snuggle down back-to-back, feeling the curious comfort that position gives. She reaches in the drawer for another tissue, making sure that she can easily grip the pistol-butt. Yes. Easy . . . but now instead of flying, the minutes are crawling to a stop.

"I wonder where Henry is."

"Oh, god, don't let him be on the bed.—But don't get up, there isn't time."

"Hold it." He wiggles, cranes his neck. "All clear. I can just see his tail hanging off the sofa. I wonder—"

"Ssssh! Don't even talk about it, he might get curious and come in."

"Right. But still, I can't help—"

"*Shshsh!* Let's go to sleep fast . . . Oh, my darling. My dear . . ."

"Yeah . . . as a matter of fact, I *do* feel . . . oh, love . . ."

"Yes. It's starting. Goodnight my darling dear . . ."

"I wonder what our younger . . . s-selves . . . were . . ." his voice trails off. She herself feels a mist trying to take her mind, and clenches her fists. "My darling . . ."

His body has sagged away from hers, his breathing slowed. Moving as quietly as she can, she reaches into the drawer . . . and gets it. Now get it out, quietly, that's right . . . the metal's so cold . . .

The room is whirling round her liquidly, like a scene deep in flowing water. Is he unconscious? She moves to lift her arm toward her head, and inadvertently causes herself to roll toward him. He doesn't move, or react in any way. She feels as if the water has got into her arms, her head, that she is flowing. *Wake up!* Oh god, her eyes are closed! She jerks them open, rolling again so she can just see his back.

And then something happens—the light seems to change. Her eyelids have dropped again, but she is sure that if she opened them she'd be in a different room. Not the school time-tunnel; she can hear foliage rustling, beyond that, unmistakably, the sound of the sea. No air-conditioner noise. And then, loud, explosive—a birdcall breaks out. It's a cardinal, and they don't exist in Enclave 47.

She trembles, her breath falters. Is she right now passing through other possible futures? If she were to rouse now, would it be in some place like Hyannisport? But she is passing the wrong way in time, on her way to youth. If she'd known, could she have stopped here, on the first time-trip, with no Don to hold her to this future? No matter—she should go *now*. Suddenly it seems very important for her to die in some place other than Enclave 47; some place without Don.

Her gun hand is stuck under the sheet. In a world loose from any moorings, she manages to transfer the pistol, to start it moving toward her head. Her eyes see his back now. So thin, so young . . . is he changing as she looks? Is she? There is something odd right between his shoulder-blades. She focuses on it sharply.

It's a scabby spot of acne.

She's sure that wasn't there before. A flicker of revulsion touches her. She hated that acne—hates it now. It's the symbol of her Enclave 47 bad, wrong future.

A dark shadow moves across his back, across the scabby spot. Oh god, it's the gun-barrel. She's letting it slip. With a great effort she holds it up. But the few inches on to her head are more than she can do just then. She rests the muzzle against that hateful spot of acne, gasping, exhorting herself silently. Move! You MUST!

But she *is* changing. Whether she's changing physically or not she doesn't care. But something internal is coming back. It's not that she's afraid; she cannot, will not fear putting that cold metal to her forehead and pulling the trigger. In fact, she has thumbed back the hammer already, to make it easier. But her past emotional self is coming back to her, a hate, a disdain—her cold shallow schoolgirl self is returning, within her body. Her effort to hold back is distorting things, she is not whole but a mix of time-parts.

And love has left her, even the memory of it. Confusedly, she's glad—it was love that was her undoing, his love for her that reached out and plucked her from the world of sea and bird-song. Her love for him, holding her here—love is to blame, somehow, for it all. She must pull free now or be lost forever. *Now.*

But the gun-barrel which is finally wavering to her forehead never makes the last inches. Whatever the ultimate reason, it is with a grimace of hatred that, using all her strength, she points it at the red and ichorous blemish on Don's back. One last convulsive effort; she pulls the trigger, and blows his loving heart out.

When she comes to, Jeffrey Bowe is propped up on his elbows beside her, looking at some disturbance down the tunnel-hall.

"Wh-what is it?" she asks groggily, not caring.

"I don't know. I think somebody came back dead."

"Oh . . ." She has no memory of anything but going to sleep beside him here; she has never fired a gun in her life.

"Wow!" He dismisses the accident, stretching. "*This* sure is better! . . . Hey, have you been to that new place, Miro's? Want to have supper with me there tonight?"

She gets up for the robe, finding herself a bit wobbly. Dinner with Jeffrey Bowe? Well, why not? He is still lying comfortably stretched out, nude, looking a trifle complacent. Just as she's about to plead fatigue, he laughs and says, "Now, Princess, don't try to tell me you made a date for *this* night, seventy-five years ago!"

His humor is contagious. "Oh—all right. I'd love it." Then she turns serious. "Only there's something I should warn you about, Jeff. I don't, uh, do sex. Not until I marry, that is."

"Oh Christ, the whole school knows that. *Lady* Diane. Look, I just want to eat somewhere new and I bet you do too. You can drip ice all over the shrimp cocktail if you want." He gets his clothes from the locker and starts to dress. "How about it?"

She gets hers out too. "I didn't mean to sound shitty. But it's always best to get things straight early. You see it's part of my philosophy."

"Tell me all about it with dinner . . ." He produces a comb and sets to work. "You're cute when you're solemn."

"Puh-lease leave the area now," says the P.A. voice.

As they go out they have to make way for a stretcher team. Jeff asks about the accident.

"Dead, all right," he tells her. "It was that poor drip Don Pascal. Would you believe, somebody shot him? In the back!"

"No! Whatever for, I wonder."

"We'll never know . . . How about I come round at six and we'll eat early? They say this business makes you dead tired."

"Lovely."

And this time, as the scenario unrolled, it included a few meaningless dates with Jeffrey Bowe before the prom. The letter from Yale Admissions arrives on schedule.

At the prom Jeffrey proposes to her too, making four this time, but of course she chooses Bill Armitage. And the script takes over in force then, all the way to the telegram and the last night at Miro's and the Mark Cross luggage. The only difference is that Bill puts four twenties in her purse instead of five; the causal chain there would be beyond decipherment.

Then comes the Martha Washington Hotel, and the modeling, and the end of that first and only job, and the dropping in at

Swingles—and the nice-looking older man with the slight accent, who spells his name Nico this time, and all he brings with him, to the unspeakable months and years on the street. And sometimes she approaches apparently solid human figures, male or female, who inexplicably turn to shadows under harsh streetlights, so that she thinks her eyes might be going. And sometimes she sees a young black cat.

Finally comes the rainy night and the hurrying man whose arm she seizes (she can scarcely stand up) and "Diane! Diane Fortnum! Oh my god!"

But of course it isn't Don come to save her.

It's Jeffrey Bowe, and he grabs her and fumbles out his wallet and stuffs everything—except one bill he hastily takes back—into her purse, and takes off running into the rainy night like a man who has bumped a hornet's nest.

And she stands there bewildered with the money in her hand until her pimp, who has been watching her, comes out and relieves her of it. And since she looks pretty bad he takes her into an all-night eatery and treats her to a bowl of hot soup.

Counting the bills—five hundred and thirty—he gets curious. "You know many jokers like that, kid? Wyncha give 'im a call?"

"No . . . no . . ." she mumbles. "Don't know number . . . never." And indeed Jeffrey Bowe is out of her life forever.

But forever isn't long, in that script.

Her cough really sounds horrible, so he puts her up at a hotel he services. It's a place where everything movable is nailed down, and you do your own laundry at a coin machine in the back of the lobby. After one night they tell her to leave. You wouldn't think anybody so frail and runty-looking could make such a terrible noise.

On the street the weather is a little better, the rain has quit and the last snow-plats have melted. She wanders along, carrying a small bundle, wishing she had something for her headache. She's at the steep edge of a new enclave, no people around, no traffic. Sometime toward twilight she comes on a pile of trash by an unused entrance. There's a big cardboard box there, and some dry newspaper. She crawls inside.

Later three kids come along and are amused by the coughing box. After they have finished with it they throw in some gasoline and a lighted match.

Agony propels her, burning, upright among the burning ruin of the box. And in the last seconds before her eyeballs burn out she sees, unseeing, the heavy enclave portals, sealed against the outside. And above them the numerals 47. Nothing more.

The Earth Doth Like a Snake Renew

Looking back—insofar as the dead can look back—it is difficult to discover how P. came to believe that the Earth was male.

We see her first as a solitary child with the habit of taking off her clothes in the woods. The woods belonged to her family, and from her first summer P. understood that this forest was magical, which is to say, real. The city, she knew, was not real. Too many buried pipes and wires, perhaps; certainly too many people. To P., her winters in the city *did not count*.

What counted were her months of wandering alone through the extravagantly senile forest, of lying bare on mulm, roots, rocks and mosses, in silent rapport with a deep Presence which she identified unquestioningly as male.

How did she define maleness, this female baby? Well, she knew it was something different from father, Oh yes! She felt . . . she felt in contact with a huge hardness to which she belonged in an unchildlike way, and which had some unspecified, slow, enormous *intention* toward her.

If she had told her family, her learned uncle would have dismissed it as garble—the myth of Antaeus, say, or Atlas, which he had told her. Her fat uncle and her genius uncle would have blamed it on her infant glands. A masculine Earth? Her beautiful mother would have gurgled like the nightingale; she had wild talents and knew that Earth was a ball of rock inhabited by (a) baboons and (b) English literature.

Only P.'s father might have glanced up from his labor of keeping the whole dotty family afloat and said H'mm? He was a thin Pict with lavender eyes which still remembered Viking massacres. In fact he was in a small way to blame for P.'s problem.

One day when P. was ten he had a laughing fit, and invited her to view the stand of *Mutinus caninus* behind the garage. This was a ferny place which P. usually avoided because she knew it was the unofficial gents' pissoir.

Her father pointed; P. stared. Bursting from the moss in front of her nose were twenty startling pink naked dogs' pizzles. They were very lifelike; the smallest might belong to a Yorkshire, the largest to a Dalmation. Each rosy glans was capped with an ochre ooze, visibly succeeding in its aim of attracting bluebottles.

"They come up every year." Her father shook his head. "Aren't they awful? It's a mushroom. I never told your mother."

P. was silent before this evocation from the ancient loam. From that day the Earth to her was explicitly HE.

Surprisingly, P. was already familiar—indeed, given her family, over-familiar—with the mythos of female Earth. She had been told that Greek and Druid and Goth viewed Earth as SHE, as Gaea or Freya—a female body to be ploughed, sowed, "husbanded" by man. She learned that assorted aborigines believed this, too, and even the immense Chinese bloc held firmly that the Earth was female: dark, moist, passive, Yin. The dry harps of science confirmed it: Earth was clearly Terra Mater, the womb from which had teemed proteins and pterodactyls, gerbils, generals, herself and the Green Bay Packers.

All this never troubled P. To her, these people were talking of another planet. Their "Earth" might be female or a cuckoo-clock, what did it matter? THE EARTH, her Earth, was male. Every cell of her small body knew it. She lived on and was carried through stellar space by a being who was a functional male. And she also knew that however that function might come to define itself, its name would be Love.

The fact of love between herself and HIM, the Earth, was so deep that she held it in perfect silence, as a fish holds its convictions about water.

Function, as always, following form, there came a summer when P. was suddenly grown large and bemused by glowings in the crotch. She invited Hadley Morton to her woods.

Hadley had attracted her attention during the unreal winter at school by happy grapplings at her erogenous zones. He would, she felt, be a suitable initiator and the forest a suitable site. And Hadley proved a wise choice. In public he was fresh-faced and polite, in private unstintingly erectile. By the third week they had managed to consecrate not only her own woods but several acres of the adjoining Northlands National Park.

It was then that the first real event of P.'s life took place.

They had whiled the afternoon away on top of a large boulder which a glacier had abandoned by a nameless lake. This rock had been a special sacred refuge of P.'s childhood. Now she sat up stuporously, feeling Hadley drying on her legs, and looked out over the golden reeds to see if events had worked changes in the view.

As she looked, summer visibly ended. Green floodlights died among the frowsy trees and the first high strobe of autumn flared. A squirrel stopped eating a pine cone and decided to bury it. The heart of the air developed an icicle; an invisible arrow from the North crossed the sky, leaving it a wilder blue—a crow shouted—and it was Fall.

Seeing this P. felt a misgiving, rather like the moment before she had discovered all her credit cards were lost. She looked down. Hadley was dozing in the fern chaff, his blameless torso molten in the sun, his kneecaps somewhat abraded.

"Go home, Hadley," she said involuntarily.

"Uh?"

"I said, we should go. It's getting late."

Always agreeable, he retrieved his Finnish hiking shorts and they clambered down and set off along the soft deer trails. P. felt unreasonably, increasingly frantic to be rid of him, but there was no way. She ran ahead, trying to sense whatever might be unfolding around them. Hadley plodded amiably up, whistling "Greensleeves." P. decided to walk behind, watching to left, right, above, beyond. A partridge covey froze by their feet. "Neat," said Hadley. At the marsh two does stared unnaturally. "That's you," Hadley said, "except you have better ass." P. felt a touch of fear.

Presently they came to a dark shore held by old climax hemlocks who had slowly, slowly outlived the bright succession now rotting underfoot. Among the dim aisles P. saw a strange pale spear. She darted to it.

Hadley turned back to find her holding a huge, white, erect, human phallus, veined and lipped with perfect fidelity. It was as long as her forearm and ended in a single large wrinkled testis.

"How did that get here?" Hadley frowned about for some feral sex-ware merchant.

"It's a mushroom," P. muttered unwillingly. "A something *impudicus*. I never knew they got so big."

Hadley poked at it in disbelief.

"Look out, it's very old. The gunk is all washed off."

It was indeed a ghost's glove; frail, almost transparent.

"The common Stinkhorn. There's other kinds." P. tried to laugh, setting it back upright in the mold, and they went on. But not as before.

She knew now. Sadness. Reproach in that spectral erection of the Earth. Its mournful pallor told her she had committed betrayal. More had been expected of her, intended for her, here in HIS sacred grove. To bring a Hadley here was impermissible.

Mortification blurred her eyes as she followed Hadley's well-filled shorts. But underneath, excitement welled. HE had spoken! HE had sent her the first sign of love!

Hadley must go—and to her relief Hadley was already telling her that he must leave in the morning. The encounter with the appalling fungus might have touched him too, she thought; like the junior baboon who senses a senior eye fixed on him from beneath a brow-ridge and departs.

As soon as the throb of his peach Corvette faded, P. ran back to the hemlock grove. The *Phalloides* was gone. She stripped and fell prone on the dark loam, sending a wave of feeling downward to HIM. Nothing responded. The deeps below her were mute. P. sighed; she had learned that the offended male was often silent. But why had HIS reproach been so delayed? Why had HE not warned her before, rather than after such an amplitude of Hadley? No answer. Well, the male (she also knew) was often a bit slow. Or perhaps HE had other matters to attend to?

This thought humbled her; she began for the first time in her life seriously to think. What she thought on then—and for most of her short life—was a simple question. Like the Indian who loved the mermaid she asked herself: How?

How? How would HE come to her? How should she offer herself to HIM?

That HE—the Earth—would claim her physically she never doubted. She also took it for granted, being barely sixteen, that HIS love would be supremely satisfying, spiced with just a bit of thrilling discomfort. Caresses, penetration, climax—a divinely amplified Hadley filled her young dreams. Her faith was perfect; she did not for a moment consider being, say, penetrated by stalagmites or caressed by an avalanche. No, HE would be incarnated, like Zeus mounting Europa. Or perhaps Danae's shower of gold? P. frowned; the gold seemed an unsatisfying method. Surely HE would do better. But how? And when and where?

So began the first stage of P.'s quest, the naive invitation of Earth to her nubile female parts.

But what of the long winter months when she lived in urban schools encapsulated by humanity? Oddly enough, these interruptions of real life did not annoy her. They were merely long dreams; P. hibernated in herself, amused to learn the names of French kings or the rites of triangles. She was not aware that she had grown quite beautiful, and she was only vaguely aware that she was also growing very rich, from a persistent mortality among her monied relatives. When all this made her the focus of erotic strivings, she responded with her usual, dreamy largesse. She felt quite unsupervised by her destiny in these trivial human scenes, and the educational effect might be beneficial.

Her human lovers were sometimes disconcerted by one of P.'s rare fits of sexual intensity—which faded in a night. How could they know that she had fancied HIS aura in a pair of muscular thighs or a surly peasant profile? A lesser girl might have been called schizy; at her increasing income-level she came only to be known as delightfully absent-minded. This diagnosis was confirmed when a yacht bearing all her mother's real-estate cousins went down in the Bahamas leaving no other heirs.

But the summers—ah, the summers of real life, when she roved in her solitary quest for HIM! Where would HE come to her? Here? Here? She lay naked and half-mesmerized in leafy deers' nests; she sprawled dreaming in sun-warm bracken; she even curled up in something's rather smelly cave. Once she lay shivering in the blue moonlight of an early snow. *Love, come to me, come to me*, she called in silence, sending out her young pheromones like the urgent moth.

And things happened—almost. As she was dozing on a log in the sunny shallows of a lake, feeling the bluegill fry nibble her lax legs, a shadow fell. She dared not open her eyes; unbearably excited, she felt vast hands taking form upon her. And then—

hard haunches seemed to be parting her own. Aching with welcome she arched, everted—and just as the Presence broached her—she fell off the log.

When she had the water out of her eyes there was only a swaying of the alders where something huge and golden might have vanished.

Another day, lying prone on the rock once profaned by Hadley, she heard again the sky-crack from the North and in the same instant the rock beneath her came alive. A warm current invaded her, a vast life thrumming toward her loins. She opened to it, forcing her body onto the stony hardness, feeling Something rise, radiant—only to sink back to nothing, leaving her half-coming and alone.

Disappointments, but they only confirmed P.'s faith. And her quest for HIM began to cover a wider area as her schooling escalated through ever more expensive locales. She had high hopes of a narcissus field in the French Alps, she vibrated to HIS nearness on an Aegean isle. She was almost sure of HIM all one afternoon in the Marquesas and took a terrible sunburn.

But it was all to no avail, and with each vacation she grew more desperate, more daring in her offering. *Oh Love, where are you?* her body pleaded, feeling HIM around, beneath—everywhere but where she was most needful. *Are you HE? Is it YOU at last?* her soul cried to assorted rural vagrants, who couldn't believe their luck. Toward the end of this phase her experiments included an unwilling flautist with a crippled foot and a small Shetland horse. There was also the exhausting episode with the Merino ram.

Such extremes (she afterward realized) signalled the end of this phase. Maturity was swelling within her girlish chrysalis; she was ready for a new stage.

But first an interlude. It began with tragedy: her beautiful mother boarded an Aeronaves jet which took off straight into the crags of Popocatépetl. At the funeral P. was shocked to see her father's grief. Her uncles too seemed to have aged. She returned sadly to her off-campus apartment in Bronxville and perceived that she was coming down with the flu.

Opening a pill bottle, she thought of her mother's quaint belief that Earth was a lifeless ball of rocks, and wept anew. Fragments of the organized gossip which she had been taught under the rubric of Psychology drifted through her mind. Suddenly she froze. The pills showered to the floor.

What if her mother was right?

P.'s mouth fell open in a horrified gape. All her life she had believed, had loved without question this supernal being: HE. The very Earth. Suddenly, for the first time, the doubt raked her. Was it possible she was crazy? Did some term like projective delusion apply to her?

Stunned, she sank upon the commode, recalling how her fat uncle had explained and explained that Earth was dead matter, governed by various laws of motion and inertia. At the time she had smiled unheeding. Now the fearful possibility struck her. Could the foundation of her life be wrong? Was Earth really only a dead rock on which she, a biological mite, was projecting her hallucinations?

All night she wrestled, weeping, with the nightmare, gulping ampicillin as her fever rose. With every sneeze the desolating idea appeared more probable. The Earth—her lover? Surely she was insane. How could she have been such a fool?

By next morning she was convinced that it was her duty to dismantle the reality-structure of her life, even though it killed her. *The Earth is not alive*, she told herself drearily with her head in a vaporizer. *HE does not exist*. Dozing in antibiotic hazes she repeated it: *The Earth is not alive. I must unbelieve it all*.

As she opened the second box of Kleenex she discovered that the effort was becoming easier, was becoming, in fact, almost amusing. *The Earth is not alive*, she snivelled, aware as she did so of a vast I AM lurking beneath her, palpable even through the noisy world of man. *The Earth is not alive*—what a willful joke, to disregard HIM thus! *The Earth is not*—why, it was like the week when she had tried to believe in Berkleian solipsism, jerking open her closet door to catch her skis in the act of reappearing. *The Earth* . . .

With the last broad-spectrum spansule this new fantasy of an inanimate Earth had taken its place among such curiosa as the doctrine of the perfection of virginity (or was it the other way round?) in which a Jesuit lover had once attempted to instruct her. With the first cup of chicken broth all doubt had evaporated forever. She rose from her couch feeling profoundly refreshed and afterward thought of that weekend as the time when she had thoroughly probed alternative viewpoints and found them wanting.

But the experience had changed her. When her mother's junk jewelry turned out to contain several hundred carats of cabochon-cut emeralds, P. understood. HE was providing for her. HE had in fact been taking care of her all along. All those regrettable deaths—she saw now how strange they were. Mysterious wrecks, natural disasters: HIS handiwork! How ruthless! she quivered. (But how kind!) She began for the first time to realize the true enormity of HIS being, vis-a-vis herself. How absurd she had been, to imagine that this supreme male principle could be incarnated in some puny human body! Not to mention a Merino ram—she squirmed and blushed hotly, causing the junior partner of the law firm she was then entering to lose his train of thought.

P. continued on into the office of the senior partner, who had summoned her to hear another will. She greeted him absently and sat by the window, her mind far away. I am now nineteen: *I am a woman*, she told herself. *No longer a mere girl*. The thought excited her. A woman's love was different; girls merely fucked, while women did—she was not quite sure what, but something more complex, profound. She gazed out over the gray corrosive waters of Lake Michigan while the lawyer droned on about some dull tract in Montana on which an unknown cousin had perished. A suspicion came to her.

Maybe, up to now HE had been playing with her! Patronizing her with tweaks and throbbings like a baby! She flushed again, realizing how ludicrous her idea of love had been. Well, now she had grown up. But how could she show HIM? How could she make HIM take her seriously?

Her eye fell on a Sierra Club brochure, wandered to the smog and the dead waters outside—and inspiration came.

P. knew, of course, of the shocking destruction of the environment at the hands of man. She had read dutifully of the forests raped, the animals slaughtered, the mountains gutted, the oceans and air befouled. But to her—in her by now very special tax bracket—these were abstract wrongs. Because she didn't see it; her money carried her to the remote unspoiled enclaves of the rich. As to her own sacred forest, her father had long since bought the lumber company which was pulping the surrounding Northwoods Park.

Now P. realized she had been blind.

While she had been mooning, HIS body was being poisoned, devastated, destroyed! HE was in danger, was perhaps even suffering, and she had not understood. How terribly childish of her, how callous! What should she do?

She turned to the elderly lawyer and saw, like a light above his head, her answer. Her duty—her mission as a true woman—was to stop the destruction! She would save Earth!

"Yes!" she breathed aloud.

The lawyer looked up irritably. "I have not finished."

P. sighed and turned back to the lake. Suddenly to her delight she perceived that a rainbow was forming itself above the leaden waters. HE had heard her, HE approved! How beautiful!

Patiently she waited while the lawyer mumbled through an incomprehensible list of assets and investments he was supervising. She listened only enough to assure herself that there was indeed a great deal of money; hundreds of millions, it appeared. Good. When he had finished she turned on him a gaze of great beauty and exaltation.

"Mr. Finch, I want to use all that to save Earth from pollution. I want to start right now, this minute. Do you have someone who knows what all these organizations"—she tapped the Sierra Club bulletin—"*do?* Which one is best to give money to?"

"Ah, ah—ah—" said Mr. Finch and slumped clutching his chest.

After a short delay a junior partner was produced. And P. set forth her new stage: The Crusade.

Now it would be well to pause for a look at P.'s bodily aspect as she entered upon the ecological scene, credit-case in hand and lawyer at elbow.

The general effect was quiet, slender and expensive. Her voice was soft and she swathed herself in natural monotones of smoke or honey, snow or willow or heath. The public eye tended to pass over her, troubled only by an obscure feeling that its zippers were showing. The male eye that roved back discovered the elegant outrage of her haunches, the slim dove's breast. Moving upward the eye encountered a sorcerer's smile (from her mother) and her father's clear lilac gaze. If the eye lingered too long it received a lethal communication of something like lascivious virginity. After which other women acquired a distressing resemblance to drum majorettes.

Her lovers called her various kinds of goddess, angel, and so on. Hadley Morton had said she looked like a doe, and remarked on her ass. It was widely agreed she was incredible ass. But lazy.

This then was the luxurious young person who, several months later, emerged from the office suite of the Club de Rome, followed by the junior partner, whose name was Reinhold. Reinhold closed the door upon a chorus of distinguished farewells and signalled the chauffeur.

"To the airport." He handed her in and leaned back. He was tired.

"Reinhold," P. said thoughtfully, "how many organizations does that make now?"

"Forty-two," said Reinhold promptly in his clear Chicago-Anglo accent. "Not counting sixteen ad hocs, a couple of letterheads and the Madagascar lemur woman."

"I thought it would be simpler. There're so many different terrible menaces."

"Simple chemotoxins and assorted direct poisons," he ticked it off on his fingers. "Potentiation effects, mechanical destruction plus erosion, radioactives, mutagenesis. Animals die, fish die, birds die, insects perish, no pollination—famine. Or, plankton is killed, oceans die—famine. Or, CO_2 greenhouse effect, oceans rise—drowning and famine. Or, smog cuts off solar radiation, glaciation starts—freezing and famine. Or, all fresh-water lakes eutrophic, anaerobic poisons—death from thirst. Or, soil bacteria wiped out—nothing to eat. Or food doesn't give out, pop runaway, pathological overcrowding—worldwide Bangladesh. Or, energy shortages—war and famine. I forgot viral plagues. Etcetera etcetera etcetera etcetera. Let's see—estimated time to destruction of biosphere or other point of irreversible damage, five years min to a hundred years max, discounting chance of nuclear holocaust—"

He wondered as he spoke whether this time she would remember fucking him.

"Terrible, terrible," P. murmured. "It's all so much worse than I thought." She sighed, thinking of all the doomed birds and animals, Earth's bright familiars. HIS works of art. It must hurt him so.

"It doesn't affect you personally, dear," Reinhold said earnestly. "Why don't you build an ecodome? Hell, with your resources, you could build an orbital satellite."

"But I want to use my resources to help *Earth*," she repeated for the hundredth time. Reinhold clenched his jaw, hoping that Finch, Farbsberry, Koot and Trickle would understand what he was up against. Their biggest investment bloc.

"How, dear?" he said lightly. "A billion uterine loops? Free vasectomies? CNS implants? Nuclear fusion research? Even your money can't change five billion minds. Or buy all the governments."

"It's so *complicated*," she hugged her shoulders sensuously, gazing at him with lilac pools of sorrow. "Reinhold . . . you know what I think?"

"What, darling?" He contemplated throwing himself on her and crossed his legs.

"Even if I could do it all, do everything . . . I don't think it would work."

He was delighted.

"They all *know* so much more than I do. I'm terribly ignorant, I know that now. But I have this feeling. It just wouldn't work. Something would go wrong. And, Reinhold—"

"Yes, dear?"

"Reinhold, all those *men*. They're so good. So sensitive and kind. And yet, Reinhold, I couldn't help thinking . . . they're really doing it. *Men*, I mean. Not women. Women just seem to scratch around and braid string or something . . ."

"Oh for Christ's sake. You're a woman, you're riding in four hundred horsepower, you're going to burn fossil fuel all across the Atlantic. Have you any idea what your gross energy consumption is? That little pair of metal-mesh slippers—"

"I know, Reinhold," she said sorrowfully. "I *do* know. But that's because it's there. Men put it all there for us. If women were alone, do you think they would do strip-mining or ocean drilling or General Motors? Or kill whales?"

"We're to be replaced by a sperm bank, is that it?" He grinned. "Speaking of that—"

"You know what I like best?" she asked shyly.

"What?"

"I liked . . . that little man with the secret army of anti-pollution saboteurs."

Reinhold chuckled nervously, hoping she wasn't serious. With P. you never could tell.

But she had covered her face with her pale gloved hands and

was whispering heart-brokenly, "Oh it's all so hopeless, so *hopeless*—"

"Dearest! Don't cry, sweetheart, here—come to Reinhold."

She burrowed in his lapel, sobbing. "There's no *way*, what can I do? Oh, oh, oh, I've failed HIM."

"I'm taking you home right now, dear. Listen to Reinhold. That Stockholm thing is just more talking heads, they'll only upset you."

". . . Yes."

But on the plane she acted really quite strange, and later in the New York VIP suite she pulled away in the middle of his program.

"Reinhold, is there any way I could start a world war *now?*"

He tried to swear and laugh at once. Then he saw her face. Oh, no.

"I mean, if people all killed themselves off right now fast, wouldn't most of the environment be saved?"

"Ah, well, but—"

She jumped up and paced naked to the window. Maddeningly, he saw she had again forgotten his existence.

"If I could get some bombs . . . but it's so difficult, isn't it? It would be so hard. I'm so small. Oh, I can't do *anything*. Oh-h-h-h . . ."

He ground his beautiful Midwestern teeth. There she stood, god only knew how many millions and the greatest ass he'd met in years. And the mind of an amnesiac budgerigar. If she did agree to marry him she'd probably forget that too. If he switched her pills, she couldn't forget she was pregnant. Or could she?

P. turned on him, a figure of woeful voluptuousness.

"I'm so miserable, Reinhold. How can I ever help HIM? I can't, I've failed. I've failed. Oh, I have to think. Hadley, please go away."

When finally she was alone her pain would not let her rest. She paced, flung herself down, got up to pace again without noticing the passing night or day, the ringing phone. HE is sick, poisoned, dying, she thought over and over, and I have failed HIM. I'm no good.

She could not even feel HIS presence, here in this mad human heap. She longed for HIM; never before had she spent a whole summer among people, away from all communion. She felt terribly disoriented. When the phone rang again under her hand she picked it up without thinking.

"I thought you should know," Reinhold said formally, "your uncle Robert Endicott passed away last night. Some sort of food poisoning, truffles I believe. I'm extremely sorry."

"Oh, poor Uncle Robbie," she cried distractedly. "He was so fat. Oh dear."

"Yes, tragic. By the way, something else just came up, it might take your mind off. You remember that tract out in West Montana? Your lessee just called, he's peed off because his artesian wells all blew out. It seems they're shooting out a fairly high grade of crude oil. We're sending Marvin. Listen, will you marry me now, darling? You have to have someone to take care of you, you can't—"

She hung up, frowning. Oil? *Oil?* HE had sent her another gift, she understood that (poor Uncle Robbie!), but why *oil?* Oil, the poison of poisons, the cause of so much pollution and death?

She paced, chewing her hair. It was wonderful that HE still loved her, was even rewarding her feeble efforts. But why more oil? Didn't HE understand what was killing HIM? Impossible. Was this some kind of reckless gallant gesture? Or was HE trying to tell her something?

She gazed out at the jeweled city crusting through the murky dawn and enlightenment suddenly came to her. It was not HIS life that was threatened. Not at all. It was hers.

The biosphere—all those endless ecologists had told her how thin it was, how fragile. A mere film of air and water and soil and life on a huge mineral body. HIS body, what, several *thousand miles* in diameter? Why, life was just a stain on it, a kind of mildew born of sunlight on HIS outer hide! How could it mean anything to HIM? Perhaps HE scarcely noticed it, perhaps it even annoyed him, like—like acne! Was it possible that HE even wanted to get rid of all this rich biology she had tried so hard to save?

At this moment the sunrise actually burst through the smog and gilded the city spires. That told her: she was right. Her ridiculous crusade was over.

But what then should she do to be worthy of HIM? To show HIM she was a woman, no longer a silly girl?

Well, she thought hesitantly, women *know* things. Real women are distinguished by deep understanding, especially of their mates. What did she know about HIM? Almost nothing—she had found that out in her travels. Her state of knowledge was contemptible.

She must learn.

Pausing only to instruct Reinhold to send a large sum to the anti-pollution guerrilla, P. rushed to the New York Public Library. Shortly afterward she emerged with an armful of course catalogs and syllabi and boarded the jet for Berkeley.

On the flight she made out a list:

Geology, Physical.

Geology, Structural; also called Tectonics.

Geophysics, including Seismics, Core Plasmas and Geomagnetism.

Oceanography, maybe.

That took care of HIS body—ah, my beloved—and its history. There remained also Economic Geology and Mineral Sensorotics, which she dismissed as disgusting. But the list did not seem complete. A real woman should understand her lover's outside interests and relate intelligently to HIS life. And there was also the boring matter of HIS relatives, she owed HIM that courtesy. Consulting further, she added:

Astronomy I. The Solar System.

Astronomy V. The Local Cluster, Origin and Future. Prereq., Calculus III. (Oh god. Give me strength.)

She felt satisfied now. As she debarked from the plane her

feeling was confirmed; the airport was jolted by the worst fault slippage in five years. She knew she was on the right track at last!

At the university began what she thought of as her period of Womanly Preparation. (Several science instructors were to see it rather differently.) It was a time of hard labor and delight.

Discoveries! HIS skin, she learned, was much like her own, always sloughing away, upwelling, smoothing out. Horsts, grabens, klippens and other details of orogeny did not interest her much, and "bedding planes" were a disappointment. But the richness of HIS substances themselves! Where before she had thought of HIS life as only soft forests, meadows, flowers, she now thrilled to the reality of mineral magic. To think, over 2,000 kinds!

Lovingly her hands held sphlerites and amphiboles. Marvelling she counted the cleavages and complex symmetries of crystal beauty. Orthorhombic, triclinic! She learned the fascinating sequences of temperature selection from cooling zeolites to burning feldspars and olivine. The radioactive ores thrilled her—HIS pulse ticked there. And oh, the magic of X-ray diffraction patterns!

Ordinary gravel became no longer dull but the powder of HIS person. Her feet became sensitized, sexualized to HIS substance; she fell asleep murmuring of HIS states and processes: sedimentary . . . metamorphic . . . igneous . . .

Progressing from granite to diorite to gabbro to the deep, the primal basalts, she felt herself moving closer to HIS mysteries. Laccoliths and lopoliths, she whispered; stocks and—ah!—dark plutons! All forms of igneous intrusion, these. Igneous intrusion? It was all her desire!

And grandest of all were the incomprehensibly vast magmatic bulges known as batholiths. She passed her first Thanksgiving holiday roaming alone upon the gloomiest rocks of the great Idaho Batholith, dreaming in the nearness of HIS primal might.

Now here it is well to clarify P.'s concept of the nature of her lover, Earth. She did not then—or ever—think of HIM as an oblate spheroid 7,926.68 miles in equatorial diameter, massing

22×10^{20} tons and bearing at the center a pressure of 25,000 tons-per-inch. HE had these attributes and all the others of which she had recently learned, just as she had her attributes of mass and osmotic pressure. But they did not *define* HIM—any more than she was definable as a 24-volt potential-pattern in 1300 ccs of electro-chemical jelly.

Exactly what HE really was she found no need to say. If pressed she might (with her new vocabulary) have murmured something about "mega-energy configurations" or perhaps "gravito-inertial structurance." But the truth was that HE was simply HE, as she was HIS. The rest was detail. To her final hour there dwelt behind her mind the immense dark figure of a sleeping man outlined in unsleeping fire.

She now returned to campus almost unbearably excited by the subject of vulcanism. And since the bank kept converting Uncle Robbie's early Polaroid, she invited her whole geology class on an Easter charter flight to the live volcano of Iceland.

So it was that her instructor and forty fellow students presently found themselves carrying a champagne lunch up the slope of a coastal caldera near Surtsey. This particular volcano had subsided into a small inner vent and was regarded as quite safe. Beyond the caldera wall lay a plain of tuffs and pumice; P. ran eagerly out upon it in her hand-made Loslis. Small fumaroles spouted to life as she passed; she smiled fondly. Her companions hung back. Trembling with excitement, P. advanced alone to the lip of the live crater and leaned over to look.

Below her bubbled HIS molten essence! Flowing fire, laced with strange crusts: Was this perhaps HIS blood leaking from cosmic scars? Or perhaps—a more significant emission?

She stared entranced, feeling only the slightest impulse to fling herself within. (The time, she somehow knew, was not yet.)

Gouts of flame burst up, warming her face. *Oh, love!* P. gazed on, delighted.

Suddenly she was seized from behind and forcibly carried at a bumpy trot across the plain. It was Doctor Ivvins, her instructor.

"Stop! Let me go!"

"Run! Run!" he bellowed, dropping her to the ground. He towed her at a gallop over the scoria toward the caldera wall. She saw the others racing ahead and noticed a rising uproar from behind and below.

"The goddam top's blowing off," Doctor Ivvins panted as they reached the chasm leading to the outer slopes. Several large boulders were dancing about. As the others charged through the gap P. jerked loose from Ivvins and turned to look.

With a cannonade of thunder, the lip on which she had been standing erupted skyward. Explosions—grindings—a pillar of blinding light: a tide of creamy orange magma welled out of the caldera floor. Heat rolled over her. An object soared out of the fire and bounced down to her feet, glowing and spitting. P. recognized its spindle shape—a volcanic bomb. How marvelous!

In the molten surface of the bomb two long, rosy, perfectly human lips formed themselves. They smiled up at her.

P. cried out wordlessly and would have flung herself on it had she not again been seized and rushed away. Ashes were now raining all around; the sky was dark. Ivvins hurried them down the bleak slopes while the mountain roared. As their plane took off P. saw the whole caldera wall spring slowly outwards on a comber of dark flame. HIS farewell gesture! She hugged it to her soul, and wired Reinhold to repay the survivors.

Joyfully, P. returned to her studies—and met with a setback. Her courses were now taking her beneath HIS skin into HIS vast body. HIS true size began to reach her mind. The abyssal deeps of ocean, she saw, were to HIM no more than the dimples of her own back. What lay beneath? Hopefully she followed her teachers down through the SIALIC crust, past the Andesite line, into the deep SIMA layer. But all this was still epidermal. The Mohorovic probes were were only pin-pricks to HIM. Even the volcanic magmas seemed to be crustal formations, no deeper than a sebaceous cyst. Under that, they told her, lay hundreds of miles of an olivine substance called the mantle. And within that, like a planetary yolk two thousand miles wide, was HIS inner core. Ah! What was there?

To her intense disappointment, no one seemed to know. HIS vital regions were pictured as homogenous doughs, differing only in their probable states of plasticity. Earnestly she listened to theories of deep, slow convections and of mysterious currents which might be related to HIS radiant auras. Her interest was briefly caught by HIS whimsical shifting of magnetic poles; Ah yes, HE had been restless! But when she read of the superconductive properties of matter presumed to form HIS heart, it meant nothing to hers. Of plasmas in general she was told more than she desired, but of HIS plasma, nothing. What did it matter that something in HIS deeps eliminated perpendicular S-waves while speeding the P-wave compressive primaries?

She realized that her teachers knew nothing vital. Their interest ended where hers began. Pausing only to endow a geomagnetic institute, she departed for the astronomers.

And here everything went sour at once.

She was afterwards to think of this as the bad time, the time of testing. It began when her remaining uncle, Hilliard, died.

The funeral was in Winnetka, two days before classes began. P. held her father's thin arm, oppressed by pangs of merely human loneliness and love. Her father had grown gray and more harassed than ever by the avalanches of wealth. Afterwards they dined together in O'Hare's executive lounge.

"Just you and me, now," her father said sombrely. He said it again.

"Poor Uncle Hilly."

"Yes, terrible. Dreadful. What possessed him? Suspended animation, cryowhatsis. It's a wonder all that hydrogen didn't blow the town up." He prodded the butter plate. "I don't think this is butter . . . and poor old Robbie eating those mushrooms. George struck by lightning. Marion and Fred. And Daphne, that wave, a tsunami, was it? Hurricanes, earthquakes. Rock slides. Acts of God. The whole family, just wiped out."

He sighed. P. clasped his hand; she knew he missed her mother frightfully.

"Just you and me, now." Thoughtfully he studied his daughter. His lavender eyes were cold. His forebears, after all, had raised the dolmens of Stonehenge.

"I'm putting everything in your name," he said so clearly that the lawyers at the next table looked around. "Every penny. I'm turning it all right over to you."

"Oh, Daddy! I'll take care of you."

He smiled, not hopefully. She squeezed his hand, wondering what he knew.

"Your mother," he said in a low voice. "We never told you . . . before you came along she had a stone baby."

"A *what?*"

"That's what they called it. There's some name. Not a baby, really. Bones and teeth. Hair. It had to be taken out."

"Oh, god, Daddy. How awful."

"Yes." He looked at her with wry love. "Be careful, my dear."

A *stone baby?* P. thought. What had HE tried?

As they embraced at the gate he said again, loudly, "It's all going into your account, dear. I don't want any of it."

But he was not, it seemed, quick enough. That weekend a meteorite struck the fifteenth hole at Ekwanok, Vermont, killing him and a passing chipmunk.

This was P.'s first real grief. The ruthlessness of HIS love. *Cleaving the others*. She wept, with new sobriety; understanding at last that this was no child's game.

Gravely she began her new cosmological studies. It pleased her to learn that Earth's infancy, like her own, had featured an ammonia atmosphere. HIS larger relatives seemed another set of uncles—Jupiter broadcasting enigmatically, Saturn plumply beringed, Uranus travelling in recumbent pose. That Earth was only an average sort of planet she rejected; to her HE was magnificent. And then there was the yellow Sun around which they all so faithfully revolved.

Here the first pang smote her.

What, precisely, was HIS bond with that blazing body? What was this "gravity" that attracted HIM so?

She stopped dead on the steps of the Science Building and squinted up at the Sun. The center of HIS life, HIS hot star. Could it be—was it possible that that blond astral entity was HIS real love? HIS lawful, public mate?

Stunned, she sank upon the steps. Fire was in her closed eyes, humiliation in her heart. Of course, she thought. She is HIS equal. I am nothing—a toy, HIS little animal diversion. She—eleven thousand degrees Fahrenheit at the photosphere—*she* is HIS wife!

Of the rest of that day she recalled only taking several Seconals.

Next morning she awoke to find this first nightmare gone. How could she have been so stupid, she wondered; not to have seen the simple gestalt. Small ones around a big one—the Sun was not HIS mate, she was HIS mother!

Relieved, she returned to class. But only to be stricken anew.

Earth had, she learned, been circling HIS stellar parent for a very long time. About five billion years, in fact. Even in astral terms this struck her as much too long a time for a son to hang upon his mother. Why did HE not break free? His planetary siblings also seemed content to remain forever at their mother's side. How sad! But wait—what about those asteroids? Perhaps there had been a planet in Bode's fifth place, a being who had somehow burst loose, hatched and flown away, leaving bits of shell behind? Then Earth might do likewise!

She questioned her professor, and hope died. Those confused rocks, it seemed, were by their mass only addled fragments of a planet unborn. Or early dead, like—she shuddered—a stone baby.

No, none of them had escaped. HE was stuck forever in HIS dull maternal round. The thought depressed her; the certainty of brilliant consummation in which she had lived so long withered away. Was her great love only to end like a bourgeois French farce, where the son brings his bride home to revolve for dreary eternity under his mother's rule? NO! Surely HE had a greater destiny. Surely HE meant somehow to be free. Perhaps she could help!

She sought out the professor again and questioned him on the force required to break Earth from HIS orbit and set HIM free in space. (The professor watched her young lap quiver and told himself that teaching was a sacred trust.) His somewhat disjointed answer dismayed her so that she never recalled it exactly. To move Earth, she saw, was quite beyond any capability of man. Even if Earth were somehow to discharge HIMSELF like a rocket, it would do no more than widen HIS orbit. HE was trapped!

She went drearily away to walk the winter beach, longing to sense HIS presence, HIS deep sustaining rapport. She had not, she realized, felt HIS nearness for some time. What was wrong? *Oh my love, where are you? Speak to me*, she pleaded silently. The surf splashed emptily. Nothing.

The blasphemous thought crossed her mind that perhaps HE did not leave because HE was quite cosy here, was stolidly content with HIS mother. To distract herself she glanced at a letter crumpled in her hand. It was from Reinhold. Another boring increase in her wealth. Another of HIS gifts—but not the one she craved.

As the moon rose over the coastal mountains, a terrifying idea rose with it. She had once had a great deal of bother from an elderly admirer who kept hiding diamond ear-clips in her broiled grapefruit. And waylaying her with pathetic obscenities and gifts, gifts, gifts . . .

Could Earth be . . . *old?*

Oh, no! No!

But as she eyed the raddled moon, certainty grew. Oh yes—it would explain everything. All the illusory fondlings and ticklings, the promises leading nowhere. The interminable useless gifts. The destruction of her whole family, leaving her so alone—was that not the act of senile jealousy?

Five . . . billion . . . years?

HE was no young virile lover, HE was old—old—old!

And that decrepit moon up there—was she not in truth HIS old wife, hanging on? Why, HE had even arranged to send her emissaries. Oh, yes. *Old*. It was too desolating to be borne.

She dropped to the sand and cried like a child. But when her weeping was over, she knew another truth. She loved HIM still. HIS age, she thought painfully, is not HIS fault. She must accept it, find what joy she could in the afterglow of HIS life. She had loved HIM too long to stop. HE was all she had.

Soul-sick, she wanted only to flee. Departing from the college, she made herself assign Uncle Hilliard's main patents to the observatory, but she would not look again at the stars. When someone joked about the "ancient sands of Mars" she broke into tears.

Where to go, what to do? On impulse she flew to the forest that had been HIS first temple; it seemed shrunken and dead. She did not even walk to the great rock but only sent the keys to a realtor—an unthinkable act—and fled back to her New York penthouse.

It was the absolute nadir of her life, bar one.

Fearing to be alone she accepted invitations at random, but laughter was intolerable; she fled among the hellos. She took several lovers and forgot their names. Reinhold caught her praying to HIM and sent round two psychiatrists. When she refused to talk with either he sent another disguised as an electrician, who burnt his hand in the fusebox.

In these depths began what she was later to call the Time of Omens. But she was too miserable to understand.

They started quietly. Her florist's bill was misrouted to Alaska. She phoned her garage and found herself speaking with a child in Labrador. As spring came on her mailbox filled up with ads for arctic outfitters, and a travel agency kept sending her elaborate schedules for a Hudson Bay charter they claimed she had requested.

Desperate, she let a new lover take her to a private ski preserve in Montana. Mortally offending him by morning, she skied out alone to meet her rented Mercedes. Animals seemed to be behaving oddly. Three antelope came close enough to touch; a lynx actually loped alongside. When she rested a coyote came up and softly pulled her parka with its teeth.

"You're as crazy as I am," she told it sadly.

On her drive to the airport a flock of snow geese buzzed the car until she had the driver stop. They circled at eye level, yelping their urgency. *North! To the North!* She shook her head and drove on to board the jet, noticing vaguely that the car compass was spinning.

It was on this plane that ACTION began at last.

A servile youth named Amory had come to escort her home; the lawyers seemed to feel him needful. Amory was a harmless youth, with a mania for telephoning. As he installed her in first class he chattered about something in the news. She huddled in her furs, enduring a world without meaning. They flew on through darkness. There was some sort of disarray in the command cabin ahead; comings and goings, tense reassurances on the speaker. Amory ran about fussing. P. couldn't care less.

Finally the plane was landing. At Cleveland. Correction: It was not Cleveland, but some strange place called Val d'Or in Quebec. This attracted her attention. When the doors opened she sent Amory out and waited for the pilot.

"Captain, what is happening?"

He looked sharply at the pale luxury rising from the lounge chair. Unwisely, he looked too long; his nerves were in rags. As they went to the door he babbled out an ordeal of instruments bewitched, ghost beacons, radio garble.

"The damn jet stream has gone crazy," he told her, "we're five hundred miles north of Ohio. Excuse me. Look at that!"

They were at the top of the ramp. The night above them blazed with auroral lights. Ropes of green fire wreathed, rayed eerily, arrowed into a torch on the black horizon, rippled out and re-formed instantly.

She gazed, recognizing Polaris in the arrow's heart. North . . . ? A lodestone in her soul shuddered, the lost feeling of connection awoke in her bones. All the meaningless signals of the past months meshed. She laid her gloved hand on the pilot's arm.

"Captain, I shall get off here." She smiled tremulously. "Please . . . try your machines again. I think the call is for me."

Amory found her in the small charter office engaging a Beaver seaplane for Churchill via Moosonee.

"You go on home, Amory. I won't need you. Besides, it might be dangerous."

This was an error; one of Amory's telephonic clients was her insurance firm. When she saw he would not be left she changed the charter to an Otter and told him to find rooms in the airfield motel.

Her legs were trembling so that she could scarcely walk to her quarters; she sank onto a chair in darkness and watched the silent heavens burn. Cold fire, white, rosy, green—cosmic veils writhing and parting, repeating always the torch, the luminous arrow to the north. *HE is calling me at last*, she whispered over and over. *At last, at last.* Her eyes streamed tears, all over her body the sealed springs were melting. *My love is calling, HE needs me!* Old, ill, dying—what did it matter? *I am yours, I come, I come. . . .* She sat by the window all night.

At dawn she and Amory boarded the Otter and began to chug north. What about Amory, she wondered; was he wanted too?

At Moosonee she was answered. Hastening across the field to telephone, Amory yelled and vanished as a sump-line caved under him. P. left him in the Moosonee infirmary with a concussion and her AT&T card. The Otter churned on north.

The muskeg below her was a monotone moire plain of lakes and scrub, shadowed by islands of rain, occasionally grayed by burns or the garbage of a camp. P. watched the winding water-patterns change from dark to light with the changing sun. *Beloved, I am coming—coming—coming!* her heart sang to the piston drone. They landed to refuel at a bush cache. She sat quietly oblivious to the blackflies swarming in the cabin.

At the second stop the pilot began to stare openly. He was a beet-faced veteran, used to being the taciturn one. He offered her insect dope.

"No thank you." She smiled. He slapped his neck and took off rather roughly, whistling a tune that had been obscene in his youth.

An hour later she startled him by asking for his chart. He scratched out their heading with a pencil stub. She checked the chart legend and sat back, her face radiant.

She had confirmed that her course was approximating the line of zero declination. The arrow had summoned her, not to the axial north, but to HIS magnetic pole. Of course; the mysterious font of HIS radiances. Where was it exactly? 75° N by 101° W, somewhere above Boothia Peninsula. Bathurst Island, that sounded right. *Oh Love, I hasten!* The plane was so miserably slow . . .

The pilot's headset began to gabble. He listened intently, changed channels, swore, listened again. The Churchill coastline was ahead. He pointed down. She saw two long wakes curving away to the east. Only a solitary tanker was left in port. The airfield too looked empty. Surprisingly, they had to circle in the sunset while two planes took off and fled away southward.

When they were down she followed him through a crowd in the office, looking for the big wall charts.

"Can you take me up to there, to Spence Bay? And then on north?"

"Sure." He signed off his clipboard. "Next week."

"Oh, no. I mean tomorrow. Early."

"Na-ah, soon as it's light I'm scooting for Chiboo. Big front coming up from Winnipeg."

"But I *must!* It's—it's very important, I'd be glad to pay double, anything—" Her beautiful eyes misted, her hands squeezed his arm.

"Lady, I wouldn't stay here for a solid gold, uh, lollipop."

"Oh, please—look, could you possibly find me a plane? I *have* to go, my—someone very dear to me is up there."

He frowned down at her, abruptly banged his clipboard on the wall. "Anybody for Spence Bay in the morning? Lady says she'll pay heavy."

The men around the weather ticker glanced up and turned away again. Only one face kept attentive, a thin boy with a black-widow's-peak pompadour.

"Frenchy, you still got those tanks on?"

"It is stupid." The boy moved a step closer. Unobtrusively P. took out her pale mauve bill-clip and began to peel hundreds.

"One would puncture a pontoon, perhaps worse."

She peeled another, another, until the boy made a quick bow and approached.

"You understand it is hazardous? Madame is prepared to sit among the ducks?"

"Lady wants to find somebody."

"Ah."

"Please load all the gas you can," she told him. "We may have to go beyond Spence Bay. I'll leave all my other bags. How early can we start?"

"At three, Madame."

So began the last stage of her voyage to HIM, which she still thought of as a mission of comfort.

That night she spent sitting in the airport waiting room, her cheek against the storm window, watching HIS glory. Churchill was used to the auroras; there was an aurora research station here. But this display was epic. Colored arcs, rays, racing floodlights, sky-wide fluted draperies of fire, a silent conflagration. From time to time dark figures wandered out on the tarmac, bottles in hand, faces to the sky. The zenith wept emeralds, rubies, zircons, swirled in diamond spokes.

P. gazed avidly, hoping HE might reveal something of his need. Auroras, she knew, were linked to solar flares. Could HIS mother be calling too? She bit her lip and noticed that the radio man was asking if she was all right.

"Yes, thank you."

He slammed off his static-ridden consoles and went to his cot.

Presently she heard him snore. The celestial fires quickened. They seemed to be pulsing now, flowing in sensual rhythms. P.'s heart began to thud. Somehow this light-show did not suggest debility. It did not seem like a cry for . . . help. What was HE conveying?

Suddenly the midnight rainbows spun, rippled gigantically and parted. To reveal a fiery hieroglyph of such starkly erotic menace that her belly cringed.

Could *that* be senile teasing?

No! her body answered.

The scandalous shape exploded up the sky, carrying with it all her sad delusions. HE was not old, not sick! HE was young! Young and supremely male, calling her to HIM at last as she had always known HE would!

She sobbed aloud as the radiance flowered outward in forms of ineffable seduction. *Oh, my love, my love, my love*—

Finally the short night paled to dawn. Her pilot arrived. To carry her on her last, her nuptial flight. To HIM.

They took off under a gray-yellow sky. The lights of other planes winked out behind them, fleeing south. In the north ahead the air was clear and still. Her pilot, whose name turned out to be Edouard, tossed his headset down.

"The barometer rises," he grinned. "Where is this famous front?"

Hours crawled by. The loaded Norseman plodded north. To endure P. let Edouard explain the dual controls. She was regretting her indiscretion when wisps of cloud scudded past them, coming from behind. She turned and saw a great bank of stratus in the south. Sobered, Edouard climbed above the scud. It rapidly became a solid floor of fleece, lit by the low sun on their right.

P. noticed that the air in the vents felt warmer, almost tropical. She smiled in wonder. HIS bridal air! Even the Norseman's engines seemed quieter, more swift. But Edouard's face grew more and more pinched.

"What is it?"

"A tail wind." He tried his radio again, joggled his DDF transceiver array. "Not possible. I look."

The plane nosed down into gray wool and it grew cold. Finally they came out beneath the clouds. They were over big water; Hudson Bay? Edouard swore incredulously as his earphones squeaked. Then he banked the Norseman into a U-turn.

"Madame, I am sorry. We must go back."

"No, no! Why?"

"That crazy wind up there, it is four hundred kilometers. The RCAF tells everybody must go out. Spence Bay is evacuated, Madame, it is no use you go there."

"Oh, no, *please!*" She stared in horror as the compass swung implacably to 180. South, away from HIM.

"Madame, I have no choice. I regret."

"Edouard, how much does this plane cost?"

"This? Oh, about two hundred sixty, three hundred thousand US dollars. And the magnetometers extra."

She was clicking a combination on her dainty mauve credit-transfer unit. Then she thumb-printed its window and signed it with a tiny gold stylus. A purple credit chip emerged.

"Here, Edouard. I want to buy your plane."

He looked at it, looked again and whistled.

"Take it, Edouard, it's good. See the certified balance?" She flipped the case over, showing nine digits. "You can radio that station to confirm it, I'll pay."

"I believe you, Madame. But if I sell you this plane, what then?"

"Then you'll fly me back north. You don't have to worry, if it's my plane."

He pushed her hand gently away. "Believe me, Madame, I am sorry. But money is no use to the dead."

"*Edouard!* Please, I must go north, the one I love—can't you understand? I'll pay anything! *Please*—"

"I am so sorry, so sorry." His face worked but the controls stayed steady. "I am not a coward, Madame. *Voyons*, at the first moment after this storm I bring you to Spence Bay, anywhere! For free!" he added desperately.

"No, no, no. . . ." She sobbed. The Norseman labored on and on through grayness, the compass implacably struck at 180°. Her whole body seethed in protest, aching to turn back north. Up above them HIS bridal wind blew empty while she was carried helplessly away. What to do? Should she ask Edouard to land, and simply start walking north? But this country was impossible, she knew that. And her slippers. *Help me, Love! Help me!* But how could HE?

The plane droned blindly southward, hours or years. Finally the windows brightened. They flew out into sunlight above the clouds. Edouard's head snapped around.

"The sun!" he gasped. He began pounding his compass.

The sun? It was behind them on their left. Why, they could not be flying south! They had been flying north—the whole time! Toward HIM!

Dizzy with thankfulness she lay back in her seat. *Oh Love, how could I have doubted Your powers?* Beside her the distraught pilot was kicking and yanking his controls. The Norseman dipped one wing, then the other, and sailed steadily northward, rising into the mighty wind. The compass whirled playfully.

"The pig, it is fooked!" Edouard turned appalled eyes. "It does not do nothing!"

She was almost too happy to speak. "It's all right, Edouard. Really. Don't be frightened."

But he was, he twisted in his seat gasping at the strange things flying with them on the tide of HIS stupendous wind. She saw palm trees, roofs, billboards, tangles of nameless debris, all tumbling slowly in the clear sunlight above the snowy millrace of cloud. A huge vulture-like bird—could it be a condor?—sailed woodenly by.

"Look—a plane!" Edouard seized his binoculars. A fat four-engine jet was following them, flying crabwise. It seemed to have US Air Force markings.

"The doors are open," Edouard whispered. "They have

abandoned." He crossed himself and peered down. "I think it is Spence Bay there." There was a turbulent seam in the clouds ahead; a coast. Edouard hit the flaps again and switched off the motors.

Nothing happened; the props roared on.

His eyes rolled, he whispered prayers. The coastal rift came nearer. What was she to do about Edouard? Intolerable to have him tagging along at the supreme moment of her life. What was HIS plan? Or was this one of those details the male expects his mate to cope with?

Edouard had roused himself and was dragging out the chutes. "We must jump, Madame." He thrust one at her.

She took out the credit chip and poked it into his hand. When he looked up she was by the far wall, pointing a small gold cannister.

"You jump, Edouard. Leave me. I shall be quite all right. And don't try anything silly or I'll paralyse you with this deadly gas."

"But no, madame!"

"Edouard, go! I mean it. Do you think this is a natural phenomenon? Jump now or you'll be killed!"

"You must, I will—"

As he reached for her the cabin window beside him crashed in and the cabin swirled with warm air and chips of perspex. A large wet object with tentacles flailing plastered itself on the torn window.

Edouard made a mewing sound. He looked down past the plane's wing which was now lit with Elmo's fire and looked back at the beautiful crazy girl. His Gallic soul took over. He tucked the credit chip in his pocket, bowed, and leaped out the door.

Blissfully alone! P. laughed for joy, moving into the pilot's seat to pull the door shut. The plane seemed to be flying itself perfectly, a toy on the torrent of HIS breath. The sunlit flood of cloud below seemed to stand still as she outraced it north. The squid had blown away. A swarm of mice, or perhaps lemmings, twinkled by.

P. glanced behind. The southern sky was filled with a towering wall of darkness; it boiled and flashed murkily, following her up the curve of the world. Warm air, she knew, caused condensation. This great piston of storm must be surging up the tropic stream in which she rode. A continental carriage to HIS arms. All for her! *Oh Love, am I worthy at last?*

Rapturously she drew off her toque and gloves and began to brush out her hair. All the years of waiting, longing, striving for a sign from HIM, despairing of HIS love. While *this* lay ahead! She put the brush away, sinuously fluffed the new amethyst furs. And the charming underthing, too . . . to think she had nearly worn that dreadful puce suede! Of course HE would probably not notice such details, she thought; males usually did not; but perhaps the general effect would please HIM before . . . before her clothing ended where all bridal finery must.

Her loins were quivering luxuriously. She applied a rare scent (from the gold cannister) and lay back to wait. To be totally ready for HIM.

Outside the sun was rolling into the west, lighting green and apricot shadows in the cloud. It would not get dark, she realized; this was Midsummer night. Oh exquisite! And there was music, a bone-deep melodious booming like the pound of a great heart. HIS heart? Her own pounded; she saw the plane was losing altitude, sinking toward the clouds. *IT is really happening!*

Warmth surged within her, her limbs were heavy with deliciousness. HIS presence, HIS slightest touch would be bliss so acute as to be almost pain. Even pain would be bliss . . . a tiny thought pricked her: HE was so huge. HE—the very Earth—how, actually, would HE take her?

What if it REALLY hurt?

She pushed back the traitor thought. They were skimming the cloud tops now. There was something shiny sticking up ahead. What could it be?

It swept toward her and she saw. An enormous penis of ice! Like the long-ago mushroom but miles high and—oh—

hideous! Deformed—brutally ridged and swollen—bestial—fiendish—

P. gasped, invaded by her first fear. What really lay ahead? What did she truly know of HIM? When HE had destroyed her family she had seen it as love—but what if HE was not loving at all? What if HE was cruel? Or totally alien?

For the first time she grasped how fragile her tiny body was. A few degrees of temperature, the fall of a stone would kill her. And HE who flung mountains, HE was her world! Even HIS love would surely immolate her. She had been mad. She was rushing to ghastly death!

She wailed as two more savage ice obscenities flashed by, imagining a vast unhuman face peering at the bloody scraps of her body. Could she leap out, escape? She clutched the parachute, staring at the dreadful storm wall that loomed behind.

It writhed darkly as if alive. As she looked two immense nimbus swells joined and took on shape. Slowly it penetrated her panic. It was an eye! But an eye of cosmic grandeur, divinely carved, unquestionably young and male. Lightnings played gently within it like the beams of love.

Transfixed, P. saw the two great lids meet and open in a wink of planetary tenderness.

She fell back into her seat, all fear gone. *How* could she have mistrusted HIM? This new air told of HIS consideration. And how subtly HE had manipulated the plane's electronic controls! Of course he would be tender with her. HE understood all—whatever HE planned would be heaven. She laughed in ecstasy as another outrageous ice-phallus went by. *Oh Love, into Your hands—*

Suddenly the plane dived into the clouds and the cabin went dark. The dive seemed very steep; hesitantly she touched the controls, wondering if HE expected her to assist. Perhaps it was not fit to arrive at the consummation of her life like a blob of fondue? The cabin rocked as something hurtled over in the gloom—it was the derelict cargo plane. There was a bright place in the gloom ahead. She forced her languid limbs to action and checked the dive, just as the plane burst into open sunlight. Cold green sea lay below.

She saw she was in a vast open crater in the clouds, like the eye of a hurricane. Ice peaks towered all around, the open sea was only a narrow channel. The Norseman was still going much too fast. How to land? No matter—HE was here, HE was just ahead, she could feel HIS nearness now!

She set the flaps, trusting—and sure enough, a blast of wind struck them head-on. The pontoons hit. The plane bounced and then was floating to an ice-ramp at the water's edge. A shining path led up the ramp and passed behind an ice crag.

HE would be there! HE, HE!

Weak with love she climbed out into the balmy air, barely remembering her bag. The ice-towers were wild carvings of topaz and viridian against the dark walls of cloud.

As the Norseman touched the ice there came a loud windrush overhead and the cargo plane plunged down. She ducked. It struck with a clang that shook the peaks.

When the noise died away she saw it had totalled itself on the crags above the landing ramp. No smoke—but what was the brilliant debris showering out and rolling on the path?

She stepped ashore—and saw that it was flowers! An acre of flowers was strewn around her way! Breathless with astonishment she started up the path, recognizing orchids, cymbidiums, vandas from Hawaii. And living birds were now flying out of the wreck—parakeets, lovebirds, finches of every color came fluttering down about her in the warmth. A big blue and yellow macaw settled like a dazed sunrise on the ice ridge beside her.

Too much, too much—P.'s eyes were streaming, her heart raced. She sank down on the flowery ice to catch her breath. HIS tenderness, HIS love—

To calm herself she passed a finger over the blue plumage of the macaw. The bird shifted from foot to foot, whispering "Hello Polly." Then it added loudly, "Fuck the Navy."

P. giggled hysterically. Beautiful corsages were all around her feet. She picked up a magnificent cattleya spray. A riband lay under it: SECRET EYES ONLY. THE UNITED STATES AIR FORCE WISHES SENATOR BAFREW A VERY HAPPY BIRTHDAY.

Her heart calmed; HIS current was thrilling through her, calling her, upholding her. *Oh Love, I come*. She rose unsteadily, clutching the orchids and her bag. The short path before her seemed the longest in the universe. She forced her legs to move, to carry the gift of herself to HIM. Around that icy cornice she would meet—what? Blinding godhood? A storm of radiance, a divine beast? HIS love, certainly. Perhaps her death, it did not matter now. Only that HE waited there.

Her eyes were blurred with light, her whole body trembled with the sweet terror of sacrifice. Doves cooed, birds fluttered about her as she walked around the shoulder of ice.

Before her lay a sunny ice-floor like a stage. An ice-proscenium arched over it, the noble entrance of a great shadowy cave. In the sunlight before the arch lay a single bright orange object. It was a huge cushion or couch. Waiting.

P. gasped, vision and body melting. There, on that vast bed she would—HE would—

Carried on HIS urgence she moved forward, not hearing the singing birds. Only the great sacrificial couch, coming closer, larger—

Her heart stopped. The couch was occupied.

Protruding from the orange billow was a massive golden foot. P. stared, blinking. The foot seemed human. It was beautifully formed and big—but not inhumanly big. And there was a bronzed hand resting elegantly on the far edge . . .

She drew a long sobbing breath. The last fear fled. HE had chosen the incarnation best suited to her fragility. The classic way.

She moved breathless toward the foot. In a moment HIS perfect face would rise, HIS eyes meet her own. *Oh Love I am Yours—Yours—Yours!*

The golden foot lay unmoving, the hand was still. Closer

yet—and then she understood. In HIS gentleness HE wanted her to find him in mock-sleep. HIS frail human creature would gaze upon HIM exposed and gain confidence. Flooded with gratitude, with sweet fancies of how she might "awaken" HIM, P. reached the couch and looked upon HIS form.

It was several heartbeats before she took in the enormity. The young, blond, naked man upon the couch was not asleep but squinting listlessly up at her. Her dazed eyes registered thc stubble on his face, the peeling sunburn everywhere. At his side lay a bottle of Chivas Regal.

"Hallucinations are getting better," the apparition remarked hollowly.

Her jaw, her soul fell open. The ice peaks swirled among multiple visions of the blasphemous body on HIS sacred couch.

"H-H-Hadley!" she croaked. "Hadley Morton! No! No! No! No!" Screaming she dropped to her knees and beat her fists against the orange plastic. "No-o-o! Darling, where are You? Where are You?" Her head rolled dementedly, she rocked to and fro with her eyes shut.

But between her cries something was touching her from within, calming her paroxysms. She checked herself, listening. HIS impress? Yes, unmistakably. Slowly she opened her eyes, avoiding Hadley, and looked up. The gleaming ice-arch, the singing birds . . . it was all still true. She had been magically borne here to HIS holy place. And HE was here, soothing her. It had to be all right. She had made some foolish mistake, misunderstood HIS plan.

The plastic she was leaning on was stencilled, DO NOT INFLATE BEFORE DEPLANING. OSHKOSH SAFETY SYSTEMS. Hadley was peering at her over the edge.

She blew her nose resolutely and got to her feet, dislodging a cascade of little airline bottles.

"Don't I know you?" Hadley's brow wrinkled. "If you're real, that is."

"What are you doing here, Hadley Morton?"

He shrugged in an eerie way. "About what you are, I guess. Waiting for the end of the world or whatever. Listen, I'm sorry. I've been under terrible stress, I can't seem to recall your name."

She told him.

"Fantastic." He sounded like a talk show. "Hey, you look great. I apologize, I mean, you're dressed differently."

"You aren't." She brushed off her furs, wondering what HE meant her to do. How was she to get rid of this wretched intruder? Hadley was going on about how his jet had crashed in the Atlantic. He had found himself alone on this life raft being carried by an ocean current for days and nights among the icebergs to wherever this was.

"It was all water here yesterday," he waved his hand. "Things change a lot. Everything's going crack, you know."

"What do you mean?" The mysterious-current part of Hadley's story bothered her. Had HE brought Hadley here? Why, why?

Hadley pushed a crumpled *Wall Street Journal* at her. "See for yourself. It's today's, it came in on that Sabrejet over there."

She saw that there were quite a few wrecked planes scattered among the ice crags.

"There were two bluepoint Siamese cats in it, for Chrissake." He shook his head. "Lots of planes come in, you're the first with people. I got pretty bombed for awhile." He gulped some Chivas Regal, wiped the bottle. "Care for some?"

"No thank you." She glanced down the stories of earthquakes in South America . . . tidal waves, eruptions . . . some catastrophe in Australia . . . HIS surface had been unquiet. Why, of course—this must be what was delaying HIM! Some problem to see to. She must be patient.

Everything was all right. She let the paper fall, puzzling over Hadley. Why was he here? Did her huge lover think she needed some sort of human companion? A servant? It would be typical of the extraordinary gifts males thought of . . .

An idea struck her.

Had HE remembered that (Oh, dear!) Hadley had pleased

her once? And possibly planned to use Hadley, to incarnate HIMSELF in Hadley's—she looked at him sharply—yes, still blameless body? Apart from the sunburn it seemed to be in really splendid condition. Taller and filled out; even more adequately male. Superb, in fact . . . well, really, what could be more suitable?

That's it, she told herself, her heart leaping with relief. *Oh Love, I understand! Yes, Yes!*

She gazed, glowing, at Hadley who was now pulling on his plaid briefs in a rather pathetic way. Strange; he had been so charming as a boy. But, Hadley the man was marvellously built, his smile was still so winning; yet he was unmistakably a slob. Well, no matter, the human personality would go when HE—when HE took over. Oh, it was hard to wait! *(Darling, hurry, please if YOU can)* . . . meanwhile she might as well be polite to poor doomed Hadley, who was groping for his shoes.

She sat down on the raft and said kindly, "What have you been doing with yourself?"

He pulled on a black blucher. "Gehricke and Kies, medical instruments. Big line in proctoscopes. I guess you wouldn't know." He reached for the bottle, trying to grin. "I was on my way to take over the B-Berlin office."

Behind him a large animal walked uncertainly out of the cave.

"Hadley! There's a giraffe!"

"Yeah. There's two of them, came in yesterday. Other stuff too. Some zoo shipment. I dragged their alfalfa in the cave, I thought they might break a leg running around out here." He flapped his hands at the beast. "Shoo! Shoo!"

The giraffe curvetted, its hooves clicking on the ice, and sidled back into the cave.

"Pair of ostriches, too." Hadley rummaged in the bottles and brought up a Pan Am snack box. "Pair of little wallabies, they got loose. I don't know how long the food will hold out. Have some?"

Unwrapping the sandwich he looked so much like his boyish self again that P. felt a pang. It was like watching the live lobster one had picked out for dinner. "Later, thank you," she said gently.

"All those birds." Hadley munched, looking around. "Quite a few of each kind, I see. Except maybe the big fellow." He waved his sandwich at the macaw who was sharpening its beak on the ice, muttering.

"Its poor feet, we should make him a perch."

Hadley nodded. "Couple of raccoons, too. Couple of cats." He nodded again, swallowed. "And now there's two of us."

He grinned.

She laughed incredulously. "Hadley, you don't know what you're saying!"

"Yes I do. I know it's all smashing up out there. And here we are, safe and warm. Two by two. What does that suggest to you, h'mmm?" He opened another sandwich, looking at her in a doggy way. "Your pills won't last forever."

"Hadley, are you actually imagining that you can repopulate the world starting with two kangaroos and a macaw? What will they all eat? You need soil and plants and—" She laughed again. "Do you think you can milk a giraffe?"

"Ostriches lay eggs," he said stubbornly.

"Oh, nonsense."

She was saved from the ridiculous discussion by a boom overhead. Another plane burst out of the cloud wall and crashed into the ice beyond the cave. The arch reverberated.

Hadley stood up. "No fire. They're usually out of gas. I wonder if it has any beer?"

"You go."

She watched him clamber out of sight in tartan briefs and black Supp-Hose and boots. An absurd figure in HIS glorious icescape. The great ring of cloud around them seemed to be looming higher. The sun shone; the birds sang in the sweet air. HIS charmed refuge . . . only where was HE? *How long, Oh Love?* She bowed her head; the disappointment had been so cruel. But she must be brave, be worthy . . .

A tapping roused her. The giraffe was coming out again. It

was a male, she noted. She rose and walked into the great cave. It was luminously green inside, like a vast vault. HIS handiwork. For her? The other giraffe was picking at a bale of alfalfa. It was a male too. A Siamese cat paced away with its tail high: neutered.

So much for poor Hadley's theory.

Two ostriches moped about in the dimness beyond the bales. There seemed to be nothing here, no communication from HIM. *How long, Oh my Beloved? Where are You?*

HERE, replied the deeps. BE CALM. WAIT.

Unspeakably happy, she walked outside again. A raccoon was shuffling potato chips in a runnel of icewater. She smiled at it and picked up Hadley's newspaper.

When he came back she was reading feverishly.

"You won't believe what was in that one." His arms were full, stacked with frozen dinners and wine bottles. "A fucking redwood tree, that's what. One big old tree, roots and all, wrapped up. Wild." He flopped down and started opening the wine.

"Hadley, do you know what orbital perturbation means?"

"Yeah, earthquakes, all that. I told you it's blowing up. Meteor's going to hit the South Pole." He studied the label. "Apple-nasturtium-ginseng. Jesus."

P. looked up, her face exalted.

"Listen, Hadley. Orbital perturbation means the Earth is going to leave HIS present orbit. They're trying not to say so but it's all here. And it's not meteors. Arecibo estimates that this so-called wandering planetoid has more mass than Earth."

Hadley drank, staring at her.

"It isn't going to hit us, don't you understand? It's only coming near enough to pull us loose from the sun."

He wiped his mouth. "If it's so big why don't we see it?"

"Because its perihelion is due south, there aren't many observatories there. And its albedo is low."

"You know a lot, don't you?"

She stood up, startling the birds. "Hadley, Earth is going out, away from the sun. Our atmosphere will freeze. Everything will die, everything. Crustal instability. The continents will probably break up."

"End of the world," he sighed. "I told you."

"End? No—the beginning!" She raised her rapt face to the sun blazing low above the cloud wall. "HE is breaking free at last. At last! Oh, my darling!"

"Still on that," Hadley remarked.

She frowned at him. "What?"

"You and your communion with the earth-god or whatever."

"*I never told you that!*"

He chuckled depressedly. "Oh man. You were one weird kid." He drank again, shuddered. "Incredible ass, however. Never deny that."

She turned away furious and then checked herself. He couldn't help being so repulsive. "Try to think, Hadley. Doesn't anything strike you as a little unusual? Are you sure?"

He rubbed his sunburnt, stubbled face. "What do you think I got so smashed for?" he said thickly. "Riding on that raft, everybody dead, like a goddamn Flying Whosis. I saw things . . . maybe you aren't really here."

"I'm here. It is HIS plan. You'll see."

"Totally insane." He shook his blond head, suddenly showed his teeth. "I got a plan too. While there's life there's nooky."

Just in time she leaped away from his lunge.

"Hadley!"

But he had stopped and was staring beyond her.

"*Those clouds are getting closer.*"

She turned and saw that the wall of storm enclosing them seemed to have drawn in; the open space was smaller. Prudently she walked away from poor Hadley along the path up which she had come. Birds flocked by, heading toward the cave. A small red kangaroo hopped after them among the tumbled ice.

The far end of the water was now hidden in a churning cliff of gray fog, with brilliant sunset colors on its crest. Awesome . . . amid all the upheavals now going on HE had made her this sanctuary, away from the worst effects of the passing planet. Or whatever this dark stranger was whom HE was going to follow—she caught herself. No more jealousies! Not with the evidence of HIS precious love all round her. Think only of sharing HIS sacred liberation, the dawn of HIS new life.

How wondrous . . . as P. strolled back toward the arch the thought passed fleetingly through her mind that HE might be quite young. Five billion years? Perhaps this was only HIS divine boyhood!

She smiled with a new maternal voluptuousness, and noticed that Hadley was all bent over, making a ragged snoring noise. Why, he was crying. And holding up an open wallet, running his fingers over the photographs. How kind of HIM to have sent liquor to ease the poor Hadley while he waited for extinction.

"Have some more wine, Hadley."

While he drank she studied him. Magnificent; Hadley had really kept in shape. What would that body be like when HE entered, transfigured it with HIS glory? Her body melted; to distract herself she looked at the animals and birds now thronging into the cave. The space before the arch was full of charming creatures. Was it possible HE intended to preserve them in whatever unimaginable dwelling HE had planned for her? A lovely idea. But perhaps they would have to be really preserved, that is, frozen. A pity. Still, they were only animals.

She picked up a sandwich and began tossing crumbs to the birds, seeing the rosy spires of ice around them wink out one by one as the clouds drew in. The macaw clambered down, rasping, "Navy? Polly?" The light was changing, deepening to weird amber and violet.

"I'm cold," Hadley groaned.

"Don't worry. Everything will be all right."

The air was turning chill now. And the great cloud walls had come quite close. Her furs rustled with electricity. She realized that tension was building all about them. *Soon! IT will happen soon!*

"Christ!" said Hadley thickly, "How I wish I'd never met you!"

For an instant his fear infected her. She looked up at the roiling cloud cliffs. They were about to cover the sun. Would she ever see it again, see blue skies? A booming shuddered through the ice underfoot. Her throat knotted in panic. HIS coming? HIS immensity—a God loved her—

A sneeze recalled her from her fright. It was the macaw, waddling into the cave. Behind it paced a raccoon with a flower in its mouth. "Oh, please save them," P. whispered.

She and Hadley were alone in the last sunlight now. The ice boomed again.

"It's coming for us," Hadley said hoarsely. "Look—"

The orange raft was silently sliding away from them. She saw that it was being towed by little arctic foxes. They drew it into the shadowy cave and lay down, panting.

"By god," Hadley croaked, "it's a zoo. Something is collecting us. D-don't go in there."

At that moment the sun winked out, swallowed in the looming cloud. A mushy crumbling sound rolled around them. It was starting. HE was breaking free. P. thought of the terrible havoc that must be wracking the puny cities of men now. HIS fires bursting out, whole cities tumbling.

Suddenly something poked between her buttocks. She spun around. A small polar bear was pointing its nose at her crotch. She stumbled backward toward the cave, bumping into Hadley. The bear followed, weaving its long neck.

"It wants us inside," said Hadley faintly.

They backed in together, P. fuming with indignation. Really, to be goosed at such a moment! But as her leg struck the raft her indignation melted. How boyish of HIM, how—how Earthy! Thrilling with sexual submissiveness she sank upon the cushiony raft.

The bear stopped. A deep crack jarred the cave and ice showered down outside the entrance where they had been. P.

felt Hadley's arm tighten around her hips. She flung it off and stood up.

"Really, Hadley!"

"Look out!" He pointed behind her. The white bear was advancing again with its fangs bared. She sat back down. It stopped.

"See?" said Hadley in a high, abnormal voice.

"What?"

Only silence answered her. The creatures around them had become unnaturally quiet, the stir of life was stilling in the green-lit vault. P. shivered; the warmth seemed to be fading too. Shafts of apocalyptic light wheeled past the cave entrance, the ice groaned distantly and ceased. Was HE about to enter at last?

The macaw squawked, making her jump. "Fuck!" it screeched and fell over stiffly on its side.

"That's it," Hadley said. He was kneeling in the center of the raft. "We end as we began and all that sort of thing. Take it off."

He flipped up her furs and grabbed her breast.

She wrenched free and floundered away from him across the orange plastic, distracted by the bear. Hadley fell forward at her, clutching her thighs.

"Are you out of your mind? HE's coming for me—don't you know I'm HIS? Get away or HE will—HE'll punish you."

Hadley grinned horribly like an exhausted dog, his hands were cold and shaking. Thunder pealed outside.

"*He's* not coming, Princess. He's going. We're dead." He licked his lips. "Just remember I got here too. I'd say it wants us both. Hurry up!" He tore at her clothes.

Desperate, she kicked him—and suddenly to her infinite relief a globe of violet light appeared in the cave-mouth and floated toward them. Hadley moaned; the light hovered behind him like a halo.

This was the moment! HE was about to take over Hadley!

The air was terribly cold now, but a current was moving in her belly, tensing her sex. *Oh Love, is it You at last?*

The current pulsed stronger in her, like an unseen hand. She saw the white bear had hold of her slipper, was pulling it off. It slumped to the ice and lay still . . . *Love?*

YES.

Oh yes! yes! yes! Love! Wildly she sent her numb fingers down the closure of her amethyst silks, her eyes on Hadley's face. *Love, show THYSELF!* Her clothes fell open, letting in more cold. Hadley was jerking like a golem, trying to tear his shorts free from a gigantic erection.

"God, it's cold. C-Come on." The face was still only mortal Hadley, mouth shaking loosely, eyes bleary with fear. But the halo seemed to brighten. *Hurry, Love!*

Her teeth chattering, she unpeeled the delicious cache-sexe, and at that moment saw Hadley's face change. But—oh!—it was not the change she expected, it was only the crumpling of his features, tears welling out and rolling down his jaws. He ripped his briefs open and the tears splashed onto his great swollen glans. A terrible doubt opened in her soul.

"Stop! Hadley, stop!"

But he flung himself heavily onto her, his icy hands expertly parting, inserting with brutal thrusts, his face buried in her neck.

She writhed, trying to hope. Was this a god's probe in her, this cold tearing pain? Her body was freezing—and yet she could feel her sex rocking mechanically, driven by a cold itch, answering Hadley's thrusts in agony. Could she be dying? She became aware that Hadley was whimpering as he bucked and crushed her—a woman's name, Jenny or Penny. Horror rose. No god was in her, but only Hadley Morton ten years overripe.

"Help me!" she shrieked to the icy darkness. "Oh Love, Oh my God, where are You?"

And as before the enormous silence answered.

HERE. I AM HERE.

"*Save me!*"

But the cold lust in her loins only quickened unbearably, her sex was smiting and grinding against Hadley as if they were dolls jerking on a grid. She screamed, screamed under Hadley's frigid chest.

GOOD. GOOD. GO ON. I AM HERE.

Terrible understanding stilled her screams.

HE was not coming in to her, HE was outside—*a spectator*. HE wanted this, only this!

Grief, degradation colder than the ice drained her heart. She whimpered in torment, as her back slid on the freezing plastic. Hadley's assault was slowing now, her own dreadful zombie jerks were slowing down. Like dying toys. Her tears had frozen against Hadley's flesh.

They were dying. As the realization came to her, a long agonizing spasm rose and gripped her sex and shuddered out through their joined bellies.

GOOOOOD, said the unhuman void.

And with that her last illusion fell away. HE had never loved her, HE did not want her at all. What HE wanted was this—herself and Hadley. A toy, an amusement that had somehow attracted HIS notice in that long-ago summer, had titillated HIM. HE wanted only to put it together again.

All the rest, all her lifelong dialogue of love—it was all garbage.

Her tears were stones of ice on her eyes, her lips were crusted with ice. Cold sparks flickered on her upturned thighs. Snow. No warmth remained now, the great cave was utterly silent and dark. Hadley seemed to have stopped breathing. A lost impulse of human solidarity moved her; she tried to press his back, but her hand was frozen. Locked under his cold body, she waited for death.

They would go out to space with HIM, ludicrously conjoined for eternity. Along with the frozen forms of flowers, giraffes, birds, a redwood tree—whatever had diverted HIM among the brief creatures of HIS skin. Not a zoo. A museum . . .

Snow was piling around her now. The cave will presently fill, she thought. Very quiet . . . very deep. . . . In the cooling axons of her brain the ion crests formed their last faint thought and stabilized forever.

—AS WITH IMMENSE SLOW JOY THE VERY YOUNG BEING WHO HAD BEEN KNOWN AS EARTH FOUND HIMSELF ABLE TO ANSWER THE CALL OF HIS NEWFOUND PLAYMATE, AND, STOWING SAFELY A FEW SPECIAL TREASURES OF HIS CHILDHOOD DAYS, HE SWEPT AT LAST FROM HIS DULL BIRTH ORBIT TO SEEK ADVENTURE AMONG THE STARS.

In Midst of Life

The first sign of Amory Guilford's mortal sickness showed up in the spring when he was forty-five.

His wife heard him stirring. When she looked up, he was sitting on the edge of his bed, his head in his hands.

"Is anything wrong, dear?"

"No. . . . I don't want to get dressed."

She sat up. "Do you feel all right? We shouldn't have stayed at the Blairs' so late."

"It isn't that. I tell you, I just don't want to get dressed."

"But—"

"I'm sick and tired of getting dressed. My pants—left foot in, right foot up and in. I've done some figuring. Call it four hundred times a year, counting dressing for dinner. That's four thousand times a decade—sixteen thousand times now. Add in changing into exercise clothes, breeches—call it twenty thousand times I've put my pants on so far. I'm *tired* of it. Bored! And I forgot the pajamas, that's another sixteen thousand."

"I'll ask Manuel to help you get dressed, dear."

"No—I don't *want* Manuel to help me get dressed. I don't want to get dressed, I'm bored with getting dressed, that's all. . . . Do you know what would happen if I went down to the office this way?"

"Oh dear—"

"I'll tell you. They'd all say Good Morning Mr. Guilford as if nothing was different. And if I went over to the computer and pulled up our position on a couple of random stocks and then sat down looking thoughtful, Tony would have George on the modem before I said a word. And that would be all that would happen except that some time in the afternoon those stocks would go up a tick because of that leak I still haven't spiked . . . I have a good notion to do it. Except that Mrs. Hewlett would phone Peters to bring down a suit of clothes, and I'd still have to get dressed. Like she did when they found me still in my dinner jacket that time . . . God, I'm *bored!*"

"With getting dressed, dear? Perhaps you want a vacation."

"No, I don't need a vacation. Besides, I'd still have to get dressed."

But he was grinning now, and going into his dressing room where Manuel awaited with his business clothes, and it all passed over.

The next time came a couple of months later and was more serious.

"Amory, dear! What are you doing home? Did you forget something?"

"No . . . I just couldn't face it."

"Face the office? But you love the office, your work. And isn't this the morning when that firm you're taking over was supposed to make you some kind of offer, you told me about that."

"Yes, yes . . . Pickering Drill. They'll pay up, I've got them over a log. . . . But I don't know, at the tunnel I just suddenly didn't give one damn about the whole thing. I told Peters to make a U-turn at Palisades Avenue and bring me home."

"You *do* need a vacation. And I think you should see Doctor Ellsworth; some little thing may be bothering you. I'll make an appointment. This isn't like you, Amory dear."

"I know."

He sat down heavily, dropping the morning paper. "Suddenly I don't *care* what Pickering offers. Another thirty-forty million, god knows we don't need it. I just don't care about Pickering Drill, or Yamahito, or Aleman or Four-L Bits—my empire-building!" He gave a derisive snort. "I've worked so hard putting it all together—and now I don't care."

"Tony won't understand," Margo said thoughtfully.

"No. None of them will. All they see is my go-go-go."

"And you'll be go-go-go again, dear. This is just a mood. But I'm sure Doctor Ellsworth—"

"No. I don't want Doctor Ellsworth . . . I want—I don't know *what* I want . . . just to *stop*, maybe."

"Oh, Amory!"

"No, I don't mean that . . ."

"Well, I better call Miss Hewlett and tell her something has come up," she said after a pause.

"Yes—no, wait. I don't know." He got up and paced around the room. Was his mood lifting?

Yes. Sure enough, a little later he called Peters and went on his way into town, right in the old groove. And Pickering Drill came up with an offer that netted him thirty-five million, which he accepted, and turned to other targets. And the days passed as usual.

But the next week the "mood" came back and settled in heavily, so that he twice went into the library and opened the drawer where lay his old forty-five Colt, and looked at it. The second time, he reached in and touched the cool chequered grip. But then he closed the drawer decisively and let Margo talk him out of cancelling the dinner they were giving that night.

At dinner he behaved normally, except that he disturbed a few guests by giving them long probing looks in silence, so that conversation died. And next day he agreed to go away for three weeks on a newly opened Caribbean beach that Margo had got wind of.

Those weeks, and the four months beyond them, were the most appalling time of Amory Guilford's experience. The engines of his life seemed to have stopped, and nothing he could do would start them. He could find no motivation, no zest or joy or the mildest interest in anything at all, though he stoically went through the motions. He felt literally bored unto death.

He and Margo had long lived, like most of their friends, in friendship without passion. Their children were both in colleges and effectively out of their lives. It had been tacitly understood that his passion was invested in his work, and incidentally in his stream of more or less mechanical erotic investigations of the new faces in his company. It says much for Amory's desperation now that he twice attempted to revive with Margo the activities of former days.

But he could in no way keep this up, and presently turned to the girl they had brought down with them in case his interest in work resurfaced. This ended as abruptly as it had begun.

By the end of their stay at Saint Antrim he could barely make the effort to get into his swim trunks, and looked with blank eyes at the scuba gear he had used to enjoy. He took to slopping about permanently in an old terry beach-robe, until Margo brought him home.

Of the next four months nothing more need be said. The end of them came one afternoon when he walked into the library, took out his gun, and without ceremony thrust it into his mouth and pulled the trigger.

There was a blinding, soundless crash.

Then to his amazement, he found himself rising to his feet. He was facing the door, through which people were now rushing. He looked behind him and perceived—something—on the floor behind him. He looked away. People closed around.

Avoiding the people, he made his way from the room.

Movement was light and easy, without pain. He was, he thought, walking—with an utter lack of effort that he had never known before.

"But, but—" he murmured silently.

Leaving the uproar behind him, he came out into the entry foyer. Here he hesitated a moment. The feeling of finality was strong; he sensed that what he left now he could never return to. So be it.

After a minute he went on through the foyer and out the front door, and began walking down the curving drive. Peters was there, standing beside the town car and looking up at the house.

"Hello," Amory said.

Peters did not seem to hear or see him. Amory went on, and came to the wrought-iron gates. Here he stopped and looked back one last time.

A milky sort of mist or film already lay between him and the house.

He knew now, absolutely and finally, that he was dead.

And, apparently, in the land of death.

It did not appear much different. Outside the gates lay the familiar two-lane blacktop road, set about with big trees. The day was overcast, the light vaguely greenish.

He went through the gates, he was not quite sure how, and began walking along the road.

He had no goal, and for a time needed none. He was content to pace along through an increasingly ambiguous landscape. All was silent, he saw no people nor did cars pass him. Presently the road changed, imperceptibly, to the streets of a small town. But it was a silent town, without traffic or people. After a time the street changed again; it became, block by block, a street in a silent city.

He walked and walked, and still the pale light held steady, though he knew it was time for darkness. His watch, he found, had stopped at three forty-eight.

But now and then a car silently crossed the street ahead of

him, and disappeared in the side-streets. Once one came so close that he shouted and ran after it, but when he came to the corner, still shocked by the sound of his own voice, it had vanished.

He strolled on, bemused by a growing feeling of familiarity. This corner, that building—he had seen them before, he knew; perhaps many times. But here they seemed oddly jumbled together, misjuxtaposed.

He passed a block of luxury condominiums. Among them was the well-known building where friends lived on the penthouse level. Should he go in and see what he could rouse up? He peered into the lighted lobby. It was empty. There seemed to be a dark, moveless shadow behind the front desk. Was this someone who could tell him where he was? He doubted it, and found himself walking on.

Still everything was overlaid with the feeling of déjà vu. Never did he see anything unexpected or strange, except for the emptiness. He couldn't be sure what city he was in. But were these not the streets which he passed on his daily commutings? Or were they from an earlier time? He couldn't tell.

Ahead lay a smoggy, mistlike curtain through which he could not see very far ahead. When he turned around, he found the same curtain hiding the blocks he had already passed.

He found himself wishing to be out of the city. On this street he passed route-signs, though he was not familiar with the number. But they must mean that this street turned to a highway at the city's outskirts. Good. It would be a long hike, but this gait was untiring, and there was no alternative. He hastened his step, moved more purposefully.

He was beginning to be puzzled—more than puzzled, resentful—of the lack of any reception. Surely he had passed a significant boundary, from life into death. Was he not due some kind of recognition or explanation? A sign, anyhow, to tell him where he was or what was going on?

This strange existence was nothing from any religion he had ever heard about. He himself was a quiet unbeliever, but he had read a bit and Margo occasionally took him to church for weddings or memorials. He knew he wasn't in Hell or Heaven; if he had been judged, he'd had no notification of it. Could it be that he was in some Eastern scenario, waiting to be born again? As, he hoped, a human being rather than some animal. He wasn't aware that he had done anything so wrong as to deserve being, say, a cockroach. Indeed, he wasn't aware of any particular wrongdoing, outside of being born rich and making himself more so. He had always given freely to charities, if that counted as virtue, and he had helped several people along the way—Margo had seen to that. What was he being held here for?

And where was here?

It came to him that in some doctrine there was a place called Limbo, which was neither Heaven nor Hell. He seemed to recall that certain doubtful cases ended there—unbaptized infants, for example. He hoped this wasn't Limbo; it sounded unbearably tedious, and the sentences as he remembered them were indefinite. No, please, not Limbo, he murmured to himself.

There occurred to him then the explanation for all this world. It was all a patchwork of his memories, old and new, conscious or forgotten. Everything here was from his own mind—he was in effect living in his mind, wandering through what was nothing but that which he had seen or heard of or experienced. "Wandering in my wits," he mumbled, and made a bark of laughter which echoed crazily in the bare street.

The thought displeased him, yet he couldn't get rid of it. It threatened an eternity of boredom, if this was to be eternity. Or perhaps, like a story he had read, all his walking had taken place in an instant of real time, the instant between the bullet's entry and the stoppage of his brain—and he would presently "awaken" to die for real. Certainly he had expected that death would be a nothingness, a total erasure of Amory Guilford. That had been what he longed for, not this vapid excursion through random memory.

And why were there no people? Of course he remembered people, too. And traffic. Was this some kind of a morality-message that he hadn't paid enough attention to people? Some corny hint for him to repent? Well, what of? He'd paid as much attention to people as most men of his class and type, he thought defensively. He didn't deserve this—this isolation ward. . . . And if he did repent, what good would it do? This was a nasty retribution, and useless, with no people here for him to notice.

Or was this a hint that he really *was* going to be reborn, to have another chance? He scuffed his feet, resentful again. The idea of becoming a helpless, squalling infant did not appeal to him.

And now he noticed something else, which shocked him.

The misty curtain in which the street ahead ended seemed to be *drawing closer*. He wheeled about, and saw the same effect behind. So few blocks were visible now! He counted ahead—five, six, and he could make out no more. Surely there had been eight or nine only a short time ago? The clear space that travelled with him was *shrinking!*

Oh, no! He became frightened, his pulse raced. Yet he could do nothing but walk a bit faster, dreading what would happen if his space shrank to nothing. The thought terrified him—to be swaddled into the mist, alone with his own mind.

Could this be some kind of substitute for the night which should have fallen?

He couldn't know, but merely hiked on, almost at a run now. He was so eager to be out of the city, into free air, where, he thought confusedly, the mist couldn't close him in as easily.

And suddenly he saw that he *was* getting out of the city. On both sides now were big gas stations, and then a shopping mall—signs of suburbia. He hurried on.

And now another thought came to him. He had heard of men who got shot in the head and yet did not die, but survived as horrible vegetables, living on tubes and machines. Maybe that had happened to him! Maybe his body was even now in a hospital, invaded by heart-lung machines and metabolic supports, while his mind walked free. Maybe the apparent closing-in of the world signified his return to his body, to take up the "life" of an idiot!

"Oh god!" He invoked a purely verbal deity, then flinched, wondering if he had offended some Unknown.

Well, if he had missed killing himself, the obvious thing to do was to complete the job now. To kill himself dead, right here. But how? There were no weapons to be had here.

He surveyed the line of shops in the nearest mall. No gun shop, of course. No hardware store, even. And no one manned those stores. Well, if he could spot a hardware he could just walk in and pick up a knife. That would be messy, and painful as well. But he thought he could do it.

He passed another mall on his right. Still no hardware store. But there was bound to be one soon, he remembered them so clearly.

He strode on, watching alertly, until a sound behind him made him turn.

On what was now clearly an interstate highway, a big truck was overtaking him at speed.

He could throw himself in front of that! Surely it would finish him.

People managed to kill themselves that way, he knew. And his body was agile and well-coordinated. He could try. Yes.

He scrambled off the verge and crouched behind some bushes.

The huge twelve-wheeler bore down frighteningly fast. It was blue and white, with a great glittering grillwork nose. He caught a flash of "LEROY'S TRANSPORT" over the windscreen. Quickly—*now*—

He leaped out, directly in its path.

But even as he jumped, he knew he had done it too soon. There was a blare of brakes, and the monster swerved by him, bowling him over in its air-blast.

As he picked himself up, he saw the truck stopping. For some reason he tottered futilely towards it.

"What do you want to do, get killed?"

The driver was climbing down from the cab, a shiny wrench in his hand. To Amory's relief, he was a short man, though brawny, with thinning red hair. As they neared each other, he repeated his query. "You trying to get dead?"

"Yes," said Amory humbly. "I missed."

"Oh, a jumper, huh? Well, you didn't miss, I missed you. You ought to be grateful. You jumpers never think what you could do to the rig. The driver. Never think a-tall!"

"I'm sorry," said Amory distractedly. He was noticing something. All around the truck and driver the world seemed different. The landscape was brighter, more detailed, and the mist had receded to be barely visible. And there were ordinary noises again. A man shouted at the filling-station ahead, and Amory could see live people there—not dark ghosts like in the lobby, but real men, moving. And there was sunlight. Wonderful!

"Are you Leroy?" he asked the driver slowly.

"Yeah. That's my rig, you could have trashed it."

"I really am sorry. I didn't think a human body could damage anything that big and hard."

"Ah, you never think. I ought to turn you in."

Amory was thinking fast. He had never known a truck-driver. Leroy must be real, another dead man like himself. If this was Leroy's world, it was very different from his. Preferable. Not to lose touch with him, that was it.

"Please don't. Look. My name is Amory. I'd like to ride with you a ways. To someplace, someplace cheerful. Could you take me?"

"'Gainst regulations. No riders."

Amory found his wallet was still in his pocket and took it out. Inside were a couple of hundreds and his gold credit card. He fingered out the bills.

"Would this help, Mr. Leroy? I could give you more if you'd stop by a bank. And you could always say you picked me up wandering crazy and are taking me to a hospital. . . . The first part is true, but I don't want the hospital. What do you say?"

Leroy didn't look at Amory's hand, but somehow his hand took the bills neatly.

"I guess I could do that," he said slowly.

"Great!" For a moment Amory felt an actual surge of cheer. "So let's get going—if your ah, rig is all right."

"Oh, she's okay, no thanks to you. Go on, get in."

Amory went around the big nose, reached up and climbed in. All he knew about trucks was that they had many gears, and, he had heard, a bunk up back of the seat where the driver could nap. Sure enough, there was one here. It was empty.

Seeing the fresh paint, the newness, he said, "This is a beautiful truck. You said 'she.' Does she have a name?"

Leroy was stowing the wrench in a built-in tool box. "Daisy," he said with a trace of shyness. "I call her Daisy because she's a daisy."

"Beautiful . . . where are you headed?"

Leroy set the gears and put the giant motor into action. They rolled ponderously off the verge and picked up speed.

"I have a load for Chicago," he said.

"Do you plan to drive straight through? I'm afraid I'm not a qualified driver so I could spell you."

"Oh, hell no. On this run I usually stop at Overlook. That's a big trucker's rest. De luxe. They have everything there, at Overlook—stores, theatre, yeah, a bank. You could spend a week there."

"Oh, good. I meant it about the bank, I need some money too. I can get it with this type of card." In Leroy's world, it was clear, the usual rules held. You paid for what you got. Good enough, he could use some reality. But Amory was becoming more and more cheered. Certainly a trucker's rest was well outside his own experience! He wondered; was it normal here for the dead to meet? Perhaps the recently dead? Mysterious . . .

"How long have you been here?" he asked.

Leroy's head snapped around at him, wearing a strange, hostile look. Amory regretted his question; things were tenuous enough without trying to probe.

"What do you mean, here?"

"Oh, I misspoke myself. I mean here in this cab. Driving."

The little man relaxed again. "Thirty years come March. This rig, one year—it's the first one I've ever owned free and clear."

"I can see why you were so mad at me for nearly damaging it. Truly I didn't think it was possible."

"They never do," Leroy said glumly. His eyes sought Amory's face again. "Say, are you after—are you an investigator, about that hassle back at the Pennsy docks?"

"What hassle? I never heard of the Pennsy docks, Leroy. And I for sure am no investigator—I'm just what I look like."

Leroy slowly seemed to believe him. "H'mm. I guess no 'spector would jump like that. Okay."

But Amory had the idea now. There must have been some accident at those docks. And Leroy was killed. But he wasn't admitting it, he was simply denying that anything had happened to him, living in his ghost-world. How could he be driving his truck? Well, his truck was as much a part of his persona, his self-image as Amory's clothes were of his. And he had walked away from, from that library in his suit. These must be ghost-clothes, though—he fingered his vest—they felt perfectly solid and had his wallet in the pocket. Just so, whenever whatever had happened at the Pennsy docks killed Leroy, he must have driven off in his ghost-truck as easily as Amory had walked away in his suit.

He must be careful not to disturb the little man's belief in the reality of all this, or he might collapse the world Amory found so reassuring. But there seemed no danger of that—he was sure that if he told Leroy he was dead, he would get only laughter. "What do you mean, I'm dead?" And indeed, Amory thought, what do I mean?

They were barrelling on through the endless sunset, the big truck eating up the road. It wasn't empty, now, Amory saw. Occasional traffic met them or passed them, the drivers seeming notably well-behaved; perhaps a happy memory of Leroy's.

Desultorily, they conversed, discussing makes of cars and the ways of drivers. Amory was charmed, learning about trucks and trucking. If he ever got back to a computer, he thought, he had a couple of names of firms to look up. Nothing like firsthand reports from the consumer! It seemed incredible; he reminded himself that he was *dead,* and most unlikely to have a use for the information.

The only hint of his state was that the gold sky did not fade. It was the beautiful time of the evening, when neon and arc lights bloomed against the colored sky. And it remained that way. Leroy did not comment on the unnatural length of the day. As they neared a big triple overpass the little man pointed ahead.

"There's Overlook!" he said with satisfaction.

On the upper level was a substantial group of buildings topped by a big sign: OVERLOOK – TRUCKERS BAR AND GRILL. Below it said, BEDS AND BREAKFAST – ALL SERVICES – 24 Hours – No Private Cars.

It looked like a medieval castle on a hill, Amory thought.

They pulled off the overpass into an enclave ending in a parking lot full of big trucks and trailers. On their left was a K-Mart store, on the right the two-story Bar and Grill. All the roadways and turns were truck-sized.

Leroy trundled Daisy into the parking lot, and took a ticket from a cute girl in a uniform.

"Full tonight, Patty."

"Yes sir, Mr. Leroy." Professional smile from Patty.

"They all know me," he confided to Amory with a grin, skillfully backing into a slot between two behemoths. As they walked out Amory felt impressed and exhilarated by the sheer size of the great trucks lined up here. This really was something new to him!

"The bank's in here," Leroy was leading him into the K-Mart.

"At this time of night?"

"Twenty-four hours. You'll see. Nothing closes at Overlook."

Beyond the aisles of clothing and appliances, in a back corner, Amory saw the grilles and counters of a small bank branch. Not one Amory had an account with. He made another futile mental note; an enterprising outfit.

After a brief, completely normal hassle with another cute girl, he got five thousand on his gold bank card. While she was making her phone check, Amory wondered who or what was on the other end. Limbo Central? Impossible to believe that all this, and the five bills she presently handed him, were substanceless, figments of his memory.

He pulled off a thousand and pushed it at Leroy.

"Just so you won't forget and pull out without me," he smiled.

The little man protested, but finally allowed himself to be persuaded to put it in his dog-eared wallet.

"I tell you where I'm not going tonight," he told Amory. "Not with this."

"Where?"

"To the blackjack table."

"Oh, so there's a casino too?"

"I told you. *Everything*." Looking up at Amory with a shy smile, he added primly, "Girls, too. *Hostesses*."

"Oh yes?"

"Oh, yes. Man!" Leroy slapped his cap on his leg.

They came out into the golden light and crossed the roadway into the Bar and Grill. Convivial sounds rose, two or three voices called out to Leroy. He waved. The bar was a cheerful, heavily wood-trimmed big room, with an oak bar and booths, just beginning to be full. All the guests were clearly truckers, mostly huge mountains of men like their vehicles.

Amory felt like an interloper in his dark three-piece suit, among Leroy's friends. Among Leroy's *imaginary* friends, he corrected himself. For god's sake not to forget that he was a ghost, living in another ghost's memories!

But it was all so real, so persuasive . . . the solidity, the detail of Leroy's mental world!

The big TV was showing what was evidently a sports cable. Music was also coming from a side-room, where dancing seemed to be going on.

Leroy made straight for the bar; Amory followed.

"Yo, Leroy," said the bartender, a husky individual with curly black hair.

"Two light," said Leroy, smacking his cap on the bar.

Amory had felt no thirst or hunger, indeed, no physical needs. But the beers looked tempting. He tasted his—and found it flavorful. Some of Leroy's zest must be spilling onto him. He drank more.

A woman came from the dance-room and circulated professionally through the bar. Finding no takers, she went away.

"Dot here tonight?" Leroy inquired of the bar-keep.

"Oh yeah, sure."

"Wait till you see her," Leroy told Amory. "Oh, hey—there she is now!"

A tall, well-built young brunette was coming in.

"Hey Dot! Dottie! Over here."

"Hey, my man!" Dot undulated toward them, looking curiously at Amory.

"Friend of yours, Hon?"

"Yeah, he's with me. He's no trucker, though."

"So I see." She smiled at Amory, her eyes nearly level with his.

"Find him a nice girl, will you?"

"Oh no, no," protested Amory. "Thanks but no thanks—I'm still a little shook up." Have sex with a ghost or whatever—no way, he thought.

"Okay," said Leroy. To Dot he explained, "He had a near miss out on ninety-one."

"Oh well, Mister, a nice girl would just fix you up."

Amory's protests finally ended the matter. Dot had a beer, and Leroy downed another, showing signs of impatience. Amory noticed that there was a staircase up off beyond the bar.

"Rooms up there," said Leroy. "Real nice . . . hey, Georgio, give us a key, will you?"

He pulled out a hundred, and got back twenty-five in change. Amory saw Dot and the barkeep exchange nods.

"C'mon, Hon." He boosted Dot away from the bar.

"What I like," Dot laughed at Amory, "is these long engagements."

"See you."

With that, Leroy hustled Dottie to the staircase, seeming undisturbed by the slightly ludicrous figure he cut with the woman; she was a good head taller than he. Like his big truck, Amory thought.

As they left him, he felt a pang of loss. The lights seemed to dim down a bit as they ascended into the shadows above. And a kind of slowness came over the scene, though the noise of the room stayed the same.

It was as if Leroy's world was weakening behind him as he left the scene. Would it vanish, if he removed himself too far? Panicked, Amory saw that the bartender had turned static, pouring a shot. Yet the liquid didn't overflow.

In a surge of fear, Amory ran to the staircase and called up.

"Hey! Hey, Leroy!"

They didn't hear him. He was about to call again, louder, when a voice spoke almost in his ear.

"Are you out of your senses, man? Let the poor ghost have his privacy."

Amory whirled. The man who had spoken to him was sitting at the bar alone. Amory had noticed his sharp black eyes.

"But—but—" Amory said, utterly confused by his need. "Who are you?"

"Don't you recognize me?" the man asked. "You called me in yourself."

"Called you in?"

The man gestured to Amory to take the seat beside him. Amory saw he had a very white face, in which his eyes burned like black embers, and felt a thrill of fear. When he was seated, the man said neutrally, "I am Death. To be more accurate, his delegate."

In spite of Amory's fascinated horror, he felt a prick of

satisfaction. At last some explanations were about to begin. The man who called himself Death's delegate was unremarkable, save for his eyes, and clad in a suit no darker than Amory's own. This was no ghost, no figment . . . What was he? Before Amory could speak, he went on, "Now you can do something for me."

Another woman was turning through the room, a cute little blonde, moving as slowly as a zombie. Hers was the only movement in the room now, but still the noise of an active bar went on, rising up the stairs. The blonde bent toward Amory, her open mouth making a kind of low moaning, like a slowed-down tape.

"What?" said Amory, distractedly. "Look, without him everything goes wrong. It's—it's grotesque, horrible."

"That bothers you? Of course." The man raised his hand and snapped his fingers. At once the lights came back bright and everything speeded up to normal tempo. The blonde whirled away, laughing.

"Better?"

"Oh, yes. Uh, thank you."

The man looked him over. There was something clinical in his gaze.

"Do you understand all this?" Amory asked.

"Yes."

"Then where are we?"

"In the country of the dead. One of them."

"And all this is just memory, right? Someone's memories?"

"Right."

"Then why were my memories so weak? And foggy?"

"Because death touched you while you were still alive."

Amory thought this over. It sounded like what he had felt, back then. The touch of death. Yes.

"Why?"

The man didn't answer him directly. Instead, he said, "We are of a kind. I smelled it as soon as you came near. You will too."

Amory thought some more. "But this *is* death?"

"Yes."

"It isn't like what I believed. I believed I'd simply stop. Nothingness. Zero."

"That's the one belief that's not fulfilled."

"Why not? I mean, it's logical. Where does a candle flame go when you blow the candle out?"

"Perhaps the spark of consciousness, once ignited, is not so easy to put out."

"No, it should be easy." Amory summoned a lifetime of quiet but impassioned argument. "Look, consciousness is one of the last developments. The last. So it should be fragile. It is, too—look at the effect of a few drinks, a tap on the head. Gone. Poof!"

"Perhaps," the pale man said noncommittally.

"You say it's the one belief that's not fulfilled," Amory said thoughtfully. "You mean, you fulfill all the others? If I'd believed in the usual stuff, Pearly Gates, Saint Peter, Judgement, Heaven and Hell—I'd have found that?"

"Yes. Or any other faith."

"What if I'd believed I was going straight to Hell?"

"You'd have got that. If you really believed it."

"But that's terrible! Hell . . . for how long? Forever? And when does *this* end? What happens?"

Death's delegate looked down at his hands. "I said this was just one of Death's kingdoms. For a special type. The unbelievers, do you see?"

"That's me."

"Exactly. But as I also said, you're special, too." Abruptly his tone changed. "Would you come outside with me for a moment? There's something I want to show you."

Casting a perfunctory look upstairs, where there was no sign of Leroy, Amory followed the pale man out.

Outside the golden daylight still held. Two big semis were rolling in. His new acquaintance halted near the entrance.

"Look at the sky over there where it's dark. Can you see a kind of light on the clouds?"

Amory squinted, and made out a patch of pale luminescence, like a reflection of a light below. As he gazed it seemed to shift a little, as if whatever was reflected was moving internally.

"Do you think you could drive over there, to the light?"

"Sure, if the road leads there. What is it, a town?"

"All roads lead there. . . . No, it's the main arrival point for this area. I should be there now but I'm making a swing around to catch the incomers I missed." He made a gesture to Amory to follow him around the corner of the building. "The numbers keep increasing, increasing, you see. The old policy was to meet everyone individually, but—" he opened his hands in a helpless gesture. "Now we can only cope with the active questioners. You'll soon get to sense them, they stand out. People like your friend don't call for attention. They're satisfied. Maybe after awhile he'll start to need help, but not soon. Anyway, there's where I need your help."

"*My* help? What do you mean?"

"Oh, just to drive around until you sense somebody who needs attention. Then you stop and talk with him. The ones who seem satisfied you don't need to bother with."

"You mean you're trying to delegate your job to *me?*" Amory demanded incredulously.

"Oh, only a portion of it, I assure you. There's plenty for me too. Ah, here's my car."

They had come to a small parking line for ordinary autos; he was pointing at a dark maroon BMW much like Amory's own, and getting out his keys.

"As I said, we're alike. Here—" Before Amory could resist he found the keys thrust into his hand. "I'm giving it to you."

"Why? What's all this about? I don't want it."

"Yes, you do. You'll feel more comfortable, at first anyway. And it's nothing—here one gets such things by simply wishing —in the right way."

"Huh? You mean . . . I'll get anything I wish for?"

"Yes. Virtually anything. Except living people. Try."

"Try wishing for something?"

"Yes."

As Amory stood nonplussed, to his surprise he found he had a wish. For a dog he'd owned in his youth, a black Labrador. He wished for it, finding it awkward to phrase. At the last moment he remembered to ask for Dory as he'd been early on, not the old dog he had become.

Nothing happened.

And then, suddenly, a black shadow that was a dog came bursting around the corner—stopping to pee as Dory always had, then galloping toward Amory. Despite his conviction that the thing was a phantasm, a figment, as the dog approached, so real, so living, Amory couldn't help holding out his hand to him—and then going down on one knee to receive the Labrador's familiar, enthusiastic greeting. Strangely, he felt a sense of comfort.

The man beside him smiled. "Nice dog."

"Yeah . . ." Amory got up and dusted off his knee. "Sit, Dory."

Dory did.

"You see?" Death's delegate was taking off his dark jacket. He looked away, oddly, for a moment as if concentrating. A moment later, long dark wings extended themselves from his shoulders and spread wide. "Well, you'll be all right now," he said to Amory.

"Wait!" Amory cried. "What do I *tell* them? You haven't told me a thing!"

The wings seemed to enlarge. "I've told you all I know," the man said. "That's all the one who recruited me told me."

He gave an experimental wing-flap. "I specified that these should be easy to work," he confided to Amory.

"But—but—"

Beside him the Labrador gave a low growl in his throat, and raised his hackles at the winged man.

"Leroy," Amory said helplessly, "my friend—"

"He'll be all right." Death's delegate flapped again, and rose a little in the air. "Oh, I almost forgot," he said. "Remember this: *Death is not mocked.*"

With a great sweep of his new black wings, the man lofted over the near roof—and went soaring out of sight in the sunset.

Amory stood looking after him dumbfounded, the car keys in his hand. Dory was looking up at him expectantly. But he couldn't go back in the bar with his dog, and he didn't want to wish him out of existence. What to do? Should he start out on this crazy business he'd been dragooned into? That seemed to be what the man expected. And he acted as if he had some kind of authority here. Or did he? "The one who recruited me," he'd said. Did that mean he was just another ghost who'd been hustled into being a reception committee? And what did that make Amory? Death's delegate's delegate? Or were there more behind that? This could be a whole chain of delegations, with nobody knowing anything. . . . And what did that mean, *Death is not mocked?* It sounded ominous. Maybe some kind of warning to take this seriously.

Dory gave a little whine. Amory remembered that he loved riding in cars. He looked up at the dark sky again; the light patch was still visible. And the road seemed to run straight toward it. He might as well try, he'd nothing to lose.

He opened the car door. "Up and in, old boy."

Dory jumped in eagerly and settled himself in the passenger seat. The car smelled new. And he liked BMWs. The motor started, purring out its happy song of good engineering.

The man had said he'd spot people in need of help. How? Maybe he should lower the window, to let vibrations or whatever in. And what *would* he tell them? Anything he liked, it seemed. But that caution against mockery might refer to this—not to tell too fantastic a tale.

At least I'm not bored, he thought. As he thought it, a dire premonition hit him. Even this job could get boring, with time and repetition. He checked himself hurriedly. Not to think that way! Not to believe it. What you believe is what you get, here.

Determinedly he pushed the thought away, and eased the car into gear.

Rolling out to the highway, an old quotation came to him. He twisted it around: *In midst of Death I am alive*. He gave a snort of laughter. Dory barked, startling him. He had forgotten that habit the dog had of barking when anyone laughed. Did that mean that Dory was at least a little real? That he too was a "spark of consciousness?" He hoped so. And what would happen if he wished for Dory to be real? A big sign in the sky, saying TILT? Better not try.

He headed down the highway, to encounter the existential Unknown.